HERE FOR THE DRAMA

Kate Bromley lives in New York City with her husband, son, and her somewhat excessive collection of romance novels (it's not hoarding if it's books, right?). She was a preschool teacher for seven years and is now focusing full-time on combining her two great passions – writing swoon-worthy love stories and making people laugh. *Here for the Drama* is her second novel.

Also by Kate Bromley

Talk Bookish to Me

HERE FOR THE
DRAMA

KATE BROMLEY

ZAFFRE

First published in 2022 by
GRAYDON HOUSE
in arrangement with Harlequin Books S.A.

First published in the UK in 2022 by
ZAFFRE
An imprint of Bonnier Books UK
4th Floor, Victoria House, Bloomsbury Square, London, England, WC1B 4DA
Owned by Bonnier Books
Sveavägen 56, Stockholm, Sweden

A CIP catalogue record for this book is
available from the British Library.

ISBN: 978–1–83877–813–2

Also available as an ebook and an audiobook

1 3 5 7 9 10 8 6 4 2

Typeset by IDSUK (Data Connection) Ltd
Printed and bound in Great Britain by Clays Ltd, Elcograf S.p.A.

Zaffre is an imprint of Bonnier Books UK
www.bonnierbooks.co.uk

For Chris — my wonderful husband, my forever rom-com leading man and my very best friend.

1

"I'm here and I have coffee!"

After five years as a personal assistant, I have found that entering a chaotic scene with caffeine is the quickest way to ease panic. It's a distraction, it boosts morale, and if you're working in the ever-intense theater world, it's often as necessary as breathing.

Roshni, our second assistant, is quick to approach as the penthouse door swings closed behind me. She's wearing a knee-length floral romper, and her flawless ebony hair is parted just off to the side. If I wore a romper, it'd look like a man's bathing costume circa 1916, but on Roshni, it's the ultimate embodiment of summer fun. I'm still not positive if I want to be her or marry her, but we've happily settled on being ride or die work friends in the meantime.

"Thank you so much," she says, scooping her iced hazelnut coffee out of the to-go tray I'm carrying and casting a nervous glance over her shoulder. "Okay, so, two things. One, I accidentally knocked a pile of papers off Juliette's desk, which then led to her calling me an anarchist and threatening to have me arrested. And two, she thinks you're going to London."

"What makes you say that?"

"She straight-up told me you were going to London."

"I am *not* going to London," I announce, making my voice loud enough to carry through the spacious four-bedroom apartment. With almost a decade of drama study under my belt, my vocal projection is legit.

"Why are you always so resistant to anything remotely exciting? To stand still is to go backwards, Winnie."

I hear her before I see her. Juliette Brassard. My boss of five years, my pseudo-mother, my often-combative sibling, and the perpetual bane of my existence. Working for her is tiring, demanding, slightly monotonous and bizarre, but I love every second of it.

She looks the same as she does most days. Wide-legged pants and a layered top. Always layered. Today it's a beige cotton shirt and a charcoal vintage vest. Her straight gray-brown hair just reaches her shoulders and thick-rimmed glasses cover her ceaselessly curious chestnut eyes. Her style is a fair reflection of her life—eclectic and casual but secretly expensive.

"It was never the plan for me to go to London," I tell her. "Roshni is going with you, and you were perfectly happy with the arrangements yesterday."

"Yes, well, happiness is fleeting, and I realized today that I need my whole team with me if this trip is going to be a success."

"I checked with the airline this morning," Roshni says, taking a tentative step forward. "And apparently there's one seat left in first class." I shoot her a loving glare as Juliette raises a victorious arm in her direction.

"You see? It's a sign from the universe."

"It's not a sign from the universe," I counter. "It's a ridiculous amount of money to pay, and you're probably the only non-tech billionaire who's willing to spend that much for a fully reclining seat."

"A noble sentiment. You should preach that sermon to the bare foot that caressed our cheeks the last time we sat in coach."

"Okay, we had *one* uncomfortable flight from LA, and you know full well that the guy was wearing socks."

"I don't know that, Winnie. I've repressed the memory so deep into my subconscious that I'll be shuffling around this apartment and whispering about phantom feet until I'm ninety." She spins away with her typical dramatic flair, opting to walk over to the windows and gazing out at the traffic below. She also covertly checks to see if I'm still watching her.

I choose to ignore her attention-seeking behavior and instead place our drinks down on an antique side table. With my hands now free, I pick up a stack of opened event invitations that I left there the day before, giving them one final look over before handing them to Roshni, who's still standing nearby.

"I'll reorganize the papers on her desk," I tell her. "Just RSVP to these, and then we can go over tomorrow's itinerary. Blue Post-its are a yes. Yellows are a no."

"Blue, yes. Yellow, no. Got it." She exits the room with her coffee and the invites, seemingly happy to get out of the fray. If only I was so lucky.

Juliette's been dropping hints about me going on this trip with them for the past week, but I've always managed to sidestep the issue. And now, she's brought the battle to my doorstep. Or I guess it's really her doorstep, since she lives here. And what a doorstep it is.

Twenty floors up on a cobbled Tribeca street, you'd either

have to be born into money or wildly successful to own one of these grandly scaled units. Juliette is both. Already a border-line heiress thanks to her Manhattan real-estate mogul father, she then went on to become one of the city's most celebrated playwrights. She was given everything but still hustled like crazy for her career and threw all of her time and energy into mastering her craft. Luckily for her, it proved to be a lethal combination.

As a native New Yorker and a fiercely proud West-Sider, Juliette's lived in this apartment for as long as I've worked for her. The furniture is mismatched and romantic, and white walls are splashed with green from her dozens of potted plants. Every available surface is covered with old scripts, books, or half-drunk cups of tea. It's scholarly chic. If Jane Austen ever traveled forward through time, I like to imagine that this is what her apartment would look like. Alas, dear Jane is nowhere to be found as Juliette steps away from the windows, moving through the space to sit on the arm of her tufted couch.

"Give me one good reason why you can't go on this trip."

I roll my shoulders, trying to relieve a sudden stress knot before taking a much-needed sip of my latte. "Because you're leaving tonight. I'm not mentally or physically prepared, and this is supposed to be my yearly vacation time. I have projects that I need to work on, too."

"Yes, your grand opus of a play that you're forever editing. Maybe the change of scenery will inspire you. 'In London, love and scandal are considered the best sweeteners of tea.'"

"Don't try to mind-trick me with John Osborne quotes."

Juliette groans and pushes up off the sofa. "I'm only trying to help you."

"It would help me if you read my play and told me what you think."

She just looks at me then and says nothing, no doubt trying to come up with another lackluster excuse. I've asked her to read my play dozens of times over the years, but she always finds a reason not to. She's too busy, her mind is clouded, she's not in the right mood.

"I'll read it when it's finished. Whatever I say now would alter your creative course."

Ah, so she doesn't want to sway my process. Not likely. Juliette's perpetually happy to give her two cents on everything, especially on another playwright's work.

"As far as London," she goes on, "you just need to think about it more. Mull it over, let the idea sink in, and if you could agree to come with us in the next ten to fifteen minutes, that would be great." She goes to leave the room after that but stops short when her cell phone starts ringing. She looks around but doesn't find it. I do the same until she digs into the couch cushions and eventually plucks it out. She checks the caller ID and smiles as she answers.

"Liam! To what do I owe the pleasure?"

A little out of breath from her impromptu sofa wrestling match, she twists around and away from me, walking over to the windowsill and picking up a small watering can. She sprinkles her first row of plant babies as she listens to his response. Liam is her nephew and lives in London, which is also where her sister, Isabelle, has lived since she moved there in her twenties. I've never met her or him, but I have sent Liam gifts on Juliette's behalf every Christmas and on his birthday.

"That's right," she says, moving on to the next row of plants. "I'm getting in tomorrow at 10:00 a.m. Will I be seeing you?" She tries to water the oversized ficus in the corner, but the can is empty. "Sounds great! Here, I'm passing you over to Winnie for a second. Do me a favor and convince her to come on the trip with me. She's being obstinate."

"What? No." My protest is in vain as Juliette's phone is already in flight. I barely catch it as she disappears into the kitchen, shaking the empty watering can over her shoulder in response.

I clear my throat and put the phone to my ear. "Hello, Liam."

"Hello, is Winnie there, please?" he asks with mock seriousness.

I fail to suppress my involuntary smile at his polite request and inviting British accent. "This is she," I answer back.

"Excellent, just the person I was hoping to speak to."

"My sentiments exactly. To be honest, I've secretly been dying to talk to you for years."

"Have you really?" he asks, surprised.

"No, not really. I don't even know you." He says nothing, and I think I might have scared him a bit. "Sorry," I lightly amend, "I thought we were pretending that we actually meant to have this conversation."

"Yes, well, that was my initial intention, but it turns out you're much more convincing than I am. I can only assume that you've had formal training?"

"That assumption would be correct."

"I should have figured." His voice is surprisingly calm, sounding more like one of my old improv buddies and less like a stranger who's thousands of miles away. "So," he goes on, "I've been instructed by my aunt to convince you to come to London."

"She does seem to have that idea stuck in her head."

"There's much to recommend it, of course. Red buses. A phenomenal bridge. How do you feel about museums?"

"I hate them," I tease.

"Absolutely. Nothing to be learned from there. And what about parks?"

"Not into them at all."

"Couldn't agree more. I'm violently allergic to pollen, and why should I be forced to carry an EpiPen just so everyone else can enjoy natural beauty? Pure selfishness on their end."

I smile to myself and pivot around so I'm no longer standing still. "I knew you couldn't be as normal as you originally sounded. It's to be expected, though, since you do share a bloodline with Juliette."

"Yes, we had hoped lunacy would skip a generation, but apparently not." He pauses then, and I somehow know that he's smiling, too. "So, how am I faring on my quest so far? Are you packing your bags at this very moment?"

"Unfortunately not. I somehow forgot to bring all my luggage and clothes with me to work today, but still, this has been a very pleasant verbal exchange thus far."

"For me as well. Can I ask what's holding you back from taking the trip?"

"You may, but I may also choose not to answer."

"Ah, a lady of secrets, are we?"

"Oh yes," I answer dramatically. "A lady of many secrets and a play that I need to finish in seventeen days if I'm going to make a contest deadline."

"Really? I take it that you're a playwright as well, then?"

"Afraid so."

"In that case, as you have a very good reason to stay at home rather than crossing the Atlantic, I won't try to sway you any further...but know that I do so very reluctantly."

"I appreciate that."

Juliette sashays back into the room then, the watering can

forgotten as she plops down onto the couch with one of her many notebooks. I'll have to see to the rest of the plants later. She props her feet up on the coffee table and begins to write as I make my way towards her.

"Alright, well, your aunt is now back, so I'll get going."

"It was very nice meeting you, Winnie."

"We didn't actually meet," I say, correcting him.

"But it sort of feels like we did."

I find myself grinning once more and shift away so Juliette won't notice. "I guess it does," I admit. "Bye, Liam."

"Goodbye, Winnie." I pivot back around and hand the phone over. Juliette looks at me with a mischievous sort of smirk as I shake my head and step away to hang my bag in the entryway closet.

"Hello again. Did you enjoy your chat with Winnie?" She raises her voice just enough so I continue to hear her. "Yes, she's exceedingly bright and even more so when you see her in person. Everyone adores her. She has a level of relatability that I wasn't born with."

I roll my eyes and close the closet door with a loud thud.

"Okay, I'll see you tomorrow. And let me give you Winnie's number in case you can't reach me." I immediately power walk back into the living room and gesture *no*. I don't just give out my phone number, even to a charming British guy with a seemingly good sense of humor.

"You know what, I'll text it to you. It'll be easier. Yes. No, I know she says she's not coming, but she's probably coming." She pauses then, begrudgingly listening. "I'm not bullying her, Liam. I'm trying to steer her in the right direction." She withstands another unhappy pause. "Okay, well, you're breaking up, so I can't quite hear you. I'll see you tomorrow. Bye, darling!"

She hangs up the phone and quickly rolls into a text, deftly moving her fingers across the touch screen.

"You really don't need to give him my number," I say, not even trying to disguise the underlying frustration in my voice.

"It's fine. If you come on the trip, he'll need it. If you don't, he won't use it. I'm texting you his number, too."

I step over to the side table once again, this time picking up Juliette's Earl Grey tea with milk. I sit down next to her on the couch and hand it over.

"I got an email from your contractor last night. He says if you still want to make those bathroom renovations, he can give you an updated estimate. Also, I heard from Cindy at the Women in Theater Foundation, and they want to know if you'll host another webinar. If you're open to it, they'd love for your talks to become a monthly or bimonthly thing."

Juliette takes a sip of her tea before placing the cup onto the coffee table. "No to the renovations, yes to the webinar or webinars. I'll do it as soon as I get back."

"Sounds good." I pull my phone out of my back pocket and program a reminder into my ever-growing to-do list. "They said they want you to focus more on the process of getting a play produced this time. Like a how-to type of thing rather than the basics of playwriting."

"Fantastic," she says in an ironic kind of way. "Maybe I can dig up a memory from one of my past lives where I was actually successful."

"You *are* successful, Juliette. You're arguably the most successful female playwright of your generation."

"Right," she says, smiling as she seems to remember better days and then frowning when she realizes she's not still living in them.

Juliette hasn't written a new piece in eight years but keeps herself busy with speaking engagements and guest lectures. She shines in them, too, until someone asks what she's currently working on, and then she deflates. It only lasts a moment, but it's always there. After that, she throws them off with a witty comment that garners a laugh and makes her escape, leaving people thinking that she just *has* to be working on her next masterpiece, because how can someone as brilliant and charming as her not be? I often wonder the same thing.

I look over at her now and see that flash of vulnerability. That split second when her formidable exterior fades enough to reveal the insecure writer who isn't so very different from me. She slumps deeper into the couch and leans her head back against the cushions, looking up at the ceiling before turning to catch my gaze.

"I need you to come on this trip with me, kid." Her doe eyes dig into mine, even through the thick lenses of her glasses. "I haven't restaged a play of mine in forever, and I need you there to support me."

"You're going to have Roshni with you," I assure her.

"I know that, but as amazing as Roshni is, she isn't even involved in the theater. She's here for a fun summer job, and then she's becoming a pharmacist."

Juliette isn't exaggerating there. Roshni's mom is her lawyer and longtime friend and was the main facilitator in organizing this two-month position we created just for her.

"Even so," I say, "you're not going to be on your own. There's a director and a cast and a crew already in place. You're really just going to oversee everything and offer advice."

"Yes, I'm aware that I'm basically only invited for a glorified photo op, but what if this is make-or-break for me? This trip could be exactly what I need to get things moving again creatively, and maybe it's what you need, too."

I sigh as I feel my resolve starting to weaken. I think about the playwriting contest I'm planning to enter. The contest that can finally wipe away my former theatrical humiliation. The contest that can give me the validation that I wish I didn't desperately need, but I do.

If I go on the trip, I can still get work done. Of course, it won't be the same as having uninterrupted free time, but it's doable. I just have to finish off the ending and polish the rest. Some of the best playwrights on earth have found inspiration in London. (I'm looking at you, Caryl Churchill!) Maybe a little jaunt across the pond wouldn't be the worst thing in the world.

Or maybe it will be a jaw-dropping mistake.

Indecision gnaws at the back of my mind as I focus back on Juliette, knowing that I need to give her a serious answer, one way or another. I make a mental note to call my dad. I was supposed to have dinner with him this weekend.

"What do you say, kid? Are you in?"

When she says it like that, when she calls me "kid," it's so easy to think that she's saying it in a maternal way—that she thinks of me like a daughter. I'm not positive that's how she means it, but that's how I hear it, and it pulls at my heartstrings with undeniable force.

I shake my head, already half regretting my decision.

"I'm in."

2

So, this is me taking back every negative thing I've ever said about flying first class. Much as I enjoyed my previous moral high ground, I am beyond comfortable right now and feeling fancy AF. Is this experience completely unnecessary? Yes. Do I feel like an imposter? Undoubtedly. Am I going to turn Juliette down if she offers to spring for the same seats on future flights? Hell to the no. I'm currently half-reclined, sitting up with my legs fully extended and covered by a luxurious blanket, with a shiny little table suspended over my lap. I'm working on my play, as I always do, while simultaneously finding a reason to procrastinate, as I also always do.

As I look at the laptop screen, my open document is more in the background than in the forefront as I read through a group chat I'm in with some of my graduate school friends and our favorite professor. We all talk fairly regularly, forever inviting each other to shows and workshops. But now, more often than not, everyone is announcing the staging of their plays or a producer they're meeting with or something else along those lines. Everyone moving forward as I stay stagnant. Comfortable, but stagnant.

Avery just told us she signed with an agent. And I'm happy for her, of course I am, but a twinge of jealousy inevitably reverberates through my psyche. I know this is incredible news for her, but it also sometimes feels like there's only a finite amount of success to go around, and if I don't get my share now, I never will.

I close out the chat and attempt to channel my emotions into my writing, into the same play that I've been tweaking and twisting around in my brain for the past four years. It's a nonlinear comedy with what I hope has plenty of depth and thought-provoking moments. I've always felt a little out of place writing comedy while my friends penned hard-hitting dramas, but I've also enjoyed etching out my own little artistic space. A place that offers laughs and sighs as well as complexity and social relevance.

I scroll through the document now, going back to adjust a scene in the second act, when I hear Juliette quietly *psst*ing at me, trying to be mindful of the other travelers who are already asleep. I glance over to my right and find her across the aisle, half-reclined. Roshni is passed out to her left with a silk mask over her eyes that says Beauty Sleep Mode.

"What are you doing over there?" she asks, nudging her chin towards my computer. "Discreetly reading fan fiction?"

"Don't judge fan fiction. It's the next literary frontier." She rolls her eyes, and I twist my body to face her. "I'm just trying to finish up my project."

"You still haven't given it a title yet?"

"I will when it's done. Like how some parents don't name their babies until they're born—I have to see what it looks like first."

Juliette nods. "I came up with the title for *The Lights of Trafalgar* a year before I wrote it. I just kept saying it over and over in my head until I willed it into existence."

"Maybe that's where I went wrong. I'll have to start referring to this as *The Award-Winning Play that Saves Me from My Looming Mental Breakdown.*"

Juliette smiles and reclines her seat a little more, looking up at the overhead light above her before turning back to me. "At least you still have time. When I was your age, ideas and plots sprang from my mind like fruit from the branch. Now I'm nothing but a termite-infested stump."

"You are not a stump. The fact that we're currently traveling internationally to restage one of your plays proves how un-stump-like you are."

"Restaging," she scoffs. "Now, that's a generous description."

I try to think of something to appease her, but I know nothing will work. The fact that *The Lights of Trafalgar* is being mounted in an outdoor pop-up location at Regent's Park rather than a traditional theater always rubbed her the wrong way, and clearly, she's yet to get on board.

"A pop-up play is still a play, Juliette. Some would say it's better. When you shy away from convention, you unlock aspects of a piece that may have never been explored before."

"Ah, to have your hopeful naivete for just one day."

I say nothing then, painfully aware that it's near impossible to get her out of one of her moods once it's taken hold.

"Do you remember what the critics said about my last play?" she goes on. "That it was a pale reminder—a sad, weathered husk of a show that didn't belong in today's theater. That through trying to re-create my past success, I was left flailing. Flailing, Winnie. That one hurt."

"Only a few critics said that. Plenty of the other reviewers thought it was delightful."

"Right," she says with a bitter laugh. "And whoever did say that was probably just as much of a hack as I am. One bad play can be forgiven. Two and you should get nervous. After three, you need to accept your fate of being buried in an un-marked Broadway grave."

"You're being too hard on yourself." I push the button to lower my legs back down to the floor, quickly glancing around for a flight attendant. I make eye contact with a kind-looking blonde and gesture for two more glasses of champagne. Maybe the alcohol will cheer Juliette up, or, fingers crossed, put her to sleep for an hour or two.

I face across the aisle again and now find her fully reclined, no doubt trying to appear as corpse-like as possible as she covers her eyes with her hands. "I'm being forgotten, Winnie. And what's worse, I'm *letting* myself be forgotten."

The flight attendant comes over with the drinks, and I gratefully take them. She looks over at Juliette and gives me an encouraging smile before walking away. I take a generous sip from one of the glasses and focus back on the task at hand.

"You just need to decide to write something and then do it. We're living in such a dynamic time where millions of stories are buzzing around us wherever we go. There are hundreds of plays waiting to be written by someone as talented as you."

"But that's just the problem! I'm detached now." She whips her hands down from her face and looks over at me, bereft and hopeless until she notices the champagne. She maintains her sad demeanor but presses the control button to un-recline her seat. "I'm not the woman I was in my twenties, going out and meeting the people who breathed life and energy into my work. I eat dinner at six, and I'm in bed by nine. And as far as love, it's a definitive no to the creepy old men or slimy younger men who are only after my money."

"Not all men are like that. If we signed you up for a dating app, I bet you would get a ton of responses. Lots of my friends use Vibefinder, and they love it."

"Me on a dating app?" She takes the champagne that I obligingly offer her. "Yeah, I'm sure I'd be all the rage online. We can post a sexy selfie of me divvying up my calcium supplements."

I shake my head, understanding her hesitation but also knowing that there's so much more to be had out there for her.

"And what about you?" she asks. "Are you on this dating app?"

"Me? No."

"Why not? You seem as solitary as I am."

"I guess for the most part I am. There is a guy I talk to on occasion, though."

"Define 'talk to.'"

How to phrase this? "I mean 'talk to' in a semi-romantic sense. We text every so often and hook up once in a while."

Juliette seems confused but intrigued. "And this is in the hopes of eventually forming a relationship?"

"Not really. He's just a friend I enjoy spending time with occasionally when I'm feeling lonely."

"I see. And I'm assuming you two…have the sex?"

"The sex?" I repeat, coughing on my champagne a bit. "Yes, he and I sometimes have the sex."

"But you're not interested in dating him?"

"I don't think so. I doubt he and I would work in the long term, plus I don't really have time to date."

Juliette continues to gaze at me, a mischievous gleam slowly taking shape in her eyes. "Okay, I just had a thought that's actually kind of perfect. And I want you to really hear me out before you get all up in arms and say no." I take a breath, bracing myself for whatever hit is about to come my way before she says, "We need to sign you up for this Vibe Selector app."

Well, it's finally happened. Juliette Brassard has lost her mind.

"Alright, first of all, it's Vibefinder, not Vibe Selector, and second of all, no. I'm not signing up. I'm not even trying to meet anyone right now, plus dating is awful."

Juliette tucks one of her knees under her as she curls up in her seat, looking animated and girlish and very much ready to bring me nothing but stress. "Just think about this for a second. I need to write a new play, but I have no material, and you're the demographic I'm supposed to be writing for now if I want to stay relevant. If you do this, you can gallivant your way through romantic adventures in London, and I can write about it. It's a brilliant, foolproof plan."

"Hard pass," I say with absolute certainty. "One hundred percent hard pass. If you want material, then you can go on out there and get it yourself. A play about your own emotional and sensual pursuits would honestly be kind of amazing."

"Oh, really? Because last time I checked, audiences weren't beating down the doors for geriatric love stories. Also, I have no time. I'm supposed to be concentrating on the oh-so-wonderful and innovative pop-up production, aren't I?"

And now she's trying to turn the tables on me. Like her putting solid effort into the pop-up is somehow doing *me* a favor.

"I don't have time either, Juliette. I'm only here right now because you emotionally coerced me, and I have my own play to work on."

"And what, you think traipsing around London with young British men will send you into a creative rut?"

"Shockingly, I don't need the male validation of horny strangers to magically reinvigorate my writing."

"Okay, if that statement was directed towards me, it is both wildly offensive and categorically not what I mean. I've written multiple plays about toppling the patriarchy from the inside out and passed them off as romantic comedies. I 'Trojan-horsed feminist revolution into '80s mainstream theater,' and that is a direct quote from the *The New Yorker*."

"Yes, I'm aware, so please get to the point and tell me what you're saying."

"I'm saying I need your help! My writing is tired and outdated, and I can't create from a new and fresh perspective if I don't know anything about what's going on in the romantic world around me. I need you to be my millennial muse. My eyes and ears. You can also have fun and put yourself out there, and we can all win."

I down my champagne in an irritated gulp. "Me doing this would not be me winning, Juliette. I'm entering the Twenty-Fourth Annual Arthur Brady Playwriting Contest, and I have to actually finish my play if I want to do that. I only have seventeen days to submit it, and I'm already cutting it close by being on this trip."

Juliette must be slightly moved by my deadline and looks off to the side before facing me again, determined as ever.

"How about this: you help me gather the writing material that I need, and I'll help you with your play."

"You'll read it?" I ask, shocked. "You'll read it in time for the contest?"

"Now, that will probably be difficult given how busy we're about to be, but I will absolutely get to it once we're back to New York. I'll read it, I'll give in-depth line notes, I'll even write you an editorial letter and put you in touch with a producer if that's what it's going to take."

I'm inwardly thrilled, but also hurt that Juliette is only willing to read my work because it's now in her best interests. She's not doing it for me, she's doing it for herself. But I also happen to be desperate enough to consider it. True, I won't have her edits before the contest, but it's better than nothing. And at least if I end up losing, her help would be a great opportunity to fall back on.

"To be clear, what exactly are you expecting out of this arrangement?"

"Barely anything, in the grand scheme of things. What I need from you is to sign up for this app so we can choose some guys for you to go out with while we're in London. And obviously you in no way need to do anything sexual or even romantic with these people. Just ask them questions and get stories out of them to bring back to me. Once I have a feeling for the character I want to write, everything will click into place."

"And how many guys am I supposed to meet?" I ask.

"Nothing too bad. How about seven?"

"Are you insane? I'll agree to two."

"Three, then. We're in London for twenty-one days, so one meetup per week or however you decide you want to space it. And if you hate it or feel unsafe for even a second, we immediately call it off."

I pause, thinking there's no way this is going to pan out the way she wants it to, but also knowing that I could probably handle it, even if I'm not looking forward to it. Years of theater school prepared me for working intimately with quasi-strangers. My embarrassment threshold is basically nonexistent. But still, this whole situation doesn't sit right with me. This isn't Juliette wanting me to pick up her laundry or to go to the store for her—this is an inappropriate ask.

"I have to think about it," I tell her.

"Yes, you think about it," she says. "I'll just lie here and wallow in self-doubt until you decide."

I give her a knowing look as she slowly reclines her seat back down. Rubbing my eyes, I focus again on my computer, which is now alerting me to an email. I click into my inbox and see that it's from my friend and former professor, Jack. I'm somewhat surprised, since we were all just talking a few minutes ago in the group chat, but quickly open the email and begin to read.

Winnie,

I know you're currently en route to jolly London-town, but I wanted to reach out to you privately so I could run something by you. As you're aware, I've recently left teaching to become the Director of Development for the West Lane Theater Company (please hold your applause, but present monetary gifts directly). Anyways, I've just found out that we're going to be looking for a new Managing Artistic Director, and I immediately thought of you. The pay isn't astronomical, but it is competitive. You'd be in charge of curating the season, working with the programming committee and supervising/supporting guest directors.

I'll still have to post the position online, but if you want it, the job could be yours, pending your interview process and the board's approval. And before you start second-guessing yourself, I want to assure you that I wouldn't be putting you forward for this if I didn't think you were qualified. I know you've been in your current spot for quite a while, but there's room for growth here as well as it being an incredible creative outlet. I hate seeing all your talent go to waste. Just think about it, and if you're interested, I'd be more than happy to discuss things further. Or you could just tell me to "bugger off," as would be more geographically appropriate for you at the moment. Either way, let me know.

Best wishes,
Jack

And just when I think my mind couldn't be any more ready to explode, here we are.

Adrenaline pumps through me, and I'm absolutely dizzy with the world of possibilities that has just opened up to me. A real job in theater, being immersed in the world I love, creative liberties and experiences. Pure giddiness emanates from my every pore until I look to my right and find my current employer still staring up at the ceiling. My racing mind comes to a screeching halt.

Could I ever really leave Juliette? Would I even want to? A guilty sinking feeling settles in my gut, even though I have nothing to feel guilty about, especially considering what she just asked me to do. And it's that exact thought that emboldens me to immediately email Professor Jack back, telling him the job sounds like an incredible opportunity and that I'm very interested in hearing more. I hit the send button and glance at Juliette again, wondering how she'll take it if I do leave. Not well, I'm sure. She'll be angry and hurt, but I can only hope that she'll understand with time.

It crosses my mind that I could help soften the blow by going out on a good note. If I agree to participate in her highly unethical dating experiment, maybe she'll be more empathetic when and if I hand in my notice. I would have proven that I would literally do anything for her. Because the truth of it is, even if we do go our own ways professionally, I don't want to lose her. Yes, she's demanding and out there and slightly self-centered, but I also know that she cares about me. That I mean something to her. I may be ready to stop being her assistant, but I don't want to stop being her friend.

I quietly close my computer, tucking it into the ample storage space beside me as I once again consider what I'm about to do. A half hour later, I'm still torn and wary, but my decision is made. I make a *psst* sound to Juliette, who looks lethargically over at me.

"I really do think this idea of yours is utterly ridiculous."

Juliette's eyes light up as they always do when she gets her way, and she immediately raises her seat. "We have a deal, then? You're going to do it?"

I pause for several seconds until I eventually nod.

"Yes!" She springs up from her chair and leaps over to give me a hug that is chock-full of excitement and tangible relief. I can't stop myself from returning it, albeit without my usual zeal. She hops back into her seat soon after, clapping her hands together. "Thank you, thank you, thank you! There is a method to my madness, Winnie, trust me. This is going to work."

"Famous last words," I mutter to myself. I gesture to the flight attendant for another champagne as I pull the ultrasoft blanket in my lap up to my chin. Frowned upon or not, it is absolutely exiting this plane with me come morning. If one finds themselves on the verge of an existential crisis while also throwing their dignity to the wind for the sake of their boss's creative process, they at least deserve a fluffy blanket.

3

Slipping out of the sleek silver town car that picked us up from Heathrow, we're now standing in front of a white stucco building lined with multiple terraces. A short wrought-iron fence encloses the front, and two rows of lush bushes lead to a pair of black double doors. Juliette takes a deep breath as she gazes up at the period building, her cheeks pulling back in the smallest smile before striding forward towards the entrance.

"Yeah, no, we'll get the bags," Roshni says jokingly. "You think she'll tip us?"

"Oh, exorbitantly," I answer with a smirk. Between the two of us, we manage the luggage after five minutes and two trips up and down the pristine elevator. And when we finally do enter Juliette's apartment, my breath catches in my throat.

It's similar in size to the New York penthouse, but that's where the similarities end. This space is dreamier, softer, shimmering with a quiet elegance. It's staged to perfection with clean lines and timelessly fashionable decor. Tan and white make up everything—the expansive walls, the plush carpets, the herringbone wood floor. Brass lighting features and chandeliers remain unlit but beautiful as natural light pours in from the stately vintage windows.

Roshni nudges me with her shoulder. "Is it just me, or do you suddenly feel like a French diplomat?"

"*Oui*, Madam Ambassador," I say in my best Parisian accent. "This place is next-level. Do you think we can convince Juliette that we should all live here permanently?"

"Whatever plan you come up with, I'm down. If all else fails, we can just start wearing glasses and baggy designer clothes as we slowly steal her identity."

"I support that course of action."

Roshni gasps as she steps deeper into the living room and looks over at the open kitchen off to the right that seems to be made entirely of marble. I follow her path, and we're both standing there with mouths agape as Juliette returns from the bedroom and tosses her bag down onto the floor. She strolls over to the center of the room and falls back onto the luxurious cream-colored couch.

"I can't believe I'm back here," she says lazily. "It feels like I've entered some kind of time warp. Any chance my body reverted back to its twentysomething glory?"

I move in her direction to sit on one of the armchairs, which I swear molds to perfectly cushion my entire body.

"You look as vibrant and lovely as ever," I answer.

"Womp, womp. So that's a no."

"Seriously, why don't you live here year-round? This place is incredible."

"Trust me, it gets old fast."

"I find that hard to believe." I burrow down even deeper into the bewitchingly comfy cushions. "And for the record, if you'd decide to relocate me here for work and change my job title from assistant to estate manager, I want you to know you have my unequivocal blessing."

"Fabulous. But before you apply for dual citizenship, let's not forget that we're only here for three weeks."

"Three weeks, a month, a year. What is time, really?"

"Time is something you're running short on, as a matter of fact. You're due to meet British Boyfriend Number One in a couple of hours."

Still investigating the kitchen, Roshni clears her throat and graces me with a disapproving gaze when I glance at her over my shoulder. She woke up on the flight just as Juliette and I put the finishing touches on my Vibefinder profile, and she is most certainly not a fan of this faux romantic endeavor. I give her a resigned shrug and turn back to Juliette.

Setting the profile up was easy enough. We used the acting headshots I had taken just before graduate school and mixed them in with some more casual recent photos. I'm not a stunner, but I'm decent. My eyes have always been my best feature. A sapphire kind of blue that stand out nicely against my untamably curly brown hair. I used to try to straighten it, but have since let the dream go. Sure, it sometimes looks like a family of squirrels lives in the unruly locks, but I like to think that they're a happy family of squirrels.

"Arranging to meet someone today was a mistake," I mutter. "I smell like an airport, and I look like death."

"Nonsense. You're adorable and exotic, and you're only going for a stroll in the park."

"A Manhattanite is hardly exotic."

"Well, that's all about perspective, isn't it?"

I continue to glare at her, and it only seems to energize her more. "So," she goes on, "have a bath, don't overthink things, go for your meetup, and then come back with stories that will undoubtedly cure my dry spell and save my career."

"No pressure, right?"

"None at all," she says happily. "Off you go!"

Two hours later, I'm showered, changed, and feeling significantly more human as I walk through the Italian Gardens of Hyde Park with a fresh cup of coffee. I weave my way through the four main water features as I enjoy the calming mist and relaxing ambiance. I'm dressed in jeans and a white T-shirt, and my hair is wrangled back in a casual bun. I've always liked buns. They make me feel like an off-duty ballerina, plus whenever I did tech in theater camp, it was imperative to keep my beast of a mane safely tucked away.

All talk of buns aside, can I just say that I am loving this London weather? I tend to sweat a fair amount, so the end of May through August in NYC often feels like my yearly summer share in the seventh ring of hell. Yet here I am, in the middle of June, and I couldn't be more comfortable. It has to be at least twenty degrees cooler than it is back home. My arms even feel the slightest bit chilled as I take a comforting sip of coffee. I'm still marveling at just how idyllic the day is when an attractive man appears a few feet in front of me with a little wave. He has messy black hair, plenty of stubble, and a devil-may-care manner. The red plaid shirt he's wearing is just the right amount of vintage. He looks like an updated, younger version of Captain Hook, and I have to say, I. Am. Into it.

"Winnie?" he asks.

I lift up my coffee in greeting and smile as I step closer. "Colin?"

"That would be me." We both stop walking with guarded smiles, now standing a couple of feet apart.

"It's nice to meet you," I quickly say. I reach out for a handshake, but he goes for a hug, and my left arm ends up trapped in the middle as my right, coffee-holding arm sort of strains around his back. He offers an awkward laugh as he backs away, and I end up doing the same.

"Alright, so not at all an uncomfortable greeting," he teases.

Always a fan of someone who can poke fun at themselves, I immediately give Colin some extra credit. "Don't worry. It's almost physically impossible for me to be embarrassed, so whatever happens moving forward, don't trouble yourself about it."

"Really?" he asks. "I'm the opposite. I once laughed so hard that I weed my pants at a dance when I was twelve, and I still think about it at least once a week and try not to scream."

I give him a pitying smile, and he seems to get embarrassed all over again. "And apparently, I also bring it up in conversations with girls I just met, so that's great as well."

"I promise you, it's fine. It's good that you're honest."

"Well, that's very kind of you, and great to know in this circumstance."

"Absolutely." A pleasant silence spreads between us as we both turn to walk side by side. "So, Colin, why don't you tell me a little bit about yourself. What were you like growing up?"

His brows jolt up in surprise as he looks down and over at me. "You really want to hear about that?"

"Sure, why wouldn't I?"

"I don't know. I just figured you would want to get to it straightaway."

I take a small sip of coffee. "I'm sorry, get to what straightaway?"

"You know," he says, his voice dropping. "Going back to my place, or to yours, if you prefer."

And just like that, Colin sucks. This is what I get for lusting after Captain Hook.

"Oh, really?" I ask. "And what have I said or done that gave you that impression?"

"It's just what this usually entails. Girls who come here on holiday and sign up for a dating app. They're looking for a little adventure or just doing it for the story."

"That's been your experience, then? You do this often?"

"I mean, more or less. We can take some pictures for your social media first, if you'd like. That way it can look like we hung out for a good amount of time. I'm better in videos than I am in photos, though, so maybe we can do a few Boomerangs instead. What do you think?"

"I think that sounds fantastic," I answer. "Actually, it works out perfectly because I'd much rather have a video of the stranger I'm apparently about to bang on vacation than a photo. But I'm a little worried about the lighting. Any chance you have an iRing handy? Or should we maybe delay this rendezvous until sunset?"

Colin stops walking, looking at me with what I can only guess is *so you're not going to have sex with me* disappointment in his eyes.

"I get the feeling that you're joking," he says.

"Yeah, me too."

A bitter kind of smirk appears on his face as he scratches the back of his neck. "To be fair, what was I supposed to think was happening here? You told me you're only visiting for a few weeks and wanted to meet new people."

"Um, plot twist, maybe I meant just that?"

"That's not what I've found when meeting up with girls in these kinds of situations. Particularly American girls."

Okay, and now he's trying to slut-shame my fellow countrywomen? This guy is two-point-five seconds away from receiving a very American kick to the balls.

"Wow, you're awful, aren't you?"

"I thought you appreciated honesty?" he counters.

"Yes, I do," I answer evenly. "And I would also appreciate it if you would go share your pee-your-pants seduction story with a therapist or a priest instead of with unsuspecting tourists from now on."

He pushes his shoulders back and turns away to glance across the park. "Right, then. I can't believe I wasted cab fare on this."

"I know, such a bummer, right?" My tone is all sympathy, and it earns me a minor scowl in return. I smile brightly up at him as he turns on his heel and walks away. It's understandable. I'd be pissed if *my* anonymous midmorning sexcapade got canceled, too.

I shake my head, then try to enjoy what's left of my coffee as I begin walking towards the exit/entrance where I came in. I'm not overly fazed by my brief and gross encounter with Colin, but I'm certain it's not the romantic material Juliette is looking for. I'm just leaving the park, and hoping she won't be too disheartened, when I hear a strange sound coming from the bushes beside me. It's a rustling of the leaves and a quiet cry, and I immediately stop walking. I inch a little closer, inwardly hoping that I'm not teeing myself up for a rabid raccoon bite when a small dog crawls out, trembling and looking terrified.

A pup-pup!

I don't hesitate to drop to my knees. "Hi there," I coo, trying to draw it closer. "Hey, baby. It's okay, you can come over."

The poor thing is beyond dirty and shaking like a leaf, and after a little more coaxing, he comes close enough to let me pet him. I can tell he's not really a puppy, but a few years old and some kind of cocker spaniel. He looks even older with the layers of dirt that are matted into the fur under his eyes. My insides tighten as I think how uncomfortable he must be. I slowly pick him up and almost implode with maternal rage when I realize that he's frighteningly underweight. Seeing that he's not wearing a collar, I'm not positive what the exact protocol should be in this scenario, but I do know that this dog is leaving the park with me. Once I get back to the apartment, I'll research what I should do, and I'll take him to a vet as soon as possible. I'm sure they can tell me what my next steps should be. Also, henceforth, his name is Ollie.

Continuing to pet Ollie's tangled caramel-and-white fur in comforting strokes, I head back to the apartment and try to anticipate how I'll be received. I don't think Juliette dislikes dogs, but I haven't seen her interact with one either. We get to the penthouse and take the lift up with little incident, but I feel a stirring of uncertainty as we stand just outside the door. Forcing my nerves away, I turn the key in the lock and ready myself for whatever reaction I'm about to face. No sooner do I swing the mahogany door open than Ollie leaps from my arms and sprints inside. My mind flies to the flawless beige carpeting, and my heart drops.

"Ollie, wait!" My fear has me rushing into the apartment after him, running through the entryway and into the living room, where I stop dead in my tracks.

Ollie is now vigorously humping the calf of a very tall and dashing redhead.

Said redhead appears as shell-shocked to see me as I am to see him, his hands whipping up in a startled kind of surrender. "I swear I'm not an intruder. I'm just here visiting my aunt Juliette." I remain momentarily frozen as his eyes shift between Ollie and me. "Assuming I'm telling the truth, which I'm sure my aunt will attest to when she comes back out in a second, do you think it would be possible to call off the dogs?"

I shake my head and break out of my stupor long enough to quickly cross the room and lift Ollie up into my arms. "Right, I'm so sorry about that," I say, unsure of the proper etiquette after a sudden, random dog-humping.

"No, it's alright. Believe it or not, this happens to me fairly often."

"Does it really?"

"No, that would be quite odd, actually."

I have to laugh a little, and the man gives me a comforting smile.

"Yes, that would be pretty weird," I agree. "And you seem like a very un-weird kind of guy."

"Do I?" I nod, and he appears pleased. "Fantastic. My daily affirmations must be working, then."

I give him a look that conveys his weird factor is increasing by the second, and it prompts him to take a small step forward.

"Let me just quit while I'm ahead and reset things a bit." He takes a breath and extends his hand. "Hello, I'm Liam."

I take his warm hand in mine and throw on my best neutral poker face in the process. This is very much necessary because, full disclosure, Liam is arguably the most handsome nerd I have ever seen.

To clarify, I have no idea if Liam really is a nerd—and in no way do I mean it in a disparaging way. I, myself, am a nerd, but I'm a standard issue drama nerd. No, this guy looks like he lived through a teen movie, but the popular girl never gave him the makeover she thought he needed to make him a viable option for her. Instead, he got through high school just fine on his own and filled out in all the right places and in all the right ways on the road to adulthood.

"Nice to meet you, Liam. I'm Winnie."

"Ah," he says, "would this be the Winnie I had the pleasure of speaking with yesterday?"

"That it is."

"This should probably be the part where I tell you that you don't look like your voice but, in this situation, you actually look exactly like your voice."

"Really? And how do I look and sound?"

He hesitates for a second, seeming unsure before he quickly says, "Enchanting."

I try to quip back with a snappy reply, but nothing comes. My cheeks threaten to stain red before I swiftly pull myself back together. "I'm sorry, but isn't that a little corny?"

"Yes, well, sometimes the truth can be corny."

"And you're coming on a little strong considering you're still holding my hand."

We both look down between us to see what I'm talking about, but he doesn't let go. And neither do I.

"As it happens," he says, "I believe it's *you* that's still holding *my* hand."

I realize that he's right and immediately release his hand from mine, stepping away as I clear my throat. "Sorry about that. It's been a bit of a morning over here." I watch as Liam slides his hand into his pocket, and I have to say, I'm sorry to see it go. "So, you said you're here visiting Juliette? Did she have to suddenly run out or something?"

"Not quite, she just stepped into the other room to take a phone call from her manager."

"Oh, great," I say unenthusiastically, hoisting Ollie up to hold him more firmly against my chest.

"You're not a fan of her manager, I presume?"

"No, he's fine, but it just means we'll most likely be going to an event or a function tonight, and I was hoping to have some time for myself."

"Do you always accompany my aunt?" he asks.

"Mostly, and the places we go to are typically interesting, but I have a lot of work to do at the moment."

"Right, your play. I'd love to hear more about that, by the way."

Pleasantly surprised that he remembered, I'm about to reply when Juliette strides into the room, holding her locked phone and what I can safely assume is her third cup of tea, judging from the abandoned mugs I see scattered on nearby tables. I turn on the spot and place Ollie down behind the couch in front of me and out of her line of vision.

"Well, if it isn't my two favorite people in the whole world. Winnie, how was your hunting expedition?"

I open my mouth to answer, training my face to appear calm and collected, when Juliette goes on instead, turning to Liam. "Winnie was just out with a very distinguished young man who loves the outdoors as well as photography."

"Sounds like a pervert."

"Excuse me!" Juliette gives her nephew a scandalized glare, but I just grin. "Ignore him, Winnie. Tell us, how did it go?"

"He was a pervert."

Liam doesn't try to conceal his satisfied smile as Juliette huffs and spins away towards the kitchen.

"Well, they can't all be winners. Better luck next time."

"What did Dan want?" I ask, my eyes shifting stealthily from Ollie to her as she opens and closes the refrigerator with a lazy swing.

"Apparently one of the arts foundations I support is having a performance benefit tonight. He wants us to go."

"What's the show?" I ask.

"I don't know, I wasn't fully paying attention. *King Lear*, I think."

"How uplifting," Liam gibes.

I shoot him an unappreciative glare myself, and he smirks before looking down at his feet. I turn back to Juliette, and she's watching the both of us with her ever-observant eyes. I don't have time to dwell on it, though, because Ollie suddenly begins to nibble on the tip of my sneaker.

"You should take Roshni," I blurt out. "She'd love to see a show, and I know she's dying to experience the city."

"I'll take her to the next one. Isabelle is going to be there tonight, and I need all the reinforcements I can get."

"Is she going because she wants to see you?"

Juliette pretends she doesn't hear me as she strolls away from the kitchen and back into the living room. I turn to Liam, who says, "My mother is on the board of the London Fine Arts Society. I'll be there tonight as well."

"Of course," Juliette mutters as she drops down onto the couch, "she's on the board because when they offered the place to me, I turned them down." There's resentment in her voice, but I don't play into it.

"Well, can you at least ask Dan for another ticket for Roshni? Then all three of us can go."

"It's sold out. I'll take her with me to the Ashford gala next week. I'm looking forward to that one, and she'll enjoy it more than you."

I absently nod my head, still trying to figure a way out of tonight when I notice that the nipping at my feet has abruptly stopped. My eyes dart around the room in a panic just in time to watch as Ollie hops up onto the couch beside Juliette.

We're all dead silent as she looks at Ollie, then straight ahead, then back to Ollie.

"I'm sorry," she says to no one in particular, "but can someone please tell me why there's a deeply adorable puppy on my couch that looks like he's carrying every germ known to man?"

I spring into action, forcing a laugh and stepping forward.

"About that, he's actually my maybe temporary, maybe not temporary dog, depending on whether or not I'm actually allowed to keep him. I was leaving the park, and he was scared and abandoned and hungry, so I took him. His name is Ollie."

Juliette doesn't look the least bit surprised, saying, "This would only happen to you." Ollie moves closer to her side, and I'm stunned when she doesn't shift away. Rather, she reaches out her hand, which Ollie begins to lick.

"I think he likes you," I tell her.

"No one *really* likes me," Juliette answers. "And as sweet as Ollie is, I'm afraid he can't stay up here unless he's potty-trained. On a scale of one to ten, how in love with him are you?"

Ollie and I gaze at each other, and I then gaze back at Juliette. "He just called me 'momma' telepathically."

Juliette chuckles. "So I figured. Well, as luck would have it, you two can stay in the studio I own a few floors down."

"You have another apartment in the building?" I ask, surprised.

"I do. It actually was my first London flat."

"Really? Is that why you bought this place?"

"I suppose it was a slightly sentimental purchase, but it was mainly just a real estate investment."

Amazing—I've been working with Juliette for five years and there's still so much I don't know about her. But then again, there's plenty of things she doesn't know about me either. I'm still considering it all when she gets up and goes to her desk drawer along the far wall, pulling out a key and tossing it to me. "I haven't been down to the studio for years. It isn't as nice as it is up here, but it has a certain sweetness. It's apartment 2B."

"Apartment 2B. 2B determined, got it."

"If you'd like, I can show you the way," Liam quickly offers.

"No, no," Juliette tells him. "I need to talk to you, and I'm sure Winnie can find the studio on her own. In addition to being an avid animal advocate, she's also very resourceful."

"She's also still here," I add, moving to scoop Ollie up.

"Yes, you are. So, go get settled, and then we can recap our little project later on."

"Sounds good." I situate Ollie more comfortably in my arms and begin to make my way through the space.

"I'll just see you out," Liam says, crossing the room and walking ahead of me to open the door. I follow his lead and pause as we stand alone in the entryway.

"Well, it was very nice to officially meet you, Winnie. Even under the unexpected circumstances." His disarming blue eyes shift to Ollie before panning back up to meet mine. "I hope to see you again while you're here."

"I'm sure we'll see each other off and on." I keep my tone light and am just preparing to walk away when I suddenly notice what he's wearing. "Wait, is this the sweater your aunt got you for Christmas?"

Liam's gaze moves from his navy pullover to me, his eyebrows scrunching together a bit. "It is. When I was younger and had family visiting, my mom always forced me to wear whatever that person had sent me. She said it was a kind gesture, and I suppose the sentiment stuck."

That is wildly adorable, but I choose not to mention it.

"Push your shoulders back," I say instead. He does, and I notice how the sleeves look baggy and that they're rolled up several times at his wrist. "I can't believe I've been buying you the wrong size sweaters for the past five years. Juliette swore you were an extra-large."

"Am I to understand that you're the one who's been choosing my Christmas gifts for me?"

"And birthdays," I confirm. "Did you like the singing messenger I sent you this year?"

"In truth, it was equal parts enjoyable and mortifying. I was just about to head out for dinner, and the singer insisted on performing multiple aggressive verses of 'Happy Birthday.' I didn't even know 'Happy Birthday' had more than one verse."

"You only turn thirty-five once. Anyways, I went through that singer's portfolio several times online, and he exuded nothing but star power."

"No, I agree with you there. It was just hard to fully gauge his obvious talent through the chicken suit he was wearing."

I let out a laugh but then try to cover it up. "Yes, I forgot about that part."

"Unfortunately, it wasn't so easy for me to forget. I think my ears were red for a week."

"Aw. Do they always turn red when you're embarrassed?"

"For the most part, yes. It has also been known to happen when I'm nervous."

Looking up, I notice that his ears are visibly rosy at this very moment. "And why would you be nervous now?" I ask.

Liam begins to speak but stops himself, appearing almost guilty until his says, "I think it probably has something to do with you being incredibly nice to talk to and me generally not liking to talk at all. And I'm afraid of saying the wrong thing."

Great. So he's a shy, thoughtful, rugged redhead, and why does this entryway suddenly feel unbearably warm? I should be sprinting for the elevator, but I keep talking instead.

"I have a nervous gesture, too," I tell him. "I'm a leg bouncer. It used to drive all my friends crazy before a performance, but they got used to it. Now they like to tap my knee for good luck."

We both slowly glance down, watching as my right leg bounces nonstop. It's not as noticeable as it would be if I was sitting, but it's still very much there.

Liam says nothing, only continues to look at me, and I feel like it's better that way. Both of us have the smallest smirks on our faces as I turn on the spot and start towards the elevator.

"I'll see you around, Liam," I call over my shoulder. I'm a few steps away and still basking in just how smooth my parting line was when Ollie promptly farts in my arms. It's loud and it smells putrid, filling the hallway like a professional grade stink bomb. I don't turn back, but I can hear Liam laughing quietly behind me as I then forgo the elevator and head for the stairwell instead.

Well, coolest and smoothest exit of my life, we had a good run. Goodbye forever.

4

When I get down to the studio, it's nothing like what I expected. Whereas the penthouse upstairs is crisp and cool, this apartment looks and feels like a cozy jewel box. A large desk is set off to the side, books are stacked every which way on a wall-to-wall windowsill, and an antique bed that's covered with a bright patchwork quilt is tucked diagonally into the corner. I place Ollie down, and he walks the perimeter, sniffing everything. I do the same, minus the sniffing.

There's a small kitchenette along the side, and an old teapot still sits on the outdated stove. Varying teacups dangle from hooks off a hanging wood shelf above the sink, and I touch each of them with the tip of my index finger. I then move to a thin bookshelf in the far corner, quickly skimming through the titles. Playwright autobiographies, romances, Shakespeare—the gang's all here.

And tucked away on the top shelf, all the way to the right, I notice what appears to be a scrapbook. I pull it out and run my palm along the surface. The leather cover is worn and slightly tattered, but not falling apart. I open it to the first page and find a picture of Juliette when she must have been around twenty years old. Her pants are flared and she's still wearing as many layers on top as possible—I smile to myself as I realize that some things never change.

I turn to the next page, where ticket stubs and playbill covers are now mixed in with photos. I also notice that one particular woman is in most of the pictures with Juliette. A majority of the shots are candid, and the two women seem playful and full of life. They're in the studio, in pubs, and, of course, constantly at the theater.

I'm flipping through the book at a leisurely pace when I find that a certain man then starts to appear on every page as well. He constantly has his arm draped around Juliette or is holding her hand. There's one photo of them where they're laughing and he's carrying her on his back. The last picture he's in features him sitting on a stage with Juliette beside him, her head resting on his shoulder. She looks so happy—more so than I've ever seen her. I'm just closing the book, and wishing I knew her then, when Ollie lets out a little sneeze. I pivot to find him, and a thin piece of paper falls to the floor, having slipped out from between the pages. I lean down and pick it up, carefully unfolding it and reading the name that's printed at the top of the stationery—Paul Davenport. My eyes move to the opening lines.

My darling Juliette,
After the manner in which we parted, I know the last thing you must want is to hear from me again. But as is our way, "the course of true love never did run smooth," and as I sit here now, my soul reaching out into the void and finding nothing but traces and echoes of you, I know with absolute certainty that you and I have made the gravest of all mistakes.

Realizing what I'm reading, I avert my eyes and fold up the letter with clumsy, fumbling hands. My breath is accelerated as I tuck the paper back into the middle of the scrapbook, which I immediately return to the top shelf. That was way too personal and in no way meant for me. Still feeling like an emotional Peeping Tom, I decide to busy myself by fixing Ollie a snack. I grab my bag from the counter and pull out an apple that I swiped from the plane, along with the large fluffy blanket. One of the flight attendants gave me a speculative glance when I disembarked, but didn't say anything. After working a seven-hour flight with Juliette, he probably understood that I needed it to self-soothe.

Once I cut the apple into tiny pieces, I place it on a plate and lower it to the floor along with a bowl of water. Ollie gobbles it down as I run him a makeshift bath in the sink and, soon enough, he's all dried and looking much more at ease as he curls up on an oversized pillow beside the window, serenely sleeping in the sun. It takes all the willpower I possess to not take a nap myself, instead looking up local veterinarians on my laptop. I find one fairly quickly and schedule an appointment for a few days later. Once I make sure that Ollie's physically alright, I'll ask them what I should do in regards to looking for his former owners or potentially keeping him. Granted, my apartment and work hours aren't ideal for a dog, but still, I'm sure I could find a way to figure things out.

An hour later, I'm in the midst of my twentieth dog article, this one titled "Eight Tips for Caring for a Malnourished Dog," when I hear the steady sound of knocking at the door. Ollie springs up, and I give him a comforting pet before answering, finding a smiling Roshni in the hallway, holding up a large paper bag with a paw logo on the front.

"Greetings, is this the Winnie D'Angelo canine rescue center?"

I smile tiredly back at her and pull the door open further. "That it is. Welcome and do come in."

"I've brought treats for you," she says, handing me the bag. "Or rather, treats for your furry friend."

"Are you serious?" I ask. Living in New York, you often forget that kind people often do incredibly kind things, totally unprompted. "How did you even know about him?"

"Juliette told me all about him after you left. And I don't want to steal credit here, because she was the one who asked me to pick this stuff up, and she paid for everything, saying the budget was unlimited. I got you dry and wet dog food, a harness, a leash, and a bunch of toys."

"Well, all the same, thank you for going out and getting all of this. I still don't know how we ended up with a real-life Disney princess for our first-ever second assistant."

"I can't be sure either," Roshni teases, "but I'd assume a wishing well was involved. Or a rare form of ancient magic."

"Either one is good with me. I'd be equally pumped to attend a tea party or a witch's coven." Roshni smirks, and I reach into the bag, pulling out the container of wet dog food and opening it up at the counter. Thankfully, it's high in protein, which Ollie needs, but I'll still have to run out for some eggs and rice to help supplement the rest of his meals. And possibly some chicken. I'm about to ask Roshni to keep her eye on him while I go in search of a supermarket when I find her looking around the room in amazement, just as I did when I first arrived.

"This place is kind of incredible," she says, moving to sit on the white-painted radiator cover and looking out at the picturesque street below. "I'm getting all the enchanted cottage feels."

"Me too," I agree. "It makes me wonder what Juliette was like when she lived here—when she was closer to our age."

"Probably exactly the same but more carefree. Just bopping around and chasing her dreams, like you are now."

I audibly scoff as I scoop one cup of dog food out of the container and place it in a bowl on the floor for Ollie. "Oh, yeah. I'm living the dream, alright."

"You are! Your life is exponentially more exciting than mine. I'm going to be dishing out beta-blockers and erectile dysfunction pills until I'm sixty while you write brilliant plays and pursue the stage."

"I love how you have the ability to glamorize everything. That's why you dress like the high-fashion lead in a Netflix drama and I look like a lost extra who accidentally walked into the shot."

"That is one hundred percent not true," she asserts, switching over to sit on the bed and bouncing around slightly. "And good news, I'm going to the benefit with you guys tonight! We scored another ticket, so now you and I can engage in super serious theater discussions while Juliette mingles."

"Wishful thinking, my young apprentice. At social events, you and I are more like ladies-in-waiting/bodyguards, but we do get sporadic breaks once she finds people she wants to hang out with."

"That sounds manageable. I'll have to practice my at-rest intimidation face."

"I'm sure it will be flawless," I tell her. "Now, is there any chance you can stay with Ollie for a bit while I run to the store? I'll be quick, I promise."

She hops up from the bed to join Ollie on the floor in the sun. "That would be an aggressive yes. We'll cuddle as we get our daily vitamin D."

"Thank you so much!" I quickly grab my bag and head for the door. "You're amazing. I mean it. I came alive when I met you."

"Yeah, yeah, that's what they all say. Also, Juliette told me to tell you that as long as you make sure he goes to the bathroom first, you can bring Ollie up to the penthouse whenever you want. She seemed kind of hopeful about it, actually. And she's paying the daughter of one of her neighbors to babysit him when we go out tonight, plus while we're at rehearsals during our stay. She was afraid he'd feel lonely without having someone with him."

I shake my head, still shocked by Juliette taking to our newest addition so fast. "Did we just find our boss's soft spot that she's somehow kept hidden for years?"

"It seems like it. Although, who wouldn't catch feelings for this perfect boy?"

"Good point," I agree.

She and Ollie promptly begin their cuddle-fest, and I slip into the hallway, locking the door behind me and switching into bloodhound mode, hoping I can sniff out the nearest grocery store in record time.

Later that night, after having watched a riveting performance of *King Lear*, Roshni and I mill around the lobby with Juliette walking a few steps ahead of us.

"That was sensational," Roshni gushes, sounding a little breathless. "Do you go to shows like this with Juliette all the time?"

"Not all the time, but often enough. Once a month, maybe."

"You are so lucky. When the lead actor gave his monologue, it felt like he was speaking directly to me. I was depressed to my core in the best way possible."

"He really was great," I agree. "Anytime I had to perform a monologue in college, I always dissected it a million ways after. I'd wish I had adjusted my voice or taken a breath in a different place. That's why so many film actors never want to watch themselves in movies, because they can't go back and change anything."

"I can get that."

"And that's part of what makes stage acting so freeing. If you don't like how you delivered a line or tackled a scene, you can try something new in the next performance. Theater is this living, breathing thing that's always evolving and moving and shaking and..." I trail off then, well aware of how often I get carried away when talking about the theater without stopping to gauge my audience. I look at Roshni and find her enthralled, her eyes bright. No need to pump the brakes here.

"I have a book of monologues with me, if you want to borrow it. It concentrates more on contemporary pieces, but I still think you'd like it."

"I'd love that," Roshni replies without missing a beat. I have to smile at her enthusiasm. I know the acting bug when I see it. Just then, Juliette floats to our side, having successfully evaded whoever she was just talking to.

"How are we on time?" she asks, shifting her stance to form a mini-circle with me and Roshni.

I look at my phone and see that it's 10:40 p.m. I tell her we need to stay for twenty minutes, or until she can talk to the theater company's PR person. Juliette groans and turns around so we're now standing in more of a U shape.

"So, Roshni, what did you think of the performance?"

"Oh, I thought it was amazing. It's crazy how the stage was so huge and there were so many people in the audience, but I still felt so connected. Like I was somehow part of it even from a distance."

Juliette looks over at me with a shrewd grin, also recognizing a fellow theater addict. "And another one bites the dust." A second later, her smile falls when her eyes lock on something—or someone—across the room. My sight line follows hers until I see a striking woman in a tasteful rose-gold wrap dress making her way towards us, weaving effortlessly through the glittering crowd.

Juliette squares her shoulders and stands up straight. "Here comes her highness, herself."

"Here's who now?" Roshni asks, scooting over to take a look.

"That would be my sister, Isabelle. The charity board member extraordinaire."

My eyes dart back and forth between the two women, trying and failing to find some similarity between them. Their hair, their style, the way they carry themselves are all so starkly opposite. It's only when Isabelle is directly in front of us that I finally see their one striking resemblance. They have the same chestnut eyes.

"Juliette," she says, her voice as light and soft as her elegant silk dress.

"Isabelle," Juliette replies with feigned enthusiasm.

Isabelle is the first to move, placing her hand on Juliette's shoulder and prompting a double air-kiss. "It's so wonderful to see you. Every time you come to London, we seem to miss each other."

"Yes, I know, bad luck that. I'm just so busy. Lots of obligations and, obviously, I'm always writing."

"You're nothing if not dedicated." Isabelle pauses then, waiting for Juliette to respond. She doesn't. "You haven't returned any of my calls."

"Haven't I? Must have been technical difficulties. My phone's been on the fritz of late."

Of course, I know that this isn't true, since she would tell me in a heartbeat if she was having problems with her phone. I finally convinced her to upgrade a few months ago, and she's now addicted to FaceTime and verbally dictating her text messages.

"We should get lunch while you're here," Isabelle then says. "We've gone too long without seeing each other."

"Absolutely, we'll have to get something in the books. Winnie can see what my availability looks like, but it might be hard with all the upcoming rehearsals." She blasts me a plastered-on smile before turning back to Isabelle, wordlessly telling me that she has zero availability whatsoever.

"Yes, *The Lights of Trafalgar*. I can't wait to see it again. Hopefully you won't mind if I come."

"Of course not," Juliette says. "You were there when I thought of it, after all."

Hearing that, I take a closer look at Isabelle. At her glossy brown hair that's cut in an elegant bob. At the delicate lines of her cheeks that seem more pronounced as she tries to smile, despite her sister's amiable but guarded tone. She seems indecipherably familiar until I realize that she's the woman who appeared so often in Juliette's scrapbook. In those countless photos, you'd think she and Juliette were the best of friends. Inseparable, even. It makes me wonder what must have happened to bring them to this point of strained civility.

If I had a sister, I would be intensely attached. As it is, it's just me and my dad, and growing up, I would have done anything to have a sibling. Not that my dad is cold—he's not. I know he loves me, but reimaging my childhood with a live-in best friend, a confidante, it would have been such a gift. A gift that Juliette and Isabelle seem to have set aside.

"Liam is looking forward to attending the pop-up as well," Isabelle then says. "For someone so preoccupied with computers, he's surprisingly drawn to the arts. He would have been here tonight, but he told me you needed another ticket."

"What was that about his ticket?" I ask, suddenly jumping in and earning surprised glances all around.

Juliette looks at me for a drop longer than normal before

speaking up. "Liam heard you talking about Roshni wanting to come tonight, so he gave us his ticket for her to use. That way, both of you could enjoy the show."

"That was really nice of him," I say, trying to downplay my initial reaction and turning to focus on Isabelle. "Your son is very thoughtful."

"He is. Thank you," she answers with a warm smile. "And what's your name, dear?"

"Oh, I'm Winnie."

She reaches out and shakes my hand with a genteel but steady grip. "Do tell me if you need anything while you're in London, Winnie. Both of you," she adds, looking at Roshni. "I'm a bit swamped with work at the moment, but I'm always available for friends of my sister. Let me give you my number..."

Before she has a chance to finish her sentence, Juliette places her hand on my arm.

"Actually, we're all going to be quite busy this trip—so busy, in fact, that we better get going, unfortunately."

A flash of disappointment crosses Isabelle's face before she sets it back to a neutral expression. "Alright then. And you'll let me know about lunch, Juliette?"

"Absolutely. Without question. Winnie, why don't you just go on ahead and let the driver know that we're ready?"

"Sure," I say, starting to walk away but then turning back to Isabelle. "It was very nice meeting you."

"You as well, dear."

I offer her a quick smile before I continue walking, stepping outside onto the pavement and calling the driver. With my task done, I look in my text history to where Juliette sent me Liam's contact info. I can't stop myself from typing out a quick message and pressing Send.

Hello, kind sir. This is Winnie. I heard you gave your ticket away so Roshni could see the show. That was very gentlemanly of you.

Blinking dots appear seconds later.

I was happy to help. I hope you all had a good time.

We had a great time.

I then add:

Also, I hope it's okay that I'm texting you. I know Juliette gave me your number in a work capacity, so if you're busy or this is weird, feel free to not answer.

He soon texts back:

It's very much okay that you're texting me. I may or may not have given my ticket away in the hopes that this very text exchange might happen.

I shake my head with a disapproving smile even though I'm enjoying every second of this. I quickly type back:

So friendly conversation is acceptable then?

He answers right away:

Entirely acceptable. Now we just have to establish how friendly. Are we thinking business casual?

I grin and try to figure out how to best continue. I end up texting:

Friendly like we went to grade school together and always got along but weren't close, but now we're adults and I bumped into you on the street and we were both like, "Wow, we should catch up sometime, let me give you my number." And now we're nonchalantly texting.

There's a bit of a pause after that, but the telltale dots soon reappear.

That backstory was so convincing, I actually thought it was real for a second. Keep going.

Keep going? Feeling emboldened that he's encouraging my weirdness, I let my fingers fly across my phone with comfortable excitement.

It was Saturday. I was out getting coffee. I had old leggings and a sweatshirt on because it was laundry day. You were listening to headphones but pulled them off when we physically bumped into each other. Turns out you were late to a friend's birthday brunch, but you didn't mind because you actively hate the concept of brunch.

He starts typing again:

I mean, it's either lunch or breakfast, right? Pick a side.

I'm in the throes of selecting the perfect assortment of food and laughing emojis when he texts again:

That was a very immersive experience, by the way. Was I just the subject of an elaborate writing exercise?

I quickly answer back:

To a playwright, all the world's a writing exercise.

My head darts up then as Juliette and Roshni walk out onto the sidewalk beside me. I look ahead to find that the driver is directly in front me and that I somehow missed his arrival.

Duty calls. Good night, Liam.

Good night, Winnie. I'm very glad you came to London.

I manage to shoot out one more text before sliding into the car after Juliette.

Me too.

5

I'm now on day three of my trip to London as I find myself sitting in a cozy café awaiting the arrival of British Boyfriend #2. I figure the quicker I book these meet cutes, the quicker I can hit my dating quota and be done with it. The space itself is lovely, dusted with twinkle lights and playing soft jazz, the scent of coffee filling the air. I'm sitting at a small table with my laptop open as I try to sneak in as much writing as possible. Roshni and Juliette are keeping an eye on Ollie in the penthouse, so I was even able to leave early. I'm just trying to figure out how to rework the opening scene when the sound of someone saying my name pulls me out of my flow.

"Winnie?" the vaguely familiar voice asks. I look up to see Liam standing above me, looking surprised but pleased. "What are you doing here?"

"I…" I honestly don't know what to say, but that doesn't last long. It never does with me. "I could ask you the same question. Wait, did you follow me here? Is this the part of the movie where my vacation takes a hard left turn into *Taken* territory? Because even if I come off as initially intriguing, I promise it's surface appeal only. People always get sick of me over time. I hum a lot. Like, a lot, a lot."

"Okay. Well, that's a no to the stalking inquiry, considering I get my coffee here every morning."

"A likely story, but how do I know that it's true?"

Liam's expression is both amused and determined as he turns to look over at one of the baristas. "Morning, Tom," he calls across the room.

The barista glances back with a smile. "How goes it, Liam? You want a large or medium today?"

"I'll take a medium, thanks."

Liam faces me again with an air of victory, but I'm not ready to concede. "That easily could have been staged."

"Really? You think Tom has been lying in wait all morning, pretending to work here so I could stumble in and pose as a regular?"

"I know a method actor when I see one."

"Right." Liam chuckles, pulling back the chair across from me and sitting down.

"Actually, I'm saving that seat," I quickly tell him. "I'm meeting someone, so I don't really have time to chat."

"I'll get up when they arrive. Who are you meeting? My aunt?"

"No, not your aunt." He waits for me to elaborate, and I begrudgingly do so. "As it happens, I'm meeting a man."

"Are you?" he asks. "Not the park perv from the other day, I hope."

"No, a different one."

"A different park perv?"

I push my computer away a few inches and rub my eyes. "No, hopefully there will be no park pervs involved in today's festivities. But I do need the seat, so if you could just pretend that I'm not here, that would probably be best. Trust me when I say that this situation is more complicated than it seems."

Liam makes no move to get up, and we both then hear the barista call out his name. I give him another *it was nice seeing you* smile as he hesitantly stands and tucks in his chair.

"Well, I better get that then." He seems the slightest bit dejected, and I feel bad but unsure of what exactly I can do about it given the circumstances. "I guess it was nice bumping into you."

"You, too," I reply.

Liam gives me a stiff kind of nod that almost looks like a bow and walks to the counter to pay for his drink. Pulling my laptop closer again, I reenter my password and try not to watch as he heads for the door. I'm attempting to ignore the faint disappointment brought on by his absence until I hear the chair beside me being unceremoniously scraped back. I turn towards the sound just as Liam settles himself at the table directly to my left. I'm momentarily flabbergasted as he takes a sip of his coffee and begins scrolling through his phone.

"Beg your pardon," I say with layered-on sweetness. "But what exactly are you doing?"

"Just checking some emails," he answers, keeping his eyes glued to the phone.

"And you need to do that right here? You're two saucy leg maneuvers away from straddling me, and not in a good way."

Liam coughs on his coffee, the smallest bit staining his white Henley shirt. "I told you," he says once he's recovered, "I come into this café every morning. I'm just abiding by my daily routine."

"And you have to abide by it at a table that's adjacent to mine?"

"It's a crowded café, Winnie. It's not as if I can sit just any-where."

I look around the spacious coffee shop that is currently filled to a quarter of its capacity. "There's a minimum of fourteen other spots where you can sit."

"But this chair is my favorite. I've tried all the others over the years, and this one is best suited to my shape and weight."

I scoff and close my computer, crossing my arms across my chest. "For the record, your British accent doesn't make you any less annoying in this moment."

Liam shakes his head with a little laugh, and I may or may not be inwardly elated by the sound of it.

"You fail to see that me sitting here is a purely chivalric gesture. What if the person you're about to meet is a hardened criminal or prefers opera to the theater?"

"Then I'll blast him with my Taser and leave England a hero."

"I doubt you were able to get a Taser through customs."

"I'm surprisingly stealthy. I could hide a grenade launcher in my hair and no one would ever know."

"I like your hair," he says genuinely.

"Lies do not become us, Liam."

He puts down his phone then, looking at me in a calm and honest way that leaves me feeling a little dazed.

"There's more to this story than you're letting on. Why the back-to-back meetups while you're traveling on a work trip? And why is my aunt so keen to hear about them?"

I take a dramatic breath and turn to face him. "You've riddled me out, Mr. Holmes. Your aunt and I are working undercover to catch an international jewel thief, and your presence here is putting our entire operation in jeopardy."

"Of course I am. But still, if my aunt has something to do

with sending you around London on dates, it clearly must be benefiting her in some way."

"I already told you, I'm doing this for god and country."

Someone walks in then, and I'm almost certain it's James. British Boyfriend #2. I'm filled with dread, then relief when he sits down with a group in the corner.

"Look," I say, turning to Liam once again, "if you must know, I'm working on a project with your aunt. She needs stories about the current dating arena, so I signed up for an app and am meeting up with guys while I'm here."

Liam seems taken aback but not as much as I would have thought. "So, you're not actually interested in meeting anyone?" he asks.

"Not particularly, no."

"Then why do it? Surely this is a bit outside the realm of your job description?"

"I agreed to do it because in exchange, Juliette is going to help develop the play I'm working on."

Liam considers me carefully before saying, "That sounds like a pretty manipulative request on her end."

The café door opens again, and I start to feel a little frantic, not wanting to explain a random British guy to another random British guy. "Okay, so now that you know everything, will you please leave?"

"How about this. Let's grab a bite to eat later on, and then we can figure out this situation of yours together."

"No," I say, instinctively digging in my heels.

"Why not? I have plenty of stories you could bring to my aunt, and I'm not a stranger. I also carry the added bonus of not being a secret psycho."

"That fact remains to be seen."

"Listen, I'm only trying to be helpful. If you truly want me to go, I will."

I know he will. The problem is, I don't want him to.

"Fine," I ultimately answer. "But this can't be a full-fledged date or anything. Drinks only."

"Deal. Meet me at the Red Lion in Westminster at five o'clock." He gets up and takes my hand. I know I should pull it away, but I don't. "I wish you the best of luck on your upcoming liaison. No doubt we'll be hearing the chime of wedding bells before the week is out."

Then I do snatch my hand back. "Thank you for the well wishes. Now please go back to the depths from which you came."

"I'm on my way." He picks up his phone and coffee and turns to leave, making it two steps until he's suddenly back in front of me. "Quick question, though, before we take things further. Is there any chance that you're currently still pining over your college ex-boyfriend who you're desperately hoping to reunite with someday?"

"Ugh, no. My college boyfriend is gross, and I'm pretty sure he's currently doing a stint in prison."

"Excellent, just had to double-check. See you tonight!"

An hour later, I walk back into the penthouse where Juliette is typing on her computer at her living room desk. She twists around and gazes up at me as I close the door behind me.

"Well?" she asks hopefully.

"James was a no-show."

Juliette drops her head down with a groan before whipping back up to look at me. "Why is this happening? What is wrong with your generation?"

"I've been asking myself that very question for years," I tell her, doing my best to sound as crestfallen as she does.

"Maybe he was hit by a bus," Juliette muses. "Or better yet, maybe *I'll* get hit by a bus, and then I won't have to keep enduring this endless agony."

I look around at her glorious penthouse and give her a knowing look. "It feels like you might be slightly out of touch with reality at the moment."

Juliette shakes her head, turning back to the laptop and refocusing. "We've just had some bad luck. You're a lovely, inquisitive girl, and there is no reason whatsoever that suitors shouldn't be lining up to take you out."

I shrug my shoulders, perfectly content with being stood up. Fingers crossed British Boyfriend #3 does the same.

"One other thing I wanted to talk to you about," Juliette then says, twisting back around from her computer and facing me sideways in her chair. "I couldn't help but notice that you and Liam talked quite a bit yesterday, and I feel like I may have picked up on a little spark forming there." I stay quiet, not really sure how to respond. "Anyways, I know I don't have to tell you this, but I'd obviously be uncomfortable with anything starting up between you two."

I nod my head, and my stomach plummets.

"It's just that he's my nephew, and you work for me, so crossing that line would probably be weird for everyone involved."

I haven't stopped nodding and now force myself to. "Right. No, yes, I completely agree."

"Okay, great. I wasn't even sure if I needed to say anything, but then I figured I should, just in case."

"Absolutely. I totally get it." Sweat pools behind my neck, and I have to physically keep my leg from bouncing. Juliette closes her laptop with a pop.

"Alright, well, I'm off to meet up with an old friend of

mine before rehearsals begin tomorrow. What time do we have to be there?"

"Rehearsals start at eleven, but we should get there at least a half hour early to meet with the director."

"And who is that again?"

"Eloise MacClare. She's young but very up-and-coming. Her take on Chekhov's work has been described as near genius."

Juliette stands up and grabs her gray messenger bag from off the couch as she makes her way to the entryway. "Ah, to be young and revered. I can tell you from personal experience, it doesn't last. Also, I took Ollie for a walk this morning, and he was pretty exhausted after. I ordered him a little bed with rush delivery to keep up here just in case, so if someone buzzes to drop it off, you can go ahead and let them up."

"Will do. Thanks, Juliette."

"No trouble at all," she says, opening and closing the door behind her with a smile.

The silence that follows is almost deafening as I stand there alone in the expansive room. Luckily, Roshni comes out ten seconds later, holding the bouncing Ollie himself.

"Hey!" I say, snapping out of my stupor. "There you guys are." She sets him on the floor, and he sprints over to me. I squat down to give him a nice long pet.

"Sorry, I only took him into my room so I could call Nick really quick." Nick is Roshni's boyfriend of over a year. I met him once when we got drinks after work, and the pair of them were so adorable, I nearly vomited from cuteness overload. I then attempted to drink my loneliness away and vomited for real. *C'est la vie.* I still killed it at karaoke that night.

"And Ollie was an angel, of course," she goes on to say. "He really is so well-behaved."

"That's good to hear. Hopefully it holds since he and I have an appointment at the vet soon. Has he eaten?"

"Mmm-hmm. Just a few minutes ago. Homeboy really likes the new dog food, and I've been letting him snack on the chicken you made."

"Perfect," I say, sitting down on the floor so Ollie can snuggle into my lap. "I still can't believe that Juliette's so into the idea of him being up here."

Roshni situates herself on the couch. "She definitely seems to be a huge admirer of his. They were more or less canoodling for a solid majority of the time. And speaking of Juliette, I couldn't help but overhear the last bit of your conversation."

"Oh yeah? Catch anything interesting?"

"Mainly just her saying that she didn't want you to date Liam."

Reality crashes over me again, and I concentrate on stroking Ollie's coat rather than dwelling on my own conflicting emotions.

"Yes, well, she may have a point there," I eventually say.

"Really? I thought she was way out of line, especially considering how she just asked you to go out with total strangers for the sole purpose of getting her material."

"I know," I murmur, "but still, why blur the professional boundaries even further?"

"How are you blurring boundaries by casually seeing the nephew she visits once in a blue moon? The same nephew who gave up his ticket last night because he knew you wanted me to go. Don't lie, that was beyond sweet."

"Yes, it was," I admit.

"Do you like him?" I choose not to answer, so Roshni does for me. "Of course you do. Who wouldn't? Just catching a glimpse of him the other day gave me my first ever redheaded sexual awakening."

"Okay, let's relax for a second."

"I just don't see anything wrong with you dating him. Liam is attractive, he's nice, and he's a billion times more normal than the first freak you met up with. Don't even try to tell me that you're not attracted to him."

All Roshni's arguments are sound. There's clearly something between Liam and me, and pretending otherwise would just be childish.

"Fine, I will admit to a certain...attraction."

"I knew it! And regardless of what Juliette says, if he asks you out, you should absolutely say yes."

"I may have actually done that already."

"Scandalous!" Roshni instantly leans forward in excitement and curiosity, and it's hard not to feed off her bubbly energy. "When are you meeting him?" she asks impatiently.

"I'm supposed to see him tonight for drinks, but now I feel like I should cancel."

"Winnie, please don't think this is me trying to commandeer your decision-making, even though I kind of am, but I really don't think Juliette should dictate what goes on in your personal, private life. She knows you love your job and that you want to make her happy, so she feels comfortable asking you to do things that go way beyond the call of duty. Not to be harsh, but she's fully taking advantage of you, and you're just letting her."

Her words sink in, and I know she's right. But I'm also so used to taking Juliette's side that going against her wishes feels inherently wrong.

"For the record, though, it's not like Juliette is some monster with no regard for my well-being. Last year a director put his hand on my butt at an after-party, and she basically flew down from the rafters and swore to physically and professionally disembowel him if he ever came near me again."

"And I fully believe that," Roshni says. "But it still doesn't make what she's doing okay."

I nod with reluctant acceptance. "How old are you, again? I feel like I'm talking to an HR supervisor who moonlights as a therapist."

"I'm twenty-three going on forty. It's rumored I exited the womb inquiring about my 401(k)." I breathe out a giggle and look down at Ollie as Roshni goes on, "All I'm saying is, if you want to spend time with Liam, you should. You're a good person and an amazing assistant. You deserve to do what you want to do and to talk to whoever you want to talk to. Plus, Ollie is basically my child, so the more you go out, the more he and I get to bond."

"I would be honored to co-parent this puppy with you."

"Same here."

I give Ollie one more pet and then stand up to stretch my legs. "Okay, I guess I'll still meet up with Liam, then. It's just drinks, after all. And I can tell him what Juliette thinks about us spending time together." Roshni gives me a satisfied smirk as I flop down into my favorite armchair. "Who would have thought that you would be such a bad influence on me? I thought you were so innocent when we first met."

"Yes, well, it's always the quiet ones, isn't it? I'm just pumped I'll get to experience a forbidden love affair through you, since I definitely won't be having one of my own."

"I'm sure your boyfriend appreciates that, and I wouldn't get your hopes up. All of this talk might lead to nothing. Liam is strange and slightly infuriating. I don't think I even like him."

Roshni swings her legs onto the couch, pulling Ollie up to sit on her stomach as she lies flat on her back and smiles up at the ceiling. "Said every romantic leading lady ever."

6

With my classic London taxi pulling away from the curb, I'm now left standing on Parliament Street in front of the somewhat iconic Red Lion. After reading online reviews, I learned that Charles Dickens used to come here quite often. (I may or may not be a Victorian fiction fangirl.) The wooden pub sign hangs overhead, adorned with gold and black paint, and, of course, emblazoned with the fierce image of a red lion. My gaze shifts as a double-decker bus turns a corner in the distance, and the whole scene feels so quintessentially British that I just may develop my own outlandish English/American accent à la Madonna by osmosis.

The glass pub door opens a second later, catching my eye as Liam walks out in jeans and a navy polo. "Glad you could make it," he says, moving to stand directly in front of me. He looks so good that everything around him seems to blur as his hopeful blue eyes sear into mine. He leans in to kiss my cheek, but I hold my hands out in front of me, genuinely concerned about the repercussions that will follow if I catch a stronger whiff of his pheromones.

"Before you do or say anything else, you should know that your aunt explicitly told me she doesn't want me spending time with you. So please be aware that I'm violating a very sacred and professional code of ethics by meeting you right now."

"Right," Liam says slowly. "That's a lot to unpack. And here I was nervous we might end up having nothing to talk about."

"That will never be an issue when I'm around. So, here's what I'm thinking as far as a game plan. I'm thinking we go into this pub, we have a drink at the bar with an empty chair wedged between us, and then that's it. We shake hands if we must, and we go our separate ways like two completely platonic, friendly ships passing in the night."

Liam seems taken off guard but is quick to regain his mental footing. "Fair enough. And while that does sound like a solid option, the thing is, I have a weird aversion to eating alone, and I'm actually starving, so how about we just share a meal together and then we do as you suggested with the ships and whatnot?"

"The platonic ships passing in the night."

"Yes, entirely platonic. No romantic chemistry between ships whatsoever. Just food and very bland conversation, on my part, obviously."

"I thought we agreed this wouldn't be a sit-down dinner date?"

"Yes, you did stipulate that, so I have another idea in mind."

Ten minutes later, we round a corner, and I'm left stunned and speechless. We're now standing on a cobblestoned street, and there's nothing but food vendors for as far as the eye can see. We're not even in the thick of things yet, just standing on the outskirts, but I can already read signs for the first three stalls: Greek souvlaki, Spanish padrón peppers, and Turkish rice pilaf. A cacophony of aromas storms my system and beckons me forward like an old-timey cartoon.

"What is this place?" I ask in foodie wonderment.

"The Strutton Ground Market. It's only open on weekdays, and I like to pop in for lunch or an early dinner every month or so."

"I want to live here."

"Many people do, but I don't think they issue permits for that."

I smile as my eyes continue to wander hungrily. "How do you pick which cart to eat from?"

"Yes, that is indeed the tricky part. Most times, I just go with what calls to me. Other times, I'll set a short timer on my phone and then see which vendor I'm standing in front of when the alarm sounds. There are so many good spots to choose from that it's often best to let the Fates decide."

"I'm game for that."

"I thought you might be," Liam says with a grin. He then pulls out his phone and sets a timer for eight minutes. I clap my hands together in eager excitement as we start off down the street.

"So, if you come here that often, I take it that you're a pretty adventurous eater?"

"Not by nature, though I have been trying to broaden my horizons lately. I traveled to Italy for about seven months last year, and now I regret how little I branched out."

"You were in Italy for seven months?" I ask, forcing my eyes away from the specialty coffee stall that's nearly causing me to salivate. "How'd you swing that?"

"I took an extended leave of absence after I sold my company. I should technically be working for them now, but…"

"But here we are," I finish for him.

"Here we are. I admit I may be dragging my feet a bit."

"Slacker. Though I should hardly be one to judge. I like to think of procrastination as my unhinged roommate who I always have fun with but then hate because she somehow convinced me to watch four hours of some dude building his dream hobbit cottage in the woods on YouTube when I should have been working on my play instead."

Liam snickers as I look off to the side, continuing to take in the vibrant buzz of the street and all the people milling about. And it's not just food stalls that dominate the area. Bakeries, sandwich shops, and even small restaurants line the space as well—not in competition but in a pleasant kind of harmony that I doubt would exist if we were back in New York.

"Yes, your play. What is it called, by the way? I've been meaning to ask you."

"I stink at titles. In my head, I think of it as *Death of a Prom King*."

Liam smiles in earnest then, and I suddenly feel oddly exposed. I can't believe I just said that out loud. I haven't revealed my possible title to anyone. Not even Juliette.

"Ah, the famous American prom. Tell me about it."

"About the prom? Its depiction in movies is pretty spot-on. Gowns and suits, barf in the hair, shattered dreams. As you can probably surmise from my description, I had an *amazing* time at my prom."

"Clearly. No, I meant tell me about your play."

"Oh," I say, feeling a little hesitant. "You don't want to hear about that."

"Of course I do."

He slows down his pace in our already leisurely stroll,

physically showing me just how intent he is on hearing about it. Taking a breath, I figure there's no harm in telling him.

"Well, to sum it up, it's about four quasi-outcast friends who are all locked in a jail cell together on the night of their ten-year high school reunion after they're suspected of killing the former prom king. Throughout the play, we learn that they each have their own unique emotional tie to him and their own specific reasons for potentially wanting him dead."

"Wow," Liam says. "It's a little darker than I expected, but sounds exciting. Is it a drama?"

"No, not a drama. I write comedies."

"Comedies?" Liam seems even more interested. I've found that happens quite a bit. Whenever non-theater people think of theater, they always assume it's solemn and serious. A lone man reciting the *Iliad* under a glaring spotlight. They forget that theater can be anything. Everything. There are no rules. It can be fun and nonsensical while still shaking you to your core.

"So, the way I imagine it, the stage is divided in two identical halves. In one jail cell, you have the characters in the current day, and in the other jail cell, you have the characters in their high school form. They can sporadically hear and observe each other, but they don't interact directly. The older characters watch as the younger selves act out past memories. The younger ones look and listen to their older selves and wonder how they got there."

"That actually sounds very compelling."

"Thanks. Also, the prom king is there, too. As a ghost—as both the older and younger version of himself."

"And you think my aunt can help you with this? It doesn't really sound like her area of expertise."

"I guess it's not. Even so, getting her eyes on it would be

invaluable. Our plays might not be alike, but similar themes are there. Love, anguish, humor, unknown pasts, undetermined futures—all that good stuff."

"Clearly her input is important to you. Important enough that you're going along with her dating scheme."

I quickly wonder just how open I should be here—not yet ready to explain that this very well might be my last hurrah with his aunt. I also slow down our walking pace to a near crawl since we're now nearing the kebab station, and I'm desperately willing his timer to go off.

"It's not just her input," I end up saying. "I like to make her happy. And I know she shouldn't have asked me to do this, but I agreed, so I might as well just see it through. All I'm really doing is collecting some stories, anyways."

"Well, if stories are all you need, I can help you with that." He's about to go on when the timer sounds. If we're going to continue delving into my moral/ethical dilemma, at least we can be consuming tasty chicken kebabs as we do it.

Five minutes later, we're doing just that. Liam and I continue walking.

"So, here's what I propose," he says, after taking a hefty bite. "Rather than soldiering on in your internet dating marathon, I think you and I should continue to meet up instead. I have plenty of stories of my own, or I could tell you stories from friends of mine that you could bring back to my aunt. That way, you fulfill your obligation, with the added bonus of not having to go out with people who may or may not be looking to dabble in their very first violent crime."

"A thoughtful offer," I tell him. "And I get the appeal for me, but what about you? What will you be getting out of this arrangement?"

"I'll get to spend time with you."

His says that so calmly and matter-of-factly that I can't help but to be thrown by it.

"And why would you want to do that?" I ask.

"Because I like you."

"You don't even know me."

"Which circles us back around to me wanting to spend time with you. I want to get to know you."

That thought makes me happy. Too happy for my own good.

"As much as I'd like that, this conversation is pointless. Juliette told me, point-blank, that she doesn't want anything going on between us. I can't just go against her wishes or risk getting fired because we feel like hanging out."

"Well, now that we've established that you do, in fact, want to spend time with me as well, we can focus just on the aunt issue. Honestly, I doubt she would fire you for being friends with me. I'm not exactly a people person. She should be pleased."

"She should be, but she's not," I tell him.

"Then she doesn't have to know."

Fabulous. A sneaky, flirty, high-stakes rendezvous. I'm sure that won't lead to anything inappropriate happening at all.

"How many more people are you supposed to go out with?" Liam asks.

"The negotiated number was three."

"Okay then. So cancel this last one and be with me instead."

Be with me instead. I don't know if he intended for that line to sound quite so tempting, but that's definitely how it was received.

"And what if after tonight or our next meetup you decide you don't want to carry on with this and then I canceled my last date for nothing?"

"I highly doubt that will happen."

"It might."

"It won't."

He's certain. So certain, and I don't know why. No one is ever fully sold on me, at least not without me putting in a tremendous amount of effort first.

"And you think it's fine that we'll be doing this behind Juliette's back?"

"I think what goes on between you and me is up to you and me. Much as I love and respect my aunt, my private life is my own, as yours should be as well."

"I've never really lied to her before," I tell him quietly. "It feels wrong."

"Don't think of it as lying. You're going to be passing along real stories, just through a slightly different messenger. It was unfair of her to put you in this situation in the first place."

He's not wrong. But I also know that I need to take ownership of this. Juliette presented me with a choice, and I made it. She's a woman I admire and who I haven't let down in five years, and I'm not ready to start now.

"I can't," I eventually say. "I'm sorry, but I can't break Juliette's trust like that."

I could say more, but I don't, and an accepting look crosses Liam's face.

"I understand," he replies. Silence goes on and on until he slides his hands into his pockets. "So, I suppose this will be it for us."

"That's what it's looking like."

"Well then, we should enjoy it while it lasts."

I raise a questioning brow, but Liam says nothing, only nudges his head down the street and begins walking. I follow until we're side by side. A minute later, we turn a corner and

I stop in my tracks. Big Ben towers ahead just in front of us. It's crystal clear and all lit up against the subtly darkening sky, and for a second, I forget to breathe.

"Wow," is all I manage to say. I continue to stare, lost in its timeless beauty and still overcome that I'm even standing here. My heart feels as light and bright as Peter Pan's, like at any moment, I just might fly away.

I look over after a while to see if Liam is as hypnotized as I am, but he's not looking at the clock tower. He's gazing down at me. "What are you thinking?" he asks.

I turn back to face ahead, smiling to myself and taking a deep breath. "I'm thinking how this is one of those incredibly vivid moments of happiness that I'm never going to forget. After something really good happens, people think how wonderful it is and that it's important, but over time the memory slips, inch by inch, until finally you can't reach it anymore. But this…now… I'm always going to remember it. This is unslippable."

I peek up and a languid smile pulls at the corner of Liam's mouth. We continue to stand there, drinking in the sight before us in comfortable silence until I feel his fingers brushing against mine, just skimming the surface until they slowly tangle together. His hand feels solid and strong in my grasp, almost like it's supposed to be there. "What are you doing?" I ask, making no move to pull away.

"I'm holding your hand," he says.

"I can see that, but why?"

"Because now I'll be unslippable, too."

The truth of his words hits me like a freight train. His thumb strokes the inside of my palm, and breathing isn't as easy as it was a second ago.

"Are you always like this?" I ask, my voice betraying me with its breathless undercurrent.

"I'm never like this. I wouldn't be surprised if I'm actually having some kind of a mild, days-long stroke."

I grin lightly up at him, happy in the knowledge that I'm not the only one losing my mind. "Well then, we really should enjoy it while it lasts."

A bittersweet expression crosses his face, and Liam says nothing as we turn forward once again. My head somehow ends up on his shoulder, and his hand squeezes mine just a little bit tighter—sweetly possessive and not at all typical for two people who have only seen each other twice before. It sends a warm wave sailing through me, and I feel it in my knees, in my stomach—everywhere, really.

It should scare me, but it doesn't. Instead, I feel anchored. Safe. And, unfortunately, I really, really don't want it to stop.

7

I have always loved first rehearsals. Some people hate it—the nauseous, nervous knots it ties in your stomach. The uncertainty. The adrenaline. But not me. For me, it's like the first day of school, but it's my dream school, and all I want to do is prove that I belong. That I'm worthy. I'm addicted to that initial excitement. The thrill of seeing the other actors. The moment where the concept of being part of a play becomes a reality.

And this, by no means, is going to be a typical production. We're under a massive time crunch, and as such, we have fourteen straight days of rehearsing, from now until opening night. All of the actors are expected to be off book by today, and I cannot wait to see what they bring to each of their roles.

Juliette, Roshni, and I are seemingly the first to arrive, walking through the large rehearsal space where a circle of about twenty chairs is arranged in the center of the room. Even with a skeleton crew, there's a sizable number of people involved in this production. The director, the cast (two main actors and two supporting), the production manager, the stage manager, the props manager, and all the designers (lighting, sound, set, and costume). Roshni and I will fill in for any odd jobs that need doing, and a handful of interns will arrive in the final few days to help more.

Speaking of Roshni, she's all but vibrating in anticipation and is flushed with nerves. Juliette is harder to read. Not indifferent, exactly, but not thrilled either. Like she's just taken a bite of her favorite meal but it's being served cold and outside in the rain with no utensils—but maybe she's still enjoying it a little because it *is* her favorite meal, after all.

"The space is nice," I hear myself saying, my voice echoing through the room.

"It is," Juliette agrees. "I'm just wondering when our fabulous director will arrive."

As if on cue, the door opens, and in walks a woman who looks to be not too much older than me. I'm twenty-nine and she seems around mid-thirties tops. She's wearing comfortable jeans and a gray T-shirt, no makeup, and her long blond hair is pulled back in a high ponytail. Thin-rimmed glasses, the total opposite of Juliette's, are perched on her lightly freckled nose.

"Good morning, all!" She puts her paper coffee cup down on the refreshment table and strides directly over to us. "Sorry I wasn't here to greet you. I just popped out for a minute. Juliette Brassard, I presume?"

Juliette remains undecipherable but pleasant as she shakes her hand, no doubt inwardly sizing her up. "And you must be our brilliant director, Eloise."

"I don't know about the brilliant bit, but I am Eloise. Feel free to call me Ellie."

I like her. Sometimes you see someone, and you just know

you're going to like them. For all our sakes, I'm sending up prayers that Juliette feels the same.

"Will do, Ellie," she says almost too sweetly.

There's a twinge of awkwardness creeping in, and I immediately spring forward, eager to diffuse it. "Hi, I'm Winnie, Juliette's assistant. I emailed you last week."

"Yes, I remember. Quite a long email, I think?"

"Just a tad. And this is Roshni, our second assistant."

They shake hands, and Ellie steps back with an easy smile. "Well, you three are quite the contingent. I'm looking forward to working with all of you. The rest of the group should be getting here soon enough, so why don't we take this chance to have a quick chat?"

"By all means," Juliette says with a nod. We all move to take seats in the circle of chairs, and Ellie pulls one out towards the center to face Roshni, Juliette, and me. It's a silent power move, and judging by Juliette's sly smile, I think it's one she actually respects. Ellie gets comfortable and leans in, her eyes bright and clear. She seems genuinely excited.

"So, before I start blathering on, let me just say how much I enjoyed revisiting this play. I originally read it a few years back, but returning to it now whilst knowing I was going to be taking it on was a really invigorating experience."

"Was it?" Juliette asks, half curiously, half skeptically. "And, if you don't mind me asking, what made it so invigorating?"

Ellie smiles even more. She isn't afraid of a challenge.

"Well, first off, while I very much enjoyed the dynamics between our main characters, what I think reached me on a deeper level was their mutual assertion of powerlessness in their shared situation. That's the true driving force of the play. At first glance, *The Lights of Trafalgar* reads as fairly straightforward. Two opposite people accidentally rent the same flat, and neither can give it up for various reasons. George stays, lest he admits defeat to his family, and Jocelyn stays because she's paid her deposit, and leaving would be an extreme financial strain. Both characters rail against their circumstances and each other for a majority of the first act, but really, neither of them are forced into anything."

My eyes dart to Juliette, waiting for her to scoff, but she's eerily quiet. Drinking in Ellie's assertion as she boldly goes on.

"If either of our characters truly wanted to leave that flat, they could. They would face difficulties, to be sure, but nothing insurmountable. They cling to the idea that destiny has somehow schemed them into this alleged torment, but really, they choose to stay together from the start because neither of them has the emotional fortitude to face the world on their own. They hold all of their own power from the very beginning but continuously refuse to wield it. They safeguard their 'powerlessness' and offer their agency to each other every time they choose to stay in that flat because surrender is easier and infinitely more indecent. The play is innately rooted in fear, and yearning, and conformity, and eventual rebellion, as well as love, which any audience can relate to. People, especially people today, shy away from power in one breath and then gorge it down in another. That's what I'm really looking forward to exploring in this production—the delicate but riotous struggle for balance."

The three of us are silent after that. All of us watching Ellie like she's some bespectacled theater nymph that we've somehow happened upon.

"That's an...interesting interpretation." If another person said that, it might be considered vague. Coming from Juliette, it's earth-shattering. She starts to lean in a little too, bracing her wrists down just above her knee. She and Ellie almost look huddled together.

Dear god. Is this going to be a healthy collaborative experience? Please excuse me while my soul leaves my body.

"And clearly you're passionate about the project," Juliette says.

"I am."

"So, what approach are you thinking of taking here?"

"To start, there's two things in particular that I feel strongly about. Firstly, I've decided to do a gender swap. A woman is going to play George, and a man will be playing Jocelyn. Honestly, I knew I was probably going to do that early on, but once I saw it played out in front of me during the casting process, it only confirmed that gender-bending was the way to go."

Juliette tilts her head off to the side. "Really?"

"I think it unlocks a lot of elements for people to dissect and consider. You have a character like Jocelyn, a musician battling stage fright who has essentially raised herself. She only reveals her true feelings through her guitar, but a majority of the time is too closed off to even allow herself that necessary outlet and release. She's soft and wounded and starved for touch while also being terrified of it. I'd personally love to see a man taking on that character, and I think we can portray her essence in a very meaningful and thoughtful way."

"And what about George?" Juliette asks.

"Oh, I think a woman assuming his character is equally compelling. Someone who's confident and fearless in the professional and social world, but who then has crippling bouts of anxiety in the safety of his own home. Who finds momentary purpose and excitement in the pursuit of physical pleasure but is unbearably lonely at his core. He's the main catalyst of the play's humor, but every joke is entrenched in insecurity and his desperate need to be accepted. I think the audience will deeply appreciate the dimension an actress can bring to that specific role."

"And would we be switching the characters' names?"

"No. Josie will be playing George, and Zachary will be Jocelyn."

Juliette doesn't say anything, but I know what she's thinking from the look in her eyes. She's here for it.

"And what was the second thought you had?" she asks.

"Secondly, I really think this performance needs to be an immersive experience."

Oh no. And here we were doing so well.

Ellie watches as Juliette visibly cringes. "I can see we're not quite on the same page with the idea," she says jokingly.

"I'm sorry, it's just, immersive theater isn't for me. I find it intrusive and chaotic, and I always have. How is the audience supposed to open themselves up to a piece if at any moment something could jump in front of them or brush past them or touch them? It just feels like a lot of unnecessary confusion and doesn't positively contribute in any productive way."

"I get what you're saying. But I do think there's a way to include the audience while also respecting boundaries and expectations. For me, as I was reading *The Lights of Trafalgar*, I was so carried away and enthralled that all I kept thinking to myself was, I have to get into that flat. I need to be there. I want to *feel* the vibrations through the floor when Jocelyn picks up her guitar and frees herself from everything that's holding her back. I want to stand beside George as he succumbs to his anxiety in the dead of night and *smell* the cold sweat that drips down the back of his neck."

"But what's best for you isn't necessarily what's best for everyone."

"Exactly," Ellie says, turning Juliette's own words back at her. "People love *The Lights of Trafalgar*, and that's why we're here having these discussions. My feeling is, we can absolutely respect the play's inherent fans while also welcoming in an era of new ones. But what we cannot do is hold on to the past forever, and that's why I'm so thrilled this show is going to be a pop-up production. Because no matter what people say, art doesn't feel sustainable anymore—it doesn't feel accessible, and we need to change that. We need to show up at our audience's door and stare them in the face because if we don't, we're going to be pushed aside until we're gone from their minds altogether."

Juliette sits back at that, and Ellie does the same. Roshni and I are too afraid to move.

"You're right," Juliette eventually says. Ellie grins, and I can't help but feel like I just witnessed a monumental event.

"I'm so glad you agree. I really do think this production is going to be something special. And we can compromise on the immersive parts."

"No, I'm looking forward to it." Juliette looks truly interested, and I am speechless. And elated.

"Fantastic," Ellie replies. The doors fling open then, and people begin to file in. "Alright, before we start, can I get anyone a coffee?"

Juliette gives her head a little shake. "I'm good, thanks." Roshni and I gesture the same, and Ellie stands, gracing us with another infectious smile before she walks away to join a group standing by the refreshment table.

"Wow," Roshni says. "Is this what football players' huddles are like? Because I feel so amped up that I could run through a wall right now."

"This show is going to be amazing," I throw in. "I can't

wait to get going." Stressing my point, I whip out the specialty scripts that I made for the three of us. They have the scripted pages minimized just slightly and printed on larger paper, leaving ample space for notes. I also have unlimited highlighters and pencils in my bag for anyone who needs them. Never pens. Pens are the enemy.

Twenty minutes later, the cast and crew settle down into their seats, and Ellie begins to speak, again with the steady, quiet confidence that's often a telltale sign of an effective director. "Alright, everyone, before we begin the read-through, I want to take a moment to acknowledge the living legend that we are lucky enough to have with us today. A woman who needs no introduction, but I'm giving her one anyways—please help me in welcoming the unspeakably talented Juliette Brassard."

The room claps, and a shy smile crosses Juliette's face, a smile that I haven't seen in quite some time. It fills me up with unadulterated pride.

"Thank you," she says graciously, waiting for the cheers to die down. "You know, when I first wrote *The Lights of Trafalgar*, I had been living in London for almost a year. I wasn't sure what my play was going to be about, but I knew where I wanted it set. I think everyone is biased in their love for a certain city, and for me, that city is London. It will always be London. To this day, the air and sounds light me up in a way that I can't quite explain. And it was that same inexplicable force that enabled me to write the play we will be reading today. All of us being here, now—in this city, in this moment—is something that will never happen again, and in a way, it makes us immortal. So, thank you for being in this moment with me, and I couldn't be happier to be having this experience with all of you. Thank you."

The room spirals into thunderous applause, and I am very much a part of it. In one breath, I'm entirely happy, and in another, I feel so cheated that we haven't been doing this every day for the past five years. Living and flourishing in this world is clearly what Juliette is meant to do, and it's clearer now than ever before. Ellie briefly addresses the group again after that, and then we go around the circle, introducing ourselves and explaining our role in the production. It takes a few minutes, and after that, we're off to the races as the read-through begins.

Four hours later, Roshni, Juliette, and I are back in the penthouse. Having just returned from a nice walk, Ollie is perfectly content on his luxurious new bed, and Roshni and I are both still on a high from the read-through as we sit side by side on the couch.

"That was seriously so amazing," Roshni says. "Just being in there and vibing off everyone's energy, it really felt like I was part of something."

"I couldn't agree more. Not bad for a first day, right, Juliette?" I turn around to find my boss at her desk, typing away. She hasn't even taken a sip of the tea that I fixed for her a minute ago.

Closing her laptop with a thud, she gets up and settles herself down in my favorite armchair. "It was fine," she says tonelessly.

"What do you mean, it was fine?" I counter. "It was great. The cast is electric, and Ellie's ideas were incredible."

"Yes, yes, Eloise is indeed a revelation."

All the excitement drains from the room as Juliette's mood instantly casts a cloud. Before I can question her about it further, my phone rings, and I see it's my dad.

Crap. I was supposed to call him yesterday for one of our scheduled biweekly catch-ups.

"I have to take this. I'll be right back." I quickly get up and walk down the hallway, stepping into the spare bedroom that was originally intended for me.

"Hey, Dad," I say as soon as I pick up. "I'm sorry I missed our call. Everything was thrown off with the time difference, and things have been really hectic ever since. Wonderful, but hectic."

In my defense, I did text him when I decided to come to London, but Dad's never been much of a texter. If anything, he'll shoot me back a one-word answer at best.

"It's alright, Winnie. I'm glad you're having fun." He sounds older than I remember. I thought he'd be more relaxed since retiring a few months ago, but maybe not.

"So, what's new with you?" I ask. "How's Cassie?"

"Cassie's good. She has some minor allergies, but nothing too serious. I suggested an antihistamine twice daily."

My dad has always preferred discussing treatment plans to small talk. If it wasn't for Cassie, his longtime and only girl-friend, I doubt he ever would have stopped working.

"Listen," he goes on, "part of the reason I'm calling is because I have some news. I'm going to be putting the house on the market this week."

His words hit me like a sudden punch to the jugular.

"Putting the house on the market?" I ask. "Why?"

"Cassie's been ready to leave New York for some time now. You know Becky still lives in Arizona, and she's having a baby in the fall. Cassie wants to be there for that and then to help her after. She moved out here to be with me for sixteen years, and now it's time I did this for her. Plus, I don't really get to see you that much, anyways."

Guilt swarms me in a thick, unforgiving wave. I know I haven't been visiting my dad as much as I used to, but I never expected him to move. That's the house I grew up in. The house my mom lived in. The house we were a family in.

My throat feels tight, but I force myself to speak. "No, I get it. I'm just surprised."

"I know, Winnie. I should have told you in person, but you've been so busy lately."

I nod my head even though I know he can't see me. "As soon as I get back from London, I'll come see you guys. I promise. I'll be there the very day I land."

"Okay, Winnie. That'll be nice. We really miss you."

His voice is as calm as ever. If he's feeling even a little of what I'm feeling right now, he doesn't show it.

"Bye, Dad," is all I can muster.

"Bye-bye." He hangs up, and I'm left reeling. My dad and I have always had an unconventional kind of relationship. We're polar opposites, really. He was a spinal surgeon, and I was this theater creature that existed around him. He's all facts and figures, and I'm a charging torpedo of words and emotions.

He encouraged me plenty, in his own way. Since I was young, he took me to tons of shows, signed me up for any theater program or class that was available. He held the VHS recorder for any at-home productions I set up in our living room and always took me to community theater auditions when his schedule allowed. He's attended every opening night performance I was ever in and presented me with two dozen white roses each time. He was dedicated to his career to a fault, but even the hospital staff knew that opening nights were untouchable for him. He was never particularly verbal with his emotions, but he constantly showed me he cared.

He started dating Cassie when I was thirteen. They reconnected at a college alumni function, and with her daughter, Becky, being away at college, she uprooted and moved in with us soon after. She was always nice. A bit of a hippie, which struck me as odd, since my dad is so straight and narrow. He's all about schedules and science and having his clothes hung up in the closet just so. Cassie is big into gardening, constantly tracking soil with her everywhere through the house. She makes her own soap and prizes sustainability above all else. But she loves my dad, and that makes me happy. And I know she cares for me, too. I wish we connected more than we did, but she always felt more like a quirky aunt-in-residence than a mother figure.

And now her daughter is having a baby, her daughter who's only a handful of years older than me. Drawing Cassie back to Arizona and taking my dad with her.

I exit the spare room still in a daze and am no better off as I enter the living room. Everyone is where I left them—Juliette in the armchair and Roshni on the couch. Roshni looks up from reading her script notes as I sit down a couple of feet from her.

"You okay?" she asks.

I place my cell phone down softly onto the coffee table. "I don't know. I just found out my dad is selling our old house."

"And I'm guessing you're not excited about it?"

As if he's reading my emotions, Ollie gets up from his bed and snuggles against my ankles. I unconsciously reach down and nestle him onto my lap.

"It's just affecting me more than I thought it would. I understand his reasons for selling, and I really am hardly ever there. But I guess I never imagined that someday a time would come when I couldn't go home." Roshni nods, and I stroke Ollie's fur in calming strokes.

"I know I'm probably being overdramatic, but it just feels wrong that strangers are going to be living where my mom lived. I get that it's just a house, but with her being gone, it feels like more than that. Like it's one of the only things that still ties me to her."

Roshni looks at me empathetically, seemingly understanding the conflicting feelings that are swirling through me. She goes to speak when Juliette suddenly jumps in.

"I'm sorry," she says from her spot on the armchair. "I know this will probably come off as insensitive, but I just had a really tough time at rehearsal, and I don't think I can handle any more doom and gloom today."

The room falls silent, and Roshni and I stare at Juliette after sending mutually confused looks to each other. I wait another few seconds for Juliette to announce that she's kidding, or something along those lines, but she doesn't.

"Okay," I eventually get myself to say, "sorry about that."

"I'm sorry, too. I've just had a very draining morning and am dealing with a lot. Plus, you need to get in a more positive headspace since you're going on your day-date with British Boyfriend #3 tomorrow. He's the painter who also dabbles in stand-up comedy. I have a good feeling about him."

Roshni continues to look at Juliette, still stunned silent by her tone-deaf response. I nod my head and try to regroup as quickly as possible.

"Me too. It can only go up from here, right?"

"Exactly," Juliette agrees, taking one sip of her tea and then leaving it beside the coaster on the coffee table. "Okay, so I'm going to go unwind for a bit. We'll all order in for dinner tonight, okay? My treat."

"Sounds great," I say with a smile.

Juliette grins, stepping over to give Ollie a doting pet before she exits. She's gone for less than ten seconds when Roshni whips around to face me on the couch.

"Excuse me, what in the hot hell just happened?" she seethes.

"It's fine," I tell her.

"Um, it is most certainly not fine. You were just having an emotional moment and Juliette completely invalidated you."

"It's not a big deal. She's my boss, and I was talking about personal stuff that has nothing to do with my job."

"Yeah, and you going out with strangers has nothing to do with your job either, yet here we are. She's cool with crossing personal boundaries but only when it suits her. Remember that."

I stretch my neck from side to side, and Roshni stands. "And now I'm going to reread the play in anger. Maybe some of the passages will hit differently."

She picks up her script and the book of monologues that I gave her and disappears down the hallway. I have to smile despite myself, still endlessly grateful that she's here with us for the summer. It feels good to have a friend at work. Of course, Juliette is my friend, too, but not in the same way.

I'm not going to lie. Juliette's response hurt. I live for the vulnerable moments she has with me, but clearly the feelings are not mutual. Her response stung, my dad's news sucks, and I suddenly feel so tired that the last thing I want to do is meet up with some guy I don't know tomorrow, a guy who just happens to be available for a day-date during the workweek.

I think again about Juliette's reaction. How she made the situation about her, because that's what she does. She looks out for number one and does what she wants to make herself feel better. Sure, it's self-centered, but it's also self-preservation, and maybe I should try that out for myself for once.

Before I lose my nerve, I pull out my phone, swiftly sending out an apology text to British Boyfriend #3 and canceling our meetup. I then draft a new message to Liam. I'm surprised at how easily I do it, sitting back on the couch with Ollie as I hit the Send button and await a response.

I'm sorry, Juliette. I think to myself. *But I know you would do the same if you were me.*

8

I find Liam at our designated meeting spot on Kensington High Street, just outside Kensington Gardens. Cars zip past near where he's waiting at the crosswalk, the sounds somehow blending easily with the birds chirping and dogs barking in the lush green space behind us.

"Well, hello," I say.

"Hello there. I'm glad you changed your mind." He's wearing jeans and a gray zip-up jacket, and he seems a little unsure of what to do next. "Sorry, I'm just wondering if I should hug you or go for a casual cheek kiss. Wouldn't it be great if there was only one socially acceptable way to greet people? Then we could all relax, and I wouldn't have to long for death each time my awkward handshake is forced to morph into an even more awkward high five."

"But then you wouldn't be able to talk about how much you hate saying hello and in doing so, drag the experience out even longer and more painfully."

"Yes, and as I'm so masterfully demonstrating now, I do

excel at that." He pauses again and squares his shoulders. "Alright, after much deliberation, I've decided to go with the casual but friendly cheek kiss. Brace yourself. I will commence leaning in shortly, giving you ample opportunity to swat me away."

I nibble on my lip as he does indeed give me a very sweet cheek kiss, and because torturing him is so much fun, I then scream out in pain and clasp my hand to my cheek. "Oh my god, you bit me!" I yell in horror. "Why would you do that? Am I bleeding?"

Liam turns pale and looks horrified as several people stop to watch us. "What? I didn't bite you!"

I lower my hand with a smile. "I'm just kidding. Don't hate me."

Liam visibly exhales and stress-wipes his hand across his forehead. "You are a wretched human being. I'm fairly confident you've just traumatized me for life."

"Does that mean you don't want to hang out, after all?"

"No, for whatever reason, I still do. I must be a glutton for punishment."

I swear I can still see his heart pumping through his chest, and I really do start to feel guilty.

"In all seriousness, I am sorry. That was quite mean on my part. For future reference, I'm terrified of sharks. If we're ever out deep-sea fishing and you see an opportunity for payback, I'll understand."

"I'm pretty sure you being savagely eaten alive by sharks isn't a fair trade-off in this scenario."

"You're such a softie," I say.

"And you really are a strange woman."

"So I've been told."

Liam shakes his head, seemingly clearing his mind. "Alright, time to take on the day. I thought we could do an afternoon of classic London sightseeing. I figured with my aunt keeping you so busy, this might be your only chance."

Even with my teasing, he's still so incredibly thoughtful. For some reason, it makes me a little nervous. "Are you sure? Won't that be boring for you since you live here?"

"Not at all. *Because* I live here, I rarely go to any touristy spots. I'm looking forward to it."

"Alright then. In that case, sightseeing sounds perfect."

"Excellent, and since we're agreed, I got you a gift for the occasion."

He reaches inside his zip-up and dramatically pulls out a bright red T-shirt with the British flag and "London" stamped across the front in big bold letters.

"Stop," I say, eagerly pulling the shirt from his hands and holding it up. "Yes! Are we going to be those people?"

Liam then unzips his jacket, revealing the matching T-shirt that he's currently wearing. "We're absolutely going to be those people. If we're having a tourist day, we're doing it full blast or not at all."

I instantly pull the shirt on over my lightweight tan sweater. "I'm so down. How do I look?"

"Like the easily excitable, artsy American that you are."

"I want that description inscribed on my tombstone."

"I'll inform your loved ones. Shall we?"

"We shall."

An hour later, we're inside the London Eye. Liam bought us fast-pass tickets, which he refused to let me pay for, that allowed us to skip most of the line. We're now halfway to the top, suspended over London in a sturdy glass-and-metal compartment with a panoramic view of the city. There are only a few other people inside with us as we sit on a plastic bench in the center.

I look over at Liam innocently. "Is this a good time to tell you that I have feverish hallucinations at high altitudes?"

"At this point, nothing you could say would shock me."

I smirk at his words and stand up, moving to lean over the metal guardrail. My forehead rests against the glass enclosure as I look down to fully take in the view. "I still can't believe that I'm here. Last month, the most exciting thing that happened to me was that I earned a free burrito after getting twelve stamps on my membership card."

"A free burrito is nothing to balk at," Liam says, getting up to stand beside me and also looking down, but stopping short of putting his forehead on the glass. "So, you're glad you came, then?"

"I'm very glad. The pop-up is going to be great. Plus, we're only two rehearsals in, and I've already learned so much from Ellie."

"More than you've learned from my aunt?"

I shift backwards to stand up straight. "Just different things, really."

Liam shifts a little closer to me as more people begin to line the guardrail. I've never felt so cozy four hundred feet in the air.

"What was it that first got you involved in the theater?" he asks.

I smile to myself as a soft, dreamy mist coats my mind. "It was my mom." My smile fades a bit as I continue. "She died of ovarian cancer when I was four, but growing up, my dad always told me stories about her. My dad is a doctor—a spinal surgeon. And he was very into everything that you'd expect a spinal surgeon to be into. Medical journals, biology. But when he started dating my mom, who was a preschool teacher, she told him it was important to have varying interests to stay well-rounded. So the two of them started going to the theater once a month. It was their special thing. And once I got old enough, maybe ten or so, he started taking *me* to the theater, and then it became our special thing, too."

Liam glances down at me, a small grin gracing his face.

"I like to think my mom would be happy I went into the arts. Maybe it's morbid, but when you're on stage, the lights are so bright that you can't really see the audience. And I always loved that, because whenever I was in a show, I would pretend that she was out there watching me."

"That's a very nice thought," Liam says quietly. "And I think your mother would be incredibly proud of you."

I can't quite articulate how much I want to believe him.

"I doubt she is these days. All I do now is grunt work and busywork, and I basically just get paid to keep Juliette company."

"I don't believe that. Whenever my aunt speaks about you, she always makes you sound irreplaceable."

"That's only because I make her tea the way she likes it."

"Well, what's more important than a good cup of tea?"

I shake my head as my eyes trail along the Thames, from Big Ben to the perfectly Gothic architecture of Parliament. "Tell me about you—about your work," I then say.

Liam stiffens. Barely enough to notice, but we're pressed so close that I feel the muscles clenching up his arm and into his shoulder. I didn't expect a normal question to strike such a nerve.

"Right, well, I started off as a web developer. I got into it at university and I loved it. I was somehow good at it, which

was a bit of a revelation considering I'm spectacularly mediocre in all other areas of my life."

"Doubtful."

"No, I am. In primary school I was literally voted 'most
spectacularly mediocre.'"

"I'm sure the eleven-year-old in you was deeply honored."

"Very much so. Anyways, after university I started working
and got lots of experience. Then after a few years, I decided
I wanted to branch out on my own. I started a web consulting firm and brought on some of the developers I knew. We
would primarily work for companies who didn't have established web teams and set them on the right track. We'd sign
a contract for six months or so, and then do work that other
developers would take a fiscal year to complete, thereby saving the company the time and money that they'd otherwise
use to hire full-time employees."

"How very savvy."

"Yes, as it turns out it was. We did shockingly well and
expanded until the final number was two hundred and eight
developers. We were a great group. Soon after, I received an
offer to be acquired, and I took it."

"Just like that?" I ask. The compartment stops moving for
a moment as we've now reached the very top.

"Well, it wasn't quite as rash a decision as that. Considering
how quickly and successfully we were growing, I had received
a few acquisitions offers over the years, but with the last one,
it just felt like the right time to sell."

"That's good, then. So, what about all your employees?
They're with this new company now?"

"They are," he says, a little strained but trying to hide it.
"The transition went smoothly."

"Smoothly enough that you're yet to go back, right?"

"That would be correct. Good memory, by the way."

"I do my best."

Liam smirks and takes a deep breath, seemingly trying to lighten the mood. "Well, it all worked out since I now have the time and the extreme honor of showing you around London."

"Ah," I say easily. "So really, your interest in me is just an elaborate means of procrastination. As a lady, I'm offended. As a writer, I appreciate your creativity and zeal."

"I'm glad. And in the spirit of procrastination, which landmark would you like to see next?"

It takes the exact amount of time until we're back at ground level for me to make my choice. Several bus stops later, we're standing outside our newest destination.

"And here we have the Tower of London." Liam extends his arm out like a proper tour guide, the fortress/palace standing formidably in front of us as Tower Bridge sits attractively off to the side. "A site not to be overlooked, it is the historic location of hundreds of years of wrongful imprisonment, overall general torture, and countless unjustified executions." We both stay where we are, tilting our heads as we take in the suddenly morose-seeming structure. "Well then," Liam says, turning chipper. "Shall we go in?"

"Yes, please!"

Two hours later, we're now at the final sightseeing location, when Liam looks at me with a slightly uncomfortable gleam in his eyes. "I have to say, I'm a bit surprised that this is where you wanted to close out our tour. Given your slightly hardened exterior, I didn't peg you for a royal wedding enthusiast."

"I'm a three-dimensional character, Liam. My ice-cold heart is inlaid with layer upon layer of fairy-tale optimism."

"So I'm discovering."

Strolling deeper into St. Paul's cathedral, Liam looks off towards the side, gazing up at the awe-inspiring glass windows as I determinedly walk to the middle of the space.

"What are you doing?" he asks when he eventually notices my position. I smile back at him and let my inner princess flag fly as I take a meaningful step forward towards the front of the church, clasping my hands up in front of me as I hold an imaginary bouquet of flowers. "You're not doing what I think you're doing, are you?"

I shrug and continue to smile angelically as Liam makes his way to my side with quickened steps. For my part, I continue on in my bridal procession, completely unbothered.

"Are you truly going to walk the entire length of the cathedral?"

"Yes, I am."

"People are staring at you."

"That's fine."

"You really going to do this? You're fully committed to the idea?"

"Of course I'm committed. I'm at Princess Diana's wedding venue and I'm supposed to not stage a full reenactment? You're lucky I didn't know we were coming here in advance or I'd be in a ball gown. Now, step away. You should be waiting up front."

"Oh, excellent," he chuckles, "so now we're meant to be getting married?"

"You wish. As much as your accent and height give you a certain princely demeanor, I pictured you as the weakly abbot performing the ceremony."

Liam grins, now seeming much more accepting. "I strangely agree with that casting choice."

"I thought you might."

And an hour later, we're back at Juliette's building, exiting the elevator and heading towards the studio with light steps and rosy cheeks.

"I have to say, this was probably the best day I've had in a long time."

"Me too," I reply. We reach the door, and I turn around with an easy smile. "Thank you again for showing me around. I don't think I would have planned something like this on my own."

"I was happy to." Things turn quiet for a moment, the small hallway abandoned as we stand facing each other. "Do you think you can sell my aunt on the idea that your Vibefinder meetup took you out sightseeing?"

"Not sure if John the painter/comedian would be quite selfless enough to plan a date of that caliber. I'll just tell her he and I went for drinks instead."

"Not a bad idea. Say you went to Coach & Horses in Mayfair. You can tell her that John plays soccer on the weekends and goes out with old school friends every Tuesday and Friday. His parents split up when he was twelve, and his mother is still in London, but his father moved to Leeds. You had a good time at first, but he drank too much for your taste. And he despises the theater, an unforgivable offense."

"That's an impressive backstory. Where did it come from?"

"A work associate of mine. Carl Umber, in fact. Not a bad guy, but I doubt you two would hit it off. You would terrify him."

"I'm really not as feral as you make me out to be."

"I know that. And honestly, I wouldn't change a thing about you."

I smile as a sudden nervous fluttering starts to spread inside my chest. "You only think that because you don't know me well enough. Once we spend more time together, you'll find I'm inundated with a plethora of annoying habits."

He takes the smallest step forward at my words. "Does that mean we'll be spending more time together, then?" More delicious jitters have me instinctively shifting backwards, my shoulders brushing up against the door.

"I wouldn't be opposed to it. And I'm sure Juliette would be happy that I'm volunteering to go out on more dates."

"Yes, I forgot we're meant to be dating in this scenario." He takes another step forward, and now we're toe-to-toe. "Assuming this is indeed a date, I suppose this is when I would tell you that I had a wonderful time."

I have to crane my neck to meet his eyes. I forgot how tall he is. "And I'd tell you I had a wonderful time, too."

"I'd thank you for breaking the rules for me. Sneaking out on a work trip and all."

"Secrets can be fun," I say, a little breathless.

Liam shifts even closer then, his hands sliding around my waist. His touch is so soft, like he's afraid I'll disappear. I can hear myself breathing, and I hear him, too. My skin feels hot beneath my clothes as he continues to gently cage me in against the door. My blood is rushing, and my mind's spinning. He continues to look down at me, watching me with soft but hazy eyes. It feels like I'm suspended over an abyss that I'm wildly ready to leap into.

"It's alright," he says quietly, his hands still gripping my waist. "I can be your secret."

Not needing to hear anything else, I push up onto my toes and press my lips against his. I inch back a second later to catch his heady gaze, and he doesn't seem surprised, only relieved. Apparently, he was waiting for me. I flash him the briefest smile, and he answers me with one of his own before swooping down to bring his lips back to mine. His arms weave around me completely—one hand sliding up my spine to palm the nape of my neck, the other encasing my waist to pull my hips flush against his. It feels like sinful heaven, and I don't want it to stop. He kisses me again, over and over, his mouth warm and disorienting. I drag him forward even more and he follows my lead, effectively pinning me against the door.

I tilt my head up further, and Liam deepens the kiss, sweeping his tongue into my entirely willing mouth. If I thought I wanted more before, it pales in comparison to how ravenous I am now. And that's why I could almost cry when he slowly leans back a few seconds later, his stormy blue eyes trained on mine as we both struggle to regulate our breathing.

"That was unexpected," I find myself saying. My voice is velvety and low, sounding very much like a woman in the aftermath of the hottest kiss of her life.

"Sorry," Liam answers, swallowing as his eyes slowly begin to clear. "I've just thought about doing that since the first time I saw you. Since I first heard your voice, really."

I fail miserably at disguising my grin. "No need to apologize. I clearly enjoyed it."

"As did I." He returns my smirk as he gives me a brief kiss and gradually steps back. Breaking free of our self-made fog, we both begin to return to reality. Before I know it, sex god Liam drifts away, leaving behind the lighthearted guy I spent a perfect afternoon with. It's like sweet Dr. Jekyll and Mr. Sexy-Ass Hyde.

"I want to thank you for today, too," he quickly says. "I think you're amazing, Winnie. And I understand that the position you're in is complicated, so whatever you want to do moving forward, just know that I'm in. Whether we're just friends or friends who…"

"Passionately make out in hallways?" I offer.

Liam gives me a good-humored nod. "Yes, or that. Whichever you choose, I'll go with it. I just don't want our time together to be cut shorter than it's already going to be."

His words wrap around me like a calming breeze, and it grounds me in a way that feels relaxed and right. He's not feeding me a line. He's not telling me what he thinks I want to hear. He wants me for me, in whatever capacity I choose.

"I don't want that either," I tell him.

He smiles then, quiet and happy and perfectly reflecting my current feelings.

"Excellent," he says.

I clear my throat and tuck my somewhat wild hookup hair behind my ears. "Should we go ahead and shake hands now, so you don't have to go into panic mode about saying goodbye?"

"No, I think I'm just going to slowly back away, so as not to ruin our tender moment." He does just that and, unfortunately, trips a bit as he goes.

"*A* for effort," I tell him. "Don't get discouraged."

"Yes, thank you. I'll just wait for the elevator now." He turns around and pushes the button, waiting patiently and rocking back and forth on his heels as he tries not to look at me.

"I'm going to head inside, then," I say to his back.

"Right, good idea. I'll call and/or text soon."

"Goodbye, Liam."

"Goodbye, Winnie." I spare him one more look over my shoulder before I unlock the studio door with a shake of my head. I'm still grinning like a fool when I close it behind me and find Roshni lying in the center of the floor with Ollie sprawled out beside her.

"Change of plans," she says. "I've decided to tell Juliette all about your torrid affair so I can claim Liam for myself." She's looking at me upside down from her spot on the rug, and I angle my head to the side to see her more clearly.

"Trust me, he's more trouble than he's worth." I set my bag down on the counter, and Ollie strolls over to nuzzle my shins as Roshni sits up, twisting around to face me.

"Is that what you really think?" she asks.

I wish I could say yes. I wish I could say that I don't care about Liam at all. That there's zero zing factor there and I could easily forget all about him. But, regrettably, I can't.

"No," I answer honestly, "as it turns out, he's actually very much worth it."

Damn it.

9

I'm just bringing Ollie in from a walk when I stop in the entryway, taking out the key for Juliette's mailbox. He sits down beside me and scratches behind his ear, and I can't help but smile just looking at him. Tests confirmed he had no registration chip and judging from his state when I found him, the vet figured he was most likely abandoned for months. I reported Ollie to the local council, and they told me that if they can't locate the owner, I'll be allowed to keep him. I really hope that he and I are endgame, but the idea also leaves me feeling slightly nervous. My apartment is small, even smaller than the studio, and with working in the theater, my day-to-day schedule is constantly all over the place. Maybe I can look into hiring a dog walker? It'll probably be expensive, but regardless, I'll figure something out, and we'll find a way to make it work.

I'm still staring unabashedly down at him when a man with sandy-blond hair appears in the stairwell, on his way out. He stops by the mailboxes as well, now standing directly beside me as he turns his little key in the lock.

"Morning," he says. His pale green eyes catch mine as he flashes me a quick smile.

"Morning," I chirp back.

He pulls a couple of letters out and looks them over as he locks the mailbox back up again. I'm doing the same when he then goes on, "Are you new to the building?"

Sliding my set of keys into my pocket, I turn to face him. "No. Well, sort of. I'm Juliette Brassard's assistant. We're here in town for work."

"Oh, nice. I think my mum knew Juliette back in the day. I took over her flat on the fourth floor a few years ago. I'm Phillip."

He extends his hand, and I don't hesitate to shake it. "Winnie."

"Nice to meet you, Winnie. And this is?" He's now looking down to where Ollie is gnawing on the edge of his loafers.

"That's Ollie. He's the newest member of our entourage."

"An excellent addition," he says, squatting down to ruffle his fur. "Very distinguished. I've been meaning to get a dog for ages but have yet to take the plunge."

"Most parents say you're never truly ready, so it's probably better just to go for it. Granted, they're referring to human babies and not fur babies, but still, I'd assume it's the same sentiment."

"Yes, I can see that saying being somewhat befitting." He stands up then with a friendly grin, and I think how nice it would be to have friends in my building back home. Too bad I live in a six-floor walk-up where everyone mean-mugs each other on a nearly competitive level.

"Alright," I say, "well, I'm off to rehearsal. Juliette has a new pop-up production coming out, so we're on a bit of a time crunch."

"I can imagine. And hey, if you ever need someone to walk Ollie or to visit him during the day, just let me know. I teach maths, so I'm free for the next two months while school's out."

"That's really nice of you. I'll let you know."

"Think nothing of it."

I give him a smile and head towards the elevator with Ollie loyally following along behind me. "Have a good day," I add over my shoulder as I hit the call button.

"You, too!" He's about to exit but stops short of the door a second later. He sniffs the air, prompting me to do the same and quickly realizing that Ollie just unleashed one mother of a silent assassin fart. Phillip turns back towards me just as I shield my nose with the back of my hand.

"It wasn't me," I instinctively claim.

"I didn't say anything." Phillip seems to be doing his darnedest to keep from laughing.

"I'm slowly learning that Ollie is prone to gassy spells when in shared, enclosed environments. I suggest you escape with your life while you still can."

"I'll do that, but are you sure you'll survive the fumes?"

"I'm attempting to build up an immunity."

"A daunting task. Good luck!"

I nod my head as he finally exits, and the elevator arrives a second later. Ollie trots inside after me as I keep my hand to my nose and press the button for the penthouse.

"You need to chill with the farting around boys," I tell my companion. He looks up at me with that perfect little face of his, and I once again can't help but smile. "Though it is pretty funny. And I'm still obsessed with you."

★ ★ ★

We're in the thick of rehearsals three hours later as Ellie stops a scene to speak to one of the principal actors.

Roshni flips through her script, reading ahead, and I peek down at her pages. She's taken copious notes in the margins, questions are highlighted, and certain speeches are underlined for emphasis. I'm entirely beaming in older sister pride when Ellie's voice suddenly has us both looking up.

"Roshni," she calls for a second time. "Would you mind standing in for a moment? I want Josie to see Zachary moving through the space from the audience's perspective."

"Are you sure?" Roshni asks, already starting to get up. "I don't know how helpful I'll be."

"The talent of an untrained actor knows no bounds. No offense, Zachary."

"Offense very much taken. Are you aware of the acceptance rate for the Royal Academy of Dramatic Art?"

"No, I don't, Peter O'Toole, but I'm sure you're about to tell us."

"Amateurs," our leading man jokes as Roshni power walks to stand across from him. "Don't upstage me or I'll never hear the end of it."

"Your legacy is safe," she assures him.

Zachary grins and promptly begins. Ellie and Josie move back several feet as they watch Roshni read in, and I inch forward in my chair as much as possible without making a sound. I'm completely enthralled with watching my friend in action when Juliette plops down into the vacant seat next me.

"Her methods are a little unorthodox, no?"

I begrudgingly turn my attention away from the scene, pivoting instead to face Juliette. "You mean Ellie? I think she's great."

"She's good, but she's too sure of herself. Artists that lack debilitating self-doubt are always concerning to me. It means they haven't been beaten down enough by the world to be rightfully terrified."

"I don't think trauma necessarily begets talent. I have faith in Ellie. This show is going to be remarkable."

"Well, Roshni is certainly thriving. I never knew she had an interest in acting."

"I don't think she knew either. But just look at her..."

We stop talking then, watching and listening as she runs through the scene. Her inexperience is obvious, but her instincts are solid. And when she finishes a couple of minutes later, she bounces over to us on an utter adrenaline high.

"That was incredible," I tell her, meaning every word. "You were so good, Roshni."

She's breathless and giddy and all but glowing in excitement. "I really tried. Did I ever tell you that I won my eighth-grade oratorical contest?"

"What speech did you do?"

"Severn Cullis-Suzuki at the 1992 Rio Summit."

"And did you light the auditorium up with fiery, impassioned rhetoric?"

"I may have or may not have burned it to the ground."

I have to smile as I sit back in my seat. "Honestly, you are such a treasure. I can't even."

"Oh, stop," she says, seeming embarrassed. "I sounded like a babbling freak just now. Zachary obliterated me. I was—"

"You were delightful," Juliette interjects. Her words hang heavier, her decades of knowledge giving a certain weight to her opinion that you're somehow forced to accept. Roshni's cheeks streak red from the praise.

"Thank you, Juliette. That means a lot."

Just then, Ellie claps her hands together, getting the room's attention. "Alright everyone, let's take a quick break and be back in fifteen." A quiet buzz falls over the space, everyone figuring out what to do with their allotted time.

"I'm going to run out for coffee," Roshni quickly says. "Can I get anyone anything?"

Juliette perks up. "I'll take another Greek salad from the restaurant we tried yesterday, and an Earl Grey tea with milk from the café around the corner. And a granola bar, but only if they're organic and sugar-free. If you can't find one of those, then just two chocolate chip cookies."

Roshni's eyes go a little wide but she nods. "No problem. Winnie?"

"I'm good," I say.

"Okay, be right back." Roshni picks up her bag and heads for the exit.

Juliette opens her notebook in her lap but doesn't write anything. "I'm glad Roshni came with us on this trip. I forgot how thrilling theater can be to a newcomer. I feel like I'm finally getting how Christmas is better when you see your child's excitement."

"That's a nice way of looking at it," I tell her.

"Well, you know me, I'm just the nicest," she jokingly agrees. "By the way, I think it's time for us to give up on your online dating pursuits. It's clearly not working, so let's just focus on the play since that's what we're here for."

I sigh in relief and surprise at Juliette's sudden declaration. Though I should have known that she'd lose interest in the project quickly enough without immediate success.

"Sounds good to me," I say as I sit back. "The pop-up will keep us plenty busy. No need for me to belly flop into the British dating pool if it's not even helping with anything."

"Exactly. And I'll read your play as soon as I can spare a few hours. Hopefully in the next day or so."

I beam at Juliette's promise, fully ready to thank her profusely when Ellie sits down beside us.

"How are we doing?" she asks. "What do you lot think of the scene?"

Juliette sits up straighter and takes a breath. "We're doing well. And the scene seems to be going smoothly."

Ellie studies her with a deciphering gaze. "You don't like it."

"I didn't say that."

"You didn't have to. Which part isn't working for you?" She's asking in such a genuine way, entirely present and not at all condescending or defensive. Quite rare in our field. Juliette seems encouraged, shifting sideways to face her more directly.

"I'm just wondering if we should give George something else to do. This is a character who is larger than life and is constantly on the move. And as much as I'm opposed to immersive theater, I'm wondering if you could maybe be implementing a bit of that here for Josie to play around with."

"I'm listening. What did you have in mind?"

Juliette closes her notebook with a pop. "I was thinking we should give George a hobby. Nothing verbal that requires explaining, but maybe he could be into photography. So instead of having him just walk through the apartment as he talks to Jocelyn, he could be taking photos of her during the scene. He could even photograph the audience throughout the play."

Ellie slowly nods, her pace picking up as she considers the idea. "Yes. Photography. I can absolutely see that."

"And maybe there can be some kind of payoff at the end or near the end, too. Like, Jocelyn discovers the photos George has taken and can then see that he clearly has feelings for her through the images he captured."

"I love that," Ellie says, moving forward in her seat, eager to spring into action. "Better yet, we can use a Polaroid camera and have him pin the photos up on a bulletin board throughout the show so there can be a visible progression of their relationship. And then at the end, the audience can come up and collect their own photo, if George took their picture during the performance. We'll obviously have to tinker with the camera so there isn't too much of a flash, but I really think this idea has a lot of potential. I'm so glad you were willing to share it with me."

Juliette's smile is shy but genuine as she busies herself with her notebook that's still in her lap. "It's fine. It was just a thought."

"It was a wonderful thought. Also, what if we..." Ellie's words trail off as her gaze lands on something behind us. Surprised excitement washes over her face. "Sorry, can you just excuse me for a sec?" She gets up, and Juliette and I low-key peek over our shoulders to see what or who caught her interest. We turn just as she reaches a pretty brunette in scrubs and a jean jacket. Ellie gives her a swift kiss before pulling her back towards us as we quickly stand up.

"Juliette, Winnie, I'd like you both to meet my wife, Chloe. Chloe, this is Winnie and, of course, the legendary Juliette Brassard."

"So good to meet you both," Chloe says with a soft grin. "Juliette, Ellie's been talking of little else for the past three months."

"Oh, I doubt that."

"You shouldn't. Whenever she starts a new play, the fixation sets in quite early. I've heard *The Lights of Trafalgar* repeated back to me so often that I'm officially off book."

Everyone smiles and it's blatantly obvious that Chloe is just as instantly likable as Ellie. I'm going to need them to adopt me ASAP.

"I think it's actually ingrained at this point," Chloe goes on. "I even discussed it with a patient this afternoon. They're very interested in attending the pop-up, by the way, assuming their lesion heals in time."

"Recruiting at the hospital! Now, why didn't I think of that?" Ellie teases.

"Don't worry, I'm happy to be your in-house promoter. And once you start printing out fliers, I'll be sure to leave some at the nurses' stations."

Juliette tucks her notebook under her arm. "That would be wonderful. You're a nurse, then, I presume?"

"A physician's assistant. And, unfortunately, I actually have to get going. I only stopped by to say hello and to bring this one lunch. If I didn't throw food at her while she's preparing for a show, she'd never eat."

Ellie rolls her eyes and steals her arm around her wife's waist. "Someone please explain to her that being a starving artist is a lifestyle."

"It's also metaphorical," Chloe asserts. "And I really do have to run. But it was so nice to meet you both."

"You, too." I shake her hand, then watch as Juliette does the same.

"I'll see you out," Ellie says.

We both wave as they walk off, and I can barely conceal my sigh as we sit back down. "Is it me, or are people just nicer in England?"

Juliette only shakes her head. "Eloise is lucky she found someone who's so supportive. Spouses typically aren't in this line of work."

"They did seem very power-couple-esque," I agree. "It must

be nice. Ellie gets to live her dream and have love. She's got it all."

"No one can have it all." Juliette turns to look at Ellie and Chloe one more time before twisting back around. "But hopefully they'll be the ones to prove me wrong."

For some reason, her words make me think back to the letter I found in her scrapbook. Before I can stop myself, I ask, "When you used to live in London, did you have any grand love affairs?"

Juliette immediately grins. "Oh, I had many." She pauses after that, but soon goes on, "Though there was one in particular."

I shouldn't push, I should just leave it at that, but I can't resist confirming my suspicions. "What was his name?"

Juliette looks around, almost as if she's about to tell me a salacious secret. Little is she aware, I already know far more than I'm meant to. "Paul," she answers quietly.

Paul. *I knew it was you.*

"What was he like?" I ask.

Juliette smiles to herself. "He was funny. Funnier than me, that's for sure. But he was quiet-funny. You'd never know he was joking by the even tone of his voice. And he was smart. Talented. An excellent writer. Being around him pushed me to be better."

I find myself smiling along with Juliette, envisioning the pictures of the two of them in my mind, but now they're coming to life. She looked so happy then, and she's starting to look that happy again now.

"One thing I vividly remember is that he was a terrible driver. He was so good at everything else that when I hopped into his little sports car to go meet his parents, I just assumed he couldn't be more perfect. And then we pulled away, and

I thought, 'Nope, he is most certainly *not* perfect, and he is going to kill me and every single person on this highway.' And granted, I didn't have the most dignified reaction…"

"Meaning?" I inquire.

"Meaning I screamed bloody murder. And then he started screaming bloody murder, and then we were both screaming bloody murder, and cars were honking and racing past us and by the time we made it a mile, he finally pulled over and we were both sweating and in shock. Ten seconds of silence later, we ended up having the biggest laugh. I don't think I ever laughed so hard in my life."

"But you did end up getting to meet his parents, right?"

"Oh, yes, we switched spots, and I drove the rest of the way. Paul was confident in all things, but behind the wheel, he just didn't have a warrior's heart."

"Did he write plays, too?"

"Oh, no. He was focused on classic literature and writing short stories. Those…those were extraordinary. And he was always so calm about writing. Whenever inspiration came to me, I was like a madwoman, scribbling away through the night and barricaded in my studio. He could sit anywhere—at a pub or at a crowded party—and just put pen to paper like it was the most natural, nourishing environment in the world. Any surface was a cozy desk to him."

"So, what happened?" I ask hesitantly.

"What always happens in love stories," Juliette answers. "It ended."

"Not all love stories end."

"The real ones do. One way or another."

Her words hit home, and I guess she's not wrong, but I also know that she's not entirely right either.

"Did you guys keep in touch at all?"

Juliette adjusts her stance again, straightening out her shirt and seeming to separate herself from the memories she just allowed herself. "We didn't part on good terms, so there were no friendly interactions after that. And it's not like today, where you could just shoot someone a drunken text whenever you feel nostalgic."

"Would you like to? Send a drunken text, that is?"

"I don't know," Juliette says softly. "Strange as it is to realize, this is the first time I'm even saying his name out loud in years."

"Do you regret not staying in touch?"

She doesn't answer right away, but I know her well enough that she doesn't need to. "I do," she confirms. "I do regret it, but it's pointless to dwell on the past."

I consider probing the situation further when we're both snapped out of our tête-à-tête as the rehearsal door slams shut. Looking around, I find that nearly everyone is back from break. We didn't even notice. Juliette groans and gazes back at me, clapping her hands against her thighs.

"Well, thanks for that fun trip down memory lane. Reminiscing about my biggest heartbreak definitely makes me super excited to dive back into this hopeful romance we're currently staging."

"I'm sorry. I didn't mean to upset you."

"I'm not upset. I just wish I…" She trails off with a stricken look in her eyes, and it somehow prompts me to jump in to help cover up her hurt.

"In other news, I may have met the son of an old friend of yours today. His name is Phillip, and he said he moved into his mom's old apartment on the fourth floor."

"Phillip?" she muses, slowly but surely recovering. "Oh,

that must be Tessa's son. God, I haven't spoken to her in ages. How was he?"

"He seemed nice."

"Why did you say it like that?" she asks.

"Like what?"

"I don't know, I just sensed a tone."

"There was no tone. Maybe we should adjust your hearing aids."

"As if I wear hearing aids, you villainous child."

I'm ready to answer her sarcasm with an equal dose of snark when Ellie gets everyone's attention once again. "Alright, let's take it from where we left off at the top of the scene. Juliette, can I have a word?"

"And the hits just keep on coming," my boss mumbles, standing up with a smile.

I feel like I should say something, but nothing comes as Juliette crosses the space to Ellie, leaving me alone to replay our conversation in my mind.

She spoke about Paul like a woman in love, or at the very least, the way she would talk about a dear friend. Whatever animosity she carries towards Paul, it's obviously inlaid with fondness and respect and definite deep twinges of regret.

Watching her now from across the room, remembering the way she looked at Ellie and Chloe like they had something she desperately wanted but was never able to have…it makes me wonder what kind of person Juliette would be if she could have that. Would she need me less? Would she treat me differently? Would her being with the right person take some of the sting away if I were to leave for this new job with Professor Jack?

It's all these questions that send an idea spiraling through me. A crazy idea. It shouldn't be more than a fleeting thought, but for some reason, it puts down roots inside my brain. I'm filled with a strange, determined sense of resolve as I think back to the way she talked about her grand London love affair. She might end up hating me. She might even fire me. Or maybe I'll be the maid of honor in her wedding, and she'll be eternally grateful to me forever.

I guess I'll just have to wait and find out, because one way or another, I am going to find Paul.

10

"Can I please open my eyes now?" I ask, trying to steal a look through Liam's fingers, which are still covering the upper part of my face. I can sense people milling around, but not a huge number. Snippets of conversation peppered with laughter and faint car honks fill my ears. It's a pretty warm day today, so I opted for just a T-shirt and jeans, and Liam steers me away from someone or something that just bumped my arm.

"Not yet," he answers.

"Why not?"

"Because then you'll know where I'm planning to hide your body."

I huff in protest and give him a light elbow to the ribs. "You know, it's bad form to make murder jokes while covering someone's eyes in a foreign country. Where's the British charm that should have been paddled into you at some fancy, horrifying boarding school?"

"Luckily enough, I was spared the paddle."

"More's the shame." Liam chuckles near my ear and

continues to move us carefully forward. I do open my eyes a bit then, but only see small slits of light and the outline of fingers. "Can you at least tell me where we're going or if we're there yet?"

"We're almost there, and don't blame me for how long this is taking. Your hair is blinding, and it's making this walk far more treacherous and time-consuming than I anticipated."

My hand instinctively drifts up, brushing through the end of my high ponytail. "I thought you liked my hair?"

"I do," he says defensively, "but standing directly down-wind from it also feels slightly akin to sustaining a physical attack. An enjoyable and fragrant attack, but an attack none-theless."

"That's because my hair is a sentient being and is fully capable of sensing evil. It's obviously trying to warn me of whatever nefarious plot you have in store."

"You're going to be eating those words in a matter of seconds."

"I'd rather be eating fish and chips. I thought we were going to the Red Lion?" My stomach rumbles in protest at the thought. It's probably half past five at this point, and having skipped lunch today in favor of periodic snacks throughout rehearsal, I'm on the dangerous cusp of becoming hangry.

"Forget the Red Lion," he tells me. Just then, his hands gently fall away, and a warm breeze brushes across my now uncovered face. "Look."

I open my eyes, and they slowly start to refocus. My breath catches in my throat as I find myself gazing at the *Globe The-atre*, less than a hundred feet away. Obviously, it's not the original *Globe Theatre* that burned down, was rebuilt, and then was later torn down by buzzkill Puritans, but the new

Globe Theatre that was reconstructed with painstaking accuracy along the Thames.

"Wow," I say, a note of wonder in my now awed voice. "There it is."

Liam steps around me to stand at my side, smiling down as I turn my eyes from him back to the theater.

"Is there a show going on? Is it open to the public?" I ask.

"No, as a matter of fact, they're closed for the night."

"Oh." I'm disappointed, but I do my best not to show it. It's cool just to be here. To look at it. "It's still fun to see it. Did you know that Shakespeare was part owner of the original theater? He invested ten pounds to put towards the lease, giving him roughly 12.5% ownership. And they used to hang flags outside the theater to let people know what kind of play was being staged. They flew black flags for dramas, red for historic plays, and white for comedies."

"I didn't know that," Liam answers. "Were you an original owner as well?"

"Yeah, as a matter of fact, I was. I forgot to mention when we met that I'm four hundred years old."

"I've always been drawn to mature women."

"Well then, you've met your match. I'm glad we finally have everything out in the open."

Liam snickers and takes my hand, promptly ushering us forward. "In that case, we better get a move on."

"Where are we going?" I ask, keeping my feet planted.

"Inside, obviously."

"But I thought you said it's closed?"

"It is, but I have a friend of a friend that's high up on the board, so we get the place to ourselves for one hour."

My jaw drops. My eyes shoot back to the theater. "A friend of a friend? Is this your subtle way of letting me know that you're currently banging Shakespeare's great-great-grand-daughter?"

"A gentleman never tells. Shall we?"

I shake my head in disbelief as I let him pull me forward. I don't know how he swung this, but I'm more than happy to tag along for the ride.

We end up going around the corner and stopping in front of a side entrance, where Liam knocks on the door. We're let inside by a smartly dressed security guard, who shakes our hands and locks up behind us. He walks us down a wide hallway, then directs us to the left and says that he'll be in his office. Liam thanks him and holds open the next door as the man disappears down the hallway. The whole thing feels very *Goodfellas*-esque with a Shakespearian twist, and I am fully game.

Step by step, I pass through the open door and move deeper into the theater, until I'm gradually enveloped in the glow of the house lights as they pour down from the rafters. The stage is front and center, intimidating but inviting all at once. I turn around, looking at the intricate wooden structure of the theater itself, which is composed of multiple levels of seating, before focusing back on the pit, where Liam and I are now standing. We're modern-day "groundlings." I look up to the partially open-air ceiling, seeing the sky beginning to darken above us, but only just. It's magic hour—day but night, and bathing London in a toasty orange haze.

"I can't believe we're in here alone right now." I twist to face Liam, finding him quietly watching me. "Do you know how lucky we are?"

"Strangely enough, I've never considered myself to be very lucky."

I tilt my head with a skeptical raise of my eyebrow. "Right.

I mean, look at you—a man who's seemingly enjoying a life
of leisure, living in one of the best cities in the world, and
who has a family who adores him. Poor boy, you must really
be having a tough go of it."

"You think you know me so well, do you?" He steps closer,
still curiously gazing at me.

"I feel like I do, but I probably don't. Bearing that in mind,
why don't you tell me more about yourself? Just the basics.
And by the basics, I mean reveal something deeply personal."

And upon hearing that, he stops moving forward. "Upon
extensive consideration, I've decided I'd rather not."

"Shocker," I say through an unsurprised grin.

"Maybe I'll be in a more sharing mood after we eat. I didn't
set up a romantic dinner table, but I did bring sandwiches."

"Sandwiches and the Globe? Have you been reading my
manifestation journal?"

A moment later, Liam and I are sitting cross-legged on the
stone pit floor, both enjoying lovely turkey sandwiches. I've
just finished taking a delicious bite when I say, "In the interest of saving time, I think you and I should discuss red flags."

"Red flags?" Liam asks, taking a sip from his mini bottle
of water and setting it down between us.

"Yes. Typically, when people like each other, they go out a
few times, maybe meet each other's friends, and very quickly,
they start to have all these expectations about the other person.
Then, a month or two down the road, they let their guards
down, and all the red flags start popping up, and then one or
both people end up running for the hills. So, as you and I only
have roughly two more weeks to get to know each other, I
think we should both just reveal our red flags now. Then we
don't have to waste any more of each other's time if we find
out we're actually no longer interested post–red-flags."

"That sounds both sensible and efficient." Liam quickly takes another bite of his sandwich before going on. "Alright then, you first."

"Okay," I say, squaring my shoulders. "Obviously, my dedication to my job can sometimes be concerning to guys I date. Juliette is my number one priority, so there have been several occasions where my romantic prospects have had a problem with that."

"I suppose that makes sense, but professional satisfaction is crucial in relationships. You focusing on that area of your life doesn't seem like such an issue to me."

"It will when it's your birthday and I ditch you to help Juliette finish up a DIY upholstery project that she decided to start on a whim."

"Well, I suppose that depends on the fabric choice used in said project. Velvet is highly offensive to me, but a nice durable cotton, that I could forgive."

I have to smile, both at his quick response and at the realization that he seems completely honest. Maybe excessive work wouldn't bother him. Emboldened by his acceptance, I go on.

"And I'm a pushover when it comes to the people I love. Friends, family, and, of course, Juliette. I've always had a deep need to be liked."

"And what do you attribute that to?"

"It could be because of what happened with my mom or how my dad raised me. He was pretty hands-off, even if he was a good father. But when I would go above and beyond, whether it be with a play I was doing or with school or helping him with something, then he'd finally give me the validation I craved. To this day, I'd do anything to make the people I care for happy, even at my own expense."

Liam shifts around a bit, untangling his legs to sit more

comfortably. "Not to minimize what you're saying, but it seems that all your red flags are steeped in good."

"That doesn't necessarily make them good. Not for me, anyways. Also, I don't think I want to have children."

Kaboom. I've dropped my biggest red flag of all.

"Really?" Liam asks, surprised.

"I've just seen so many of my friends go off and have babies, and they always seem to lose themselves after. Not in a bad way, but they're just different. And with the career I want, I don't know if having a family is a realistic goal. Working in the arts is very consuming and draining, and the hours can be erratic. I don't know how I could balance that with having a child or children. Would it be fair to them or me? Because if I have them, I know I'll love them, and I'll want to give them everything and all of me, and that would mean surrendering my dreams, and I don't want to do that. I shouldn't have to."

"It doesn't have to be like that, though. Having a family isn't necessarily one-size-fits-all."

"That's what it seems like. Obviously, I might change my mind down the road, but as of now I can't guarantee that it's in the cards for me. Understandably, that can be a deal breaker for some people."

Liam doesn't say much, or anything at all after that, only nods, and I'm left wondering exactly what his silence means.

"Okay," I then go on, eager to keep things moving. "Your turn. Tell the truth and admit to your hidden freaky-deaky nature."

Liam sits up straight and rubs his hands together, wiping away any loose crumbs. "Where to begin. Alright, well, like you, I can be very focused on my work." I give him a doubt-ful look, and he shrugs. "Perhaps not at this current juncture in my life, but typically, I am very career-oriented. Another thing, I like routines. Going on my latest trip to Italy was the most spontaneous decision I ever made, and even then, I didn't do a terrible lot while I was there."

"No noteworthy holiday flings?" I ask.

"I thought I might, but it turns out we're better off as friends."

"What was she like?"

"She was funny, nice, fairly introverted. She's a romance author."

"Fun! I want to be friends with a romance author."

"Maybe you'll meet her someday," he says. "She lives in New York, too."

"Good, then maybe she can spill the tea and tell me all your dirty secrets, because thus far, your red flags are all very tame. You need to dig deeper."

"Dig deeper. Well, another thing, I'm a fairly recent divorcé. Not too recent, though. About a year ago."

"Oh," I reply, caught a little off guard. "Going to be honest, I did not see that one coming."

"Yes, I suppose I was saving my big reveal for the finale."

A few sensations course through me at the thought of Liam being previously married. Surprise, bewilderment, and, most prominently, jealousy. And it's that sharp, possessive pinch that's the most disconcerting feeling of all.

"So, what happened there? If you don't mind me asking."

"What happened," Liam repeats with a sigh. "I'd like to say it was complicated, but in retrospect, it really wasn't at all."

I put my sandwich down on its paper wrapping, dust off my hands and give him my undivided attention.

"I met my ex-wife five years ago. We got on very well. She was completely out of my league, but somehow didn't notice. Our relationship progressed as one typically does. We dated

and eventually moved in together. My business was growing, and things were great between us—everything seemed
to be lining up, so I proposed, and we got married. We hon-
eymooned in Italy, which eventually led to my rather morbid
trip back there last year. Things were good for a while, or at
least in my eyes they were. My company was at its peak, so
I was putting in long hours quite often. I thought I was bal-
ancing things semi-successfully, but then, apparently, I wasn't.

"She would try to plan time for us, but I would be stuck
at work, or I'd be too tired. When we did go out, I was usually answering emails or was on my phone. Looking back, I
see how she tried. She did what she could, but I just didn't
meet her halfway."

Even I have to sigh as I take that all in. "That really stinks.
And it's odd, because as a single woman, I'm definitely into
you, but as a storyteller, I'm kind of hoping you guys work
things out and get back together."

Liam shakes his head with a little grin. "We clashed over
her work, too. She's an interior designer. At first it was nice,
because our flat looked like something out of a magazine. But,
as I'm sure you know, a huge part of business is now based
on social media. So she started posting videos and photos of
our place and soon after about her life in general. She always
wanted me to be part of them, but I was terribly awkward.
And when I looked at the comments of the pictures or videos
I *was* in, what I read was far from favorable. Lily would obviously delete the ones that were downright cruel, but I almost
always saw them first."

Liam looks down, forcing a smile, and it sets off a certain
stab in my gut that I immediately identify as slowly simmer-
ing rage. I have been a complete and utter pacifist for my en-

tire life but, no joke, I want to go and find everyone who ever cyberbullied Liam and karate chop them in the face.

"After all that, I started to pull away—wanting no part of her online presence, which in turn made her resentful towards me because that was becoming such an important aspect of her career. The end of our marriage was really just a perfect storm of issues. And by the time I realized, it was too late. When she wanted to fix things, I wasn't there. And when I wanted to fix things, she was emotionally too far gone. And that was that."

With his story finished, I just look at Liam for a few seconds in silence.

"Man," I eventually say. "Honestly, I thought your biggest admission was going to be that you actually hated the sweaters I bought you each Christmas."

"No, unfortunately not."

"But I don't know if all that is so much a red flag as it's just a really sad thing that happened in your life."

"It was sad, but there were ripples from there on out, too. I started doubting myself—on a personal level and in business. And now, in the event that I'm ever actually starting to feel good about myself, I then have the opportunity to check in on Lily's social media to see how fantastic her life is without me in it."

I give him an empathetic look as my phone dings. I pull it out of my bag and see a text from Roshni:

Just an FYI, Ollie is sleeping in the penthouse with us tonight (he and Juliette are having a movie night on the couch), so if you'd like to stay out or have someone stay over for a clothing-optional sleepover, the time is now. All it will cost you is detailed notes and descriptions. Bye!

I roll my eyes a bit and am about to put my phone away when I suddenly rethink it, instead opening up Instagram. "What's Lily's last name? Would it be weird for you if I looked her up?"

"No weirder than your typical behavior. Go ahead." He tells me her name, and I quickly type it into the app. Then I gasp. "Holy hell! She has half a million followers!"

"Yes, and they unanimously hate me."

I continue to scroll, seeing gorgeously curated picture after gorgeously curated picture of Lily's house and vacations and then a disturbingly handsome brunet specimen of a man. I keep scrolling and soon see a stampede of flawless wedding photos.

"She remarried that quickly?" I ask, already knowing the answer.

"She did. It was a whirlwind romance, and with a professional football player, no less. But she's a good person, and I'm happy she's happy. He's much better suited to her life than I was. And her followers, of course, continue to give him rave reviews."

I glance up from my phone then, switching the screen off as I look over at Liam. He's smiling, but I'm starting to see the bruises—the ripples, as he calls them. It makes me want to shield him. Keep all the trolls away so he can have enough time to heal. Going through a divorce is hard enough, but going through a divorce and then continuing to compare yourself to a lusted-after athlete seems particularly harsh.

"Sometimes things just aren't meant to be," I offer weakly.

"Yes, that was the quote on the Valentine's Day card I got from my mother this year."

We both laugh a little, and the fact that Liam can joke his

way through what must be one of his biggest disappointments speaks volumes.

"So, this was fun, right?" I ask sarcastically.

"Tremendous fun. A terrific bonding experience."

"Yeah, in hindsight, maybe this wasn't the best third date icebreaker I've ever come up with."

"Possibly not, but we do have twenty minutes left. Are you ready to take the stage?"

"I couldn't," I say with feigned shyness, immediately standing up.

He smirks and reaches for my hand, both of us pulling each other into a standing position. He walks with me to the stairs that connect to the very front of the stage. I start to ascend, but he stays where he is.

"Come on," I say, giving his arm a tug.

"No, I'm distinctly an audience dweller. You go ahead."

I begrudgingly let him go and slowly wander the space until I find myself center stage, looking out.

"When I auditioned for my college drama program, I had to perform a piece from Shakespeare. I was pretty proud of it in the end."

"Which piece did you do?" he asks.

"Titania's monologue from *A Midsummer Night's Dream*."

"I can see why you'd be drawn to it. You do look quite spritely."

"Thank you. I appreciate that."

"Will you perform it now?"

I hesitate for a second, but it's half-hearted. "What if the security footage leaks and I end up getting torn apart on YouTube?"

Liam has now moved towards the back of the pit, stopping to lean against one of the perfectly reconstructed wood railings. "Then I'll protect you," he promises. "We'll move off grid, and you and I can be social media pariahs together."

His words send a comforting sensation sweeping through me, and it's all the encouragement I need. I don't even think before I launch right into it, reciting the monologue carefully and meaningfully. I attempt to play Titania as the regal, strong-willed character that she is. Independent and fearless. I end a minute or so later, breathing heavy with exhilaration as I find Liam still watching me, almost in a trance. He's smiling softly and is unmoving until he starts clapping, his eyes remaining locked with mine all the while. I offer a sweet curtsy and descend the small flight of stairs, crossing the space until I'm standing directly in front of him.

"A fairy queen, indeed," he says melodically.

I shake my head and glance down before my eyes find his again. "Did you like it?"

"Of course I did," he answers.

Before I can stop myself, I lean forward and wrap my arms around his midsection, locking him into a tight hug. He embraces me back, holding me firmly to his chest. In his arms, in the Globe—I'm in a world within a world, and I don't want to leave. Seconds seem to slip past, and I'm not sure how long we stay like that until I finally pull back.

"Will you spend the night with me?" I ask, tilting my face up to meet his gaze.

He doesn't answer right away. Instead he looks down and runs his hands around the expanse of my waist, unhurried and soft. "Are you sure that's what you want?"

I nod my head, feeling entirely alive even if I am a little nervous. Even if I never usually move this fast. Like ever. "Do you think I'm crazy?"

"Maybe a little, but then I must be, too. Part of me thinks I'm dreaming all of this up."

His words are soft and honest, and I feel exactly the same. "And is it a good dream or a bad dream?" I ask.

Liam slides his hands into mine, and it's really not normal how much it affects me.

"A very good dream," he answers. "And one that I won't be forgetting anytime soon."

11

In the cab to Juliette's and all the way up in the elevator, we're lost in a game of secret touches. To the outside world, we're holding hands, brushing knees—nothing out of the ordinary. To me, it's been fifteen minutes of nearly painful foreplay, and my heart feels like it's beating out of my chest. It takes all the concentration I possess to put the key in the lock and to get the door open once we reach the studio, especially with Liam clutching my waist from behind, pinning my back to his front as he drags his mouth across the side of my neck.

I gasp as the door finally gives way, and I stagger inside. Liam's eyes are locked on mine as I whirl around, and he doesn't look back as he swings the door shut behind him. I'm barely able to take a breath before he's stepping towards me and I'm moving towards him. We collide as we intended, our lips snapping together like magnets. My hand finds the nape of his neck, traveling up and twisting into his hair. I give it a pull, not very hard but not light either, and it elicits a deep, rumbling moan from him that I'm determined to hear again and again.

He pushes into me further, and I go with gravity. The backs of my legs hit the small kitchen table, jolting me a little bit, but I'm quick to get my bearings. I'm about to edge my way onto its surface when Liam takes hold of my waist and sets me on the table himself.

Kitchen tabletop sexy time? Um, yes, please! My legs lock around his waist. His hand grips the back of my neck, firm but steadying as he leans away ever so slightly, drinking in the sight of me as I inhale a much-needed breath. A little smile crosses his face, and an even bigger one crosses mine. We both know what's about to happen. I drag him forward for another kiss, my hands gripping the front of his shirt when I hear the door opening and the lights flip on.

The sexual tension instantly vanishes, and my eyes go wide, but nowhere near as wide as Roshni's as she and Ollie step into the studio and freeze.

"Oh my god! Oh god, I'm so sorry!" She stares at the floor and shields her eyes with one hand, dropping Ollie's leash as he happily canters inside without a care in the world.

"I had no idea you were home," Roshni stammers. "I figured it was early enough that you'd still be out. I forgot my script in here when Ollie and I came down earlier, so I figured I'd just grab it now. I'm so, so sorry."

"It's fine, Roshni," I assure her. "It's okay, you can look. I swear we're both decent."

She slowly looks up and forces a smile even though I can tell she's ready to burst into flames. "Again, I apologize. I had no idea you guys were in here. I'm just going to grab my script and we'll go."

I lean down to pet Ollie and look over my shoulder at Liam. He's frazzled, but he's holding himself together well.

"Don't worry about it," I tell her. "Ollie can just stay here. I'm home for the night, so there's no need for him to sleep upstairs."

"Are you sure?" Roshni asks, flashing a quick glance at Liam and then a meaningful look at me.

"I'm sure. Thank you so much for watching him, though."

"It's no problem," she says. "Honestly, Juliette watched him for most of the time. I kind of felt like the third wheel, so I just binge-watched *Schitt's Creek* on my laptop for the fifth time."

"You should think about investing in a pair of blue light glasses if you watch a lot of shows on your computer," Liam suddenly adds. Roshni and I turn to gaze at him, and he looks like an adorable deer in the headlights. "No one is safe from eye strain."

Relative silence follows, but luckily, my angelic bestie is quick to ease the tension.

"Okay then," Roshni says, clapping her hands together, "fun as it was to catch up with you both, I think I've intruded on your evening long enough. Winnie, I'll see you in the morning, and Liam, I'll be pretending that I didn't see you at all. And I will also be on the alert for eye strain."

"As everyone should be."

Roshni steps out into the hall, and I move to the doorway as she presses the button for the elevator. It arrives quickly, and she mimes an over-the-top humping motion for me before stepping inside. I laugh and close the door, turning back around and leaning against it as I find Liam and Ollie now standing side by side.

"So," I say, not quite sure how to establish the new normal.

Liam seems just as clueless as I am. "So... I guess I should get going."

"Oh, yeah? You don't want to stay?"

"You mean you still..." Liam nudges his head towards the bed, and it's not hard to guess what he's trying to ask.

"I don't mean stay to do it," I reply vehemently. "I'm obviously not going to have sex with you in front of my child."

"Right, obviously. Me either. That's why I was surprised." The tips of his ears are blazing red, and I start to get worried that I may be growing entirely too fond of them.

"I just meant, you could just stay and sleep over."

"You really want me to?" he asks.

"Kind of. It might be nice, but if you don't want to, that's fine."

"No, I want to. It's just... I feel like I should tell you that I'm not much of a cuddler. At least, not a sleep cuddler. I can cuddle when we're awake, but when I'm trying to fall asleep, cuddling throws me into a bit of a panic."

"Can you say the word *cuddle* one more time?"

"I'm a nervous cuddler."

I let out a quiet laugh as I cross my arms over my chest. "Well, you can relax, because we're on the same page. As much as I enjoy the concept of cuddling or spooning or what-have-you, I'm very easily startled when unconscious—so if you touch me while I'm asleep, there's a solid chance I'll inadvertently punch you in the jugular."

"Oh, wow."

"I have no idea how or why, but I was somehow born with violent, visceral sleep tendencies. I just wanted to put that out there before you make your decision, since you bravely gave me your cuddling trigger warning."

"I see. Because me not cuddling and you unconsciously assaulting me is basically the same thing."

"More or less. At summer camp, my bunkmates called me Rip Van Will Slap You in the Head. It's after—"

"Rip Van Winkle, no, I get it. That's very clever for young kids."

"It was theater camp," I say somewhat deadpan. "We were an eloquent bunch."

"Right. Well, after hearing all that, I definitely want to stay."

"Really?" I ask.

"Sure," he answers. "I'm never in much of a rush to get back to my place. Though I suppose that's pretty telling, since I'd rather sleep here with the threat of physical pain looming over me instead of returning to my safe apartment."

"You think too much. Let's hop into that bed and not cuddle."

Fifteen minutes later, Ollie is fast asleep on his pillow pile beside the radiator, and Liam and I are all tucked in and facing each other as we lie two feet apart. I'm wearing cotton shorts and an old T-shirt from high school, and Liam's in his boxers and undershirt. He nestles around into a comfortable position as our eyes adjust to the darkness. All the lights in the room are out, but a fair amount of moonlight slips in from the windows.

"What were you like in school?" he asks, having noticed my faded gym T-shirt.

"I was a dork. I was in all the plays and musicals and had braces until my junior year. My hair was even frizzier than it is now, and when I was a senior, a few boys actually asked me if I was a transfer student. I'm assuming because my boobs had finally arrived and I was suddenly on their radar." Liam smiles and I subconsciously inch closer. "What about you?" I ask.

"I was tall. Gangly. I was on the track team, and I played the clarinet."

"Did you truly? I never would have guessed that you played a musical instrument."

"I haven't played it in ages," he says, "but I was quite good. If I knew you back then, I would have played for you over the phone to win you over."

The inner teenage version of me squeals with delight at the idea. I can say with complete certainty that my former drama-nerd self would have been entirely obsessed with band-geek, track-running Liam. And if he ever did call me to make sweet clarinet love to me over the phone, I absolutely would have died.

"Yeah, that probably would have worked," I tell him. Understatement of the century.

"Maybe I'll have to pick it up again, then."

"You should. It might do you some good to have a hobby."

"But then I wouldn't have the time to squire you about town as I've been doing."

"Well, luckily, I won't be here very long."

A silence falls over both of us then, and I wish I hadn't said anything. I nuzzle into my own pillow and throw on a comforting smile.

"Regardless, it's nice to know that if I'm ever having a bad day from now on, I can call you up and request a solo performance. Do you still have your clarinet?"

"I think it's in a closet somewhere. Or maybe my mom has it back home in the attic. If you're going to expect spontaneous concerts, I really will have to start it up again in earnest."

"No pressure, but you should definitely prepare yourself. Which song did you play the best?"

"'Pretty Woman,'" he says with a guilty grin.

"You little flirt. Just how many girls did you seduce with your sultry woodwind routine?"

He laughs to himself and rolls over away from me. "I don't want to talk about it anymore. I'm revealing all my tricks too early."

"You're ridiculous," I tease, twisting around myself. A minute later, I'm still smiling, and I push up on my arms just enough to turn my head so I can look at Liam's back. "I'm really glad you stayed," I tell him.

He rolls over and looks at me with tired but sweet eyes. "Me too," he answers.

I can't help myself. I nudge myself forward until I'm close enough to give him a quick kiss. He seems happy to receive it and doesn't push for anything further as I quickly move back to my side of the bed.

"Good night," I chirp as I drop down onto my pillow.

"Good night, Winnie. I'd say don't let the bedbugs bite, but if they did, I'm sure you would just punch them in the jugular."

I smile one more time as I roll away again, pulling the blankets up around me and settling into a perfectly comfortable position. "It's amazing." I sigh. "Just a week and half and you already know me so well."

12

"Guess what, guess what, guess what?"

Roshni bounces over to me the second Ollie and I enter the penthouse door, seemingly on her twelfth cup of coffee as she lands at my side. Her outside excitement is a fair representation of my current mood, still basking in the leftover butterflies from my fun but innocent night with Liam and a particularly idyllic morning walk with Ollie. Cue the musical montage of me loving London set to an upbeat '90s classic! I wouldn't say I'm set on any specific song, but if it's not "I'm Every Woman" by Whitney Houston, I will have a meltdown of epic proportions.

"I have no idea," I soon tell Roshni. "But I'm pretty positive that I'm about to be hit with a whole lot of awesome."

"Indeed, you are. Awesomeness all over your face."

"That sounded weird."

"Yes, it did," she agrees.

Juliette walks in then, dressed in a sleek long-sleeved pajama set and a large pair of sunglasses. Ollie immediately rushes over to her, and she's quick to lift him up into her arms, giving him a little kiss before turning back to me. "I'm assuming Roshni told you the news?"

"She was about to," I go on to say, "but first, can you give me the rationale behind what you're wearing? Are we hiding from the paparazzi this morning, or are we just quietly recovering from cataract surgery?"

"Hilarious," she answers mirthlessly. "Your wit is truly astounding. But to answer your question, I'm suffering from a horrendous headache at the moment."

"Oh, I'm sorry. Is there anything I can do to help?"

"I'll survive. Just leave Ollie with me for the morning, and I'm sure I'll be fine in time for my dinner out tonight."

"Are you sure you don't mind keeping him if you don't feel well?" I ask.

"Of course I don't mind. Ollie is my person."

"Fair enough," I answer without argument.

"And speaking of tonight..." Roshni then prompts, despite her lack of a clear segue.

"Yes, tonight." Juliette plops down onto the couch, and Ollie happily settles down into the space beside her. "I made a few calls, and I was able to get you and Roshni tickets to the opening of that new West End show you both were talking about yesterday."

My jaw drops as my feet take an involuntary step forward. "No way!" I shriek.

Getting into that play is close to impossible. It's only been in previews, but the buzz is already astronomical beyond compare.

"I cashed in a few favors. I'm sure you girls will have a great time."

"Thank you so much, Juliette! I don't even know what else to say. I'm honestly lost for words."

"Well, that's a first," she jokes. "Anyways, you two head off to rehearsals, and we'll touch base later."

I automatically nod my head, still in merry shock as I give Ollie a kiss and disappear with Roshni out of the door.

"Didn't I tell you?" she asks, skipping to the elevator and pressing the call button. "Supreme awesomeness, is it not?"

"Complete and utter awesomeness. I agree with you profoundly."

The elevator arrives, and we step inside. "From what Juliette told me, it starts at eight, and I think it has a three-hour run time. Depending on how long the intermission is, we should be back sometime around midnight."

The doors close, and my face falls the slightest bit. "That's a little late. I've never left Ollie alone at night before."

"He'll be fine," Roshni answers confidently. "We smother him as it is. In fact, I'd put money down that he's cocooned in a blanket with Juliette at this very moment. I bet he'd appreciate some alone time."

"What if he's afraid of the dark?" I counter. "What if he gets extremely vivid night terrors?"

"Okay, helicopter mom, will you chill out for a second? Ollie isn't going to have a breakdown just because he's alone for three hours at night. We'll leave a light on and have music playing, and he'll be totally fine." I still feel uneasy, and I'm sure Roshni can tell by looking at me. "Are you genuinely concerned about Ollie, or do you just not want to go to the show?"

"No, obviously I want to go to the show. It's not that. It's just…"

We arrive at the main floor then, the elevator doors opening and revealing Phillip standing just opposite us, holding a bag of groceries.

"Hey," he says in his friendly tone. "Winnie, right? I haven't forgotten."

I answer his smile back with one of my own. "Phillip, so good to see you again."

"You as well. What, no little man today?" he asks.

Him mentioning Ollie gives me a thought. I don't think it would be too forward—he did offer, after all. And Juliette said he was a nice guy. "He's actually in the penthouse at the moment, but if you're free tonight, how would you feel about dog sitting?"

Roshni smiles and claps her hands together as Phillip looks from me to her in curious amusement. "I feel good about it," he answers.

Later that night, Roshni and I are sitting on a small sofa in the theater lobby with two glasses of white wine, biding our time during intermission. We're only halfway through the show, but I'm already a groupie. This play is so good that it makes me mad. I'm enjoying every blissful second while simultaneously cursing my own mediocrity for not writing it myself. Silent, festering dissatisfaction is the highest form of praise among writers.

Roshni takes a sip of her wine and sits back with a sigh. "I still can't believe that I'm here. Seriously, how did this happen?"

"I keep asking myself the same thing. This is far and away the best perk I've experienced since working for Juliette."

"When my mom pitched the idea for this summer job, I seriously thought I would be sitting in a corner and creeping you guys out as I stared at you and tried to find something to do. I never thought I'd be in London, helping out with a fantastic production and going to shows like this."

"You know, I've somehow never even met your mom. I've spoken to her on the phone a bunch of times to set up appointments or lunches with her and Juliette, but I've never seen her in person. She seems super nice, though. Very dignified phone voice."

Roshni nods and lifts her glass. "She does have a dignified phone voice. Fingers crossed I somehow inherit it someday."

I take a sip of my own wine and twist to face her more fully on the couch. "What were your parents like when you were little?"

A relaxed smile crosses her face. "They were awesome. Super hardworking, but they always made time for me and my brother. My parents came to the US after they got married but before I was born. They're from Gujarat, which is a state in India. They were both the first in their family to come over, but they had a huge friend group that was here, so every weekend we would get together with like, eleven other families, and it felt like a constant party. We would rotate whose house we went to each weekend, so there were always places to go and things to do. It was a lot of fun."

I listen to Roshni's words and can't deny the longing I feel for a childhood like that. Yes, I got to participate in as much theater as was available to me, but other than that, it was me and my dad in our quiet house. Or me with a babysitter when my dad was at work.

"That sounds amazing," I muse, still imagining it all.

"It was. I hope I'm half as good of a parent someday."

"I'm sure you will be."

"We'll see. Nick has to propose first, and even then, I'm

sure we'll want to be married for a couple of years before we start trying for a baby."

"Yeah, you guys definitely don't have to rush on that," I tell her. "And who knows, maybe down the line you won't even want to have kids."

"What? Of course I want kids." She looks at me with that confused disorientation I so often receive after saying something along those lines.

"How do you know?" I ask.

"I just know," she answers simply. Because for so many people, it *is* that simple. It's an unfaltering notion deep in their gut. A landmark knowledge they can always be sure of. It makes me wish that I knew with such certainty, too.

Wanting to change the subject, I decide to go out on a bit of a limb. "So, I have some news," I find myself saying.

She takes a sip of her wine, and her eyebrows shift up a bit. "Color me intrigued. Do tell."

"Once we get back to New York, there's a solid possibility that I'm quitting."

Roshni nearly chokes on her wine then. "What?" she yells. "Tell me everything immediately!"

And I do just that, telling her all about the West Lane Theater Company and Professor Jack, and how my possible departure played a part in agreeing to Juliette's crazy dating scheme.

"Well, I think this new job sounds exciting as hell and absolutely amazing. Juliette should be nothing but happy for you, but given her track record, that's a big question mark."

"Quite the question mark," I agree.

Just then, the lights flicker, letting us know that the second half of the play is about to begin. Roshni lets out a little shriek, and I do the same on the inside. "So much excitement in one night," she says as we both stand up. "By the way, did you look at the price on our ticket stubs? I didn't even realize that shows could be so expensive."

"Being trendy doesn't come cheap, my dear."

"Obviously not. I'm going to Instagram the crap out of this." She pulls out her phone for a selfie, and she and I pose side by side, smiling and lifting our wineglasses. A second later, she applies just the right filter to make us look like the influencers we definitely are not as we make our way back to our seats.

"This really is the best night ever," she continues on. "I'm not going to say I'm glad that Juliette got a headache and it was just you and me at the play, but I'm also not going to say that I'm not happy Juliette got a headache and it was just you and me at the play."

"And you've officially entered the cutthroat world of theater. Another lamb becomes a lion."

"Do all drama people talk like you?"

"What can I say? We were born expressive." Shimmying safely into our row, we slip back into our seats and get situated.

"By the way," Roshni says, "I tried looking up that Paul Davenport guy like you asked, but I haven't found him yet. I'll let you know if anything pops up."

"Thank you, that would be great. I couldn't find anything on him either, but you're much more tech-savvy than I am."

"Hardly. Why did you say we were looking for him again?"

"Just a side project," I answer in my best noncommittal manner.

"Right. And by your lack of specifics, I'm going to go ahead and assume that this side project is something incriminating, and you're deftly trying not to implicate me."

"If your assumption is correct, does that mean I have to start paying you a retainer?"

"Probably, but I'll accept one of those souvenir mugs they're selling in the lobby as payment instead."

"Done." We agree with a handshake just as the house lights start to dim. We're both turning our attention back to the stage when I quickly whisper, "Do you think Ollie is doing okay? Should I step out and text Phillip to make sure?"

"The only thing you should text Prince Phillip is a tasteful, faceless nudie."

"Stand down, lady. I thought you were Team Liam?"

"I am," she whispers back. "Fine, you can cc him as well, then. Nonexclusive vacation dating is fully permissible when you're single in foreign waters."

"As much as I respect your polygamous maritime laws, I'm going to keep the boudoir shoots to a minimum on this trip."

"That's probably for the best," she agrees. "Even with your head cropped out, I wouldn't be surprised if your hair somehow still made it in and gave you away."

"I don't doubt that in the least."

An hour and a half later, it's just past midnight when I find myself lightly knocking on Phillip's door. Roshni went straight up to the penthouse, still reeling from the spectacular play that we were lucky enough to see and leaving me to pick up Ollie on my own, which I assured her was entirely fine. I'm mentally going over a particularly moving scene when Phillip opens the door, the warm lights and lively sounds of his apartment belying how late it actually is.

"Hey," he says with a cheerful kind of smile.

"Hi," I answer back, trying to borrow some of his energy so I won't seem quite so tired. "How was Ollie? Was he okay?"

"He was great. We went for a walk, watched some TV, talked about life. I was just telling him about my summer abroad in Bali that led me to my path of self-discovery when he passed out from boredom. Rightfully so."

He steps aside, indeed revealing Ollie asleep on the floor under his desk, nestled comfortably on top of a blanket. He's basically entrenched in a comfy little fort, and I kind of want to squeeze in, too.

"I wouldn't take it as an insult," I tell Phillip. "I bet he was just riveted to the point of exhaustion."

"Not likely, but I'll try to believe that."

We stand there in silence for a second as I wonder what to do next.

"Would you like to come in for a drink?" Phillip asks. "Maybe Ollie will slowly wake up once he hears your voice, and then his departure wouldn't be so abrupt."

I look over at Ollie again, and he really does look entirely comfortable. I suppose one drink couldn't hurt.

"Sure, that'd be nice."

Phillip smiles and opens the door further, allowing me plenty of space to step inside. He closes the door once I enter, and I enjoy the coziness of the room. It's smaller than Juliette's, of course, seeming to be a one-bedroom, but it's very nice. The furniture is newish and matching, and there are several photographs of Phillip with his family scattered throughout the room. He has a bookcase tucked in the corner, but it seems more like a storage unit for picture frames and DVDs rather than a literary fortress.

"Now, what can I offer you?" Phillip asks. "Will prosecco do?"

"I love prosecco," I answer happily. "It's one of my favorite drinks."

"Mine as well."

He's soon handing me an expensive-looking wineglass that's

filled halfway as I sit down on the gray, midsized couch. He sits in a short armchair across from me, sampling his own matching drink that looks picture-perfect with just enough condensation fogging up the glass. "So, did you enjoy the play?" he asks.

"I really did. The cast was outrageously talented, and I love how the designers played with the lighting. It was poignant without being overpowering."

"I wish I got to the theater more. When I first started teaching, I thought it would leave me with so much free time, but other than the summers, I'm either working nonstop or too burned out to do anything even when I do get the opportunity."

"I can relate to that." I take a sip of my drink, and it goes down with delicious smoothness.

"Can you?" Phillip asks. "And here I was starting to think that I was the only homebody left. My friends are constantly taking the piss out of me because I'd rather stay in on the couch instead of going out clubbing. They make the argument that I can sit when I'm out, but I then have to explain that there's a big difference between sitting at a bar in a suit and sitting in my living room in fluffy pajamas. What kind of places do you like to hang out in back home?"

"Wait, I'm sorry. Did you think we were just going to cruise past the fluffy pajamas statement? I'm afraid I can't allow that. Do expand."

"What's there to say? Give me fluff or give me death."

"That's a bold statement."

"And I'm comfortable making it. I think it's entirely possible to maintain my masculinity while also wearing oversized superhero slippers and binge watching cooking shows."

"Side note, I love cooking shows, too, but the real

question is, which superhero slippers do you rock? Batman or Superman?"

He takes a generous sip of his prosecco and places his glass onto the round wooden coffee table. "Neither. I'm proud to say that they depict an underrated, though equally crucial character—Robin."

"Robin?" I ask incredulously. "Are you sitting there telling me you wear sidekick slippers? Maybe you really should get out more."

"I firmly disagree. Batman would be nothing without Robin. And considering you're an assistant yourself, I thought you would have a little more sense of comradery with a fellow sidekick."

"I guess," I concede, "but I think it also depends on how comfortable the slippers are."

Phillip looks at me with a challenging streak in his eyes. I have a vague inclination of what's to come next, and I'll say this… I don't hate it.

Sixty seconds later, I am casually sipping on my sparkling wine with slightly large but exceedingly soft Robin slippers encasing my feet.

"Fine," I admit, crossing one leg over the other. "I get the appeal of sidekick slippers."

Phillip leans back, seeming very pleased with himself. "Thank you for owning up to that. And what are we thinking? Would you like another glass of wine?"

I'm about to answer with a polite "no thank you" when Ollie saves me the trouble, getting up and yawning loudly.

"Well, it seems that his lordship has awakened," Phillip jokes as he stands up. I do the same, crossing the room to give Ollie a good petting.

"Hey, handsome, you ready to go home?"

I straighten back up to full height, and Phillip hands me the leash. "Well," he says, "after this somewhat blissful night of domesticity, I think I'm more sold on the idea of having a dog than ever before."

"I highly recommend it. Me and Ollie might still be in the honeymoon stage, but for true love, the honeymoon never stops."

"I couldn't agree more." Phillip gives him a soft little pet as I lean down to click on the leash.

"Alright, buddy, let's get going." We're soon out the door and in the hallway when I turn back around to find Phillip standing in his entryway. "Thank you again for watching him. I really appreciate it."

"It was my pleasure. Don't hesitate to ask again."

"I won't," I assure him. I'm turning to leave when Phillip quickly gets my attention, calling my name before stepping back into the living room and picking up my suede ankle boots.

"Almost forgot these," he says as he walks back and hands them over.

"I'm so sorry! And here I almost absconded with your precious slippers." I reach down to pull them off when Phillip's voice stops me.

"It's alright. You borrow them."

"What? No, you love them."

"I can live without them for a day or two. Plus, if you keep them, it'll give me a reason to see you again when you drop them off, and I'd really like that—to see you, that is."

I throw on a quick smile at his kind words.

"Okay," I tell him. "And thank you again."

"It was a pleasure."

Phillip gently closes the door, and I turn to walk away. Five seconds later, I'm strolling through the empty hallway with a tired dog, oversized Robin slippers, and a twinge of dread that I inadvertently might have just given hope to someone I have zero romantic interest in.

13

Handling Juliette's emails is probably my least favorite task in my slew of responsibilities. Not because I mind the work, but because either I have to issue an unconditional surrender to the inbox and answer the emails constantly throughout the day, or I have to let them pile up to tackle later on, which, in turn, fills me with anxiety.

In London, I've been going with the latter option and am responding to my twelfth inquiry at the desk in the penthouse living room when I hear a sudden knock at the door. Startled that it's an actual door knock and not an intercom buzz, my fingers stumble a bit against the keys as I turn my head towards the noise. Juliette is scheduled to do a podcast interview in about an hour, so I suppose whoever's in the hall may have gotten into the building as someone walked out.

Typing a lightning-fast response, I close the laptop and cross the living room. I open the door and am once again startled when I find myself face-to-face with Isabelle, Juliette's sister.

"Hi," I say cheerfully, getting over my surprise. She's

wearing a gloriously tailored pantsuit, reminiscent of a low-key, contemporary queen. I look down at my jeans, Converse sneakers, and T-shirt and quickly realize that in this scenario, I'm Bessie, the shapeless yet charismatic scullery maid.

"Hello, Winnie," Isabelle replies smoothly. "I'm sorry to pop over unannounced, but I was wondering if my sister was at home."

"I'm sorry to say she's not. She's just finishing up at rehearsal, but she should be here in a few minutes. Come in."

I pull the door back and step aside as Isabelle walks past me with a grateful smile.

"Thank you," she says. "I tried calling her, but I suppose she missed it. I believe she's doing an interview with a friend of mine this afternoon, so I figured I'd take a chance and swing by to listen in."

"Of course. I'm sure she'll be happy to see you."

Isabelle gives me a small, disbelieving grin and sits down on the couch. I slide into my armchair, which also doubles as my dream home, across from her.

"Truth be told, I doubt she'll be overly happy. I think it's fairly obvious that I'm not my sister's favorite person."

"Juliette just has a tough exterior. You know her."

"I used to know her. There was a time when we were very close. Thick as thieves, really."

I'm desperately curious to hear more. To ask what the hell happened to them, but I know I have to tread lightly.

"Will you tell me about her then?" I ask instead. "About what she was like when she was younger?"

Isabelle shifts around a little, getting more comfortable on the couch, her posture relaxing by a slight degree. "She was wild," she says wistfully. "We both were back then. We came to London with such a set of dreams for ourselves. She was going to be the world's best playwright, and I was to be a famous actress. We had liked New York well enough growing up, but we always spent our summers in England. Our mother had an aunt who lived just outside Oxford, so as soon as school let out, we were off. On our flights home, we would swear that as soon as we graduated high school, we'd leave Manhattan behind for London. And that's exactly what we did."

"Sounds like quite the sisterly adventure."

"Oh, it was. Did you know we both lived in the studio for two years together? We each had a twin bed pushed up against opposite walls like a rowdy girl's dormitory."

I sit forward a bit in the chair, viscerally thinking that if I get closer, I can somehow sneak into the stories myself. "I can't imagine two people living in that studio. It's a tight squeeze with just me and a cocker spaniel."

"It was a tight squeeze, but we had such fun there. Believe it or not, we almost always had friends staying with us as well. It's nice to remember—all of us laughing and drinking and chasing our ambitions. I often wish that I could go back for a day or two."

"It sounds idyllic," I muse.

"It was. But, of course, it wasn't always perfect. When we moved over here, our father cut us off financially, so money was always incredibly tight. The bath would run out of hot water at an alarming rate, and whenever I was the most tired, that's almost always when Juliette would be the most inspired to write. We fought like cats and dogs, but when so many years have passed, you tend to only think back on the good memories…which is nice, I think."

"I think so, too."

"I'll never forget when she started working on *The Lights of Trafalgar*. She had been working in the London theater scene for a year, but nothing huge had panned out yet. And for myself, I learned fast that my hopes of being an actress were no more than pipe dreams. Anyways, she was writing one night, and she was so quiet and serene. Alarmingly so. Usually, she wrote with a very particular environment—radio on low, no TV and certainly no talking. She would mutter lines or thoughts to herself out loud, but that night she was dead silent."

Isabelle pauses, and I'm not sure if it's for dramatic effect or if it's because she's reliving the memory for herself. "She went at it for hours and then suddenly, just like that, she turned off the light and climbed into her bed. After a minute, I asked her how it went and she said it was a disaster, but it was going to be the play that made her. She had the title stuck in her head for ages, just waiting for the play to come to her. And that night, it did."

"And the rest was history."

"That it was. *The Lights of Trafalgar* didn't come out right away, of course. She ended up working on it for several years before it was ready to be released to the world."

"And were you still pursuing acting then?" I ask.

"Not really. The year she started writing it was the same year I decided to give up. Our family had a background in real estate, as I'm sure you know, so soon after that, I started moving in that direction as well."

"And now you own one of the largest brokerages in London."

"Yes, I've been very lucky. My husband has always been tremendously supportive, and my father helped me with a lot of very valuable connections in the beginning." She smiles at me then, but it doesn't reach her ears. It gives me pause, and I end up twisting my fingers together in my lap.

"Did you meet your husband through the theater?"

"Oh no," she says, brightening back up a bit. "Freddie has worked in banking since I've known him and doesn't have an artistic bone in his body. He tried as best he could, for my sake. He called me his little Bohemian, bringing a great burst of color to his otherwise gray life. He's a very sweet man."

"Did Juliette like him?" I decide to ask.

"She did for the most part. She gave him a tough time at first, calling him my shiny ball and accusing him of distracting me. But once she started seeing Paul, she eased up a bit."

As she mentions Paul, a flash of nerves streaks Isabelle's face, giving the impression that she feels she's overstepped. I'm quick to try to put her mind at ease. "That's understandable. Juliette told me about Paul the other day."

"Did she? Well, I suppose that makes sense. They did almost end up getting married, after all."

It's difficult for me to hide my surprise at hearing that, but I somehow manage it as I simply nod, and Isabelle goes on.

"That was as close as she ever came to settling down. At least back then, anyways. I guess I wouldn't really know what her love life looked like after that. Unfortunately, we fell out of touch once she left for New York."

Still reeling from Isabelle's bombshell revelation, I try to stay focused on the conversation at hand. "It was probably hard to maintain a close relationship with so much physical distance separating you both. Sometimes it's hard for me to text a friend that lives twenty minutes away, and we can go months without seeing each other."

Isabelle gives me an obliging grin. "I'd be willing to accept any form of a relationship with my sister at this point, but I know that won't be possible until she decides to forgive me."

Forgive her?

In ten minutes, Isabelle has revealed more insight into her

dynamics with Juliette than Juliette has in the entire time I've been working for her. I want so badly to know more, hoping I could maybe help them in some way, but I don't dare press any further. Isabelle seems appreciative as she sits up a bit and tries to lighten the mood.

"But, at least through it all, she always played a part in Liam's life. She'd come see him when she was over here for work and she constantly sent him gifts and letters. He adores her. And he had no clue of the strain between us until he was much, much older. I guess that's one perk of having roots in the theater. We were able to play the happy family for his sake whenever we needed to."

I smile even though it's underlined with sadness. Isabelle's expression is the same.

"Anyways, never mind our family sagas. Tell me about you, Winnie. Are you having a nice time in London?"

Oh yes. And nearly shagging your son senseless last night has definitely been the highlight.

"I'm having a great time. I've never been to Europe before. The only time I was out of the country was to Canada, and my dad and I drove, so this is a big trip for me. Your sister is extremely generous."

"Yes, I'm happy to report that she's always been that way. And how long have you been working for her?"

"Five years," I answer proudly. "Time flies when you're having fun."

"And when you're with Juliette, fun is never in short supply."

"Absolutely. In fact, maybe I'll just shoot her a quick text to get a status update and to let her know you're here so she..."

I don't even finish my sentence before the apartment door swings open, and in walks Juliette with another woman I've

never seen before. Juliette goes from smiling to frowning to
forced smiling in two seconds flat as she takes in the scene
with me and Isabelle.

"Well, this is a surprise," she says with strained sweetness.

Isabelle quickly stands up, her effortless grace and easy
manner seeming a little shaken as she faces her sister. "Hello,
Juliette. I hope you don't mind, but I was in the area, and so I
figured I'd stop by to say hello and listen in on your interview.
I also thought I'd introduce you to Caroline, but I see you've
already beaten me to it."

"Yes, we met in the elevator."

Isabelle says nothing, waiting on Juliette, who inconve-
niently also says nothing. My crowd-pleasing inclinations take
over, and I'm keen to jump in. "Hi, I'm Winnie," I say, getting Caroline's attention. "We spoke via email the other day.
Did you need me to help you set up somewhere?"

"Oh, no. There's really not much to it, actually." She lifts
up her small but thick briefcase, which I can only assume has
all of her recording equipment, and I gesture her towards the
coffee table.

"Would right here be good?"

"Perfect." She steps on over, stopping to give Isabelle a double cheek kiss and then proceeding to set herself up. I move to
Juliette's side in the kitchen as Isabelle walks over to Caroline.

"When did she get here?" my boss asks in a hushed voice,
flipping on the sink for extra noise traffic.

"Basically, just now. Ten minutes tops."

"I should have known that she'd push her way into this.
Or that she probably bribed Caroline into interviewing me. I
ignore a few of her phone calls so she gets one of her lackeys
to strap me into a lie detector."

"Caroline seems very nice, and you're doing a podcast for the arts—it's hardly a shakedown."

"Well, you're clearly not familiar with the crowd Isabelle rolls with. They seem cordial on the outside, but deep down they're ladies' aid mobsters. Their pearl necklaces are meant to distract you from their brass knuckles."

"That seems a little over the top," I say as my phone dings. I pull it out of my pocket and see a private reply email from Professor Jack. I cautiously open it, making sure Juliette is distracted with whatever is going on in the living room before reading.

Hey Winnie. I was so happy to get your email, and I'm thrilled to hear that you're interested in the position! Would tomorrow night be a good time for you and I to talk?

My eyes shift up to Juliette, who's still monitoring Isabelle and Caroline in the next room. I write back a quick reply.

Tomorrow night would be perfect! Just let me know what time is best for you and I'll make myself available.

A surge of adrenaline starts to rise in my chest when Juliette suddenly asks, "Who are you talking to?"

I abruptly close out my email and shove the phone back into my pocket. "It was nothing. Just some spam I was deleting."

She nods and I'm about to ask her a question to change the topic when the intercom from downstairs rings.

Juliette groans, and finally turns off the water. "Now who's that? Roshni has a key, and there's no dragging her away from rehearsals, anyways. I told her she could cut out early with me, and she all but handcuffed herself to the radiator pipe in protest."

"No worries, I'll find out." I jog across the room to where a phone hangs on the living room wall and briskly pick it up. "Hello," I chirp into the receiver.

"Hello. Hi, it's Liam."

I immediately smile but am sure to reel it in as I see Juliette staring at me. "It's Liam," I tell her blandly.

"Buzz him in," she says with a sluggish wave of her hand. She twirls around then to flip on the kettle for a cup of tea, and I twist away so my back is to everyone.

"What's the password?" I ask, holding the phone tight to my ear.

"The password," Liam repeats. "Is it *Death of a Prom King*?"

"Not quite, but a good guess."

"How about *Broadway*?"

"Getting warmer."

"Is it *I can't stop thinking about you*? Because that's the password I would choose for myself at the moment."

"Are you always so corny?" I ask, even as I feel my cheeks reddening.

"Again, it isn't corny if it's genuine. I think I forgot how pleasant it was to sleep two feet apart from someone but in the same bed while facing away and in no way breathing on each other."

"Now, that's exactly the kind of romance I'm looking for. Come on up." I hang up the phone and hit the button to buzz him in.

When I turn back to the group, Caroline is wearing headphones and is completely set up with a small microphone, and her laptop is on the coffee table. Juliette is sitting next to her on the couch with a second microphone, and Isabelle has moved a chair along the far wall.

"Alright," Caroline says, adjusting something on her mic

before pivoting around to face Juliette, "are we ready to get started? I assure you, this is going to be a very standard interview. Just questions about your journey in the theater, touching on your previous shows, all leading up to dive into the production you're now working on."

"Fire when ready," Juliette says, gripping her microphone and leaning in. Caroline is finalizing one last thing on her laptop when I hear a light knocking at the door. I disappear into the entry hallway as the interview begins.

Twisting the doorknob, I try my best to repress my butterflies when I find Liam standing across from me. He's wearing jeans and a faded band T-shirt, and seeing him dressed so casually does something to me.

"Oh, I'm sorry, Mr. Neighbor-Man," I purr seductively. "Was I making too much noise in here, and you've come upstairs to scold me for being such a bad girl?"

Liam stares at me for several seconds, looking an equal mixture of turned on and petrified. "I..." His words trail off, and I quickly opt to have mercy on him.

"Relax, I'm only carrying on my tradition of horrifying hellos. Consider it shock therapy." I grab his wrist and pull him into the apartment, making sure to close the door quietly behind him.

He follows my lead and lets me usher him a few feet through the hallway. "It wasn't an entirely unpleasant shock," he says.

"Yeah, right. You looked four seconds away from crying. If I ever showed up at your place in a naughty teacher costume, it would probably take years off your life."

He plants his feet to keep us standing in the middle of the hall. "Teachers can be intimidating as well as deeply sultry. What do you say we give it a try sometime just to be sure? For research purposes only."

"Unfortunately, I wasn't able to bring my role-play wardrobe. My bag was over the weight limit at the airport, and so my meterstick and thigh-high stockings were the first to go."

"I'm sure the luggage handlers enjoyed that very much."

"One can only hope. Okay, come on through. Your aunt is giving an interview, though, so make sure to stay quiet."

I turn to step into the living room, but Liam catches me by the wrist. "Wait," he says, pulling me back deeper into the hallway. "Can I see you tonight?"

Feeling his hand on my skin and catching the want in his eyes, I'm immediately tempted to say yes. But I also know that I haven't written nearly enough while I've been here, specifically in the past few days. I need to buckle down no matter how much I may want to stay wrapped up in Liam and whatever it is that's starting between us.

"I can't," I tell him. "I'm so far behind on my play, and my deadline is coming up fast."

"No, I get that. I want you to come over and work. I know you've been preoccupied, so if you come over tonight, I'll arrange a comfy corner for you, and I'll spend the evening with Ollie so you won't have to focus on anything except your writing."

Oh, he's good. I don't know why I keep underestimating this soft-spoken gigolo.

"You won't distract me at all?" I ask him.

"Not at all. I'll be on my best behavior. Even if you launch yourself at me, I'll refuse. You could strip naked in the middle of the room, and while I may peek for a brief second, I will then turn away and adamantly refuse any and all come-hither glances."

I shake my head and consider his proposition further. Liam presses his advantage.

"If you come over and it's not working out, you can leave. But let's just try it, because I really, really like being around you. And I'll supply snacks."

Ugh, this bastard. Sold.

"Fine," I tell him after a few seconds. "Are we talking about a snack or two, or like a bunch of snacks?"

"Oh-so-many snacks."

"And Ollie will need a pillow."

"I have pillows in excess." I give him a questioning eyebrow raise, and he goes on. "I don't know why I said that. I have a very average amount of pillows, but definitely enough for Ollie."

I sigh and admit defeat. Like he said, if it's not working out, I'll just leave. "Okay. Ollie and I will be over at seven."

I then go to walk away again, but Liam only pulls me back one more time, locking his arm around my waist, ducking his head and stealing a brief but drugging kiss.

"I'm sorry," he says heavily. "I just couldn't be in the same room with you for another minute without doing that." His words feel warm against my face as his fingertips brush the delicate skin of my wrist. Standing here with him in the somewhat narrow hallway, I get a little drunk off his presence. He smells like summer and soap, and his scent weaves effortlessly around me, muddling my thought process. His eyes tell me he wants to kiss me again, and while I would like that, I'm not far gone enough to forget that my boss and his mother are mere yards away and just out of our line of vision. I give myself five seconds to enjoy his soft touch until I force myself to move away, stepping backwards with a languid smile before twisting around and heading back into the living room. I pause before I enter, taking a calming breath and then striding inside.

An hour later, the interview is done, and Caroline, Liam

and Isabelle have just left. Juliette is still sitting on the couch, staring blankly ahead until I hand her a cup of tea. She never ended up making her first one despite boiling the water earlier.

"Well, that seemed painless enough," I say as I sit down next to her.

"Right." Juliette sighs, seeming more tired than I've seen her in a while. "Why don't you just take the rest of the day off, kid? I have a headache, and I'm going to bed early."

"Are you sure?" I'm a little concerned even though a couple of extra hours to sneak in some writing would be incredible. "I can stay and answer more emails. Or we could have one of our cooking network watch parties. English baking shows are always an unparalleled delight and I bet watching them while physically in England somehow makes them even more charming."

"No, it's alright. You go. Just text Roshni and tell her the same, will you?"

"Sure. Of course. Call me if you need anything."

Juliette stands after that, taking her tea with her as she crosses the living room, moving in the direction of her bedroom. She's almost reached the hallway when she stops and turns back to face me.

"I never asked. What did you and Isabelle talk about while she was here?"

I mentally review our conversation and quickly decide that me revealing anything from my chat with Isabelle would in no way help the rift between them. I shake my head with a noncommittal expression. "Not much. Mainly just about the pop-up."

Juliette seems to accept my answer but then goes on anyways. "Did she ask you about me? About how I've been or anything like that?"

I'm not sure how to respond. Isabelle didn't so much ask as she did tell. But it's also painfully obvious that there's so much sadness there. A longing for the past. Resignation about the future.

"I think she really misses you," I end up answering. "She didn't have to say it for me to know."

Juliette stands there a moment, contemplative and quiet until she turns around and disappears from view.

I want to call after her, but I stop myself. I'm generally good at anticipating what Juliette needs, and in this moment, it's clear she needs time for herself. Even so, it still hurts to see her at odds with her closest family member. They were just together for over an hour with almost zero human connection—sitting in the same room with insurmountable distance between them. And then that thought leads me to remember that at this very moment, *my* closest family member is packing up to move thousands of miles away from me to start a new life with his new family.

I wrap my arms around my waist as the vision sinks in deeper, clawing down into my consciousness until it puts down roots. It leaves me feeling sad, disjointed and completely alone, and makes me more than ready to snuggle up with Ollie and Liam once I finish working on my play. Getting up from the couch, I choose to ignore the quiet but painfully accurate voice in my head reminding me that, most likely, it's only Ollie who will be mine to keep.

14

I'm not quite sure what to expect when I knock on Liam's door with Ollie and my tote bag filled with overnight necessities. To put a label on it, I suppose we're about to embark on a work session/puppy playdate/adult overnight hangout? I mean, I've had weirder Wednesdays, but this one is kind of up there. The weight of the laptop in my bag starts to pull at my shoulder, prompting me to knock again as Ollie ravenously sniffs the floor. He only stops a couple of seconds later when the door swings open, revealing Liam standing inside, looking almost out of breath in light sweatpants and a gray T-shirt.

"You made it," he says with a smile. "And before you try to shock me with whatever nightmarish greeting you've mentally concocted, I'm saying hello, so it's over and done with. Hello. Very glad you could be here. Please come in."

He moves back to allow me to pass through, and I decide to give him a break for once and act like a normal human being.

"Thank you for having us. We're very happy to be here." I slowly step past him and into the apartment, moving steadily deeper into the space until I stop to look around. "Oh boy," I say quietly.

Looking around, I find what I can only describe as a mixture between a dirty dorm room and an abandoned fallout shelter that was most likely overtaken and destroyed during a somewhat recent zombie apocalypse. Old mail is littered over almost every available surface, which there aren't many of because Liam's furniture is shockingly minimal—one couch, a folding chair and a TV sitting on what looks to be a bedside table. There's an explosion of food containers lining the kitchen counters, and the windows are nearly all bare, minus one section behind the TV that has a bedsheet thumbtacked into the wall above. The carpeting on the floor seems caked with spills that have long since dried, and judging from the stale beer stench wafting through the air, it's pretty easy to guess what they're from.

If a rabid pack of college freshman were living here, I'd understand. But it definitely doesn't seem like the home of a man who sold his successful business and could then afford to traipse around Italy for over half a year.

"Did you just move in?" I ask hesitantly.

"Not just. About six months ago."

"Okay, wow."

This is my fault. Through all my time with Liam, I think I subconsciously whipped up a certain fancy persona for him. That person, I imagined, lived in a stormy hilltop mansion with endless wood paneling, first edition books, a grandfather clock and a crackling fireplace. Essentially, I envisioned Bruce Wayne's study. That's why this is such a shock. I anticipated the ambient retreat of a fallen hero, only to find him encamped in "dude" headquarters instead.

"I was actually just tidying up before you got here," he says.

"Admittedly, I should have started earlier, but if you give me a few minutes, everything will be in top shape in no time."

He quickly springs into action, moving into the kitchen and shaking out an empty garbage bag. He then begins swiping his arm along the counter, dropping the food containers inside the bag like a pungent waterfall.

"If you look in the corner, you'll see that the desk is set up nicely for you. I was primarily concentrating on that area, as it were. I was hoping it would give you tunnel vision so you wouldn't notice the surrounding disaster."

"A valiant attempt," I say, turning to the corner to find the desk he's speaking of. While it does seem in slightly better shape than the rest of the apartment, it's hard to get past the large-scale bulletin board hanging directly in front of it that's pinned with dozens of web-related articles.

"What do you think?" he asks.

"I think it's a lovely work space. And as an added bonus, it's also a great spot for me to plot out my next ill-advised assassination attempt."

"Does it look that murder-y?" he asks, surveying the living room and clearly already knowing the truth for himself.

"Kind of," I answer in a softer tone. "I don't mean to complain or to put down your lifestyle, but holy red flag."

"Yes, I was afraid that might be your reaction."

"What's the deal with all of this? You said you liked routines and order. If that's the case, this place doesn't really seem to fit you at all."

Liam pauses from his cleaning then, setting the garbage bag down on the floor.

"To be honest, I don't have company over often, and I just haven't had the desire to fix the place up. I guess I don't see it as a real home, so I figured, what's the point in putting effort into it?"

"Let me reiterate again that I'm not trying to be judgy, but even if this isn't your forever home, it should still be a place that makes you feel better, not worse. And I don't think you could ever be happy or even remotely comfortable surrounded by all of this."

"I suppose after living in a staged flat for so long where everything always had to be photo-ready and clean, this was my form of rebellion."

"I get that. And again, I'm not trying to put you down. I'm just surprised."

"And I'm sorry I didn't clean more before you got here. I should have." We both just look at each other for a second before Liam goes on. "Anyways, let me show you to your station. And, of course, Ollie's has his station all set up as well." I look to where he's gesturing and see that he actually set up a very cute area with pillows and a water bowl beside the desk.

"Okay, so that's adorable. But still, if Ollie ends up swallowing a miscellaneous bong accessory that you've flagrantly discarded, know that I will have your head on a spike."

"I keep all my bong accessories on a very high shelf, and I am going to be cleaning for the entire evening. Look, there are headphones for you to drown me out so you don't have to hear my vigorous vacuuming."

I give him a small approving smile and sit down in the surprisingly comfortable desk chair, placing my tote bag on the floor.

"You don't have to clean the whole time," I tell him, twisting around a little. "This probably isn't what you had in mind when you invited me over."

"No, this is good. I should get this place in order, and you're the catalyst I needed to finally start. Your scorn fuels my fire."

I smile a little at that, and it seems to fill Liam with a certain level of relief. Looking more confident, he goes on. "Now, begin. Write at will. The next time you turn around, you will see birds and field mice happily sweeping along beside me."

"You don't really seem like the Cinderella type," I tell him.

"I may surprise you yet. Now, to work, if you please."

I scoff as I turn to face the desk again, pulling out my laptop and plugging the headphones in. I cue up my most inspiring writing playlist before glancing down at Ollie and seeing that he's already settling comfortably onto the cushions to my right. I check on Liam one more time in my peripheral to watch as he continues to load up the garbage bag before I turn back once again. *Death of a Prom King*, let's do this.

Three hours later, I pull off my headphones with a deep breath as I pivot around in my seat. I actually got a substantial amount of work done. I edited some major scenes and worked out most of the inconsistencies I was hoping to address by this point. All that's left now is the ending. Writing the perfect ending that will hopefully take the play from enjoyable to extraordinary. Ollie is now safely back on the pillows beside the desk, having gone out for a long walk with Liam a half hour before.

True to his word, our host spent the entire time cleaning, and while the apartment still feels threadbare, I'm starting to see some of the personal touches I didn't notice through the initial clutter. A framed movie poster from the '90s—a record player with a stack of vinyl albums in the corner—a kitchen that seems fairly new. Liam's currently sitting on the couch the long way with his legs on the cushions. His laptop is open, and his headphones are on. He's typing away as furiously as I was for the past few hours.

After closing my own computer, I make my way over to sit down on the other side of the couch near his feet, lifting my own feet up to rest beside his hip. Feeling and noticing me, he pulls off his headphones and angles the laptop screen down towards him as we face each other.

"Hey, there," he says. "How'd it go?"

"Very well, thank you. How about you?"

"I think I have carpal tunnel from how aggressively I scrubbed the inside of my fridge. Other than that, I'm wonderful."

"And your walk?"

"My walk with Ollie went better than expected. I felt very safe in the knowledge that he would lovingly nibble on the shoes of any assailant that dared cross our path."

I look over adoringly at my savage guard dog, who's now sleeping on his back, legs in the air, as he lies in the direct center of the pillows. I turn back to Liam with a smile.

"He's a lover, not a fighter."

"Yes, I can tell. He tried to have his wicked way with my leg again when we waited at a crosswalk, but then thought the better of it when another bloke stopped beside us. Apparently, his calf was more appealing than mine."

"Blasphemy. Your calves are without rival."

Liam grins and closes his computer all the way, then sets it down on the makeshift coffee table that he's erected from two piles of books and an ironing board. "Well, seeing as you've finished your work for the evening, we can now partake in the promised snacks. How do you feel about milkshakes?"

My heart almost stops at the suggestion. "Um, I feel fantastic about them."

"Excellent. I don't have too many talents to boast of, but milkshake making is a particularly large feather in my cap."

"Boast away, my friend. Milkshakes are arguably the best dessert in the world."

"I couldn't agree with you more. Now, prepare to be amazed."

At that, he springs up from the couch and heads for the kitchen. It's clear I'm not the only one who's pumped about this. I get up and follow after him, standing on the opposite side of the kitchen island until I settle onto the lone bar stool. Liam takes out a carton of ice cream, chocolate syrup, and a gallon of milk from the fridge and freezer. He then reaches up to the top shelf of one of his cabinets and pulls down what looks like an industrial-grade blender.

He begins scooping out vanilla ice cream into the blender, and I lean down slightly onto the freshly scrubbed counter. "Dare I ask where you learned to make these?"

"When I was a teenager, I worked in an ice-cream shop every summer for four years. I could make these blindfolded with my hands tied behind my back."

"Milkshakes and soft-core bondage? Stop talking dirty to me."

Liam shakes his head with a sly smile and continues on in his endeavor. "Do you always say the first thing that pops into your head?"

"Not in a work environment. I probably don't speak my mind enough in professional situations, so I overcompensate for it in my private life."

"There are worse ways of coping." Liam reaches into the cabinet once again, this time pulling out a measuring cup and pouring in the milk until it hits a specific line. "And now," he says, pouring in another drop until he has the measurements just right, "tell me something about yourself that I don't know.

Something that, in different circumstances, I would learn over time, but since you're leaving, I'll never get the chance."

I'm oddly pleased by his question while also being momentarily gutted. He's right. There's so much of me that he'll never know because of our limitations—both with time and distance. Pushing the depressing aspects of the question aside, I choose to focus on my response.

"Something you would learn for yourself," I muse. "Oh, I know! I love Halloween."

"Well, that's…nice," Liam answers. "Though, to be perfectly honest, given your usual outlandish responses to questions, I expected something a little more…you."

I have to smile at that.

"No, I mean I *really* like Halloween. And I don't mean that in a 'I wear some cat ears with a cute little tail and a black dress' kind of way. I'm talking a full costume that's planned out at least a month in advance. No obvious choices. Something somewhat obscure and definitely weird and that will either spark personal joy for me or will make other people laugh."

"Dare I request examples?" Liam asks nervously.

"You may one hundred percent request examples." I immediately scurry away from the counter and cross the room to my computer bag beside the desk, pull out my phone, and power walk back into the kitchen. I move to Liam's side and open it to my pictures section, scrolling through until I hit October.

"Dear lord." Liam winces, squinting his eyes and looking more closely at the image I'm proudly displaying. "What is that with you? Is it alive?"

"I wish. It's just a highly realistic prop. I attached it to the basket and strapped the handlebars to backpack slings that I hid under my jacket."

"That is incredibly elaborate."

"Yet not my most elaborate costume to date."

"How long did it take you to put that together?"

"Just a few weeks," I answer. "I have a friend who designs costumes on the side, so he helped me with most of it."

"And I'm assuming this is you being…"

"Elliot bike-riding ET back to his spaceship. Four of my friends dressed up as the other kids on bikes so we could enter into each bar in a V formation. We were a hit. Hundreds of people asked me to phone home."

"What were some of your other costumes?" Liam asks.

"I mean, there's a solid twenty in inventory for me to choose from. I suppose my highlights would be a traffic cone, a Christmas snow globe, and another time my friends and I went with a *Price Is Right* theme. Sara was Bob Barker, Min was a contestant and I was the Plinko board."

"Surprising. I would have taken you for more of a yodeling mountain game kind of girl."

"I tried, but it turns out lederhosen don't look flattering on me."

"Now, that can't be true."

"It's a regret I'll take to my grave." I walk around the counter to sidle back up on my stool. I pause to watch Liam's handiwork as he pours the milk and the syrup into the blender before I go on. "Your turn. Let's hear some fun facts."

"Yes, my turn," he says. "Alright, my favorite movie growing up and to this day is *Robin Hood: Prince of Thieves* with Kevin Costner."

"Kevin Costner? He isn't even British. He's arguably the most un-British Robin Hood that ever was."

"And yet, I love it still. That movie is pure genius, and I refuse to hear otherwise. I must have watched it a thousand times when I was younger. I even took up archery for a bit, but I wasn't as good of a shot as I thought I would be."

I nod in commiseration. "I think everyone is a better archer in their mind."

"A hard lesson I was forced to accept. I really thought righteous thievery was going to be my life's path when I was ten. And look at me now."

"A capitalist monster," I joke.

"Just a wretched bourgeois pig. When I was a child, I thought I'd be an integral member of the Sherwood gang, if not Robin Hood himself. Now I'm probably closer to one of the Sheriff's minions who dies thirty minutes in. I'm a nameless henchman."

"You are not a henchman," I assert. "A henchman would never be as nice to me as you are."

"Maybe I'm only being nice because I'm trying to seduce you. Perhaps I have many a sordid plan in store."

"Well, you've already almost seduced me once, and as far as sordid plans, I have my own in mind, so prepare yourself."

"I'm looking forward to it. Now, please hold while brilliance ensues." Liam covers the blender with the lid and promptly presses the mix button. It roars to life, and with that, Ollie is up and barking, flinging himself against my legs. I'm quick to squat down and soothe him, and by the time I have, Liam is finished.

"Done! Prepare to fall even deeper under my spell than you already have."

"Consider me ready," I say as I stand up once again.

Just then, he twists around and pulls two fountain shop glasses from out of a cabinet. He fills both glasses to the top and slides one to me across the counter, slinging a dish towel over his shoulder.

"For the lady."

"This is so much fancier than I expected," I say, rotating the glass and admiring the delightful-looking milkshake from every angle.

"Now you can almost tell Juliette the truth if she asks you what you did tonight. You can say your escort took you out for ice cream."

"I forgot to tell you, Juliette actually called the experiment off. She's so consumed with the pop-up that she's shelving her next project until further notice. My Vibefinder days are blissfully behind me."

"A cause for celebration if I ever heard one."

"Huzzah, indeed," I agree.

"And now for the moment of truth. I don't have straws at the moment, so spoons will have to do." A moment later, he drops an aforementioned spoon into the glass, and I don't hesitate to dip it down and draw out an ample scoop. I shovel it into my mouth in what I hope is a semi-ladylike manner and find myself groaning a second later.

"Stop," I mumble, quickly lowering my spoon again. "This is delicious. So outrageously good."

Liam looks more than pleased as he grips his own spoon and takes his first taste.

"I'm not going to lie," I go on to say between scoops, "you are infinitely more attractive to me now that I know you can make these. You were already close to a ten on your own, but now you're a solid twelve. I should have known it was only a matter of time until I dated someone in the ice cream industry."

"I'm honored to be your first. Now, how about we sit down and turn on some music so we can enjoy these properly?"

"First you dazzle me with your frozen dessert prowess, and

now you want to add music into the mix? Keep this up and I really will start to think that you're trying to seduce me."

"'Thou art as wise as thou art beautiful.'"

"Excuse me!" I laughingly exclaim, my eyes lighting up as I lower my milkshake onto the counter. "You did not just quote *A Midsummer Night's Dream* to me right now."

"I may have watched the movie after hearing your monologue at the Globe."

"I'm impressed," I tell him. "That's some serious fieldwork to put in just to get me to hook up with you."

Liam looks confused and then disappointed as his smile falters. "Or I might have done it because I like you and I want to understand you better?"

His words land a direct hit on an unguarded part of me, stealing my breath and leaving me disoriented. Our typical sparring feels far away, leaving me in a position where I have no other option other than to be vulnerable. It makes me nervous, and I end up scratching behind my neck.

"I'm sorry," I say. "I guess with my dating history, I sometimes forget that there are still good guys left out there."

"Should I take that to mean that I'm a good guy?"

"A very good guy." I'm being completely honest, and I know Liam can tell.

"Does that mean I can choose the music?" he asks.

His light tone instantly relaxes me, and an appreciative grin appears on my face.

"I suppose, but if you choose the world's best clarinet solos, you should know that I'm only interested in hearing you play them live."

"Fair enough. And lucky for you, I happen to have something even better in mind."

15

Two minutes later, Liam and I are sitting on opposite ends of the couch, once again facing each other, but this time, our ankles are overlapping in the middle. I give him a pensive look as music continues to fill the air around us.

"I never would have pegged you for a Barry Manilow fan," I tell him.

"Barry Manilow is one of the greatest artists who ever lived. If the best and worst moments of my life could be crafted into the most glorious melodies and then accompanied by the voice of a male temptress, we would be listening to this album, right here. *Even Now* is transcendent."

"I don't mean this offensively, but you honestly get weirder by the second."

"Does that lead you to liking me less?"

"I think it actually increases your likability. It makes me feel like we're on a more level playing field. You'd probably get along great with all my theater friends, and they're a handful even at their calmest."

He smiles and scooches back further into the couch. "Know what I've been meaning to ask you? What made you switch from performing in theater to playwriting? You seem to have concentrated on acting for a fair bit from what you've told me, so when did that end up changing?"

I take a hefty scoop of milkshake and drink it down. "It was towards the middle of my undergrad. I really liked being on the stage, but my favorite part of each production was always studying scripts and trying to get inside the characters. Sometimes I'd read a play and think of what I would have done differently if I wrote it. Starting in my teens and onwards, I always devoured scripts. And when you read so much of something, it starts to become ingrained."

"I'd say it's similar to coding, but that may be overreaching."

"No, you'd be completely right," I agree. "And it probably applies to any language, really. I think the key thing is that you have to be actively trying to learn. Like, right now, you could go to another country and be surrounded by a different language while not picking up a single word. But if you went there and wanted to learn, if you practiced and paid attention to the people around you—their dialects and tones—you could learn it. It's the same with playwriting. There's a difference between reading like a reader who enjoys plays, and then reading like someone who wants to discover the nuances of writing them. You have to have an ear for it, and you have to want it."

"So, you switched over to playwriting mid-college?"

"No, I finished out my undergrad as a drama major and then went for playwriting in graduate school."

"And did you enjoy it?" Liam asks, taking a sizable scoop of his own ice cream.

"I loved it. And in the beginning, it was magic. I was like the golden child, the top of my class. Classmates asked me for feedback, and teachers looked at me like I was more of a peer than a student." I pause at that, remembering the addictively lulling feeling of being so constantly praised, so entirely sure of myself.

"And then?" Liam prompts, rightfully assuming my nostalgic reveries are about to take a turn.

"Before graduation, each senior had to write a full-length play as their thesis. And the student with the highest GPA from the two-year program got to have their play performed as a student production."

Liam points his spoon in my direction. "You?"

"Me," I answer. "I had a comedy written. It was good. Everyone who read it loved it. But a few months before, I got into my own head. All my other playwright friends wrote these powerful dramas or these incredibly relevant pieces. My play felt campy in comparison. So I wrote something new. And that's what was performed in the workshop."

I shake my head, wishing I could go back and do it all differently. Or not do it at all. I'd completely wipe the memory from my whole existence.

"I tried too hard. I wrote what I thought people wanted to see. I wrote what my vanity told me to write, rather than the play I *had* to write. And it was a bomb. My professors were disappointed. My classmates were stunned and probably secretly happy on some level. The tweets and the reviews were so scathing that I still remember all of them. And then, when my dad handed me my flowers—just taking them from him after that felt so humiliatingly ironic that I wanted to curl up in a ball and never get up again."

"No one's perfect. You shouldn't expect yourself to be."

"I did back then," I explain. "I know better now, but I went from spending two years in the sun to then spending the next five dwelling in the shadows."

"You can hardly consider yourself to be a shadow creature at the moment. You're an invaluable employee to a world-renowned playwright, you're days away from submitting what is sure to be an award-winning play, you're enjoying the company of a moderately dashing Englishman, and you have a phenomenal dog who's devoted to you. You're in a good spot."

"No, I know I'm an incredibly lucky person. I guess I just feel like until I redeem myself writing-wise, it's hard to feel completely satisfied with the rest."

"Well, you should. You're sensational."

I nudge his hip with the tip of my toe. "Your gratuitous praise is very sweet, but also unnecessary. And for the record, I happen to think very highly of you, too."

We've both finished off our milkshakes at this point, and Liam places our glasses on the ironing board/table. "So, how are you feeling?" he then asks, sitting back against the cushions. "Are you ready to call it a night after breaking such a theatrically creative sweat?"

"Soon, I think. But let's stay here for a little longer first."

"The Manilow magic is pulling you in, isn't it?"

"Among other things," I say with a grin. Shifting to tuck my legs underneath me, I climb over to Liam's side of the couch and sprawl out across his chest. I feel rather than see him adjust his position a bit, sliding down to wrap his arms securely around me. His chin rests on the top of my head as I listen to the loud and steady beat of his heart.

"Three weeks really is a short amount of time," he says. I

feel the vibrations of his words through my ear that's pressed up against him.

"Three weeks is better than nothing," I answer back.

"But worse than everything."

"Is that what you're after, then?" I tilt my face up to catch his eyes. "Everything?"

He gives me a bittersweet kind of smile and runs his hand down the length of my back. He doesn't respond, and I don't mind in the least.

I sigh and snuggle even more comfortably into his hold. "Let's just listen to a couple more songs before we go to bed, okay? I bet they'll be transcending."

He still doesn't reply, only holds me the slightest bit tighter. We end up listening to half the album by the time I slowly fall asleep. Turns out, Liam wasn't lying—Barry Manilow really is one hell of a vocal temptress.

It's three in the morning when I wake up in Liam's bed, fully clothed. He must have carried me in at some point. I sit up and the room is dark, but I can see enough to distinguish my surroundings from the light that's still on in the living room. The bedroom itself is nice—noticeably in a far better state than the rest of the apartment. The space is tidy, and the dresser and bed look new. The sheets are tantalizingly soft, and actual curtains cover the windows while still letting in soft striations of light from the street outside.

I sneak out of bed and tiptoe across the carpeted floor, peeking out the doorway and finding Ollie asleep on the couch. Seeing that he's fine, I sneak back into the room and wiggle out of my jeans as I stand beside the bed, doing my best not to wake Liam. I then gently glide back in and hold my breath as I pull the blankets up around me.

Despite my best efforts, Liam turns over, groggy and perplexed, leaning up on an elbow as his eyes slowly focus on mine.

"Are you alright?" he asks hoarsely.

"I'm fine," I whisper back. "I just wanted to check on Ollie. I'm sorry I woke you."

"Don't be sorry. I was going to wake you before to see if you wanted to change, but I was just so satisfied that Barry serenaded you to sleep that I couldn't do it."

"Maybe it was just beginner's luck for Mr. Manilow."

Liam reaches out and takes my hand, skating his thumb across my palm. The sensation goes straight to my belly, and my breathing turns shallow.

"I suppose we'll have to test that theory out next time," he says.

How in the hell can hand-holding be so erotic? I'll have to contemplate that question further in the future, because right now, I'm far too busy dealing with the definite heat that's traveling up my neck.

"You think there'll be a next time, then, do you?"

"I'm counting on it," he answers.

And just when I think I couldn't like Liam more than I already do, sleepy sex voice Liam makes an appearance. It's official—this is happening.

Still lulling me into a state of quiet delirium from hand touching alone, I'm more than receptive when he pulls me forward with a gentle tug. I instantly slide my body across to meet his, and a swirling rush shoots through me. I've never wanted a man more. I feel drunk. He makes me feel drunk. The delectable buzz that's clouding my mind spreads all through my stomach and even lower as I urge Liam down until we're nose to nose. I'm the one to close that last inch, tilting my chin up so my lips meet his.

Our kiss is soft and slow. There's no one to rush us. Echoes of touches reverberate through every inch of me. My shirt bunches up as I slip closer still, exposing my hip. Liam drags a hand across my bare waist, leaving a trail of fire. I want to feel it everywhere. Apparently thinking the same, Liam moves his hand to graze up my back as my own hand travels to the nape of his neck. I lean up further and nudge his lips open with mine. His tongue slips into my mouth, confident and practiced. He knows what he's doing, and I'm insatiable as a result.

I all but mold myself against his front, and his skin feels hot to the touch. I'm pretty sure I've been burning for ages, already itching to tear my clothes off for any kind of relief. Liam's hand slides from my back to my thigh, pulling it up to wrap around his waist. As soon as it does, he rolls onto his back, shifting me up until I'm straddling him.

Very much happy in our new position, I pull my shirt over my head, and my bra follows seconds later. Liam's eyes seem to glaze over until he jolts himself up into a sitting position, situating me firmly in his lap as he pulls my head down for another drugging kiss. It quickly turns desperate, and I instinctively roll my hips forward. Liam pulls back with a groan that sounds almost pained, but he can't be in too much pain since his mouth moves determinedly to my chest. He licks and sucks, and my head falls back. A muffled moan fights its way out of me even though I'm doing everything I can to stay quiet. A minute passes in the same manner until I'm dizzy and wild and the rhythm of my hips steadily builds. I'm thinking things could reach the breaking point just like this when Liam locks an arm around me and twists us again, somehow pinning me onto the bed beneath him with another deep, frenzied kiss.

I'm not sure how much time goes by before he leans back on his haunches, gripping my underwear as his eyes lock on mine.

"Can I?" he asks, his voice utterly desperate and low.

I nod as I swallow and lift my hips up to help him. He pulls my panties away and then slides off the bed, pulling his boxers down and stepping out of them as he reaches into his bedside table for protection. Soon he's back on top of me. His weight feels grounding and perfect, and I'm quick to wrap my legs around him, desperate to reach the finish line even as I'm inwardly hoping we can go on like this for years.

Liam seems as impatient as I am, instantly lining himself up and nudging in little by little until he's there. Right there. I feel full and on fire and eagerly start to move. His eyes stay clenched shut as he mutters a smothered curse into my neck. "Winnie. Christ, you're amazing. You feel..." His words are cut off as I twist my head and drag his mouth back to mine.

One hand supports his weight beside me as the other continues to mercilessly roam my body, eventually slipping down between us and rubbing just enough pressure right where I need it. We continue to move against each other, alternating between feverish thrusts and measured strokes until the delicious clenching in the pit of my stomach snaps. I hide my face against the skin of his shoulder, muffling my cry as I tighten around him. Liam's hips whip forward at the sensation, his chest dropping to mine as he moans in my ear in such a dirty way that it amplifies my aftershocks by a million. I want to hear it again and again.

A minute later, we're both still panting as Liam rolls off to lie beside me and we gaze up at the ceiling, slowly coming back down to earth.

"Well, that escalated quickly," I say breathlessly, turning

my head over to look at him. "And here I thought ice cream was going to be the standout moment of my night."

Liam chuckles and glances over at me. "That was brilliant," he replies. "I mean, I knew it was going to be good, but I had no idea it would be *that* good."

"I'm glad you had fun."

"I'm actually quite proud of myself. We threw some real acrobatics in there. I may have pulled a muscle, but it felt so incredible that it didn't register at the time."

"Bold of you to admit that, Old Man River. Tell me, is discussing sex injuries typical in this neck of the woods, or are you only speaking so honestly because our super-steamy activities lowered your inhibitions?"

Liam grins and rubs his eyes. "I'll have you know that yes, while I may still be in an amorous haze, having a sex sprain is nothing to be ashamed of. It just means I'll have to up my daily stretching."

"Or get a new hip," I suggest coyly.

"You know, if you continue to tease me like that, I'm going to feel the need to defend my manhood and ravish you all over again."

"Maybe that's been my plan all along."

Liam rolls then until he's propped up on his elbow beside me. "The first second I saw you, I knew that I was in trouble. I immediately thought to myself that I was either going to run far, far away from you, or shamelessly chase after you."

"I guess it's fair to say you went with door number two."

"Was I that obvious?" he asks.

"Just a bit, and I not-so-secretly liked every bit of it." He reaches down and lazily traces his hand on the curve of my cheek as I go on. "So, now that we've slept together, does that mean you're done chasing after me?"

A sly smile crosses his face. "I'm only just getting started," he whispers, inching down to brush his mouth across my neck.

I close my eyes and tilt my head back just enough to allow him better access. "On second thought, I'm starting to think that I'm the one who's really in trouble."

16

Know how you know you're in the field you're meant to be in? When you're halfway through the day and you're already getting disappointed that you'll eventually have to go home. As in, you're genuinely upset. That's how I feel right now—borderline heartbroken because in four hours, we'll be calling it a night, and I want this experience every day for the rest of my life.

Today is our final day of rehearsal, a full run-through of the play in its entirety from cue to cue. There's no rehearsal tomorrow—so the actors will stay fresh—and then the next day, it's showtime. Usually, this would have been what's known as a technical rehearsal where we'd be at the venue, perfecting the lighting and sounds, but as we're only going to be at the pop-up for one night, this is the best we can do.

We're at the halfway point now, having our faux intermission as everyone eats a quick bite and reenergizes. I like to think that this is how I'll feel for the majority of the time if I end up getting the job at West Lane. I spoke to Professor Jack about the position for over two hours the other night, and I'm scheduled to have a Zoom interview with Suzanne, the executive director, tomorrow. I'm not quite positive what to expect from it, but I'm entirely ready to fake it till I make it. And after working with Juliette for so long, I feel like I can make anything work.

Thinking of Juliette, I look up and find her sitting off to the side with a magazine reporter who arrived a couple of minutes ago to interview her. I was going to check in and make sure everything was all set between them, but with me being wrapped up as I was, I figured they could handle it on their own. I'm subtly watching them out of the corner of my eye now and munching on a bag of chips when Ellie appears beside me, drinking an abnormally large cup of coffee.

"Hi there," she chirps.

"Hey," I answer back happily. "I've been meaning to tell you: I really love the song you have Zachary playing after the big argument scene. It's haunting but so sweet, too. I've never heard it before."

"Well, I'll be sure to pass on your compliments, because Chloe wrote it."

"Did she really?" I ask.

"She did. She's an amazing songwriter and has played guitar since she was ten. I actually met her at a café open mic night. It was love at first sight."

My heart explodes just from picturing it. "That's amazing. And now her song will be in *The Lights of Trafalgar.*"

"Yes, it's our first artistic collaboration, as it were. She's pretty nervous about it, but I can't wait."

"Maybe this will be her big break."

"Might be," she agrees with a smile. "What about you?

You're a playwright, aren't you? Are you still waiting for your big break?"

"That I am. Hopefully something will pan out soon. I have a project I'm nearly finished with, but we'll see what happens there."

A sudden crash causes us both to jump, our eyes whipping to the front of the space, where we see that one of the metal folding chairs has fallen to the floor. We both sigh, and Ellie takes a soothing sip of coffee. "Well, hey, if you'd ever like me to look at your work, I'd be more than happy to."

"Are you serious?" I ask, taken aback. I've practically been begging Juliette to read my work for years, and here Ellie is willing to do it after only knowing me for two weeks.

"Of course," she answers. "We're all in the playwriting trenches together."

Once again struck by Ellie's kindness, I shake my head a bit as a massive smile spreads across my face. "Yes, that would be amazing. I can email it to you tonight if that would be okay?"

"Perfect," Ellie answers.

"Honestly, though, please don't feel obligated to read it. I'm sure you have a million things going on with the play."

"Oh no, send away. I barely sleep as it is. And if I can't get to it now, I'll make sure to carve out time the minute the show is over." Her eyes trail over my shoulder then, something catching her eye that causes an inquisitive crinkle to appear between her brows. "Who is that that Juliette is talking to?" she asks.

I quickly turn around to follow her gaze. "That's Michael Quinton, a journalist from the *Herald*. He's interviewing her about the pop-up."

"Yes, I've heard of him," she says dryly. "How about you and I just go introduce ourselves, shall we?" She starts walking towards them before I even answer, and I have to jog a bit to catch up with her. The closer we get, the clearer I can see Juliette's face, and it gives me pause. Her typical media-friendly expression is strangely absent, replaced instead with a surprised kind of blankness. She's distracted enough that she doesn't even see us approaching, her gaze focused entirely on the reporter. We're nearly there and I'm about to step to Juliette's side when Ellie holds out an arm to stop, halting us a few feet behind Michael but within earshot.

"I think it's worth noting that you've been linked to some pretty famous men in the entertainment industry," he says, his voice nasal and confident. "Producers, actors, fellow visionaries such as yourself. What do you think was the catalyst for each of those relationships' eventual demises?"

Juliette's eyes glaze over with a coldness that she only reserves for people she truly can't stand. "Would you like me to come up with some sort of a list?"

"Let me rephrase that—do you feel like you value your career or your craft over personal fulfillment? And if so, do you stand by that decision?"

Juliette swallows then, her eyes shifting up and landing on mine with a wounded streak that I seldom see on her. It stuns me into a sort of stupor that only breaks when Ellie takes several determined steps forward, moving to stand beside Juliette.

"Hello, I'm sorry," she says, looking down at the reporter like the cretin that he is. "Just wanted to clarify something here. You are aware that you are now interviewing one of the greatest playwrights of our time, correct?"

Michael crosses one of his legs over the other, and I have the distinct urge to smack him in the back of the head. "I'm aware," he answers.

Ellie continues to stare uncharacteristic daggers at him.

"That's what I figured. And that's why it's baffling to me that you're sitting here asking her asinine and, honestly, offensive questions, when there are several other topics you could currently be broaching. Perhaps you could discuss how she brilliantly bested the male-dominated '80s theater world before she was even thirty. Maybe you could ask her about all the charitable work she does to encourage women's involvement in the arts. Or, alternatively, maybe you just continue with the path you've set for yourself and ask her to specify her bra size. Was that going to be your follow-up question?"

Still far enough away, I step forward to see his profile, and Michael's cheeks suddenly flush red. "I apologize if my tone came off as irregular, but I assure you..."

"Oh, it absolutely did come off as irregular," Ellie says, "though not at all surprising, given your reputation. Now, I suggest you take on a far more respectful approach moving forward, and that's only if Ms. Brassard is gracious enough to carry on with the interview at all, because I can tell you right now, if I was in her shoes, I certainly would not."

She flashes Michael an over-the-top smile and walks away. I'm tempted to do the same, but also adding in a snarl and some very specific hand gestures.

Michael, for his part, twists in his seat and clears his throat, no doubt trying to find his mental equilibrium after surviving Ellie's very eloquent verbal ass-whipping.

"So now, Ms. Brassard, how do you find working with your current director? Many of those in the theater community consider Eloise MacClare as a young star on the rise."

Juliette plasters on a smile then, shaking some of the hair off her brow and taking a breath. "I would agree with that entirely. Working with Ellie has been a delight and a breath of fresh air, and I'm very grateful for the time we've spent collaborating on this project. It's been transformative, to say the least."

"And would you also say…"

Michael doesn't get the chance to ask another question as Juliette promptly stands up, grabbing her bag from off the floor and slinging it over her shoulder.

"I'm afraid that's all the time I have for today," she tells him. "Thanks so much for taking the time to come out. I hope you got everything you came for."

Michael's mouth hangs open, looking down at his nearly empty notepad and then back to Juliette. "I was rather hoping…"

But Juliette has already started walking away, leaving me to trail after her, rushing to keep up and to catch what she's saying over her shoulder.

"I have a headache. Feel free to take the rest of the day off, and tell Roshni the same."

"Are you sure?" I ask her, still following her path as she nears one of the side exits. "I can go with you. Just give me a second and I'll grab my stuff."

"No, no," she answers automatically. "It's morphing into a migraine. I'll do better alone."

And with that she's gone. The metal door slams shut in front of me, just as strong as the emotional walls Juliette is fortifying around herself at this very moment.

Five hours later, I'm at the penthouse, walking into the living room carefully and quietly. It's dark inside save for the light from the TV, which casts a white glow in the center of the room and reveals Juliette sitting on the couch as she watches a British baking competition that I've never seen before.

"Hi," I say, easing down into the world's comfiest armchair. She's so engrossed that she doesn't even turn to look at me. "Hey," she eventually answers. "How'd the rest of rehearsal go?"

"It was wonderful. We finished the run-through and tightened up a few scenes. It's really so good, Juliette."

"I'm sure it is," Juliette agrees, still not turning away from the TV, where ten contestants are all baking cakes that apparently represent a beloved childhood memory.

"By the way, did Roshni call you?" I ask. "She left a couple of hours early to take a field trip to Knightsbridge with the costume director, and I haven't heard from her yet. I was going to treat her to dinner tonight as a thank-you for walking Ollie this afternoon since our dog sitter is away for the weekend."

"She called a few minutes ago and said she'd be home soon. They just stopped for a bite to eat." Happy to hear that Roshni is having fun, I shimmy down deeper into the chair as Juliette goes on, "She also said she was in a rush this afternoon and wasn't able to walk Ollie after all, so Phillip offered to do it and kept him after. She then told me to tell you that Phillip mentioned something about you bringing a pair of slippers when you pick Ollie up? Does that make sense to you?"

"Yeah," I groan, "he's talking about his Robin slippers."

Juliette looks over at me for the briefest of seconds. "Kinky."

"It's not like that," I assure her.

"Hey, to each his own. What you do in your personal time is totally up to you."

The irony of that statement isn't lost on me, considering she definitely imposed guidelines on my personal time when she asked me to stay away from Liam. A guilty wave passes through me at the thought, and I turn to watch the TV to drown it out.

"Well, if you don't need me for anything else tonight, I should go pick up Ollie."

"You can stay for a few minutes. I already went down to check on him. I planned on bringing him back up here myself for some one-on-one time, but he was fast asleep. Phillip said they went on a rather long walk."

"That was very nice of you to check on him," I tell her.

"It was nothing. I didn't mention it to you before, but I've been working on potty training with Ollie for the past few days. He's doing really well with the wee pads, but we should figure out a more permanent walking schedule for him so he can stay consistent."

Her words prompt me to scan the apartment and I look over to realize that there's not only a wee pad in the kitchen, but there's one in the far corner by the windows as well. I don't know how I missed it.

"Thanks, Juliette. That's awesome."

"No worries. I just figured he could stay up here longer this way, and he would be more comfortable."

"I completely agree. Are you sure I shouldn't go get him, though?"

"Honestly, he looked content beyond compare resting on his mountain of pillows. But it's up to you, of course."

Mulling it over, I slip back further in the chair. "I guess I won't rush, then. Phillip could always bring him up if he needs me."

"Very true," Juliette replies.

Turning my attention back to the TV, I do my best to get caught up on the show. "How long have you been watching this?" I ask her.

"Since I got home. It's a marathon, and it's entirely soothing."

I can see what she's talking about, already falling for the show's charming allure as the polite contestants whisk and mix for our viewing pleasure, their melodic voices from their interviews immediately drawing me in.

Forty minutes later, we've barely moved. We have, however, become honorary judges on this baking show's panel of experts.

"How do you forget to grease the pan?" I ask, utterly crestfallen. "Damn it, Gertrude! I was rooting for you."

"It's looking bleak for our front-runners, kid." Juliette shoves a handful of popcorn into her mouth. "Graham's presentation was completely sub-par. You can't do sloppy fondant rosettes like that and expect to advance to the next round."

"Obviously. And I have to say, after years of careful consideration, I think I'm finally ready to admit that British baking shows really are more enjoyable than the ones that are filmed back home. At least here they give you normal ingredients and sufficient time."

"Oh, I agree," Juliette says. "American cooking shows make me spiral into a panic attack after watching for five minutes. They're like, 'Okay, you have to make this tiramisu, but if you use flour or eggs, you will be shot, and substitute lobster and raw fennel for all dairy products, and if you don't finish in three and half minutes, we'll gouge out the eyes of your oldest living family member. Good luck.'"

I giggle and reach over from the chair to grab a handful of popcorn from the bowl beside her. "I think I actually watched that episode last week."

Juliette ends up passing me the bowl. "Not to brag or anything, but I think I'd be really good on one of these competitions. Contrary to what you think of me, I do exceedingly well under pressure and with improvisation."

"You wish," I tell her, stuffing the popcorn into my mouth.

"I can already picture you cursing the judges out and crying in your exit interview."

"Winners don't cry, Winnie. And I would absolutely win."

I dust the crumbs off my hand with a mischievous gleam in my eyes. "Let's test that theory, shall we? Let's have our own little cooking show right now, and we'll see how well you do."

Juliette lifts an intrigued brow and pivots around on the couch to face me. "What kind of cooking show?"

"Let's make it toned-down but American, to keep things spicy. You're not nice enough to be on a British baking show. They would totally cast you as the villain."

"True." She reaches forward and enjoys another mouthful of popcorn, and I'm pretty sure her ego is inwardly calculating her odds of success. My boss doesn't like to fail.

"Unless you're too scared," I say, goading her.

And that's all it takes. Her go-to confidence is awakened and jolting her into sitting up, tall and proud. "Is that a challenge?" she asks.

"It sure is. Are you brave enough to accept it?"

Juliette only stares back at me, and I know I have my answer.

Five minutes later, her migraine is seemingly forgotten as she stands in the kitchen donning an apron with her hair pulled back in a low bun.

"Contestants," I state, moving around the counter to stand across from her. "Tonight, you will prepare an appetizer that you feel would be appropriately served at the elegant after-party of a Broadway theater debut. The following ingredients must be included in your recipe: chicken, arugula, and any form of cheese. You have thirty minutes to complete your dish. Begin."

I start the clock on my phone and prop it up against a stack of books, which I have strategically placed on the counter. Juliette springs into action, firing up the stove and oven and grabbing vegetable oil from the cabinet. She sprinkles it into a sauté pan and briskly washes and dries the chicken I've left on the counter before tossing it inside.

She's then off to the fridge, pulling out what looks to be cheddar cheese and a red onion. She leaves the cheese on the counter and then begins to chop up a quarter of said onion.

"It seems that chef Juliette is making some interesting choices this evening. Her predominant ingredients so far are cheddar cheese and raw onion, flagrantly disregarding her primary care physician's warnings about acid reflux."

Juliette shoots me the evil eye but keeps working, now looking through another food cabinet until she pulls out a small package of flatbread. Returning to the stove to check on the chicken, she opts to let it continue to cook and returns to her prep work.

A little time passes, and I once again check the clock. "Chef, there are now fifteen minutes remaining on your allotted time. This is also the part of our show where the contestant must reveal their most embarrassing moment in life."

"Are you serious?" Juliette demands, scowling up at me from her spot on the counter, where she is now lightly oiling the flatbread.

"Answer the question, chef, or five minutes will be taken off the clock."

Juliette grumbles and looks off into the distance until she glances back at me with a little smile. "Okay, when I was speaking at a conference once, I had a very bad cold and sneezed so hard that I'm pretty sure a chunk of my brain ended up on the podium mic. There was visible splatter, and I just had to stand there until someone brought me a tissue."

"Oh god," I mutter, wincing as I imagine it. "That's a tough one."

"The show must go on. Now leave me alone. I'm concentrating."

By the time the alarm on my phone eventually goes off, Juliette has just barely finished and steps away from the food with her hands up. I then pull the plate towards me, gazing down at her presented appetizer.

"Chef Juliette, in your own words, please explain what you have prepared."

Juliette takes a breath, looking exceedingly satisfied with her creation. "I have prepared my take on a chicken flatbread wrap, handmade with cheddar cheese, arugula, red onion, celery, and baked flatbread."

I turn the plate around in front of me, scrutinizing its appearance before lifting it up and taking a delicate bite. I sit in silence for a few moments until I level my eyes on Juliette. Thinking back to all the bizarre judge's remarks we've heard in our years of watching cooking shows, I channel my inner food critic and babble away with absolute authority.

"Chef Juliette, while I found your presentation to be rudimentary, I very much enjoyed the bold, captivating taste of the cheddar. The chicken was thoughtful. The arugula was flirty. The flatbread was both quiet and profound, giving off a distinct tree-falling-in-the-forest aroma. The textures danced the tango across my taste buds with every bite, and the celery felt reminiscent of an obscure poem I read in my hometown library in the seventh grade."

Juliette continues to look at me expectantly, and I then take a gargantuan bite. "Simple translation, you win. All hail the flatbread wraps." I give her two thumbs-up in case she can't understand me through my mouth full of food.

"Well, that's very dignified," she mutters, picking up one of the wraps herself and taking a bite.

"These really are highly tasty," I tell her. "If your writing didn't work out back in the day, you easily could have become a restauranteur."

Juliette shakes her head, finishing off her bite. "In a world of uncertainty, the theater was my only constant. I never could have done anything else."

"What was it like?" I ask her dreamily. "What was it like when you finally got to dive in completely?"

Juliette smiles softly. "It felt like, and I know there must be a more eloquent way to put it, but it felt like I was finally returned to my home planet after being abducted by aliens for most of my life."

I smile back at her, knowing exactly what she means.

"Coming over here and going to theater school, it was just everything. It shook the ground beneath my feet in the most freeing way that I never experienced before. I went from being surrounded by my father's friends and his world and going to high school where subjects I couldn't care less about were shoved down my throat, to doing and studying exactly what I was interested in. I was surrounded by like-minded individuals who I could talk to and who were ready and willing to receive and respond in a productive way. I went from living life at a distance to rolling around in my classmates' sweat as we played with avant-garde and traditional theater.

"I finally had a laboratory to try and fail, to experiment. I was taught to be brave, and every day I was given the opportunity to make creative choices that might not work or that might lead to magic. It was the biggest game changer of my life."

"I wish I could have been there with you," I tell her.

"You would have hated me. How you put up with me now is a mystery for the ages, but back then, I was even more self-centered. I was absolutely single-minded in my ambition."

"There's nothing wrong with being ambitious."

"True enough," she says, picking up another wrap. "And anyways, all that matters is that we're here now, and we're doing pretty well for ourselves."

"Exactly. Not many people are lucky enough to be hosting and/or participating in spontaneous cook-offs in their gorgeous penthouse."

"Precisely. And you know, we're very alike, you and me. Maybe someday you'll be standing in your own fancy apartment, passing the time with *your* favorite assistant."

I scoff and opt to pick up another wrap myself. "I doubt that will ever happen."

"Would that be the worst thing in the world?" Juliette asks. "Ending up like me?"

"Of course not. I would love to end up like you."

"Except for the lonely bit, right?"

"Are you lonely?" I ask hesitantly.

She looks at me, seeming uncharacteristically complacent. "Sometimes I'm so lonely, I think I might collapse from the weight of it." Her words hit with ruthless strength, and I so desperately want to find the perfect response to make her feel better.

Nothing comes, and Juliette reaches over to me, placing her hand on mine like she knows my intentions even if I can't voice them. She gives the tops of my fingers a comforting squeeze before pulling her hand back and going on.

"But in life, in this industry, you have to be willing to pay a certain price to seize the things you want. And a word of advice. You should start thinking about that concept long and hard right now. Because only you will know if it's worth it or not."

"Was it worth it for you?" I ask.

"I like to think so."

I slowly nod my head, deciding to ask another question. "Do you ever wish that you had kids?"

Juliette pauses, truly thinking about it before saying, "Not really. I always figured that if I ever wanted a baby, I would do it myself, but I also wanted to wait until I had a burning desire for it. Ultimately, that desire never came."

"I get that," I say, feeling very much on the same page. And her sudden openness emboldens me to press her even further. "Do you think you'd be less lonely if you reconnected with Isabelle?"

If I offended her with my question, she doesn't show it. She only fidgets with the corner of the plate before eventually speaking. "That's a complicated question. Honestly, I could have and would have ended up with a completely different life if she didn't do what she did."

"What did she do?" I ask quietly.

Juliette looks up at me, calm and collected as anything. "She betrayed me."

I suck in a quiet breath, not quite sure what to ask or offer after that, and Juliette shakes her head, rubbing her temples and clenching her eyes closed.

"Something about Isabelle always gets to me in a way that

nothing else does. Being here and being around her again, I can't shake the headaches. It's like my brain is being squeezed too tight." She opens her eyes and inhales deep, seeming to hope that the air filling her lungs will ease her troubled mind. "It was like this the last time when everything fell apart between us. It wrecked me so completely that I made myself physically sick over it." She takes another breath and leans down against the counter, once again rubbing the sides of her head.

I inch myself closer, desperate to help find the solution that she so clearly needs. "But if that's the case, then shouldn't you both try to fix things? If not for each other, then at least for yourselves? It doesn't have to be this way."

Her gaze rises to mine at that, and for a second, I think she's about to agree. Her eyes soften a bit, like she truly wants to tell me her story—like she's finally ready to be free of it. But then they refocus on the food, and she throws on a smile, much the same way she does when she's regaining her composure as a guest lecturer.

"Don't worry about me, kid. I made it this far on my own. No use rocking the boat now."

I'm all primed to try again, but Juliette takes the last wrap and promptly walks back into the living room. She returns to her spot on the couch and turns the TV back on, resuming the marathon I initially interrupted.

I follow her in, knowing that the moment is long gone as I stand dejectedly behind the couch. "I better go get Ollie," I eventually tell her.

"Sounds good," she says, adjusting the volume to a lower level. "Make sure to say hi to Phillip for me."

"I will."

She twists around with a coy smile. "And feel free to do other things to Phillip as well."

"Don't be gross," I say, my face scrunching up at the notion.

"On the contrary, I encourage you to be very gross."

Getting the gist, I turn on my heels and head for the door, picking up my bag from the side table on my way out. "Text me if you need me."

"Have fun," she sings after me.

A few minutes later, I'm outside Phillip's apartment and am lightly knocking on his door. He once again opens it with a welcoming smile, and I match it with a slightly less enthusiastic one of my own while holding up his Robin slippers.

"As promised," I say.

"Excellent. My toes have been absolutely frigid without them, on top of me feeling generally far less heroic."

"Well, you are now free to prowl the streets in search of crime or a pillow fight once again, because here they are. Thank you for lending them to me."

"It was my pleasure," he says, taking them from my offering hands. "And thank you for continuing to let me monopolize Ollie. His company is very much appreciated."

"I'm more than glad to share my bundle of joy, and I'm sorry if he was forced on you today."

"It was no trouble at all. I practically begged Roshni to let me walk him when I bumped into her in the hallway. I was looking for a reason to get some fresh air. Otherwise I would have stayed in all day doing sudoku."

"If you say so," I tell him, "but I'm sure you're just being nice."

"No, it was a completely selfish act, I assure you."

I give him a grateful smile as Ollie trots over to the door, greeting me with excited jumps and his perpetually perfect face.

"Hello, handsome," I coo, bending down to pet and scratch him. "How are you? Are you ready to go home?"

"If you're done working for the night, would you like to come in? I was just about to make a curry, and we could always pour out the prosecco again?"

I consider it for a second as I stand back up. "That's really generous of you, but I'm pretty tired, and I have a ton of work to do. Maybe another time."

"Of course," Phillip replies, lifting Ollie's leash down from the coatrack and passing it to me. "Whenever you're free, just let me know."

"I will, and thanks again."

"No problem. It was good to see you both, and if you change your mind about the slippers or the prosecco, I'm only a Bat Call away."

"I'll keep that in mind," I say lightly. "Have a good night."

"You, too."

He closes the door, and Ollie and I set off down the hallway, pausing at the elevator as we wait for it to arrive. I'm beyond tired, but I know I can't sleep tonight. I seriously need to tighten up *Death of a Prom King* before I send it in tomorrow. I'm looking forward to working on it while also dreading it when I feel a vibration in my bag. I fish out my phone and find a text from Liam.

Just wanted to say hello. Are you gearing up for your final writing session in the studio tonight?

I quickly type back,

I might be. Or I might be willing to work at your place if snacks are once again provided.

Blinking dots appear almost instantly.

I bought fresh supplies this afternoon—eco-friendly straws and a brand-new pint of ice cream. Shall I send you some pictures to prove it?

I smile as the elevator arrives and Ollie and I step inside.

I think you may have just invented an entirely new level of sexting. We'll be there in an hour.

17

Ollie and I make our way into the studio at eight in the morning and I inhale a sharp, startled breath and nearly splatter my coffee all over myself when I find Roshni lounging on my bed, reading a script. She looks like a goddess, but even goddesses can be scary when unannounced.

"Well, well, well, if it isn't Ms. Dirty-Stay-Out," she teases as she closes the script and sits up, swinging her legs down to dangle off the side of the bed. "Or am I mistaken, and are you and Ollie simply returning home from a refreshing morning walk?"

"Why, yes, it was a refreshing morning walk," I answer innocently. "It was highly, highly refreshing, actually."

"Yeah, I'll bet. Too bad my morning strolls don't help me emit that same healthy, thoroughly debauched afterglow."

"Your time will come," I tell her. "So, did you have a good time with Christine yesterday?"

"I had a ball. I had no idea so much work went into costume

design. It was super informative, and Christine is awesome." I make a face, and Roshni catches it. "Why are you scowling?"

"No reason," I say. "It's just that your talk about other friends significantly reduces my will to live."

"Nonsense. You'll always be my favorite."

"Same here." I sit down then in the tiny armchair, taking a sip of my coffee as Ollie snuggles up against Roshni's legs. "Do you know if Juliette is up yet? Did she say what she wants us to do today? I figured we could go to the pop-up location and look for any potential problem areas, or we could help the interns pass out flyers."

"As a matter of fact, we are doing none of that, because Juliette is giving us the day off again! Don't go off the deep end, but Christine offered to show me her favorite spots around the city. Want to come with?"

I practically choke on my coffee. "Another day off? There's nothing Juliette wants us to do? Like, nothing, nothing?"

"Nothing, nothing. She's going to spend the day writing, and you should do the same, no? Isn't your contest deadline, like, tonight?"

"Yes, it is, plus I have a call with the executive director at West End tonight, too, so this day off couldn't come at a better time."

"Fabulous," Roshni says. "And before I forget, I have some news regarding our Paul Davenport spy mission."

I inhale sharply at that, inching forward in my chair. "Do tell."

"Well, I called the university she and Paul went to and said I was Juliette's assistant and was trying to organize an alumni event. They wouldn't give me his address, but the woman I spoke to told me that she knows him because he's a benefactor to the school and is now an English professor at the University of Surrey. So, then I called the university and said I was a journalist for the *Central London Art Journal*, which I made up, and that I wanted to do a piece on him and the university. They mentioned he was teaching summer classes and lived semi-nearby. I casually guessed some random village like I already knew where he lived, and they corrected me and said they thought he lived in Abinger. I looked it up, and it's an hour and a half drive from London."

My jaw is hanging open, and my heart is pounding. "This is more than a lead, Roshni. You found him!"

"Not entirely. All I know is his village." I immediately type Abinger into my phone for directions as Roshni goes on. "Are you sure about tracking him down all the way, though? I know I'm on a need-to-know basis, but if it's bad enough that you don't want to tell me about it, it must be risky. And I'm aware that you're trying to go above and beyond since you'll probably be quitting soon, but even so, maybe you should rethink this."

"I'm just going to feel things out. If it ends up being a bust, Juliette will be none the wiser, and if things look positive, it could end up making her extremely happy."

"Wait, you're going to go looking for him right now?" Roshni asks, her voice suddenly troubled.

"I have to," I answer. "This could be my only shot."

"But what about the contest? You should spend the day working on your play. That's way more important than what-ever Nancy Drew cosplay you're about to get all wrapped up in."

I know she's right, and I get a sinking feeling when I think of all the hours I squandered while being here, especially last night. I was so distracted and rushing to spend time with Liam that I in no way finished what I needed to get done.

I should have tried harder. I should have worked longer. Then another debilitating, guilty feeling starts to spread when I think maybe I intentionally didn't finish my play on time. If I refuse to give my writing to the world, then they won't be able to tear me apart. Again.

To them, all they're doing is writing a clever tweet. A harmless, entertaining little jab. I'm aware people are fully entitled to their opinion and that art is subjective, but to me, it's years of my life shot down in an instant. Sleepless nights and days of effort with burning eyes and sore muscles as I sit and stare at a screen for hours on end. I push my mental and emotional health to the limit to write a play, only to find out that it's not enough. That I'm not enough.

If I stayed home and worked today, I could get it done. It's a miracle that I have the day off when I need it most. *Death of a Prom King* won't be exactly where I wanted it to be as far as a finished product, but it would be passable. But that also means giving up on my one chance to find Paul. I could always enter the contest next year, but an opportunity to do this for Juliette will never come again. It's Paul or the play. Juliette or me.

I think for several agonizing seconds until I make my decision, committing to my choice even if I'm not sure of it.

"I'm not going to submit my play," I tell Roshni. "It isn't ready, and there's no point in me entering if I know I won't win. Juliette's going to help me with edits and put me in touch with a producer when we get back to New York anyways, so me skipping the contest isn't the end of the world."

My friend looks back at me with saddened eyes. "But you've worked so hard to finish. Even if it's not perfect, you should submit, anyways. At least then you can say you tried."

At least I can say I tried. Roshni is the kind, logical angel on my shoulder, but she doesn't stand a chance against the bitter, scarred devil on the other. I can already feel self-hatred starting to settle in, my old friend that I can't cut ties with, but I push it aside into a dark, far-off place to deal with later. Like I do with all my problems.

"It's okay," I assure her. "I want to do this for Juliette."

"I don't see why. It's not like she's gone out of her way to help *you*."

That one stings, but I guess the truth hurts. I swallow it down and throw on a strained smile.

"She will, though. She promised me she would. Now, please don't worry about me, okay? Everything is going to be fine."

"I hope so," she answers, and I have to force myself to ignore the disappointed tenor in her voice. "So, if you're not going to work on your own project, I'll also assume that you're a no to the London hotspots, then?"

"I'm thinking so. It looks like I'll be heading to Abinger."

"And how are you going to get there?"

I shrug my shoulders, but a small grin eventually appears when I take a solid guess as to my mode of transport.

Liam arrives two hours later and rolls his window down as Ollie and I wait on the sidewalk.

"And how are we all doing this morning?" he asks.

"Feeling good and ready for a road trip. Any chance you have a light vintage scarf and sunglasses for Ollie to wear? This is his first substantial car ride, so I feel like he should probably look the part."

"You know, I was *this* close to bringing those exact items, but then decided against it. Rookie mistake on my part. I apologize."

"Apology accepted. Shall we hit the road?"

"We shall, indeed." He hops out of the car and opens the back seat door, and I see that he's lined the space with a blanket and a couple of pillows. His thoughtful nature doesn't just apply to me, but extends to Ollie as well, and it makes me appreciate him all the more.

Ollie's tail wags back and forth rapidly as he walks the length of the seat, sniffing everything. I close the door and move around to the passenger side, and Liam quickly sneaks past me to get there first. "Allow me," he says, gallantly opening the door.

"How very suave," I say. "And thank you for taking us today. Are you sure you aren't busy?"

"Too busy for an adventure with you lot? Never."

I flash him a smile and slide inside. He gingerly closes the door and walks around to get in the driver's seat. "Ready?" he asks.

"As ready as I'll ever be."

"Then off we go."

He fires up the engine and pulls away from the curb. Twenty minutes pass, and we're soon heading out of London and onto the A316. Traffic is light, and there's not a cloud in the sky. The radio is playing on a soft volume, and I tilt my face towards the sun that's beaming in through my window.

"So, you never told me," Liam says as we continue cruising. "What is this new project you're working on for Juliette that has us taking this trip?"

"Just research," I answer.

"What kind of research?"

How to phrase this? I guess I have to tell him the truth since he's about to be privy to all of today's events.

"I'm trying to find a former gentleman caller of hers," I end up replying.

"A former gentleman caller? Tell me, was this before or after she was launched into Regency high society in search of a husband?"

I turn away from the window to give him a sarcastic grin. "If you must know, I'm not quite sure how to refer to him, since this is a very delicate matter."

"In what way is it delicate?" he asks, looking at me briefly before turning back to focus on the road.

"It's delicate in the way that Juliette doesn't exactly know that we're doing this right now."

"She doesn't know that we're doing this? Then why are we even here? Shouldn't you be home, working on your play?"

"It's fine. I have everything covered."

"Really? Because that's hardly the view from my seat, if you pardon the pun." I roll my eyes and look out at the highway before us as he goes on. "You told me last night that today was your last chance to finish your play."

"I may have said that."

"So why are you now dead-set on some self-appointed assignment that my aunt knows nothing about? Did you submit the play this morning and we're now going on a celebratory joyride?"

"Don't worry about the contest," I answer, more defensively than I would like. "We're driving into Surrey because I tracked down Juliette's first love/once-fiancé, and I'm going to find out if he misses her as much as she misses him."

Then Liam nearly swerves off the road.

He immediately steadies us as he stares ahead with large, panicked eyes, only turning to send me a couple of quick, sharp looks.

"Are you out of your mind?" he exclaims. "My aunt is a social extrovert who is also an emotional introvert, and she is going to be furious if she finds out that you're doing this. Not to mention that you've tricked me into being an accomplice and the getaway driver. I'm turning back. This is a terrible, completely inappropriate bad idea."

His eyes then dart up to the side of the road, no doubt searching for the nearest exit.

"No, listen to me!" I tell him. "There's no way Juliette is ever going to know about this unless Paul feels the same way that I know she does."

"You know that for a fact? She flat-out told you that she misses this mysterious Paul?"

Now, this is where he may get upset.

"Not exactly, but I could tell."

"You could tell," he repeats disbelievingly. "She's going to kill you, Winnie. No, she's going to fire you, then kill you, and then kill me when she's done. Then my mother will have no choice but to demand satisfaction and challenge her to hand-to-hand combat to avenge me, in which case one or both of them will also die. You will have single-handedly wiped out my entire family in one deft swoop. Your grand romantic gesture is nothing more but a homicidal volcano waiting to erupt."

"Okay, simmer down, Hamlet on crack. No one is going to die, because we are going to be wildly discreet. The only thing onlookers will remember about us today is that the *Pink Panther* theme music drifted down from the ether every time you and I entered or exited a room."

Liam shakes his head, in no way convinced.

"I do not support this decision. I don't support it at all. I vehemently oppose the motion."

"Just listen to me," I try again. "I know Juliette better than I know myself. She has been content enough and successful, but there has also been a void in her life. I never knew what was supposed to be there, but now I know that it was Paul. So if there's even the slightest chance that I can in some way help her get the full life she deserves, I'm going to take it."

"And what about the contest? Was all that effort for nothing?"

I look at Liam and feel painfully speechless. "I guess I'm not ready to get rejected all over again," I force myself to admit. "I thought I could enter the contest, but I can't. I wish I was braver, but I'm not."

Liam slowly shakes his head. "I think by not entering, you're setting yourself up for an even bigger disappointment."

I avert my eyes, turning to face the window instead of facing the reality that he's holding up in front of my face. Still, regardless of the repercussions, I've made my choice, and I'm going to see things through.

"That may be the case, but it is what it is, and I'm not going to change my mind. And as far as today, if you now don't want to be part of it, I understand. You can drop Ollie and me off wherever. We'll take a cab the rest of the way."

Seconds tick by with neither of us saying anything, the gentle hum of the radio now sounding out of place, until Liam suddenly speaks.

"You can't honestly think that I'd just drop you off on the side of the road because we're having a disagreement. If this is what you want to do, then I'll go with it. We're in this together."

I turn to gaze at him, his words filling me with a sense of reassurance that I grip onto with every fiber of my being. He gives me a quick smile before focusing back on the road.

"But just know that if this ill-advised crusade goes awry, I'm going to be very upset when I get raked over the coals by my aunt and mother. I know I seem like a tough alpha male, but I promise you, I will both pout *and* sulk."

"I don't doubt it."

"I mean it. I will slam my bedroom door shut with a very heavy hand, and I will blast angsty music for ages."

"Which you are within your rights to do," I agree. "I did trick you into this, after all."

"I will also write a scathing journal entry that centers on you. I may not even talk to you for an entire day, and I will only forgive you once you present me with an apology mix CD that musically transmits how sorry you are and how much you miss me."

"Okay, has this happened to you before? Because all this is starting to sound like a detailed memory from your teen years that you're now projecting onto me."

"I am just trying to very clearly communicate the kind of emotional support I will require when this ship goes down, as it surely will."

"Well, let's just focus on the positives at the moment. We have a name, we have a town, and we have a place of business. I'm going to pretend to be interviewing Paul for an article on the university he works at until I can feel him out. If it doesn't seem promising, we bail."

"We bail," Liam reiterates. "We quickly and quietly bail."

"Absolutely. I'm not looking to kick down his front door and make a scene. That's not my style."

Liam scoffs. "No offense, but that sounds exactly like your style. You're the female millennial version of a gunslinging cowboy in one of those old westerns who travels alone because you're a loose cannon and all the other cowboys are afraid to befriend you."

"Um, was that supposed to be an insult? Because I'm taking it as a full-blown compliment."

"Take it as you will, desperado. Let's just make it back to London in one piece." He's gripping the wheel so tightly, you'd think he was on a roller coaster right before the big drop, and I have to say...it's completely adorable.

"You're very cute when you're being dramatic," I tell him. "Maybe you should have gone into theater, after all."

"The only place I'm going into after this is a military-grade oxygen chamber. I think I've experienced more stress in two and a half weeks with you than I have in the past ten years."

"Oh yeah? Does that make you wish we never met?"

Liam's face softens as he steals a peek over at me. "Quite the opposite," he says. "I wish I met you sooner."

My stomach flips despite myself, and I shake my head as I look away. I'm starting to like him way too much.

"You stress me out, too, buddy. I promise you."

"Good stress or bad stress?" he asks.

"All the stress."

Liam laughs softly at that, and after a while, we fall into a cozy silence. One hour and one puppy pit stop later, we arrive in Abinger. The village is so lovely and picturesque that if Hugh Grant doesn't stumble out of a bookshop and fall madly in love with me at first sight, I will genuinely be upset.

"Where should we start?" I ask Liam as he parks the car.

"Know that I'm saying this with the intention of being helpful and not just wanting to calm my frazzled nerves, but I think we should start at the pub."

"Good idea," I tell him.

We head down a decent stretch of road, walking up to a charming bar called The Hatch. It's Tudor-style perfection with overlapping gables and wood framing for days. All the windows have diamond-shaped panes, and the stone doorway contrasts beautifully with the white stucco facade. There are several picnic tables outside, which a handful of patrons are occupying, and a wooden door—one that wouldn't be out of place on a medieval castle—leads inside. Liam, Ollie and I stand a few feet away, pausing side by side.

I'm the first to speak, saying, "I guess I'll just go in, then, and put some feelers out."

"You want me to go with you?" Liam asks.

"No, I can do it alone. You stay out here with Ollie."

"Alright. Good luck, Winnie."

"Thank you." Taking a breath, I stride confidently into the pub, trying my best to take on the self-created role of Fiona, friendly journalist who has recently moved across the pond. As I step deeper into the space, my heart skips a beat. If I thought this place was beautiful on the outside, the inside is the manifestation of a Pinterest post entitled *Dreamy Pub Aesthetic*. I try very hard to exude the vibe of a local and not at all the enthusiasm of a tourist who desperately wants to pose for pictures in front of the fireplace, the vintage bookshelves and the thick hundred-year-old beams that are lined across the ceiling (which I obviously do). Instead, I only allow a small smile as I walk over to the bar and catch the attention of the bartender.

"What can I get you, love?" he asks.

"Hi. I'll have two ciders, and I'm wondering if you can help me with something. I'm looking for an English lit professor who lives around here. His name is Paul Davenport, and I'm trying to get in touch with him for an article I'm writing about the university."

The man pauses for a moment, astutely looking me over as I pray that my performance was convincing. A few seconds later, his shoulders relax as he reaches for two pint glasses.

"Well, Paul lives a ways down the road. Maybe fifth house on the left? He has the white fence and the big garden."

Did that just happen?

"Wow, that's amazing. Thank you so much," I all but sputter.

"Of course, you won't find him there now if you go looking."

"I won't?" I ask, feeling a quick stab of disappointment. I knew it couldn't be this easy. "Why not?"

The man slides me my ciders with an expert push.

"Because he's sitting just outside."

18

"Act normal," I tell Liam, stepping so close in front of him that we're only a foot apart. "I need you to act completely normal, because Paul is sitting right over there."

Liam's eyes bulge for a moment before he trains his features back to a relatively neutral expression. "Sitting where?"

"Behind my right shoulder, reading a book."

Liam instantly looks over my shoulder and keeps his gaze there for several seconds. "He seems very studious. He looks like the type that writes math equations on library windows with chalk. Is that what they're using when they do that in movies? Chalk? I never really thought about it before."

I grab his hand to get him to refocus on me. "I don't know. I was a theater major, Liam. I didn't exactly hang out with many genius mathematicians."

"Of course not." He gives another glance over my shoulder and then back at me. "So, what's your plan of attack? Are you going over?"

"Yes, I'm going over. I'm just taking a second to get my bearings. I don't want to blow it."

"Shall I go over first? He might be more trusting of me since I'm a fellow Englishman."

That gets my attention. Fearless as I like to think I am, I suddenly feel intensely apprehensive. "If that's what you want to do, then sure."

"Really? I honestly only asked because I thought you'd say no."

"No, I'm good with you going first."

"Right," he says, squaring his shoulders. "Okay, no problem. I'm taking Ollie over with me so I seem more relatable."

"A wonderful idea."

"Excellent. Here I go, then." Liam readjusts his grip on Ollie's leash and walks around me with a deep breath. I casually turn to look off to the side while clandestinely keeping an eye on him.

I watch as Liam boldly approaches the picnic table. I watch as he gestures hello. I watch as Paul looks up. And then I watch as Liam turns on his heels and walks away as if he's confused and is now looking for someone else. I'd be annoyed if I wasn't too busy silently laughing at how perfectly on-brand a move that was for him.

I can't believe I'm falling for such a weirdo.

That last thought sends a panicked jolt through me, strong enough that I walk directly over to Paul instead of standing still to think about what it means.

So that's how I end up in front of the picnic table, looking down as Paul slowly gazes up from his book. The sun is facing me, going into my eyes a bit, but I can still make out his gray/auburn hair as well as his deep brown eyes. He's wearing a light blue button-down shirt and khaki-colored slacks, looking every bit like the professor enjoying his downtime that he is. He's handsome but not overly so—handsome enough that if a movie was being made about his life, he could possibly play himself.

"Hi," I squeak out, inwardly hoping that he likes me.

"Hello," he answers. His voice is soothing and steady, and I immediately think he'd be a marvelous audiobook narrator, which is my latest addiction in consuming fiction. I just stand there then, grinning like an idiot as Paul goes on. "Can you I help you with something?"

"Yes. Sorry to bother you, but are you Paul Davenport?"

"I am. Have we met before?"

"We haven't, actually. My name is Fiona from the *Central London Art Journal*, and I was hoping to interview you for a piece I'm doing on the University of Surrey's literature department."

Paul closes his book lightly and sets it down on the picnic table. "Sorry, did you say the *Central London Art Journal*?"

"Yes."

"No."

No? I think back to the journal I think back to the journal Roshni invented, still believing it sounds legitimate enough. "What do you mean, no?"

"I mean there's no such thing as the *Central London Art Journal*."

He states his assertion so assuredly, my confident demeanor starts to reveal the slightest crack. "How can you be so sure?" I counter back.

"Because I read everything, and I've never read that."

"We're a new publication, and we're exclusively online."

"I see," he says thoughtfully. "And who is your editor-in-chief?"

"Sloane Spalding." It's an easy enough lie. I got off the tube

at Sloane Square yesterday, and Spalding is the last name I always opted for in my improv days.

"Sloane Spalding? Is this the same Sloane Spalding who ran
the *London Times* op-ed department in 1997?"

"That's the one," I answer, thinking I finally caught a break.

"No again. That was my cousin, Lucy."

I consider digging my hole even deeper with another fib,
but then think better of it. The small grin on Paul's face tells
me he appreciates my decision.

"So," he says, "are you ready to tell me what's really going
on here? If there's a hidden camera recording us for an internet clip, you should know that my left side is more compli-
mentary and yes, I am willing to sign a video consent waiver.
Though I have assisted my granddaughter in filming many a
TikTok video and she will probably feel extremely slighted if
I somehow end up going viral before her."

Oh god. A granddaughter. He's married.

"Wow," I reply, barely managing to disguise my building
panic. "I didn't anticipate you being so informed in the ways
of TikTok as you sit there reading Hemingway."

"As I said, my granddaughter has aspirations to become
internet famous, and my downstairs sunroom apparently has
impeccable lighting." I nod in understanding, and Paul goes
on. "Now, why don't you start by telling me who you really
are?" He gestures for me to join him at the table, and I nervously sit down.

Here goes nothing.

"Yes. My name is Winnie, and I'm the personal assistant
to Juliette Brassard."

Paul seems to stop breathing for a moment. "Juliette," he
says quietly, half questioningly, half to himself. He then starts
to look around, his eyes anxious but eager. "Is she here? Has
she moved back to the UK?"

"No, she's not and she hasn't," I quickly tell him. "We're only in town for another week for a pop-up production of *The Lights of Trafalgar*, and if I'm being completely candid, she doesn't know that I'm here seeing you right now either."

Paul's soft eyes shift back to mine. "I don't understand."

"I know, I'm not explaining things as well as I should. I just wanted to find you because the other day, Juliette was talking about her life in London when she was younger, and she talked about you so fondly. I thought maybe I would look for you and surprise her—that maybe she would like to see an old friend while she was here."

Paul looks a little disappointed as he takes in my words, but a kind smile soon appears on his face. "That was a very thoughtful idea on your part, but I'm not quite certain Juliette would want to see me."

"Would you like to see her?" I ask daringly.

He pauses for a moment. "I'd like that very much, but I would never want to show up out of the blue. I don't think Juliette would appreciate it, nor would I feel comfortable."

"I understand. Liam said something similar."

"Liam?"

I look around, now finding the aforementioned Liam standing a few feet off by a tree with Ollie, pretending not to watch us while also full-on watching us. "That's Juliette's nephew," I say as Paul follows my gaze. "He thought it was a mistake to even come here."

"That's Isabelle's son?" he asks surprised. "When I saw him a second ago, he told me he was looking for a man named Sven in regard to some antique car parts."

"Yeah, Liam can get a bit tense when it comes to greeting people. If you give it some time, it actually morphs into a very charming quality."

"I'll take your word on that."

I wave Liam over, and a few seconds later, he's joining us at the table, sitting beside me. "Turns out Sven was busy today," he says jokingly.

I place a comforting hand on his knee. "It was a convincing story."

"Thank you. I tried my best."

"I could tell."

Paul watches our interaction with a discerning eye. "Sorry, so are you two dating, then?"

"Um…" Liam and I look at each other for a moment until we both start to mumble. "You know, we've really only met recently," I explain. "We're just getting to know each other more than anything else."

Liam also chimes in with awkwardness mode fully engaged. "Exactly, so we're technically undefined at the moment. It's sort of a complicated situation. Lots of potential, poor timing."

Paul only smiles. "All love stories are complicated."

Liam and I both freeze at the mention of love stories, and this only seems to entertain Paul further. "Alright, the both of you relax. I'm only having a bit of fun. I think I'm at least due that much considering my quiet pint has now transformed into a somewhat memorable life event."

"Has it?" I ask, more intrigued than ever.

"To be honest, I never thought I'd have any link to Juliette again. Even if she's not here right now, just talking about her feels…pleasantly jarring."

"She does seem to have that effect on people." Paul nods, looking nostalgic, and I pick Ollie up from the grass to sit in my lap. "Will you tell us about her?"

"I wouldn't even know where to start," he says. "When we first met, Juliette hated me. Did she tell you that?"

I shake my head with a grin and instinctively lean in. Enemies-to-lovers? So much yes.

"We were going to some play opening with mutual friends, and somehow we ended up sitting next to each other. Part of the way through, I had an idea for a story, so I took out my notepad to jot it down. Juliette got so offended, seething at me that I was disrespecting the actors and everyone involved in the show by not paying attention. Mind you, we were in the last row, but she was adamant. I told her I could write and listen at the same time, feeling the emotion of the scene even if I wasn't completely focused on it. She was not impressed."

"What did she do?" I ask, already coming up with a string of possibilities in my head.

"She took my notebook and shoved it down her shirt. She then proceeded to tell me that if I tried to take it back, she would bite my hand off."

"And you fell in love?" I ask.

"Hardly," Paul answers. "I thought she was a stuck-up eccentric who was also extremely rude. She thought I was a know-it-all square who was better suited for the library than artistic society."

Liam and I both smile as Paul continues.

"We saw each other a few more times after that. Being in the same friend circle, you learn to be cordial, even if you don't exactly get on great. But eventually, cordiality gave way to being moderately friendly, which then shifted into a friendship, which then grew into attraction, which then led to…"

He doesn't finish his sentence, and neither Liam nor I tries to finish it for him. We all know the answer.

Love.

"We balanced each other out. I was reserved and quiet; she

was a wild child with zero filter and with even less care as to what people thought of her. She made me a more exciting person and set fire to my writing in a way I had never experienced. When I was with her, I was an elevated version of myself. I constantly felt like I was on such a high, but then, once and a while, I just felt so tired. She expected so much of herself, and I felt like I had to expect the same of myself to keep up. But she was worth it. It was a heavenly delirium. An addictive exhaustion. I would have run until I dropped, but then things changed so fast."

"What do you mean?" I ask.

Paul moves his book around a bit on the table. "I shouldn't even be discussing it."

"We already know most of it," Liam lies, so coolly that it shocks me. "Juliette told us everything."

Paul considers us both until he sighs. "Something happened between her and Isabelle. There was a shift. And then they had a falling-out—a big falling-out."

I inch even closer in my seat. "Over what?"

"Over the house."

"The house?" Liam echoes.

"Once Juliette and I got engaged, we planned on moving into her aunt Nicola's house, the one that was left to her and Isabelle. Juliette was the one who kept it up, and Isabelle was pretty established in London at that point. We figured we'd buy her out over time. Make monthly payments. But then Isabelle decided *she* wanted the house."

"Did she say why?" I ask.

"She just said she had a right to it, too. And she and Freddie were well set up at the time, at least compared to us. They both had well-paying jobs. They could afford it, while Juliette and I were just barely scraping by. The girls went back and

forth arguing over it. I thought they'd eventually figure
something out, but they didn't—or couldn't. In the end,
Isabelle threatened to sue Juliette if she didn't agree to give up
the house. And with neither of us being able to cover legal
fees, Juliette had to agree. Isabelle bought her out, and that
was the end of it."

I feel an uneasy twinge in my abdomen as our friendly adventure suddenly seems to be changing into something more
intense.

Liam looks confused and the smallest bit wounded. "But
mum never mentioned her living in Oxford full-time."

"She never did," Paul says. "To my knowledge, she only
kept the house as a holiday home for a year before she sold it."

Liam and I glance at each other before turning back to Paul.

"And how did Juliette handle that?" I ask.

"When she realized she truly had to give the place up, she
was very much defeated. I tried to pull her out of it. I said we
could use the money from Isabelle to buy a place of our own.
I'd give up writing and start teaching full-time. But something switched in her after that. She was so hurt and angry,
and it suddenly seemed like we had to decide on our future
all at once. Mammoth choices were made in the blink of an
eye with tempers flaring and hearts pounding. We made our
choices…and we didn't choose each other."

"Why not?" Liam questions, beating me to the punch.

"Juliette had lived in England for years at that point, and
always told me she wanted to stay permanently. That was the
plan, and that's what we built our ideas for the future around.
We assumed we'd get married and figure everything else out
as we went. But then, after everything with Isabelle, she said
she wanted to move back to the States. She said if we stayed

here, there'd be a lingering cloud hanging over us and that she couldn't give her playwriting a real chance unless we were in New York. I wasn't prepared for that. My parents were here, my friends were here, everything I knew was here, and I think I went into fight-or-flight mode."

"Meaning?" I ask.

"I dug in my heels. I told her I couldn't leave England. I couldn't picture us moving to a city where I didn't know anyone, and Manhattan was hardly an ideal place to start a family. And then that statement set off a whole new question of compatibility. Juliette said she might not even want children, and I knew that I did. All of this piled up in the course of one heated conversation, and just like that, our world together crumbled. We couldn't find a middle ground—she wouldn't stay, and I wouldn't go."

I pull Ollie a little closer to me in my lap. Paul twists his pint glass around that's been untouched since we arrived.

"I was glad when I heard of her success. I followed her career through the papers, and in some twisted way, I felt like I played a small part in it all. I let her go, and she achieved everything I knew she would."

"And what about you?" Liam asks.

"I went on to lead a good life. I fell in love with and married a wonderful woman and had two fantastic children. I've had a job teaching about books and writers for the past forty years. I achieved everything I wanted, too. My dreams were just smaller than hers."

"And your wife?" I hesitantly inquire.

"She died several years ago. I never told her about Juliette, but I still somehow think she knew. Women have a way of knowing all the things that matter."

"And you've lived in Abinger all this time?"

"I have. It's just the right amount of quiet, and, of course, if I ever left now, my granddaughter would be furious. As I told you..."

"You have the good sunroom," I fill in. "Yeah, you can't just give up top-shelf lighting when it falls into your lap. That's basically scorning a gift from the gods."

Paul laughs in his soft, rich tenor. Silence stretches for a few seconds until he speaks again. "After Juliette and I had it out, I wrote to her a week later. I was desperate to work things out and begged her to forgive me. I honestly thought we would move past it, but she had left London before my letter arrived." He pauses before saying, "I always wondered if things would have been different had she read it."

"She did get your letter," I offer without thinking. I immediately regret it as Paul's face falls. The moment nearly spins away from me as I think of Juliette next—how I had no right to tell him that. All the events of today suddenly feel like a massive betrayal, and I want to get up and run away as far and as fast as my legs will carry me. "I shouldn't have said anything," I mutter. "I'm so sorry about this. About all of it."

"No, I'm glad I know," Paul says quietly. "Well, there you have it."

"We should probably go, Liam. I think we've taken up enough of Mr. Davenport's time. I'm so sorry again that I barged in like this." I swiftly get up, nearly knocking over the cider I never drank, and Liam rushes to stand up, too.

"Wait," Paul says. He looks around and grabs a paper napkin from the center of the table, then picks up a pen that's set beside his book. He begins writing directly onto the napkin. Liam looks at me and I look at my feet, mentally being the judge and jury to every decision I've made the last few hours and finding myself guilty, guilty, guilty. A full minute passes until Paul clicks the pen closed and folds the napkin in half, holding it out. "Will you give this to Juliette for me?"

I know I should reach out and take it, but my arms somehow feel like they're weighted down beside me. "I don't know," I say.

"Please. It would mean so much to me if you would give it to her."

His face is solemn, but his eyes plead with mine. Scared and ashamed as I now am, I remind myself that this was my idea. There's no turning back now.

"Okay," I say, forcing myself to lift my arm and take the napkin. I then safely tuck it into the inside pocket of my bag.

"Thank you," Paul says. "And thank you for coming here."

"You're welcome," I offer weakly.

"I probably shouldn't have told you as much as I did. Juliette won't like it, but it was so nice talking about her again after so long. I haven't, you know. Not for a long time."

I'm not sure what else to say, so I quickly pivot and begin to head to the car. I only make it a step when Paul calls out again.

"Winnie?" I hear him ask. I reluctantly shift back around to face him. "Has she been happy? All these years...has she been happy?"

I try to think of what Juliette would want me to say. Would she want me to tell Paul that her life has been a dream? That she's completely satisfied and wants for nothing? Or would she want me to tell him the truth?

"She has been happy," I decide to say. "No one's life is perfect, but for the most part, I think she's been very happy."

Right answer or wrong, I don't stay to find out. I whip back around, and Ollie and I stride directly to the car. I can hear Liam rushing to catch up with us, but I still beat him to the door, desperate to leave this place and my suffocating guilt behind before it swallows me whole.

19

When Liam and I get back to the studio, we take Ollie for a walk, which seems to wear him out. I put down some food for him, and he all but inhales it before settling into his beloved pile of pillows by the window, his face once again turned towards the sun. Liam and I sit down across from each other at the inconceivably small kitchen table. Our ride home was quiet and contemplative, and so was our walk, both of us absorbing today's revelations.

I'm the first to speak, eventually looking up from the table's mahogany surface. "Did I just do something truly horrible?" I ask.

Liam's eyes are empathetic and gentle. "You were only trying to do the right thing. It was a risk, but it was bold, too."

"I shouldn't have put myself in the middle of that. Now I have to deliver this note to Juliette, and she'll probably despise me. I don't know what I was thinking by pulling this stunt. The London altitude has finally gotten to me."

"The topography in London is actually very flat compared to other big cities."

"That's not helpful."

"Right, sorry."

"I should have listened to you," I groan. "You described me to a T—I'm the impulsive cowboy in a bad western, and do you know what happens to those characters? They die. They lie bleeding in the street and deliver a pithy but profound line with their last breath, and then they die. The townspeople are sad for, like, two seconds until the primary characters move on and enjoy their happily-ever-after."

"Now, I have to take argument with that. You are, without doubt, the main cowboy who gets the girl in the end and becomes the unlikely sheriff. You never thought you were meant for a small town, but you find both acceptance and peace in your new life."

"You're just saying that to keep me from freaking out," I mutter, once again staring down at the table.

"I'm not. Yes, what you did today may give my aunt initial, temporary discomfort, but in the long run, I'm sure she'll appreciate it."

"Yeah, I'm the employee of the month, aren't I? Here I agreed to help Juliette with a project to reinvent her writing, and then I lied about it for nearly the entire time. I slept with her nephew, who she explicitly told me to stay away from, and then I dug into her painful, private past love life and resurrected the ghost of her long-lost love. But no, I'm sure she'll appreciate it."

Liam just looks at me for a few seconds before venturing to speak again. "I suppose there's nothing I can say right now that will make you feel better?"

"I'm sorry," I mumble. "I shouldn't take my frustration

out on you. You've been nothing but a good sport through everything. This is all my fault."

Liam's about to speak, but his cell phone cuts him off. He gestures *one second* to me and answers it, getting up from the table and walking away to face out the window.

"Hey, John," he says. "Yes, I know, I sent you an email. Today just didn't work for me. I had an emergency."

He continues to look out the window, and I inwardly wish he would turn around so I could read his face.

"Yes, I think next week would be much better. Tuesday… I'll call you to confirm." He pauses and rubs the back of his neck with his free hand. "I will," he goes on. "I will call you back. It's just that I've been increasingly busy with other endeavors as of late. Yes. Well, I'm at an appointment at the moment, so I'll reach out in the next week or two." Another pause. "Next week, then. Alright…take care, John. Cheers."

He hangs up, and after a few unusually long moments, he turns around to me. "Sorry about that. It was one of my old work associates."

"Sounds like he was eager to meet with you."

"I suppose he is. We were meant to catch up this afternoon, but obviously that didn't work out."

I think he's going to sit back down, but he doesn't. It makes me feel a little uneasy.

"Liam, you shouldn't have canceled because of me. I could have taken a train to Abinger."

"No, I was happy to take you. The meeting wasn't important."

"It sounded important to whoever you were talking to."

Liam starts to shift around on his heels, first looking at the door and then the kitchen cabinets, but not at me. "I've known John for years. He'll be fine with meeting next week instead."

"Do you not like your job?" I find myself asking. "Sometimes when you talk about it, you seem like you love it, but then other times, you seem so detached. Why is that?"

"Those are all extremely interesting questions. Questions I will happily answer at another point in time."

"If you don't like it, why not just give it up? You sold the company. They must be doing well enough on their own. Why not move on?"

"I don't know, Winnie," he says, finally giving me the eye contact I'm after. My gaze is determined and his shoulders slump ever so slightly as he speaks again. "Perhaps I'm not ready to move on. That company was the one thing I did right. It was my only success, and I sold it to the highest bidder when I should have stayed with my employees who trusted me and who depended on me. And even now, it's a year later, and rather than fulfilling my obligation to my buyers, I'm choosing to drag the process on and on. I must get some kind of sick enjoyment from constantly reminding myself that not only did I ruin my life personally, but I'm now ruining it professionally as well."

Silence fills the room after that, and Liam takes a defeated breath. "I didn't tell you the full extent of my contract when I agreed to the sale. I told you I signed on to work for them for a year, but what I didn't tell you was that I actually agreed to work in their Paris office. So not only would I be going back to work, but I'd be going back in a completely different country. They're being incredibly lenient by allowing me to delay for this long."

The news hits me like a bit of a wrecking ball, and I shake my head as I try to clear my thoughts.

"Oh, wow," I say, my voice lacking the enthusiasm I was

aiming for. "But that doesn't sound like the worst thing in the world. You should try to see it as a fresh start."

"Maybe I don't want a fresh start."

"And maybe that's exactly why you need it."

Liam looks away at that, and I can tell he's reverting back inside himself. I opt not to add anything else, not wanting to push him any more than I already have. He slowly moves through the apartment, pausing when he takes note of my suitcase and the travel dog carrier I bought for Ollie that's sitting on the floor.

"When did you pick that up?" he asks, gently nudging the carrier with the tip of his foot.

"Just yesterday. I was passing the pet supply store, and I figured I might as well buy it, since we'll be leaving soon enough."

Liam nods, continuing to drift through the apartment. "I sometimes forget that you're leaving at all. And then I don't quite know what to make of it when I do remember."

I offer him a smile to lighten the mood. It doesn't help, but I keep it up anyways. "It's probably like when the circus comes to town. You'll be sad when we go at first, but soon enough, you'll be grateful for the silence."

"But that's just it," Liam says. "I've been living in silence for so long that I couldn't stop myself from hoping for noise. And now that I have it..." He trails off, and I let him. "I don't know. I think I'm rambling at this point."

"Rambling can be nice," I tell him.

"I guess it can be. Do you ever ramble?"

"Not as much as I'd like."

"We'll have to work on that."

The room goes quiet, the moment fraught with tension,

and neither of us moves to ease it. We just take it in, letting it fill us up until Liam speaks again.

"Were you going to come over later? There's a great restaurant around the corner from me that we could go to, or, better yet, we could get takeaway and watch a movie."

"Are you inviting me to Netflix and chill?" I ask with a small smile.

"Do they have *Robin Hood* on Netflix?"

"I'm sure they do."

"Then yes, I would very much like to Netflix and chill."

I let out a quiet laugh and glance down at my feet. "I can't," I tell him. "It's been a long day. I think I'm just going to grab a salad from down the street and call it a night."

I see a quick flash of vulnerability in Liam's eyes before he instinctively blinks it away.

"Yes, that makes total sense. Today did err a bit on the tumultuous side, so a rousing historical drama might not be the best choice to help you unwind."

"Exactly," I agree gently. I decide not to mention the main reason I need to stay in is that my phone interview for West Lane is due to start in an hour. "Another time, though."

Liam's gaze moves to my suitcase, and Ollie's carrier on the floor. "Absolutely," he says. "Another time."

I'm not quite sure how to make the situation better, so I just throw on a strained, bright smile before he heads to the door and opens it. He turns around once he's in the hallway, and I wonder if I should kiss him or hug him or give him an awkward high five, which he claims to be so famous for.

"Thank you again for driving us today. If Juliette eventually asks how I got there, I swear I won't rat you out."

"That's very kind, though I wouldn't hesitate to go down in a blaze of glory with you."

My insides light up a bit at his declaration. He doesn't want me to go down in flames alone. He wants to stay by my side through Juliette's wrath. I force myself to push away just how much that means to me as I once again resume my token playful demeanor.

"That's because you're both a gentleman and a scholar."

"True, though I do think I've amply proven I'm not quite a *total* gentleman."

His innuendo hits me like a ton of suggestive bricks, but I know I have to resist. Today was heavy, and after everything, the rational part of me knows I should spend the night alone—no matter how vehemently every other part of me disagrees.

"I'm well aware," I say softly. "Will you text me tomorrow?"

"Of course." He leans in and kisses my cheek, and I have to physically stop myself from dragging him back into the apartment by the front of his shirt. "Until tomorrow." He turns then and walks away, disappearing into the stairwell and forgoing waiting for the elevator.

It's a smooth exit, and no matter how much I don't want to admit it, I immediately start to miss him.

It's one o'clock in the morning when I quietly but insistently knock on Liam's door. It takes less than a minute until it swings open, revealing a tired-looking redhead squinting at me as his eyes adjust to the light. He's wearing nothing but boxers, and me-oh-my, sleepy, bed-tussled Liam is an absolute jolt to my system.

"I'm sorry to wake you up, but I couldn't sleep, and I can't stay long." I walk past him and into the apartment, whirling around to face him in the darkness when he shuts the door behind me. "Ollie is out cold, but I still don't feel comfortable being here for more than two hours in case he wakes up. I know you probably think I'm a psycho for showing up here in the middle of the night after you asked me to come over and I said no, but I can't shake this restless feeling, and I keep thinking about you, and I don't know, I just had to see you."

Liam continues to look at me, now seeming more lucid and understanding of the situation.

"Also, this is me rambling," I then add for good measure. "In case it wasn't obvious."

He continues to stay quiet, and I start to think that I just made yet another massive mistake. I'm considering if I should walk or run to the door when Liam is suddenly closing the distance between us, locking me into the most calming hug that I was absolutely craving.

It appears that he needed my touch as much as I needed his, because it's a solid half minute before we loosen our holds and lean back to look at each other. I breathe in his scent as his comforting presence surrounds me, and I waste no time in rising up on my toes to kiss him. I weave my arms around his neck, and my hands brush up into his hair, so soft and perfect as I run my fingers through it. He deepens the kiss, which I'm all too eager to return as his hands slide down from the small of my back to cup my bottom. He squeezes firmly, and I moan into his mouth. Just kissing him made the cab ride worth it—would have made the trip over here worth it if I ran the whole way instead.

Knowing our time is limited, both tonight and in general, I step back to pull him with me towards the couch. I sit on the cushions, wondering how to best position myself, when Liam pushes me down by my shoulders and instantly covers my body with his. I'm all about it as I steal my arms around his back to drag him even more intimately against me. One of his knees wedges itself between my thighs as his other foot remains on the floor for leverage. I can't stop myself from rubbing against him, only just obtaining the friction I'm desperate to chase down.

One of his hands braces the frame of the couch while the other trails all over me, moving from my cheek, to my hip, and then upwards to bunch my shirt under my chin. He pulls the cup of my bra down, and my breast springs free to meet the open air as he rubs and pinches in the most sinfully perfect ways. My eyes flutter shut when I feel his warm mouth on me next, but I force them back open, gazing down to watch him with hooded eyes. My hips are still moving—they never stopped—still reaching and grasping for the release I know I could probably find, but don't allow myself. Waiting will be entirely worth it.

Luckily, I don't have to wait long. Liam unbuttons my jeans and helps me to ease them off, then stands and tosses them onto the chair a few feet away. I quickly sit up, unclasping my bra and pulling it off along with my shirt. I throw them over my shoulder as he tosses his boxers away and drops to his knees beside me on the couch. He edges me down to lie flat and kisses my stomach as his fingers hook into the sides of my panties. His clever tongue traces delicate patterns across my rib cage as he tugs them down, so slowly that it almost hurts. I squirm and squeeze my thighs together in an attempt to ease the ache. It makes it better. It makes it worse.

We're both completely naked now, and Liam is looking down at me like I'm something to be worshiped. Savored. He moves his mouth back to my stomach, and I can tell where he's heading next. Nice as that would be, it's not what I came here for, and I tell him so, gripping the back of his hair until he turns his head up to look at me.

"Not right now. I want you," I almost whine, shocking even myself.

Liam nods and starts to stand again, but I don't let him go. "I need to get something," he tells me.

"I brought one." I point to my pants on the chair. I do let him go then as he grabs my jeans and pulls out the foil packet with a smile.

"I guess it's safe to say you didn't come here for a friendly chat."

"No, I didn't. Why, do you want to chat?" I arch my back as he stands there gazing at me, the muscles in his shoulders tensing as I stretch my arms up onto the couch above my head.

"Perhaps later," he says. I flash him a coy smirk that he soon kisses away as he slides over me again. The kiss starts out sweet but turns heated as his hand slips down between us, finding me completely ready. He positions himself with my legs around him, sliding forward until we're finally locked together. Our chests brush with every smooth stroke, building the tension up and up inside of me, so high and taut that I dig my fingers into his back to the point that I might actually leave marks on him.

Liam's thrusts become less controlled, and his forehead lowers to mine as I feel him starting to shake.

"I don't want this to end," he soon groans. "We shouldn't let it end."

I swallow his achingly sweet words down, not answering, but kissing him so hungrily that I know he understands. I break around him seconds later, and my whimper gets lost in the side of his neck as he all but growls into the couch cushion beside me. I don't move as I float in the aftershocks, and Liam does the same, still trembling slightly and snaking his hand down until it finds mine.

A little time after, we both shift, making room for him next to me as I lie half on him, half on the cushions. I stay perched just like that on his chest, our fingers brushing against each other's as they rest on Liam's stomach. Eventually, we stop even those soft movements, and I tilt my head up. Liam appears spent, satisfied, and sad. My expression mirrors his.

"I have to go," I whisper, positive that we're already close to my predetermined time limit.

"I know," he answers quietly.

We stay looking at each other, both aware that we're not just talking about tonight. The realization hurts, but I accept it, reminding myself that we still have some time left, and that makes the pain a little easier to absorb.

"But don't go yet," he says. "Stay for a few more minutes, okay?"

I know we're only delaying the inevitable, but his arms are so warm, and his heart is still beating so fast. What's a few more stolen moments? We're not hurting anyone—only ourselves.

"Alright," I agree, nestling down even more comfortably into him. "Just for a few more minutes."

20

I walk into the penthouse with more energy than usual the following morning. I should be tired after my night with Liam, but with the pop-up being staged in twelve hours, adrenaline has me completely wired and awake. Ollie is with me. Juliette suggested it would be better for him to spend the day up there, since there's so much more room, and we'll be gone longer than usual. She's installed a dog nanny-cam so we can check on him while we're gone, and she even bought a little machine that distributes treats throughout the day. Looking around the living room now, I'm only just noticing that space has almost fully morphed into a puppy play place. What was once a flawless London pied-à-terre is now completely Ollie-centered, and it somehow makes the space even more inviting and warm.

"There they are," Juliette says, looking up from where she's sitting at the counter, eating her oatmeal and blueberries. "Nice and early and looking bright-eyed and bushy-tailed."

Ollie pulls at the leash to run to her, and I let it drop. It's becoming more obvious by the day that Juliette's fondness for him is very much mutual. She hops off her stool to unhook his leash and to give him an enthusiastic petting. I adjust my bag on my shoulder, and Paul's note feels as heavy as a ton of bricks.

"Happy opening day," I tell her, stepping forward as she sits back down at the counter.

"Oh, yes. I feel like a debutante all over again. Pray tell, where are my fan and my gloves?"

"Already packed in the carriage, my lady." I give her a curtsy, and she graces me with a sarcastic bat of her eyelashes.

"Okay," I say more austerely, getting down to business, "so let's talk about your schedule for today. We need to be at the venue at ten. Then you're doing an Instagram Live interview at one, and another at two. We'll be working on technical aspects throughout the day. The show starts at seven, so if we go anywhere, we have to be back at the venue no later than five. We can either bring dinner and eat there or stop somewhere very briefly along the way."

Juliette takes her last bite of oatmeal. "Yes to all of that, but I forgot to tell you, I saw Phillip yesterday. He came around looking for you, so I told him you would have dinner with him at four."

"What?" I ask, completely dumbfounded. "Juliette, there's no way. Today is going to be nonstop work, and there is zero possibility that I can randomly go out to an early-bird dinner date."

"You're not going out for dinner—he's cooking at his apartment."

"No. I'm sorry, but you have to cancel that."

"Well, I think that's very unfair of you. Here Phillip has selflessly watched Ollie on several occasions, and the one time he wants to cook you a lovely dinner, you blow him off." She picks up her bowl and spins away to place it in the sink.

"I'm not blowing him off," I tell her. "We just have a million things to do today. And what do you care if I see him or not?"

"Because he's a nice boy, Winnie. I used to be friends with his mother, and I don't want her son's heart to get trampled on."

"I'm not trampling his heart, Juliette. We hung out one time."

"One time is all it takes to forge a connection. Isn't that what you would tell me if the roles were reversed?"

"Good, let's reverse the roles. You go instead." I pull my phone out of my pocket, seeing a text from Roshni asking us where we are. My foot starts to tap, eager to finish off this conversation so we can get moving.

"Unfortunately, Phillip is a tad young for me. And I'm busy tonight. I'm meant to be reinventing my career and all that." I sigh, and she goes on. "You're going to have to swing back here to walk Ollie anyways, so do that, have a quick bite with Phillip, and then you're done."

"Fine," I begrudgingly agree. "But only because I don't want to waste any more time or energy arguing about it."

"Excellent decision." She smiles to herself, seeming self-satisfied in her usual way, and I groan and look at the door.

"Can we go now? Roshni's already asking when we're getting there."

"Right, yes. I just need a minute." She quickly glances around the kitchen a little aimlessly, almost looking for something to catch her attention.

"Did you need to do something?" I ask her.

"I don't know, I'm just..." She keeps looking around. "I just need a minute."

Before I can probe further, she places her hands down onto the marble countertop, dropping her head a bit and taking a deep breath.

"Juliette?" She doesn't glance up, and I instinctively soften my voice. "Are you nervous about tonight?"

She looks up at me then, pushing her hair back off her face as she takes another steadying breath. "Show me a playwright that doesn't get nervous, and I'll show you the future leader of the undead."

I smile back at her because it's funny and also because I know it's what she needs. She's using her humor to hold up a sign that says *look at me!* so I don't glance the other way and see the terrified artist cowering in the corner.

"What was it like the first time?" I ask her. "When *The Lights of Trafalgar* opened in New York?"

Her playful smile returns slightly and I'm relieved to see it.

"It was pure, unadulterated excitement paired with dry-heaving terror. Agony in the dark that gave way to the ecstasy of deafening applause. Playwrights can be so unassuming, sitting there in the audience. Hiding in plain sight. The people beside us have no idea that they hold our entire fate in their hands. That we live or die with their choice to clap or not." She drifts off again, maybe in a memory or maybe hoping for the future. Either way, she's quick to look back at me. "What am I telling you this for anyways? I'm sure you know the drill."

"Barely," I tell her. "The only sound at the end of my play opening was the stomp of feet as they stormed the exit."

"It couldn't have been as bad as all that."

"It really was. There was also the sound of people

whispering, 'What the hell was that?' That was a very prominent sound, actually."

Juliette's gaze turns sympathetic. "For every success you obtain, there will first be a thousand failures."

"It still sucks," I say petulantly.

"Welcome to my life for the past five years. I'd like to say that you get used to it, but I don't think anyone ever really grows accustomed to an ass-kicking of the spirit."

"Well, I can almost guarantee there will be no spiritual ass-kickings tonight, because the entire city of London is about to fall back in love with *The Lights of Trafalgar*. This staging is going to change everything, Juliette."

"I hope so. After being back here and working on this revival, I feel like I've changed. I was closed off to so many things, but now I see that I've been standing in my own way these past few years. I couldn't let the past go, and by holding on so tight, I was refusing to let myself move forward. From here on out, I'm going to do things differently. If I don't take risks, I'm catering to my fear, and I'm done doing that. I'm absolutely done."

"That's amazing to hear," I tell her. "I'm so happy for you."

"This is going to be good for the both of us," she says. "Together, there's nothing we can't do." My heart flutters at her words. Maybe she's finally seeing me as a fellow writer. As a peer. Maybe she'll even want to write something together. I'm about to suggest it when my phone rings, flashing my dad's name across the screen.

"I have to take this. You just relax for a bit, and I'll meet you downstairs in ten. Also, would you be able to leave out some food for Ollie?"

"I already have his water and food bowls set. The treat dispenser is also fully stocked and ready to go." I give her a thumbs-up and check on Ollie one more time. He's lounging on the couch with his favorite toy, looking happy as a clam and barely noticing me. I give him a quick kiss and hurry out of the apartment, accepting my dad's call along the way. "Hi, Dad," I say, closing the door behind me.

"Hey, Winnie. How's your trip going?"

"It's going great. The show's tonight so I'll be running around for most of the day. How are you? How's Cassie?" I swing open the stairwell door and start to make my way down.

"She's doing good. We're both good. I have some news." He pauses, and it makes my pace falter. "Someone put an offer in on the house yesterday, and I accepted."

I stop walking then, gripping the metal banister tight in my now clammy grip. "Wow," I answer. "That was fast, huh?"

"Yeah, well, they're a young family who have been looking in the neighborhood for quite some time, so they were anxious to move forward. It looks like we'll be closing in less than a month."

I can feel something inside me starting to break, but I make myself hold the crumbling pieces together. "That's really exciting stuff, Dad. Congratulations."

"Thank you," he says, sounding a little relieved. "Cassie and I were surprised at how fast everything happened, but I suppose it's a good thing that it won't be a long, drawn-out process. And now we can go ahead and start looking for our new place in Arizona."

I nod my head, wishing my dad could see me since the tightness in my throat is making talking difficult. "I'm really going to miss you."

"I'm going to miss you, too. But anytime you want to see me, you're more than welcome to visit. We're going to make sure we buy a place with a spacious spare bedroom. Cassie says we'll call it the Winnie Suite, and it will be ready for you anytime you want it." I don't know why, but the thought makes me tear up. "And I know we're moving to be closer to Cassie's family, but I want you to know that this is very hard on her, too. She really struggled with the idea of leaving you."

Leaving me.

He's leaving me. Cassie's leaving me. My mom left me. I'm just a leave-able kind of person, I guess. As quickly as it came, I try to force that last inclination out of my head, knowing it's only clawing its way in because I'm feeling weak and emotional. I have no space for that in my life, but it feels quite at home at the moment.

I end up sitting down on the stairs as I wipe away an errant tear. "Listen, Dad, I have to go, but I'll be home in a few days. I'll come over and see you guys right away."

"I'm looking forward to it. And you know..." He trails off, and I find myself holding my breath as he goes on, "I love you, Winnie. You do know that, don't you?"

"I know, Dad," I say a little brokenly. I didn't realize just how badly I needed to hear that. "I love you, too. I'll see you soon."

"See you soon."

He hangs up, and I continue to sit there, lost and confused. I'm considering stopping in the studio to throw some cold water in my face when a stream of dings sounds from my phone. Realizing they're from my grad school group chat, I open the text conversation that's now in full swing.

Professor Jack, I just saw the job listing for your theater company on theaterconnect.com. As someone who considers themselves to be a son-like figure to you, I'm very curious on your stance on nepotism. Personally, I support it wholeheartedly.

Another text:

I would like to point out that I am both artistic and very direct—thus I would make an exemplary artistic director. Please consider this my resume cover letter.

And yet another:

Now, we all know that I'm not the kind of person who would fight or compete with my friends over a job, so I just want to let everyone in this chat to know, straight up, we are no longer friends, and this position is mine. Sorry not sorry. Also, Megan, happy birthday.

Well, it looks like the job is posted.

I feel slightly panicked as I mentally go over my interview with Suzanne, suddenly doubting just how well our phone call went last night. I'm just at the point of spiraling when I then get a private message from Professor Jack.

Hey, Winnie. I'm sure you can tell from the barrage of activity in the group chat that we posted the job position today. But not to worry, because I'm thrilled to report that Suzanne absolutely loved you, and the job is as good as yours pending your in-person interview once you get back to New York! I truly do believe that this is going to be the perfect fit, and I couldn't be more excited to see all the value that I know you will bring to the team. Let me know once you're back in the city and we'll get your final interview lined up. More to come soon!

And just like that, happiness floods my system. For the first time in a very long time, I feel genuinely proud of myself. There is a definite chance that I am going to be an artistic director. Victory still seems like such a foreign concept to me, but now it's within reach. All that's left to do is to complete the in-person interview and accept the offer. And then, of course, I'll have to tell Juliette. That brings me plummeting back to earth quickly enough, wondering how she'll respond when I give her the news.

I don't dwell on the thought, though, as I quickly realize that Juliette is most likely waiting for me at this very moment. I spring up and rush down the stairs, hitting the lobby running just as she steps out of the elevator.

"Ready?" she asks, taking in my somewhat heavy breathing and frazzled state.

"Born ready," I answer.

When we arrive at Regent's Park, it's typical opening day chaos. Our low-to-the-ground stage is constructed in the center of the grass, and lighting is still being installed on trusses above and off to the sides. Seats line the grass, but not too many, as they want plenty of room for people to stop and stand, even if just for a while, if not for the entire performance.

Juliette walks off to talk to the stage manager, and I'm heading for the costume area to join Christine and Roshni, who are organizing in the makeshift dressing tent, when Ellie pops up in front of me.

"Good morning, Winnie. Might I have a word?"

"Ellie!" I say, pleasantly surprised. "Good morning. How are you feeling?"

"Feeling wonderful. Always love the day a show opens. Why? Do I look abominable?"

I look her over, and she seems much the same as she does every day, except she now has some bags under her eyes, but with her glasses and perpetual cheerfulness, it's hard to notice.

"You look great. Confident and fully prepared."

That elicits a short laugh from our director. "Confident, yes. Fully prepared, never. No one's ever fully prepared for these things. All you can do is jump out of the plane and pray that the chute opens."

"That is a highly accurate metaphor."

"Thank you. Anyways, I wanted to talk to you because I read your play last night. *Death of a Prom King*. Love the title."

Nervous knots instantly take root in my entire body. "You did? But I only emailed it to you a few days ago."

"I know, but I couldn't sleep last night, and I needed a distraction. If I wasn't going to scamper off to dreamland, I figured the next best place for me to be was at an American prom. So, here are my thoughts—I feel like you're forcing things a bit."

Her blunt feedback is jarring, and all I can do is nod with wide eyes.

"It felt, at times, like you were steering the ship with a heavy hand, and I just wanted you to relinquish control so the winds could take us where they would. You need to let your characters speak for themselves. You cannot do it for them. And sometimes you won't agree with the choices they make, but it's my belief that it's in those moments that the most interesting concepts come into play."

Her words sink in as best they can, given her somewhat manic pace.

"I also felt like, while your characters were very multidimensional, they were also kept at a distance. Theater isn't dropping bombs from some safe, secure war room—it's brutal, in-your-face combat. Playwrights, and all theater professionals by extension, are dying breeds. If we don't seize our audiences and shake them awake by making them feel something, they're going to let us go extinct, no matter how long or how hard we keep up the fight."

Everything she's saying is spot-on, but as much as I want to do exactly what she's advising, I also don't know how.

"It's just, when I think like that...when I try to make myself move the audience, it always ends up feeling intentional, and I know it's meant to be effortless."

"I get that," Ellie says. "And so, my advice for you with this play is to just sit inside your character's heads for a while. Breathe as they breathe, think as they think, and genuinely crave their deepest desires. Tunnel down into their secrets until you hit their core. You need to fully understand where each of them is in their lives and where they want to end up, and if you do that, everything will be revealed to you and the audience just when it should."

I continue to nod, so thankful for the feedback, as I try to burn her words into my memory. All I can do now is hope that they sink in, which, judging from my erratic heartbeat and dry mouth, is hopefully happening at this very moment.

"But listen to me," Ellie says, stepping closer with an intense, serious expression. "I do not want you to be discouraged. I'm being candid with you because what you have here is a play that is good just as it is, but it has the potential to be great. Now you must hunt that greatness down with a rabid perseverance. You cannot allow fear into the world you're creating. You have to live with knowing that sometimes you are going to fail, and it's through that failure that you learn what works and what doesn't. Failure is a whetstone. It sharpens blades and it sets you free. I know that it's scary, but when it comes to your work, you have to dive in, because if you don't, you *will* be left behind."

"But I..."

"I'm sorry if my tone is a touch dramatic, but I'm not going to patronize you by handling you with kid gloves. You are a writer, and you wouldn't be in this field if you couldn't take a hit and get back up, over and over again, until your eyes are swollen shut. I'm telling you right now, if you push this play to its limits like I believe you can, *Death of a Prom King* will absolutely get produced and you will, in fact, realize that you are a truly talented writer, and have been for a very long time."

I stand there in silence, too stunned to move. I don't know if I'm about to start bawling or if I'm going to give Eloise a borderline aggressive hug.

"So those are my thoughts," she goes on lightly. "A very enjoyable read and one that I'm looking forward to reading again in the future."

I do hug her then, just as aggressively as I assumed I would. "Thank you so much. I can't even tell you how much I appreciate you critiquing my work or how awesome you are."

"No worries at all," she says, patting my back. "And fair warning, if you're counting on me to disengage first, think again. I'm very much on the verge of a nervous breakdown, and your ferocious bear hug is surprisingly soothing."

"Glad I could help," I say with a smile as we disengage at the same time. "Now, where should I report to first?"

"Check in with Mary and see if the soundboard is still acting up, and then check on the interns and ask if they need more flyers."

"Will do. And don't forget to breathe."

"Already forgot," she says happily. "See you later!"

I give her a salute and head off in the opposite direction, feeling alive and inspired and on fire for the first time in a long time. Yes, I was a coward by not submitting my play to the contest, but now I can apply Ellie's insights and try again next year, if need be, when my work is even stronger. I'm vibrating with the new hope that everything is going to work. My play is going to work. My new job is going to work. My life is going to work. I'm right where I should be—I'm surrounded by my people—and this is where I belong.

21

When four o'clock rolls around, my brain is fried and my heart's in a flurry and I wouldn't have it any other way. I'm counting down the minutes until our actors take the stage (approximately one hundred and seventy-eight minutes, give or take), which is why I need to fly through this dinner as quickly as possible. I even knock on Phillip's door more rapidly than normal in the hopes that it will save me some time. Ollie seems to be feeding off my energy and is noticeably jumpier than usual as we stand in the hall.

Phillip opens the door with rosy cheeks and with an apron on. He's smiling, as always, and I flash a smile back at him, reminding myself that he's trying to do something nice, even if it's ill-timed.

"You made it," he says happily.

"We made it," I echo. "Fair warning, I can't stay long. Tonight is opening night at the pop-up, so I'll have to eat and run. I hope you don't mind."

"Not at all. I figured that was the case. I can't wait to see it."

"Oh yeah? You're coming tonight?"

"I wouldn't miss it."

I smile then in earnest. Phillip really has been nothing but kind since the very beginning. I'm glad to have met him, and I'm sure Juliette will be happy about our friendship despite her hopes for a romance.

"That's great," I tell him. "I'm excited to hear what you think."

"I promise to give my honest opinion. And when I say honest, I mean I already wrote up my five-star review that I am going to post on every social media site in existence the second the curtain closes."

"I'm sure Juliette will love that," I say assuredly.

"I aim to please. So, come on in, dinner's almost ready." I step through the doorway and immediately take in the smell of garlic and tomato sauce. My face grows warm as the heat from the kitchen immediately hits me. "I'm making spaghetti," he goes on to say. "I hope you like it. It was either that or a highly questionable salmon dish, and I'd never forgive myself if I sent you off to your opening with food poisoning."

"Spaghetti is great," I assure him. "It's actually my favorite."

"It's my favorite as well." He gives me a wink, and I clasp my hands together in front of me as I move briskly into the kitchen.

"Can I help with anything?" I ask.

"You can finish off the salad if you like." He nudges his chin to the counter, where all the ingredients are laid out.

"I'm on it. I'm one of those people who are very ambitious when it comes to salads. Every time I go grocery shopping, I buy a ton of greens, thinking how I'm going to be super healthy and start a new chapter in my life. I promise myself I'll start meditating and go to bed earlier, but then, five days later, my untouched lettuce has turned into seaweed and silently judges me when I toss it in the garbage."

Phillip looks at me in a way that's both entertained and a little bewildered. "Does that mean you don't want the salad?"

"No, I definitely do." I promptly pick up a washed tomato and start cutting it on the butcher board. "The salad I'm about to make is going to be shockingly crisp and good. I may not have earned any Michelin stars back in the States, but over here, I feel like I'm right on the cusp."

"Oh, me as well. I mean, I can't fully guarantee that this specific serving of pasta will spark interest from an investor, but I'd also be shocked if it didn't."

"I agree with that wholeheartedly, and I wish you every success as you go on to conquer the London restaurant scene. Once you're famous, I can say I knew you way back when."

"Absolutely," he agrees jokingly, "this meal is sure to be a major highlight in your life. Though don't be offended if I don't remember it so well in the future. I'll most likely be far too consumed with all my money and fame."

"Totally understandable. If I was in your shoes, I'd forget I ever existed."

"Oh, I don't know about that. You're a pretty memorable woman, Winnie."

"You're not too bad yourself, my friend." Chopping up my last slice of tomato, I lift the cutting board and slide all the tiny pieces into the bowl of greens with the edge of the knife. "Look at that. That's farm-to-table majesty if I've ever seen it."

"I am both awed and inspired by your confidence."

I chuckle and place everything back down on the counter. "Okay, with that done, I'm going to take Ollie for a quick walk. I'll be back in ten minutes, okay?"

Phillip continues to focus on the sauce. "Excellent. I'll use this ten-minute window as an opportunity to add all my secret ingredients. Not that I don't trust you completely, but some things are sacred. Specifically fresh basil and garlic."

"Can't argue with that," I answer easily, crossing the room. "Be right back." I make quick work of securing Ollie's leash and stepping out of the apartment. After a speedy elevator ride, we're hitting the pavement, and I take a cleansing breath, happy in the knowledge that I will be on my way back to the pop-up within the hour. Bearing that in mind, we set off for a determined lap around the block.

We're just returning to the building ten minutes later when I look straight ahead and stop dead in my tracks.

Oh man.

"Hello," Liam says, approaching me with a grin and stepping away from the entrance of the building.

"Hey," I answer as he reaches me. I lean in and kiss his cheek without the slightest thought of tormenting him with a horror-inducing hello. "What are you doing here?"

"I swung by the park to wish my aunt good luck and discreetly asked her where you were. She said you were grabbing dinner and taking Ollie for a walk, so I figured I'd come by and wish you good luck as well."

"Oh, well, that's…"

Before I can get another word out, he steps even closer and wraps an arm around my waist, pulling me forward for a soft kiss. I close my eyes and lean in, inhaling deep and letting his presence wash over me. He pulls back just enough to whisper "good luck" into my ear, and a lazy smile crosses my face as my eyes drift open.

"Thank you," I answer dreamily.

Liam loosens his hold a bit but keeps his arm around me. "Are you nervous about tonight?"

"Insanely nervous."

"Are you feeling ill?"

"Violently so."

"And are you loving it?"

"Completely."

He smiles and tugs me a notch closer, and I can't believe how much I adore it. Maybe I'll need to invest in a weighted blanket when I get back to New York.

Unfortunately, my human weighted blanket then lets me go, stepping back and leaning down to pet Ollie. "And how are you tonight, young sir? Are you giving your mother plenty of emotional support?"

"Of course he is. And don't pretend like you came over to see me when you're clearly only using me to get to my dog. I know a puppy gold digger when I see one."

"Well," Liam says, standing fully upright once again, "while I do enjoy Ollie's company more than a majority of humans, you may be the one particular human who has him beat."

"Such sweet, honeyed lies. Look at that face," I say, gazing down towards Ollie myself. "Whenever he makes eye contact with me, the chorus for 'I Will Always Love You' starts randomly playing every time."

"In your head or in the physical room?"

"Both, I think."

"Right," Liam answers with a little laugh. "Well, true as that may be, it doesn't change the fact that I like you way more than I probably should."

I take a shallow breath at his words. They're scary, but they feel so good.

"You're only saying that because I'm leaving in a few days. If I lived here, you'd be coming up with a mile-long list of ways to get rid of me."

"I think that's what you want to be true," he says, once again pulling me closer. "But it's not."

I place a hand on his chest, pushing him away a foot and stepping back a couple myself. I think distance is going to be key in this conversation.

"Know what it is?" I hear myself say. "It's that we have this whole secret affair thing going on. If we were allowed to date in the light of day, you'd be over me in a week. Steamy looks and sneakily holding hands are all well and good, but things get significantly less sexy when we're participating in a fully permitted and encouraged relationship and I'm asking you to unclog my shower drain because, well, you know." I point to my hair and give it a shake. "This doesn't go down without a fight."

"Not to downplay your shower plumbing issues, which I don't doubt exist, but what would you think if I said I wanted us to give this a real shot in some capacity?"

No. No. No.

Yes. Yes. Yes.

"I would say you're crazy."

"I might be," he replies. "And I know you're going back to New York and I'm going to Paris, but I still believe we have something worth exploring here. Don't you?"

"I…"

My words trail off. I don't know what's right. I know what I *should* say, but it doesn't at all match up with what I *want* to say. I'm about to tell him just that when I hear the building door open and close behind me. I turn around just as Phillip strolls out, stepping forward and arriving at my side.

"Hey there," he says to me, wrapping an arm around my shoulder. "I was just peeking out to see if you were back yet.

The dinner's ready." He then turns his smile over to Liam. "Hello."

Liam stares blankly back. "Hello," he answers uncertainly. His eyes shift from me to the man standing beside me. "Sorry, who are you?"

"This is my friend, Phillip," I blurt out. I then casually slide Phillip's arm off my shoulder as I twist to face him. "Can you actually give me a minute? I'll be right up."

"Sure." Then to Liam, "Nice to meet you."

"A thrill," Liam answers, his voice entirely flat.

Phillip goes back inside, and I'm left with a very stern and crestfallen Liam. I'd be lying if I said I didn't feel sick.

"You'll be right up?" he asks accusingly.

"Stop. Don't say it like that."

"Don't say it like what?"

"Like you think something's going on with me and Phillip, because there's not."

"Oh, obviously not," he scoffs. "He's just waiting for you to pop back upstairs for your romantic dinner. That's what he's doing, isn't he?"

"He is, but I didn't plan it. Juliette told him I would come over, and I only went through with it so she would get off my back."

Liam lets out a humorless laugh, looking down the street before turning back to me. "Of course, because I forgot, you always do everything Juliette tells you like a good little girl, right?"

"Hey!" I answer back defensively. "Don't get nasty just because you've decided to jump to conclusions. I told you, Phillip is a friend, and I'm sorry I didn't mention him, but it didn't seem relevant whenever we were hanging out. I see now that maybe I should have."

"Hanging out? Is that really what we've been doing?"

I don't answer and Liam shakes his head. "This is ridiculous. Sorry to have interrupted your dinner." He turns and walks away, and I stay frozen in place. He makes it several feet before he stops and walks back, the tips of his ears visibly red. "That's it, then? You're just going to let me leave?"

"I don't… What else was I supposed to do?"

"How about ask me to stay? Try to make things right between us instead of being fine with me leaving you with no intention of coming back?"

Leaving. Leaving me. No intention of coming back. The words strike a dark chord inside of me and I feel my whole body tighten. Liam seems to notice, his stance instantly faltering.

"I'm sorry," he says. "But just answer me this. Have you been seeing this guy the entire time you've been here?"

I don't want to lie, but I also know the truth is deceiving. Ultimately, I end up saying, "I hung out with him one time, but not in the way you think. I told you, we're just friends."

"Then why did he have his arm around you?" he demands.

"How should I know?" I fire back. "Maybe he thought I looked cold or something? What does it matter? All that should matter is what I'm telling you, and I'm telling you, I don't like him like that. Nothing happened between us nor is anything going to happen."

Liam nods, looking down at the ground before gazing back at me, and I can tell he's emotionally checked out. Closed off. His ears even return to their normal shade—that's how detached he is. "I'm going to go. It was stupid of me to come here." He turns on his heel, and this time, I do try to stop him.

"Liam, come on! I know I could have handled this better, but you're blowing things way out of proportion."

"Good luck with the play," he calls over his shoulder, barely slowing as he disappears down the street. I think about going after him but decide against it. He needs to cool off, and whatever I'm saying clearly isn't working.

Ollie pulls at the leash, wanting to follow after him, but I hold him steady. I squat down and scratch his coat, trying and failing to process what just happened. My throat feels painfully dry as we walk inside the building two minutes later.

Soon we're back in Phillip's apartment. My mind is still in a daze. Phillip's saying something about being ahead of schedule, and Ollie is fussy, and I shake my head as I try to clear my thoughts.

"I'm sorry, Phillip, what did you say?"

He looks back at me with an obliging smile. "I said, what luck that the dinner is ready early. Now we can get you back to work sooner than we thought. And maybe after the show tonight, we could go out for drinks to celebrate?"

I'm about to answer with a polite no when a shrill beeping suddenly shrieks through the apartment from near the stove, no doubt the timer for the sauce. Ollie starts barking at an earsplitting pitch and instantly begins to run around the apartment.

"Ollie! Ollie, relax," I call to him, following his path into the living room. Phillip sets the plates that he's holding onto the counter with a clatter, adding to the mayhem as he struggles to stop the timer.

"I'm sorry, this thing is always a pain to shut off, which is typically why I never use it."

I don't respond as I continue to try to soothe Ollie, who has now barricaded himself in the magazine shelf beneath Phillip's coffee table. I'm eventually able to get hold of his collar, and I gently pull him out, inadvertently spreading a mess of papers and books onto the floor in front of us. Phillip gets the timer off a few moments later, and Ollie scampers away, seeking solace on the couch and its pillows in the aftermath.

"I'm so sorry about this," I say, wiping the hair out of my face and beginning to gather up the mess. Phillip finds me on the floor and then quickly hurries over from across the room to make a grab for the papers.

"No, it's fine, I'll get those!"

"Don't worry, I'm almost done." And I am. I have everything in near perfect order when one of the papers catches my eye. I slowly pull it out of the stack and am surprised to see that it's a headshot.

Phillip's headshot.

Confused, I flip it over and see his full résumé, complete with acting and modeling credentials as recent as last month.

"What is this?" I ask as Phillip stands up beside me. I push to my feet and face him head-on, holding up the paper.

"Bugger," he says quietly.

"I don't get it." I look at the headshot again, still trying to make sense of it. "I thought you said you were a math teacher?"

"Yes, I did say that." I glare at him, and he seems to physically shrink under my gaze. There's no way he's six foot two, as his clearly exaggerated résumé claims. "I guess that was the character I was assuming at the time," he then goes on. "The friendly teacher in the building."

"I don't... What are you even talking about?"

"Please don't be mad," he then sputters nervously. "I really do think you're a lovely person, so just bear that in mind when I say what I'm about to say."

"What the hell is going on, Phillip? I don't know if you're getting ready to kill me or what."

"What? No, of course, I'm not! It's just, Juliette...she asked me to spend time with you so I could distract you a bit from her nephew."

It feels like the world falls out from under me. The room is spinning at a stomach-churning pace, and I don't know which way is up.

"Are you kidding me?" I ask, completely aghast.

"She said something about a project you two had going on that wasn't working, and then told me about Liam, who I'm guessing I just met. She said she wanted me to divert your attention away from him, promised me a part in her next play if I could do it." Phillip starts to move towards me then, but quickly reverses when it becomes obvious that I very well might cheetah-claw his face.

"Wait a second...so you're saying that Juliette told you to spend time with me? All of our interactions...they were fake?"

"They weren't entirely fake," he offers weakly. "And I genuinely do like spending time with you. Under different circumstances, I bet we would be great friends. We still can be, if you want to."

"Yeah, I'm going to say a strong no to that, considering I have no freaking idea who you are!"

"I promise, I'm your very apologetic, very desperate acquaintance who made a bad decision but is actually a very good person. I truly am so sorry, but I haven't booked a job in ages, and Juliette's offer was too good to pass up. I swear I'm not some maniac or anything. Juliette's been close with my mom for ages, and I've known her since I was a kid. She only told me a few things about you. Just your basic likes and dislikes."

"Just my basic likes and dislikes?" I ask. He shrugs dejectedly and I shake my head for what feels like the millionth time as I start to fully grasp what it is that I'm hearing. "So everything we had in common...the prosecco and how you wanted a dog and love cooking shows...those were all lies?"

Phillip looks even more ashamed, his eyes shifting to the floor before lifting back up to mine. "I thought having shared interests would help our connection to materialize quicker."

For a second, I think I might actually black out.

"Wow," I mutter, more to myself than anyone else. "You two are sick."

"No, please, Winnie! I'm so sorry. I understand now that I shouldn't have done it, but I honestly never meant to hurt you. It seemed harmless enough at the start, but I shouldn't have ever gone along with it. I just needed a job so badly. You know what this industry is like, don't you? Sometimes you agree to anything if it helps you get ahead."

I continue to look at him, and it's not at all hard to see the self-loathing that's painted all over his face. I'm hurt and betrayed, but I'd also be lying if I said I didn't see a little bit of myself staring back at me. I'm another person who's guilty of going along with one of Juliette's morally bankrupt plans in the hopes that she'd help me. She casts her web and the world just walks on in. Including me.

Phillip notices my momentary reverie and is quick to plead his case again. "Please say you forgive me? I really have been my true self with you, minus the prosecco and cooking shows, though, the prosecco *is* starting to grow on me. It's shockingly refreshing on a warm summer day."

I hesitate just slightly as I push past him to scoop Ollie up from off the couch, grabbing his leash from the table and not stopping as I head for the door. I try to leave in stoic rage, but my soft thespian heart forces me to pivot around once I reach the hallway. "I don't forgive you, but I don't blame you either," I tell him. "I know who the ringleader is here."

Phillip's entire demeanor brightens for a flash before he tones it back down. "I really am so sorry, Winnie." I don't answer him, and his nerves seem to prompt him to go on. "So you don't entirely hate me, then?" he asks hopefully.

"I marginally hate you," I answer. "But I'll tell Juliette you did a good job. She should give you the role she promised you." I head for the stairwell then, needing to drop Ollie off in the studio before heading back to the park.

I've just pushed open the door when Phillip calls out, "I'm still glad that I got to meet you. And if you want my Robin slippers as restitution, I'll hand them over without hesitation. There will be tears in my eyes, obviously, but if you want them, they're yours."

"Your slippers are safe," I eventually say, still holding the heavy door open. "Though I probably should take them purely out of spite."

He grins at me in a mixture of sadness and relief. "You're a very good person, Winnie."

I shake my head with an unamused smile and flip him the middle finger with the hand that's carrying Ollie. Phillip offers me a final apologetic wave in return as I step fully into the stairwell, letting the door slam shut behind me.

A befitting conclusion to our entirely non-epic love story.

22

When I get back to Regent's Park, it's moderately controlled pandemonium. A sizable crowd has formed out front. Backstage, everyone is running around and rushing behind the angled curtains that separate us from the outside world. There are a million things I could do at the moment, but all I'm thinking about is confronting Juliette, determined to have this out. After a few minutes, I still haven't found her, but I have found Ellie, who is now talking to a hyperventilating Roshni, and my protective instincts kick in right away.

"What's the matter?" I ask, immediately approaching the pair. "What's going on?"

Ellie seems more than grateful for my arrival and adjusts her stance so we're all standing in a circle. "Thank goodness you're here. We're having a bit of a moment. Bethany stepped in a divot while walking in the grass and twisted her ankle, so Roshni needs to go on in her place."

I turn to Roshni, now fully grasping the reason for her terrified state. There are four parts in *The Lights of Trafalgar*–two main characters and two side parts. Bethany is one of our actors; she plays George's best friend. It may not be a leading role, but it's substantial. Substantial enough to be petrifying to a first-time actor.

"I can't do this. I really can't," Roshni wheezes.

Ellie looks at me, desperate but confident. "Can I leave her with you?"

"Yes, we'll figure it out. Don't worry."

Ellie then rushes off, no doubt having a thousand other obstacles to overcome by showtime. I step closer to Roshni, placing my hands on her tensed-up shoulders.

"I can't do this," she repeats, still looking like she's staring down the barrel of a gun. "You have to tell Ellie that I can't do this."

"Roshni, listen to me. I promise, you *can* do this. Don't you remember how good you were at rehearsals?"

"That was just practice," she says frantically. "I was reading from a script, and I was only standing in. This is the real, actual show."

"Yes, and you are really, actually great."

She shakes her head, in no way accepting the truths I'm telling her. "Not at this level. Not in front of an audience."

I release my hold on her shoulders and take her hands instead. "No one is ever ready for their first performance. All you have to do is decide to do it, and that's it. You give yourself over to the role, and then there's nothing to be scared of because nothing else exists outside the scene."

"I don't know the lines. I don't know the blocking."

"Yes, you do. You know this play inside and out, and you haven't missed a minute of rehearsal. I'm one hundred percent certain that you could take on any role in this play and perform it well, except Jocelyn, because her character plays the guitar, but I also wouldn't doubt that you've secretly been learning how to do that too via YouTube like some self-taught prodigy."

Roshni laughs, and I take it as a positive sign. "You have to believe me—I know you can do this, and you are going to feel so proud and powerful when you're done. And I'm going to be filming the whole thing, so you'll have this memory to watch and rewatch forever. You can show it to your grand-children someday. How many people can say that they per-formed a world-famous play in London with classically trained actors? You'll be the most badass pharmacist that ever walked this earth."

She takes a deep breath, and the color starts to return to her cheeks. "But I was nervous just being here and helping out today. How am I supposed to handle physically being in the show?"

"Have you ever been part of a production before?" I ask her.

"When I was younger, I used to do garba with a group during Navratri."

"So, there you have it. It's basically the same thing."

"It is absolutely not the same thing, and I was terrible in those dances. All the other girls were super graceful and on tempo, and I looked like a frazzled bodybuilder."

I shake my head with a smile, summoning all my bravado, and hoping it catches. "I refuse to believe that. Plus, Ellie wouldn't have asked you to step in if she didn't think you could do it. Did she ask me? No, and I went to theater school. She wants you for the part, and we have a full hour to run lines. I won't leave your side until you step out on that stage, and while you're on it, I'll be waiting in the wings, silently shriek-ing in excitement. I know you can do this."

Roshni eventually nods, and I breathe out a thinly veiled sigh of relief.

"Will you hold my hair back if and when I puke?" she asks.

"Holding back puke hair is what I do best."

We both smile, and in that moment, every other thought falls away. It's just me and my friend, and we are going to get through this.

An hour and a half later, the play has begun, and Roshni is waiting for her cue. We stand in the wings, side by side, as she squeezes my hand with a brute strength I had no idea she possessed. All the seats that were set out are taken, and a large crowd fills up the surrounding standing space. People come and go, leaving and arriving, allowing a glimpse to anyone who's interested, and this is what pop-up theater is all about. Opening countless eyes to possibilities.

Roshni's entrance is coming up, and I grip her hand back, fully aware that she probably doesn't even feel it. But then she looks at me, and I know she feels it. Our eyes lock, and I give her a grin as I try to magically send her every bit of confidence I have or have ever had. She must receive it in some form, because she smiles back at me and squeezes my hand one more time before letting it fall and stepping forward. She's now nearly on the stage, waiting for her cue. It comes and she's off, disappearing into the lights until my eyes readjust so I can see and hear her.

Her projection is a little low at first, but it picks up quickly, and I'm crazy thankful for the vocal exercises we rushed through minutes earlier. Tears well in my eyes as I watch her, and I don't resist them in the least.

A few minutes later, she's back in the wings. I give her water and a towel to dab her face—we're like a theatrical boxer and trainer prepping to reenter the ring. The adrenaline has clearly taken over, and Roshni's nerves seem to have reduced significantly. She's so magnetic that I have to actively remind myself to take in the rest of the play as well, but I'm glad that I do. Our collective ideas from rehearsals have now taken flight and are being executed and delivered with all the passion and subtlety we hoped for.

Every so often, I steal glances into the audience—one of the privileges of being part of the show but not a cast member. Everyone seems as rapt as I am, their eyes glued to the stage even as some whisper back and forth to one another.

Roshni goes on three more times, and each time I'm there to send her off and welcome her back. When she leaves the stage for the final time, she walks right into my hug and starts to cry as we shift deeper into the wings. I've never felt prouder of another person in my life. She's legit my little sister now, and I'm pretty sure a DNA test would confirm it.

"I can't believe I just did that," she says, wiping her tears away.

"You were amazing," I tell her. "And I'm not just saying that. You were absolutely incredible."

"I feel like my head might explode. Do you think people would notice?"

"Would people notice if you were to spontaneously combust? Probably. Let's maybe try to delay all that until after the curtain call."

"The curtain call! I almost forgot. I can't believe I get to be part of the curtain call. What do I do? Curtsy or bow?"

"You do whatever feels right. Let the spirit flow through you."

She quietly claps her hands together, brimming with anticipation, and it sends such a sense of happiness sailing through me. "Okay, so you enjoy the rest of the show. I'm going to head out front to relieve the intern who's filming for us." I give her one more hug before moving back once again. "I really am so proud of you, Roshni."

"I couldn't have done it without you," she says. "Assistant squad for life."

"For life," I repeat back. We both step apart smiling, Roshni sneaking into a better viewing spot and me slipping out from the backstage area. From there, I disappear into the crowd, maneuvering my way as carefully as possible. I find one of the interns faithfully guarding the tripod I set up, and he's quick to scurry off closer to the stage for the end of the show when I tell him I'm there to relieve him.

I stand there alone for the next ten minutes. I try my best to get lost in the show, but it's near impossible, as a million sensations surge through me at once. Pride, excitement, sadness— they all rise and fall inside me, reaching an emotional crescendo as the play ends and deafening applause fills the air. The curtains close and then open again as each actor comes out one by one for their time in the sun. I cheer at the top of my lungs when it's Roshni's turn.

Eventually, the curtains close for good, and the lights around us shift to a standard level—slowly ushering the audience and me back to the real world. The crowd is dispersing little by little when I feel a presence beside me. I don't have to turn my head to know it's Juliette.

"So, what did you think?" I hear her ask.

I swallow down a sudden lump in my throat. "It's a hit. The reviews are going to be everything we hoped for."

"You know, I'm actually starting to believe that, too." She pauses, then quietly adds, "We did it, kid."

The endearment that I typically love so much cuts through me in a sloppy, sickening slice. I let myself feel all of it as I turn to Juliette, in no way trying to hide the betrayal and hurt that's splayed across my face. "Phillip told me everything. He told me how you bribed him to spend time with me. How you both used fun little personal facts to trick and manipulate me." Juliette's smile falls, a line of fear crossing her typically confident face. She says nothing.

"How could you do that to me?" I press.

She focuses on the stage, seeming unsure and still not looking at me when she answers, "It was stupid. At first it was because we weren't getting anywhere in the dating project, and I figured he could help to move things along—but then it turned into something else, and I don't know, I should have called it off."

"Yeah, you *should* have called it off. In what world is it okay for you to have an actor feed me lies? What if I actually started to like him, Juliette? What if I slept with him?"

"That was never going to happen," she says, quickly turning back around. "I've known Phillip and his family forever, and he would never do anything untoward. I gave him explicit instructions that he was only supposed to catch your interest." I know she believes what she's saying, but I also see a flare of genuine concern—of her second-guessing herself. "He didn't try anything, did he? Because I will kill him if he made you feel at all uncomfortable."

"No, he didn't try anything," I assure her. "But what if *I* decided to make a move on him? How would you know what went on behind closed doors?"

She looks away again briefly, rubbing her face with both hands and shaking her head. "Because I'm not blind, Winnie. I know you have something going on with Liam and have for almost our entire trip."

I don't say anything, a little thrown to actually hear her say the words out loud. Juliette takes a deep breath as she moves a small step forward.

"I'm not mad at you, and I regret what I did with Phillip. It was a mistake, and I'm willing to forget the whole Liam business."

"*You're* willing to forget?" I ask disbelievingly. "Wait, are you expecting me to apologize about that? Because you flat-out demanded I stay away from him without giving any thought to what he or I wanted. I had every right to see Liam."

"I understand that now," she says. "But I also think that in a small way, I had the right, as your employer, to ask you to follow a certain code of ethics when it comes to my family."

"What happens between Liam and me is none of your business."

"But that's what you don't get!" she suddenly says, her eyes becoming a little wild. "I couldn't just stand by and let her win. Do you think that on top of her taking absolutely everything that I loved away from me, I was going to let her have you, too? No. You mean too much to me, and I wasn't willing to lose you."

"I...what are you even talking about?"

Juliette sighs and looks to the side, pushing her hair off her face when she turns to me again. "Isabelle. Isabelle doesn't get to ruin this aspect of my life. I won't let her."

"You're not making any sense," I say, utterly confused.

"If you fell in love with Liam, what do you think would happen? Do you think he would pick up and move to New York and leave his family and work behind? No. You would end up moving here. You would choose this life. Isabelle would have her perfect job, her perfect family, and then she'd have you. She would get everything. Again."

"Juliette, this isn't about some sisterly rivalry between you and Isabelle. This is about you violating my trust when I have dedicated the last five years of my life to you. I've put my own dreams and projects on the back burner to make *your* work better. To make your *life* better. I didn't even finish my play in time to enter the contest. I could have, but I chose to give you a chance at happiness instead."

"How do you figure that? I thought you loved working on *The Lights of Trafalgar.*"

"I did," I tell her. "But I should have spent my last day writing, and instead I spent hours in the car so I could find Paul for *you!*"

Juliette freezes. The gravity of my words washes over us both.

"What do you mean, you found Paul?"

I try to put on my bravest face, fully conscious that what I'm about to say next is possibly going to split our world in two. "I got his last name from the stationery I found in the studio. In the letter he wrote to you, asking you to forgive him."

Juliette only continues to stare at me. Her breath seems to catch as she turns back to the stage. When she looks at me again, her eyes are glassy. "I see," she says quietly. "And I'm supposed to be the only manipulative one here, right?"

Her accusation slithers inside me with reptilian slickness. Coiling tight in my stomach until I'm breathless.

"I wasn't trying to manipulate you," I explain. "I just wanted to help you. Paul still thinks about you all the time. He told me so. I know he wants to see you again, and if you give him the chance, you can at the very least get closure, if not something even better. He wrote me this note to give to you."

I reach into my pocket and hold the napkin out to her. She looks at it but doesn't take it.

"I reached out to Paul because I wanted to make you happy. I thought if I…"

"You thought what?" Juliette says, cutting me off. "You thought digging into my past and discovering the main character in my most painful memory was the way to bring us closer? That it would finally give you the unconditional love and acceptance that you're so obviously desperate for?"

Her words physically knock the wind out of me, and for a second, I wonder if I might black out.

"I'm sorry I said that," she immediately murmurs. "I didn't mean it."

I see the vulnerable Juliette now—the one that always pulls me in. But there's no kindness waiting to greet her this time, and I hope she can feel it in her bones.

"Oh no, I think you did mean it. Because now, more than ever, it's become painfully obvious that you never really cared about me at all." My voice cracks as I speak. In my heart of hearts, I know my words aren't true, but I'm furious enough to say them anyways. "All you ever cared about is that I was your goofy sidekick that was forever available to do your bidding. In all the years we worked together, not once did you ever think of how you could help me. You couldn't even be bothered to read my play."

"I told you I'd read it when we got back to New York!"

"After I've been begging you to read it for years!" I fire back with painful acceptance. "And you only agreed to read it now because I was willing to pimp myself out for the sake of your writing."

Juliette grimaces, my words seeming to hit their mark as she takes an erratic kind of breath.

"I didn't read it because I was afraid. If I read it and I didn't like it, it would have hurt you. If I read it and I did like it, then you'd start submitting it to places, and you'd end up leaving me. Nothing good was ever going to come from me reading it."

"You mean nothing good for *you*," I amend. "I barely know Ellie and she read my work and offered me amazing, generous feedback. She actually wants to prop up the people around her. And do you know why she does that? Because she's completely unselfish and unthreatened by the potential success of someone younger than her. She's the opposite of you. Actually, she's the person you wish you were."

Juliette's chin starts to quiver as she absorbs my words for several seconds. The real her is still here. Not the untouchable writer she presents to the world, but the unedited version of herself. That's who I want to talk to—who I need to talk to if we're going to survive this. But a split second later, her head tilts up the slightest bit, and she blinks her tears away. It's in that moment that I understand the truth—this is going to be the end of us.

"Listen," she says. "I don't know how we got here, but this whole conversation feels highly unprofessional."

My jaw sets in an unforgiving line, and Juliette runs her fingers through her hair with a defeated sigh. "I'm not articulating myself well. Let's just go home, and we can sort all this out tomorrow after we've decompressed."

She stands there then. Waiting for me to acquiesce to her wishes, because that's what I do. But this time, I don't.

"No, let's sort it out now," I tell her. "Considering this is a purely professional relationship, you should have no problem with me terminating it. I formally hand in my resignation, effective immediately."

Juliette's eyes go wide. I think about leaving it at that, but then step forward, looking at her like the equal that I now know I am.

"Though for the record, you and I both know that our relationship was never professional. You were my best friend. And I'll admit that sometimes I liked to pretend you were a mom to me, but that's only because I thought you were funny and brave and actually gave a damn about me. I see now how wrong I was. I see it because in this moment, you're nothing like my mom. My mom was kind and good, and she put everyone before herself, which is something you're incapable of. And don't worry—from here on out, you don't ever have to consider putting someone else before yourself, because guess what? You're alone, Juliette. I really hope you enjoy it."

I throw Paul's napkin to the ground, not turning back no matter how much I want to. Not even when I hear Juliette desperately calling out my name into the darkness.

23

I wander aimlessly for a few minutes after I leave the park, sticking to crowded areas and bustling streets to keep from getting lost. I eventually catch a taxi, not even sure where I want to go until I hear myself muttering out a familiar address. Ten minutes later, I'm outside Liam's flat, pressing the intercom button, and Liam tells me he's coming down. It's strange how different it is now. Every other time I've come to Liam's building, I was bubbling with excitement. Anxiously awaiting what was about to happen next.

Tonight isn't one of those nights.

Liam exits the building, looking as tired as I do, muttering a quiet, "Hey," as he steps out onto the sidewalk beside me. He slowly starts walking, and I follow suit. We're just rounding the corner when he finally speaks again. "So, is this our old Hollywood movie breakup stroll? Should I be wearing a fedora as we fade away into the mist in opposite directions?"

I get a twist in my stomach as I picture it in my head. Our bittersweet ending where we part ways, grateful for our time together, but ultimately knowing we would never work. A disappointing truth I'm not ready to face.

"I don't think we need to be quite that dramatic," I say softly. "Plus, it isn't even misty out. And I doubt we could rent a fog machine this late."

"Our last conversation was fairly dramatic," he counters back.

"One of us may have been slightly more dramatic than the other."

"And are you referring to me accusing you of adultery despite us not even officially dating? Because I feel I was being very mature in that moment. I'm not sure if you're aware, but lover's spats in the street are a telltale sign of personal growth."

I have to smile despite my lingering sadness. "You do believe that I was telling you the truth, right? That Phillip was just a friend?"

Liam swallows and nods, an embarrassed blush coloring his cheeks as he keeps looking forward. "Yes, I do believe that. I suppose it was just bad luck that your only other male friend in England just happens to look like a young preppy version of Anthony Hopkins."

I gaze up at him with exhausted but friendly eyes. "Leave it to you to have a man-crush on Hannibal Lecter."

"*Young* Hannibal Lecter. And the heart wants what the heart wants."

"Well, if it makes you feel any better, I recently discovered that Phillip was only pursuing me because Juliette was bribing him. Apparently, she picked up on the sparks between you and me and was trying to divert my attention."

"Are you serious?" he asks, his pace slowing momentarily.

"You can't make this stuff up."

He shakes his head in disbelief. "I guess I should take it

as a compliment. My romantic prowess must be so tangible that she knew enlisting outside help was the only way to tone down your interest."

"That really is the only logical explanation. It definitely had nothing to do with the fact that she thought you were going to steal me away and keep me in England forever."

"To be fair, I *was* considering keeping you prisoner in my seaside castle, but it's being treated for asbestos at the moment, so I had to scratch that plan."

"What a letdown. And here I was hoping to finally live out my *Rapunzel* role-play fantasy. I was growing my hair out and everything."

Liam laughs and I drink it in—savoring every note—every drop. But its sweetness starts to turn bitter when I realize it might be the last that time I hear it.

"We really should be assuming a more serious tone here," he says. "Isn't this meant to be our tearful farewell?"

"We can play out our goodbye scene however we want. Our relationship has hardly been conventional."

"True."

"What was the worst breakup you ever had?" I ask.

He looks down at me, knowing I'm only delaying the inevitable but seeming willing enough to play along. "Does my recent soul-crushing divorce count?"

"No, I want a more embarrassing memory. I'm thinking of you in braces, truly believing you're losing the love of your life after dating someone for three weeks, and then sprinkle in some possible wailing."

"I thought you said you *didn't* want me to discuss my divorce?"

I make a face at him, and he smiles to himself before continuing to look forward as we keep walking.

"Alright, a devastating breakup. Let me see…when I was thirteen, I was dating Nadine Lacey. It was a quite serious relationship. And by quite serious, I obviously mean that we spoke on the phone several times over the course of a month and decided to be exclusive after going to a movie and sharing a much anticipated closemouthed kiss."

"So, what you're telling me is that you've actually been married twice before?"

"More or less. Anyways, my friend Matthew was having a roller-skating birthday party. I obviously went, and when it was time for a couples' skate, Nadine decided to hold hands and skate with Norman Baxter, who also happened to be one of my best friends."

"Typical Norman," I grumble. "You know, I've never met a Norman that I've liked."

"Have you met many?"

"No, Norman Baxter is my first, but now I'm going to be biased for the rest of my life."

"You don't have to do that," he says easily, "though I do appreciate your loyalty."

"It's official, then. He's on my enemy list. Holding a grudge on someone else's behalf is a big talent of mine."

"Sounds healthy."

"Yeah, I'm super broken inside."

Liam chuckles, and we cross the street over to a more residential block, then turn to head back in the direction of his building. "Alright then, over to you. What's one of your tragic breakups?"

"I guess the one that stands out the most is from college. I was really into this guy named Trent."

"Trent," Liam mutters with disdain. "I loathe him already."

"Same. I'm sure he and Norman would get on great."

"I concur."

Liam reaches down and takes my hand then, and we stop walking, both a little surprised. Him, that he did it, and me, that I'm allowing it. It seems somehow against the rules, but I don't let go. I look down as he threads his fingers through mine, and my mind shoots back to the night we stood together holding hands in front of Big Ben. We had so much time then. We don't anymore, and I feel like I might cry.

"Anyways," I continue, hoping he misses the hitch in my voice as we continue walking. "Trent and I were casually dating for a month or two, and then we were watching a movie together in my dorm the day before Valentine's Day…"

"Ah, the day before Valentine's Day. If that doesn't warn you of impending doom, I don't know what does. What kind of movie were you watching?"

"A comedy, ironically enough. Anyways, I figured it was the perfect time to define the relationship, so I asked him what we were…"

"At which time he dropped to one knee and proposed, and you now reveal to me that you've been hiding a secret husband this whole time, and then *this* becomes my new most horrifying breakup ever."

A small chuckle escapes me at the thought of it. "I guarantee you, I'm not that diabolical. No, Trent just went on to say that I was more the type of girl you have fun with rather than being girlfriend material."

"Well, that's terrible," Liam says. "I thought there would be some kind of a funny twist, but it appears Trent was just a jerk."

"Yes, just a run-of-the-mill turd. And from then on, I was pretty guarded when it came to relationships. I didn't want to get all excited over a guy only to end up getting Trent-ed in the end."

Liam nods. "You know a guy is the worst when his wretchedness warrants being used as a verb."

"Agreed. And I'm pretty sure both Merriam and Webster would agree with us."

"I don't doubt it."

We're back on Liam's block now, and every step forward takes more effort than the last. His pace slows substantially, and I'm glad of it.

"This isn't how I thought our talk was going to go when I came down," he says.

"Me either. I don't know what I even expected by coming here... I just couldn't let that be the last time I saw you."

My words sink in, and both of us seem to be struck by them. "I'm leaving tomorrow," I go on to tell him. "Probably in the afternoon. Once I get back to the studio, I'm buying a ticket."

His hand tightens on mine the slightest bit. "You don't want to wait a few days and go home as scheduled? I can't imagine a flight to New York is cheap."

"I think me quitting would make it kind of weird to be cozied up in first class next to Juliette. I can't imagine what we'd say to each other."

"You truly quit, then?" he asks.

"After the show. It was a long time coming."

"I'd hate to think I had something to do with it."

"You're worried you led me down a path of sin?" I tease. "Would you take it back if you could?"

"No, I just... I know how much your job meant to you. Rethinking everything, it was wrong of me to force my way into your life."

I give his hand a comforting squeeze. "If I didn't want you

in my life, you wouldn't have been in it. And as far as me quitting, it was something that had to happen. I don't know if I loved working with Juliette so much as I was dependent on it. And her. And not just financially, but emotionally, too. While staying her assistant, my writing was always going to be second fiddle to hers, and it's time for me to change that."

"Sounds empowering. It makes me want to get my life back on track as well."

"Maybe you should," I tell him.

"Easier said than done."

We stop walking then, standing directly in front of Liam's building. It suddenly looks dark and sinister, probably because it's set to be the backdrop of our ending.

This is it. I'm leaving now. I won't see Liam tomorrow. Or the next day. Or maybe ever again. I look up at him and he looks at me, registering my emotions and starting to pull me closer. I keep my feet planted.

"I should go," I tell him.

"You don't have to. We can talk a little longer."

"I need to get back to Ollie and figure everything out with my flight."

"You can do that here. Go get Ollie and come back. I can help you figure things out."

It's so tempting—so tempting that it physically hurts. My throat feels impossibly tight, and I just want to hug him and feel his arms wrap around me. It's beyond cruel that I know stepping forward and falling into him would wash all my pain away. I'd feel safe and looked after. I could just let go and not think, but that's what I want. It's not what I need.

"I have to do this on my own," I tell him. "And so do you."

I move back again, but Liam doesn't let go of my hand. I

see a drop of desperation flash through his eyes, and in that moment, I know he's hurting as much as I am.

"Okay, here's a crazy thought. Come to Paris with me."

And just like that, all the air temporarily leaves my lungs. "What?" I ask quietly.

"I know that it's nuts, but it could also be a little bit genius. You can come to Paris with me. You and Ollie both. I'll fulfill my contract, you can write, Ollie can wear a beret, and the three us can all sit and eat croissants under the Eiffel Tower."

I smile and shake my head in dissent even as my heart positively basks in the daydream. "You know we can't do that," I tell him.

"Why not?" he asks longingly.

"Because we need to get our lives together. I'm almost thirty and I have nothing to show for myself. Even on this trip, I threw away a huge goal I was working towards because deep down, I was afraid of failing again."

"But you always wrote when you came over to my place."

"I know that, but I shouldn't need you coercing me to do what I'm supposed to be passionate about by tempting me with your company and snacks. I should be writing because I love it—because I'm driven and because I know it's what I'm meant to do."

"This is just a side note," Liam says, "but it made me really happy that you ranked my company ahead of snacks on the temptation list. Do continue."

I sniffle a bit, feeling the tears in my eyes even as I grin back at him. "You need to figure out what you want to do with your future, too. I know you had fun spending time with me, but you were also looking for a reason to put off your work, and I enabled you to do that. And I realize that you're doing better, maybe even better than you should, but you're clearly still not fully over your divorce. If we started something up, I'm sure it would help you feel good, less lonely for sure, but it wouldn't fix anything, not long-term, anyways." Liam eventually nods, and I take strength from his reluctant acceptance.

"Plus, I never told you, but I'm up for an amazing job back in New York, and if they offer it to me, I'm going to take it. It's a managing artistic director position and I'd get to work hands-on in the theater every single day."

Liam's eyes light up a bit and, to be honest, it means the world. Even through his disappointment, he's still so happy for me.

"That's fantastic," he says. "I knew you were going to do incredible things, and hopefully now you know it, too."

I do hug him then. Not because I'm giving in and not because I'm weak, but because every single ounce of me wants to, and more than that, I need to. I need to more than anything.

He squeezes me back with complete abandon, and even as I take in each second of our embrace, I still do my best to lighten the mood. "So," I say mirthlessly, "I guess we won't always have Paris."

I drink in and lock away Liam's light laugh as we step back from each other, our eyes never leaving each other's.

"You couldn't help yourself, could you?" he asks.

"My cynical sense of humor balances my dreamer soul."

"That's one way of putting it." He reaches forward and runs his fingers through a lock of my hair, holding it for a second before dropping his hand back to his side.

"So, this is it, then? You'll leave tomorrow, and you and I will just go on as if the last few weeks never happened? Is that truly what you want?"

"Of course it's not what I want," I admit. "I want milkshakes and Barry Manilow. I want to fall asleep next to you, but not touching you, and I want to run off with you to Paris, but if I do that, I'll never focus on doing what I need to do to be happy within myself, and neither will you."

I know that Liam knows I'm right, and the pleading look in his blue eyes softens to something steadier and more resolute. "We can still talk, though, can't we? I can call you?"

"Of course," I tell him. "But only if you promise to bring your clarinet for late-night musical seductions."

The smile that crosses his face is so bittersweet that it leads to a brief pounding in my ears. "I can do that," he agrees. "But what if you meet an actual clarinet player who lives in the same time zone as you?"

"Then I'd say you have some serious competition."

"And what if Sandra Bullock and I serendipitously meet at the Louvre and she and I fall madly in love?"

"Then you should take your shot. I know I would."

Liam shifts as he stands across from me, his brow creasing. "What I mean to say is, we're not... I mean, you and I are free to..."

I know what he's asking, and as much as the thought of Liam meeting someone else feels sickening, I also know that I have to accept that it's a distinct possibility.

"I don't want you to stop living your life because of me or because of the idea of me. If our feelings are still there in a year, maybe the timing will be right...or maybe it won't. Maybe this is all we'll end up being, and if that's the case, then I still don't regret anything. I'll always be glad we had this."

"So will I," he says. I let him pull me forward again, wrapping me up in those arms that I've come to crave. "I'm really going to miss you, Winnie."

"I'm really going to miss you, too." We step back and it

hurts more than I ever could have imagined. "We enjoyed it while it lasted, didn't we?"

He doesn't answer, just cups the back of my neck and brings my mouth to his. He leans down, and I rise up on tiptoe. Our usual heat is there, but it's also coupled with softness. Sadness. Friendship. It feels like a fitting end when I slowly inch away, putting more and more space between us.

"This isn't over," he says confidently.

I search my mind for an equally memorable response, but nothing comes. Instead, I just look at him one more time. I'm half smiling, half tearing up as I turn and walk away.

This isn't over. I repeat his words on a loop in my mind, tucking them away somewhere safe inside me. Only time will tell if he means them or not, but in this moment, they're very real. And even if they're only temporary, for right now, they're enough.

24

It's early—painfully early considering my night last night. One of my eyes is twitching, and both are red from lack of sleep. I'm moving through Juliette's apartment as carefully and quietly as a serpent, using every stealth bone in my body as I attempt to grab my computer off her living room desk without making a sound. Bless these blissfully carpeted floors. My flight is booked for early evening, and the last thing I want is to see Juliette again before I leave.

I've just reached my halfway point, safely picking up my laptop and clutching it to my chest. I'm gearing up to make my escape back to the studio and Ollie when there's a sudden and sharp knocking on Juliette's door. Startled panic saturates my entire being. I can't answer it. I can't be here. I feel frozen in place until the room once again falls quiet. Maybe whoever was outside had the wrong apartment. I take a strained breath in and close my eyes, and then there's more knocking at the door, even louder than a few seconds ago.

My eyes dart around the room, looking for any kind of

solution, when I hear a rustling coming from the hallway that leads to the bedrooms. Maybe it's Roshni. It needs to be Roshni.

It's not Roshni.

I only spot the first inch of Juliette's slippered foot, but I know it's hers, and it's in that split second that I drop to the floor and take cover behind the couch that's parallel to the desk, praying to all that is holy that she didn't notice me.

Peeking out the slightest bit from my hiding spot, I can see that Juliette is only now putting her glasses on as she crosses the space to the door, and my pounding heart slows by the slightest degree. She didn't spot me, but that's not to say she won't. I do my absolute best to level out my breathing as Juliette opens the door.

"Isabelle," I hear her say lifelessly. "What a wonderful surprise."

I keep my eyes trained on the floor as two sets of feet now enter the space.

"You know," Juliette goes on, "given all your etiquette training, I figured you would know you should announce yourself before visits."

"If I let you know I was coming, you'd feign a mysterious illness."

Juliette plops down on the couch, sitting directly in front of me. "Incorrect. I'd hit the deck and pretend I wasn't home, like a normal person. You continually appearing out of nowhere is denying me my basic antisocial human rights."

"You're hardly antisocial," Isabelle replies.

"When it comes to you, I am."

"Touché." There's more movement on the far side of the couch then, and I can only assume that Isabelle has also taken a seat but left plenty of space between them. I am now trapped on the floor with my former boss and her sister sitting a foot in front of me. It's official. I have unlocked a new level of hell.

"It seems your play was a great success," Isabelle soon says, filling in the deafening silence.

"Thank you. It was," Juliette answers unenthusiastically. "Best night of my life, really."

"I'm happy for you. You deserve it."

"Oh, I deserve it alright," my boss says. "I took what should have been a remarkable evening and opted to turn it into a complete misery. Because why get everything I ever wanted when I can self-sabotage instead?"

"Are you talking about the play?" Isabelle asks. "The reviews are all extraordinary."

"I'm aware of that, but no, I'm referring to my private life. Though I am glad that you read the reviews. Did they make you feel bad about yourself?"

"Of course not. I was pleased for you."

"That's unfortunate."

The couch shifts in front me, and I watch from underneath as Juliette's feet move to stand behind one of the armchairs.

"I didn't mean to make you feel agitated," Isabelle eventually says. "I was just hoping to spend some time with you."

Juliette doesn't move from behind the chair. "Listen, I'm depressed enough as it is. If you're here to deliver the final emotional blow, rest assured, I'm more than capable of doing it myself."

"That's not at all my intention," her sister says. "And I know I'm the last person you want to see or talk to right now, but we should have had this conversation thirty-four years ago."

Juliette does move then, her feet tracking across the carpet like a caged animal's. "Oh, spare me. Maybe you're in the mood for your big redemption scene, but I can tell you right now, I'm not feeling it."

Then Isabelle is the one to stand, though her feet remain firmly planted in place. "You know what, Juliette?" she says, her voice taking on an uncharacteristic hardness. "Forgive me for being rude, but I honestly don't care if you're not feeling it. I've given you time. I've given you decades, and clearly that hasn't worked, so we are going to have this out. Maybe you're happy existing with this festering rift between us, but I'm not."

"How convenient," Juliette says, suddenly moving closer to her. "It's amazing that you're only now plagued by the rift between us after I proved last night how capable I am of getting through life on my own. What happened between us came from your hands. You tore everything we were apart, and for what? Better clothes? A pat on the head from our dear daddy?"

"I grew up, Juliette! I moved on. My priorities changed and my dreams shifted, and the last time I checked, that wasn't a crime."

"Your priorities changed?" Juliette asks incredulously. "You abandoned me. We were each other's whole world, and then you fed me to the wolves."

"Really? I fed you to the wolves? If that's the case, then why are we now standing in your luxurious penthouse? Why have your dreams become a reality if I was seemingly so intent on your failure?"

"Because I worked my ass off! I didn't take the easy way out, and I didn't go crawling back to our family the way you did. You sold out, like all cowards do."

Still entrenched behind the couch, I roll off my stomach and onto my back, staring up at the ceiling above me. I shouldn't be here. Not in this room and not in this moment. It's all so wrong that I feel itchy in my own skin. I turn my head and watch as Isabelle takes a tentative step towards her sister.

"I sold out because I didn't have your talent, Juliette. You didn't need help, but I did."

"So why not tell me that back then?" Juliette asks sharply. "Why instead choose to hurt me in the most excruciating way possible? You ripping your friendship away from me wasn't enough, so you decided to take Paul and our future away, too?"

Both women hold their ground as Juliette's accusation seems to fall between them. It's Isabelle who speaks first. "What happened between you and Paul was your decision. Though, I admit, I could have handled things better."

"Could have handled things better?" Juliette challenges. "You sued me! You were going to take me to court over the house because you knew I couldn't fight you, and you knew that you would win."

"I *threatened* to sue you—I didn't actually sue you. There's a big difference."

"Oh, go to hell," my former boss seethes. She crosses the space and drops back down onto the couch. The material shifts, and Isabelle's feet are beside Juliette's as she sits down once again as well, this time closer than before.

"I was wrong, Juliette. Okay? In retrospect, I should have done things differently, but I didn't, and all we can do now is move forward."

"I don't have to do anything," Juliette tells her. "You're the one who has a problem with how things stand between us, not me."

"Can you try, just for one second, to see things from my perspective? I thought I was doing the right thing. You had all the talent in the world, but things weren't happening fast enough for your liking, and I could tell you were getting discouraged. And whether you want to admit it or not, I knew you looked up to me. I knew you were watching. You watched as I quit acting and went into real estate, and you saw how everything started coming together for me. I got married. I got pregnant, and you told me that maybe I had the right idea."

Juliette's feet disappear from the floor, and I can only assume she's now sitting cross-legged on the couch. "Good god, what a monster I was. I'm so sorry I had the audacity to admire you."

"That wasn't the problem, Juliette. The problem was that I could tell you were getting ready to give up. I could see it. You were going to marry Paul and move into that house, and your playwriting would have always played second fiddle, if it wasn't forgotten about entirely."

"So what?" Juliette yells. "That was my choice to make, Isabelle—not yours."

"I understand that, but even still, I don't regret pushing you. Writing was always meant to be your destiny."

"Okay, well, thank you, Great Oracle, for your stellar premonition, but you still didn't have to jackhammer my life in two!"

"Will you please take some accountability for once?" Isabelle fires back. "All I did was take the house—I didn't force you to break up with Paul. You could have used the money I gave you and bought any other cottage, but you didn't. You didn't because deep down, you knew marrying him then would have been a mistake. If everything with the house never happened, if you moved in and married Paul and then got some job— which you would have had to do to keep the place up—do you think you would have been happy in the long run? No. You would have been resentful. Every day you would look at Paul and remember what you gave up for him, and you never would have recovered. Big dreams require big sacrifices."

Juliette almost laughs. "You say that so flippantly. You have no idea of the sacrifices I've made."

"Yes, I do," she says solemnly. "Because in my own way, I had to sacrifice our relationship so your dreams could come true. And it was the hardest, most painful choice I've ever made in my life."

My breath catches, believing Isabelle's sincerity even if I can't currently see it in her eyes. Juliette gets up and moves to the far side of the room.

"You can think whatever you want about your noble sacrifice," she says, "but you started to pull away from me long before I got engaged. You and I were inseparable, and then all of a sudden I was just your eccentric sister that you barely had time for."

Isabelle crosses her ankles in front of her. "I did what I thought I had to do."

"Stop saying that!" Juliette shouts. "Are you honestly going to sit there and say you did everything for my sake? You stole the house and kicked me out of your life for my benefit?" Isabelle doesn't answer, and her silence seems to enrage Juliette further. "Admit it! Admit that you were sick of me. Admit that you were jealous. Admit that every time you looked at me, you were reminded of your own failure, and you couldn't stand the fact that I still had a chance, and you didn't."

"Of course I was jealous!" Isabelle answers with a roar. "Do you think it was easy to be your sister, Juliette? And to be clear, I wasn't just your sister. I was your mother, your caretaker, your cheerleader, your sounding board, your whipping boy. I was the one who always took care of you, and what did I ever get in return? Your friendship? Your wit? Maybe you have these glorious, glittering memories of our lives in London, but let me remind you, it wasn't all rainbows. If you weren't complaining, you were in a bad mood. If you were writing and I was in the apartment, I couldn't make a sound. You were up and down and high and low, and you expected me to cater to you all the time because that's what I always did, and eventually, I got so tired that I just didn't want to do it anymore."

"And the truth finally comes out," Juliette says, sounding triumphant and self-assured. "So maybe you weren't such a martyr after all, then. Maybe you just didn't like me anymore, and my dreams were the excuse you needed to do your dirty work."

Isabelle springs up from the couch and follows her sister's path.

"A middle ground existed, Juliette. You just refused to see it. I was in my twenties, but it felt like the weight of the world was on my shoulders. I should have been allowed to love you while also being entitled to take a break. I should have been allowed to want things for myself without being seen as some selfish, evil mastermind."

The room falls quiet, and I don't know what to make of it. Are they silently forgiving each other? Staring each other down? It feels like I'm in the orchestra pit at a Broadway musical—hearing all the action without catching a single glimpse.

"When I couldn't get any work," Isabelle eventually says, "when I knew I would never make it as an actress, I felt like I was always letting you down. I was your older sister. I was supposed to be the one who blazed the trail, but it was in that moment that I realized you truly didn't need me, and not only that, I was legitimately holding you back."

"That's not true," Juliette tells her.

"Yes, it is." Isabelle comes back around to sit on the couch, and Juliette slowly but surely joins her as her sister goes on. "Your writing was getting better and better. You were right on the verge—all you needed was your big break. In your mind you were failing, but in reality, it was me who was failing. I went to hundreds of auditions and was told no over and over again. I was too tall, too short, too young, too old, too expressive, not expressive enough. There were endless reasons why I never got cast in anything, but the real reason was that I wasn't good enough. And it hurt so much to feel like nothing all the time. I couldn't take it anymore."

Silence stretches several moments before Juliette speaks. "You could have done something else. You could have found any other job, but instead, you had to go groveling back into Dad's good graces."

"So what if I did?" Isabelle asks. "He was our father."

"He couldn't care less about us. We were invisible until we eventually benefited him."

Isabelle laughs, so soft and faint that I almost don't catch her next words. "A trait I think we both picked up." Quiet once again fills the room until she goes on. "I'm only being honest. We learned to take what we needed from people to survive and thrive, and I know you like to believe that Dad has no part in us, but we're both more like him than we think."

"We're better than him," Juliette says, her voice cracking just a bit.

"Maybe so," Isabelle agrees. "But he also wasn't the tyrant you made him out to be in your head. He was flawed, like all of us."

"I'm aware of that, Isabelle. We weren't strangers when I went back to New York. We found a relationship that worked for us."

"I'm glad to hear that. When he got sick, he told me he saw you from time to time, but nothing specific."

"We were fine. It was a bond forged out of necessity. He was the only family I had after you and I stopped talking."

I stay firmly locked in position as I watch Isabelle's feet move the tiniest bit closer to Juliette. "I turned to Dad because I was tired of believing that I wasn't enough. I wanted to do something where I could be proud of myself again. I needed to do that, for me. And then I met Freddie, and he made me feel wanted and worthwhile, and it was honestly so nice."

"I never had a problem with your shiny ball," Juliette tells her. Her voice sounds a little softer. Less guarded. It's shockingly refreshing.

"I can't believe you still call him that. He'll love it when I tell him. He misses you, too."

I wait for Juliette to stand up again. To walk off and flee, but she doesn't—she only murmurs, "I wish you would have just talked to me then. We could have worked through everything together like we always did. I didn't need a baptism by fire. I needed *you*."

Isabelle slides over again, and now they're sitting side by side. "I'm sorry," she says. "I know I should have said this long ago, but I'm sorry, Juliette. I know now how wrong I was, and all I want is for us to try to salvage whatever we can from this."

"It doesn't matter," Juliette says, her voice resigned. "Even if we do scrape together some form of a relationship, I'll only screw it up. That's what I do best. In fact, it's a pity you didn't find me after the pop-up, because you could have witnessed my most destructive tour de force to date. In the span of five minutes, I drove away the kindest, most dedicated person I've ever met, and who probably would have walked through fire for me if I asked her to."

My heart plummets into my stomach then, and I almost forget how to breathe.

"Are you talking about Roshni? I saw her last night, and she was pure sunshine the whole time we spoke."

"No," Juliette clarifies. "I'm talking about my former assistant, Winnie."

"Winnie?" Isabelle echoes. "You know, I meant to ask you if she's been spending time with Liam of late. If she has, she's been a wonderful influence on him."

"Why, yes, she was," Juliette answers with a dreary laugh. "And I'm the cursed old crone who tried to force her and Prince Charming apart, because I didn't want to lose her. And of course, that's exactly what I ended up doing."

I'm frozen in place, and every inch of me feels like it's weighted down by cement. I couldn't move even if I tried. This might be as close as I get to ever receiving an apology from Juliette.

"I'm sure you could talk to her," Isabelle says.

"I doubt that. I said and did unforgivable things. I don't have the right to talk to her anymore." The room turns so quiet that my ears ring with it. Why couldn't she care about me enough to say this to my face? Why couldn't she choose me over her pride? "She saw Paul," Juliette then goes on. "Can you believe that?"

"Paul?" Isabelle asks, her voice sounding shell-shocked. "As in Paul, Paul?"

"Yes, Paul, Paul."

"And what did he say?"

"I don't know," Juliette answers. "He wrote me a note, but I didn't open it."

I hear Isabelle gasp. "What? Give it to me and I'll open it right now."

Juliette promptly stands up from the couch. "I think not, traitor. We may be acting civil now, but I'm not forking over my personal correspondence anytime soon."

"Fair enough," Isabelle says, sounding closer to happy than defeated. "So, where do we go from here? Do we just get to know each other again?"

"I haven't changed much," Juliette admits. "I get more back pain now."

Isabelle's melodic laugh sweeps through the space like a soothing breeze. "I do, too. I also sleep with a hot water bottle next to my feet."

"Really?" Juliette asks. "I know you're getting older, but I didn't realize you were a Depression-era schoolmarm."

"Don't knock it until you've tried it," her sister says. "And what are you going to do about Winnie?"

I freeze up when I once again hear my name—anxiously waiting for Juliette's response.

"I don't know," my former boss answers. "I don't think there's anything I can do. I screwed things up beyond repair this time."

Dread and painful acceptance wash over me. It's cold and it stings. The next voice I hear is Isabelle's. "You could apologize. Maybe don't wait a hundred years to talk things out like we did."

"I tried apologizing last night and failed spectacularly. The truth is, she's better off without me. She's bright and kind, and I only stifle her. I don't deserve her. I really never did." She pauses then, and I don't breathe until she speaks once more. "I'll apologize again when the time is right. When I can prove to her that I've changed."

"And until then?" her sister ventures.

"Until then… I'll just really, really miss her."

25

When Roshni slips into the studio a couple of hours later, she finds me on the floor with Ollie. He's on his pillows, and I'm beside him. The sunlight pouring in from the windows feels almost too warm on the back of my head.

"Hey," she says gently, closing the door behind her.

I continue to pet Ollie but offer her as good a smile as I can muster. "Hey, lady."

She sits down across from me, the three of us now forming a tight-knit circle. "Are we having a meeting of the minds?"

I laugh, but it feels hollow. Nothing is right today.

"I guess you can say that," I answer. "Ollie and I are leaving this afternoon. I hope the plane ride won't be too rough for him."

Roshni doesn't say anything, but she does nod. I go on. "I think he'll like New York. I can move some of my furniture around to make more space for him. And a friend of a friend of mine is dating a dog walker, so maybe I can get some kind of discount."

"That would be good," Roshni replies, leaning forward to pet Ollie herself.

I look around the room, finding his things that I've now bunched together on the small kitchen table. Juliette basically bought him everything, so I'm only keeping the bare minimum—just his leash and the travel case I got him myself.

"There is, however, another option," Roshni suddenly says. "So, this is kind of awkward, but Juliette talked to me a few minutes ago. She knew I was coming down to see you, and she assumed you both would be leaving today. She asked me to tell you that if you were open and comfortable with the idea, she would be more than happy to keep Ollie."

My eyes dart up to hers and for a second, I think I must have misheard her. "She wants to keep Ollie?" I repeat back to her.

"She says she's going to stay in England for a while. For at least a year. She says she knows you work long hours and that if you want her to, she would adopt him in a second. And if you ever change your mind down the road, she'll bring him back to you, no questions asked."

"But she…" My words fail me as I attempt to gather my thoughts. "She's never taken care of another living thing in her life, and all of a sudden she wants Ollie?"

"It seems like it," Roshni says with a small shrug. "I know she loves him. But remember, this is completely up to you. Whatever you decide, I support you one thousand percent."

My mind flashes to every moment Juliette and Ollie have spent together. Their first meeting was cute. Their next one, even more so. A gentle friendship followed. Soon she started to spoil him. And then there was obvious love.

I look at Roshni, and she gazes sympathetically back at me. I pull Ollie into my lap and breathe in his smell, focusing all my concentration on remembering exactly what it feels like to run my fingers through his coat. I think of what his life would be with Juliette compared to what it would be with me. He won't be holed up in my tiny six-floor walk-up. He won't spend the majority of his day alone. He won't get scared when my lunatic neighbors have their screaming matches at two in the morning. He's going to be the prince of Juliette's castle and life and I know he's going to be happy.

I pull him closer. There's a painful lump in my throat, but I force myself to speak. "I guess she can adopt him," I tell Roshni. Ollie goes up on his back paws and places the front ones against my chest. It's sweet and it's magical and through it all, I feel like I'm being ripped apart. "What do you think, buddy? You want to go upstairs and see Juliette?"

Ollie springs off me with an excited leap, running to the door, where he eagerly wags his tail. Dear god, this hurts.

"Are you sure?" Roshni asks. I nod my head and stand up as she does the same, helping me to gather up Ollie's belongings from the table. "Can you please just hang out here and come home with me in a couple of days? Juliette won't be on the flight with us anymore since she decided to stay."

"I can't. I already booked my flight. I'm off to the airport in a few hours."

Roshni groans in acceptance. "Fine. But dinner in the city when I get back?"

"Of course." That seems to appease her, and seconds later, we're both standing beside the door. I pass her the bulk of Ollie's things and try and fail to suppress the panic that's steadily building inside me. Roshni looks at me as if she knows.

"I'll just bring these upstairs and then come back for the big guy. Unless you want to bring him up yourself?" I shake my head, since speaking doesn't feel possible, and sit back on the floor as soon as she exits. Ollie looks at me expectantly, and I can't hold it in anymore. I let every tear fall as I drop my head, bringing my face close to his as guilty agony threatens to engulf me.

"I love you, Ollie," I somehow manage. "I really wish I could keep you, but I know that would be selfish of me."

He nuzzles his face against mine, and I wipe my eyes and cheeks as I try to get a grip on myself.

"I really do think you're going to like living with Juliette. Yes, she's a pain, but I know she'll take such good care of you. You won't ever have to be lonely. I bet she'll take you everywhere with her even if they don't allow dogs. She'll make them make an exception for you."

Ollie once again gets excited at the mention of Juliette's name, and it's in that moment that I know I'm making the right choice.

I hear Roshni at the door then—it's a soft knock, but it almost makes me topple over. Time for goodbye. I cup Ollie's perfect face in my hands and gently rub under his chin.

"You'll always be my favorite boy, okay? I'm going to think about you all the time. Even if me and Juliette aren't talking right now, I'll find ways to check on you. I'll get Liam to turn Isabelle into my spy. And I'll send you gifts and treats every Christmas and on our anniversary of finding each other."

I stop talking then and just take in the sight of him. No dog will ever have my heart like he does.

"Thank you for choosing me to rescue you, Ollie. And thank you for rescuing me back."

Knowing I need to get up or I'll stay crouched down like this with him forever, I give him a kiss and stand, opening the door and finding Roshni sobbing.

"Oh no," I say, somehow managing to laugh.

"I heard everything," she whimpers. "That was ridiculously

beautiful. And I know he's going to have an amazing, pampered life, but that was really freaking sad."

I pull her into a hug as she continues to cry. "I know. But sometimes we have to do really sad things for the ones we love. It helps us know that it was real."

And that makes her cry harder. "Can you please not say things like that to me right now? Are you trying to kill me?"

I laugh again as I pull her in tighter, and a few seconds later, she's managed to relax as she steps back to wipe her face.

"Okay," she says, leaning down to scoop up Ollie. "So, all of this is fine, and you and I will be having dinner together next week."

I nod my head in agreement. "Yes, we will. And I'll also be obsessively texting you, because not seeing you on a daily basis feels like a fate worse than death."

"Agreed, and you better." She steps forward then, allowing me to give Ollie one more kiss before they disappear into the stairwell, saving me from the experience of watching them wait for the elevator. I walk back into the studio, and once the door is safely closed, I collapse onto the floor and cry for an hour.

When I walk up to my dad's house three days later, I can already see piles of boxes through the sheer curtains covering the windows. Not in a rush, I stand on the sidewalk and gaze at the two-story wood Colonial in front of me, knowing it very well might could be the last time I'll see it with my dad inside. The last time that I'll walk in with it still being my home. A tight, squeezing sadness starts to pass over me, so I quickly step forward as a means to evade it.

It doesn't work.

When I get inside, packing mode is in full swing. You can

tell which boxes were packed by my dad and which were packed by Cassie. My dad's boxes are sealed airtight with heavy masking tape, and highly descriptive labels are attached to all sides. Cassie's boxes are filled to capacity to reduce waste, and the top lids are folded into each other, not requiring any tape, and are labeled with one-word descriptions scribbled on one side.

"Hey, hey," I call out, my feet echoing on the hardwood floors.

My dad walks in from the kitchen with his label-maker in hand, wearing navy slacks and a short-sleeved button-down, as per his typical Sunday attire. "Winnie," he says with a smile. "You're here."

"I'm here." I give him a hug, and he patiently pats my back until I'm done.

"How'd your interview go?" he asks.

Mentally reliving my meeting with the West Lane Theater Board of Directors this morning, excitement and pride immediately appear on my face.

"It was awesome," I tell him honestly. "They offered me the job, and I accepted."

"Oh, Winnie, that's wonderful!"

I dip into a modest curtsy. "Thank you, thank you. Enough about me, though. So, T-minus how many days until the big move?"

"Two weeks," my dad answers. "Cassie's in the attic now, on the lookout for any long-lost mementos."

"Is it the colony of squirrels she's been secretly feeding and harboring up there for the past sixteen years?"

Dad lets out a quiet laugh. "I wouldn't doubt it. But it's also possible that it's more along the lines of some old books."

"That was going to be my second guess."

"I'm sure it was."

I smile and turn to look around the nearly empty living room that's littered with boxes, thinking of the hundreds of shows I performed and the millions of movies I watched in these four walls. Lazy mornings and late nights. Barreling out the door on my way to school and lounging on the couch when I was sick. All of it happened here, and *here* is about to be gone forever. It feels like I'm on a theme park ride, and I don't want to get off. I want to stay on and go again, but I know that I can't.

"Do you think I can go sit in my room for a bit?" I ask my dad, knowing it was the first room they packed up.

"Sure. Stay up there as long as you want. We're ordering out for dinner in an hour."

"Sounds great."

He sets back to work, and I head up the stairwell and through the hallway. I hear Cassie shuffling around on the floor above, but I go straight to my room, which is now almost completely empty. I do find one box sitting on the floor, labeled with a sticker that says "Winnie." I sit down cross-legged and start looking through it—finding old playbills and reviews that were clipped out. There are old pictures with my friends from grade school and high school. Tattered report cards where my right-brained self excelled in English and art while the left side of my brain played possum for science and math.

I strike gold when I find my Mary-Kate and Ashley VHS treasure trove. Regardless of what haters will say, these movies were disastrous masterpieces. I must have watched them nine hundred times, and I regret nothing. I'm just stacking them back neatly into the box when Cassie appears in the doorway, holding an unsealed box of her own.

"Knock, knock," she says with an airy smile. Her hair is pulled back in a braid, as always, and she's wearing jeans and an old T-shirt. She may have just been in the attic, but her cheeks are sun-kissed, telling me she's been out in the garden this morning as well. I'm sure she's going to miss our back-yard most of all.

"Hey, Cassie," I answer easily, looking over my shoulder. "Looks like you guys are just about finished up."

"We're getting there. I still can't believe we're actually doing it."

"It's not too late to change your mind," I tease.

"Oh, don't make me feel worse than I already do." She slides down to sit across from me with the agility of someone who does an hour-long yoga routine every morning, without fail. "It was hard enough to decide to go in the first place. If I stop and think about it now, I'll only start crying again."

"Did you cry when you first decided?" I ask, somewhat surprised.

"Of course I did," she answers. "I knew it was the logical next step for us, but that didn't make the decision any easier. We're not excited about moving away from you, Winnie."

"No, I know that." I try to brush off her sentiment, fully aware that she's just as emotional a person as I am and worrying that a sobfest will inevitably ensue.

"Do you, though?" she asks meaningfully. "I know that from the beginning—since we first met, really—you basically sort of liked me, but there was always something keeping us from being as close as I hoped."

"Don't think that," I tell her. "You were great. You *are* great. You always treated me well, and you make my dad very happy."

A dreamy kind of smile crosses her face. "Yes, your dad. I

have to say, when I showed up for that college reunion, the last thing I expected was to run into him. I really only went because I thought a change of scenery would be nice for the weekend. But then, of course, I ended up uprooting my entire life."

Self-centered as it is to realize, I never really thought about how Cassie's moving here affected her. I only pictured it from my line of vision. How her being here made *me* feel. How her relationship with my dad affected *my* life. I never stopped to consider that she was a woman who left so much behind just to be with us.

"Do you regret it?" I ask her.

"Oh, no. The truth of it is, I thought my life was over for the most part. I was married, I had Becky, I got divorced, I got accustomed to being a single mom, and then Becky went off to college and it was just me again. I was happy enough, but I figured that was it for my story."

"And then?" I prompt.

"And then I fell in love with the weird guy from my Intro to Biology class. Did you know that we were lab partners back in college? Anytime I tried to help or touch anything, he nearly had a panic attack. He was so organized and precise, and I had the best time just watching him. He'd get so wrapped up in a project that it almost seemed like he was making music with a microscope."

She grins at me, a little lost in her daydream, and I find myself grinning back.

"He couldn't get away from me fast enough at the end of the term, of course. And I didn't blame him. I was very much outside his comfort zone."

"Did he recognize you right away at the reunion?" I ask.

"Not at all. I assumed he did, though. I walked right up to him and started rambling away about how funny it was to see him again and told him all about what I did after graduation. I think I was probably ten minutes into my life's story when he finally asked me who I was."

"Sounds about right," I say lightly. "Then what happened?"

"And then he just kept on asking me questions. He never did that in college. He must have picked that up later on."

"It was probably my mom. He once told me that she would have him practice making friendly conversation with her. She told him the key to getting someone to like you was to ask them questions." I pause, feeling her memory slip around me like my favorite sweater that's warm enough for winter and light enough for summer. "I guess he wanted you to like him."

"Well, he didn't have to work too hard at it," she says jokingly.

"I think my mom would have liked you, too." I pause only a moment before I amend my statement. "Scratch that. I *know* she would have liked you."

"That's very kind of you to say, and I hope it's true. From what your dad told me, Gianna was a very rare and wonderful person." Words suddenly seem to fail me, and I only nod as Cassie goes on. "You know, being the mother of a girl myself, I thought dating someone with a daughter would be easier than it was. I'm not saying that you were difficult, because you truly weren't, but in the beginning, I was honestly scared to death of you."

"Of me?" I ask disbelievingly.

"Yes, you. I mean, here I was, some strange woman you hardly knew, moving into your house, dating your dad… I would have hated me if the roles were reversed."

"I never hated you, Cassie."

"No, I know that. I was just constantly afraid of doing the wrong thing. In my head, I thought if I overstepped even once, you'd despise me forever, and I'd ruin whatever relationship we were slowly creating. And I think, because of that, I ended up keeping too much distance between us. I was so nervous that you were going to think I was trying to take your mother's place that I struggled to find my own space in your heart."

Her words hit me so hard and so sweetly that I'm not sure how I feel. "Cassie..."

"That's why I started up this little project." She reaches into the box she set on the floor, pulling out a notebook and holding it in her hands. "I want you to know, when I got this, I had no intention of turning it into what it became. I was feeling a lot of conflicting emotions with my life here and how much or how little I should contribute when it came to you, so I thought if I wrote things down, it would help me sort things out. But then I opened it up one day when you were upset—you didn't get invited to someone's pool party—and it just happened."

"What just happened?" I ask, looking from the notebook to her.

"It's hard to explain. At first, I thought I would keep it to myself. It was only meant to be a place where I could get things off my chest. But then eventually, I thought I would give it to you when you graduated high school. Then I pushed it back until you graduated college. Then I thought maybe when you got engaged or got pregnant, but now I know I was just being a chicken. Because as much as you never fully let me in, I never fully let you in either, and I regret that more than I can say."

She hands me the notebook with slightly shaky hands. I've never seen her so nervous. "Anyways, you'll see what I'm talking about when you read it. I'm sorry if it's weird or out of line. I just want to make sure I let you in, even if it's just this once, before I go."

She gives me one more smile and gets up from the floor, leaving the room as I sit there wondering what I'm about to walk into. Wanting and needing clarity, I open the notebook to one of the first semi-weathered pages, and I almost forget to breathe.

Dear Gianna,

Winnie came home upset today. Some girl named Crystal didn't invite her to her birthday party, and is it terribly immature that I want to go over there and drop my composting toilet in that stupid pool? Winnie has been so stressed with finals and rehearsals, and this was the last thing she needed. I want to help her feel better, but I don't want to pry. Sometimes I try to connect with her, but I can tell she's not into it. It almost feels like I burnt my hand on the stove and now I'm afraid to cook.

Maybe I'll tell Ben we should do something special with her tonight. We could drive into the city for dinner. She loves the city. She swears she's going to live there someday. I'll talk to Ben. He should be home in an hour, and I know he'll do it even if he's tired.

Okay, sorry to bother you. I don't even know why I wrote that. Sorry. And if it isn't already abundantly clear, I'm one of those people who apologize a lot. Also, I accidentally broke your lamp in the living room the other day while I was cleaning, and I felt very guilty about it. I'm going thrifting at some point this month, so I'll try to find something similar. Sorry. And that's an actual justifiable sorry, not just me saying it as a nervous habit. Anyways, that's it for now. Thank you for listening.

Best wishes,
Cassie

P.S. I'm realizing now that "best wishes" is kind of formal when writing to someone's spirit, but I'm not quite sure how else to sign off in this scenario. We'll figure it out eventually. Okay, bye.

So apparently, crying is my thing now. I wipe under my eyes and turn the pages, flipping through the book and catching sporadic dates over the last sixteen years until I get to the final entry that's dated a month ago. I take a shallow breath and read…

Dear Gianna,

Ben and I decided to put the house on the market. I know I should be excited. I should be thrilled at the thought of going home, of being closer to Becky, but I can't shake the feeling that this is going to hurt Winnie.

I know I'm probably overthinking things. I'm sure she won't even mind that we're going, she's been so busy with work. But even so, I don't want her to see us leaving as us leaving her. That's the last thing Ben or I want. But the truth is, I've never fit in here. I'm a desert hippie in the thick of Long Island. It hasn't been easy. But I had Ben, and then I had Winnie, so things never felt too bad. But with her being gone so much over the years and Ben working the hours he did, I always felt lonely, even in the midst of our happy life.

Going back to Arizona will be a refreshing change. Becky needs me, and after I've been away so long, I owe it to her to come back. I think Ben will like it there, too. His joints hurt in the cold, so the heat will do him good. The house we're renting while we look for a new place is cozy and nice. It's close to the university, so I'm sure Ben will look into becoming an adjunct professor—he just can't help himself. And if Winnie ever needs a break from New York, she can fly out to see us and take in the sun.

But now, as I look through the pages we've filled together, I can't help but feel sad that this is my last letter. You've helped me through so much, and I want to thank you for being part of this with me. Maybe you can't hear me, but maybe you can. And if you can, please know that I will never stop loving your family. I will take care of Ben, I will be Winnie's number one fan, and you can always count on me. I may not have known you, but I'll never forget you.

Your friend,
Cassie

I close the book and clutch it to my chest as ugly tears pour down my face. My mom is here, I know she is. I can feel her love and her beautiful heart filling me up, telling me that all of this is going to be okay, even if I don't see it yet. I'm so strong and so loved, and even though she couldn't be with me, she saw everything for herself and heard the rest from Cassie.

Cassie. So much regret and gratitude fill my head as I think of her. I should have given her more. I should have shown her more. For the past five years, I was chasing a mother in Juliette when an incredible woman was trying so hard to love me since I was thirteen.

Without stopping to think, I get up and rush out of the room. I charge down the steps with the grace of a rhino, power walking past my concerned dad in the living room and heading directly into the kitchen, where Cassie is washing dishes. I say nothing when I flip her around by her shoulders and immediately wrap my arms around her, locking her into the tightest hug I've ever initiated between us.

"I'm going to miss you so much, Cassie. I love you, and I'm sorry I didn't tell you sooner."

After a moment of what I can only assume is shock, I feel Cassie's soapy hands land on my back, returning my hug in the way she's probably wanted to since the day we met.

"It's okay, Winnie, I know."

Her words and voice only make me hug her tighter, and we're both starting to laugh a little when my dad walks in a few seconds later.

"Is everything okay in here?" I hear him ask.

"We're fine, honey," Cassie answers. "We're just making up for lost time, is all."

"I can see that."

Now, my dad isn't classically what's known as a hugger, but I still turn my head to glance over at him, keeping one arm draped around Cassie as I lift the other for him. A little smile crosses his face as he hesitantly steps forward, wrapping his arms around the two of us.

Hours later, I'm still smiling on the train ride back into the city. It may have taken our unconventional family a long time to get where we needed to be, but I guess, as in so many other cases, it's better late than never.

26

A year and a half later

Standing in the wings, I struggle to inhale calming breaths as I hear the audience filing in, taking their seats and getting acclimated to their surroundings. The last time a play of mine was being staged, I was so sure, so excited, so ready for the next step. Now I'm all but paralyzed in ice-cold terror, doing everything I can to appear collected so I don't spook the actors. I tell myself that no matter what, I'll survive. I'd like to think it couldn't be any worse than the last time.

I peek out into the crowd then, looking for a familiar face. I find two—my dad and Cassie. My dad is holding his usual two dozen white roses, and Cassie is looking down at the tickets, trying to find their seats. Seeing them gives me a temporary moment of peace. They've been gone for almost a year and a half now, happily settled in Arizona. I've visited them more often than I ever anticipated, maybe every other month or so. My weekends in Phoenix have been a major highlight of my year, especially during this particularly harsh winter.

The five-minute warning announcement rings out backstage, and I immediately step back further, feeling another round of bone-chilling nerves gripping me. I'm just closing my eyes and trying to convince myself that my heart is racing due to excitement instead of fear when I suddenly hear an entirely welcome voice.

"Oh boy, is it my turn to give you a pep talk now?"

I open my eyes and whip around to find Roshni, looking gorgeous as always. I may be biased since I'm slightly obsessed with her, but I also think it's a common fact.

"Yes," I say, trying and failing to shake off the nerves. "By all means, pep-talk the hell out of me. I'm seriously considering pulling the fire alarm and squeezing myself out the bathroom window."

"Just relax. Remember when I was about to go on for *The Lights of Trafalgar*? I nearly went into anaphylactic shock."

"Which was strange, especially since you have no known allergies."

"The stage can do crazy things to a person," she says. "Anyways, you're way more prepared for this than I was then, and I did fine."

"Pardon me, but you did more than fine. Why you're not currently the main cast member in a modern-day reimagining of *Helen of Troy* is totally beyond me."

"Um, maybe because as fun as acting is, there's no way I could handle that stress on a consistent basis. Community theater exists for a reason, and I'm very happy with my traditional workweek and my weekend thespian lifestyle."

"So instead of living a high-anxiety life in a state of constant flux, you're choosing to live a successful and lovely life? How obnoxiously well-balanced of you."

"I try my best. Now, let me pass your own words of wisdom back to you." She places her hands on my shoulders, just as I did to her in London. "You can do this. Everything is going to be amazing, and you are going to be so elated come curtain call."

"Lies," I reply, my voice shaky. "The world is ending, my play is a disaster, and you've clearly been sent here to build me up before my non-survivable fall. Go spread your treachery elsewhere."

"Right, your play is such a disaster that it won the Twenty-Fifth Annual Arthur Brady Playwriting Contest and is now being staged in New York City."

"Did I forget to tell you? I sold my soul to the devil. At the stroke of twelve, I'm riding off with the four horsemen into a fiery oblivion."

"Eternal damnation can wait," she counters. "Last year in London you weren't ready, but this year you are. You worked on your play, you submitted it, and you won. You deserved to win, and I refuse to hear anything different."

I choose not to argue, and a smile spreads across her face as she releases her hold on my shoulders. "In other news, I'm sitting next to your West Lane crew. Professor Jack and the rest of your coworkers seem super nice."

"They're so awesome. I know I've only worked with them for a year and change, but it feels like I've known them forever. They're absolute nutcases, but the best people I've ever met."

"Aw," she says sweetly. "Our little weirdo found her niche."

"So I have."

Thinking back on my past sixteen months at West Lane Theater Company, it still seems like a dream that I somehow willed into reality. Naturally, I was overwhelmed at first. Handling all the responsibility of being an artistic director was no joke, and while I did stumble here and there, I also grew as a woman and an artist more than I ever could have imagined.

"I meant to ask you," Roshni then goes on. "Did you... and I'm sorry if this is a completely inappropriate question, but did you tell Juliette about *Death of a Prom King* winning the contest and getting staged? I mean, a fair amount of time has passed."

I don't know why, but thinking about Juliette somehow always prompts me into motion. This time, I roll my shoulders and stretch a little from side to side. "I thought about it," I say. "But what's the point? I doubt it would mean anything to her, anyways."

"I hardly think that's true, especially since the contest last year was kind of the tipping point for you guys. Your winning it this year could be a symbol of rebirth."

"Rebirth or not, it's clear she doesn't care either way. It's not like she's reached out to me since London. My number hasn't changed."

"But she did follow you on Instagram, and you followed her back," Roshni challenges. "Being Insta-official is a huge step."

"Be that as it may, we still haven't spoken."

"She's probably just scared to reach out to you directly. I told you, after you left, she was totally thrown. And she never even came back to New York. For all we know, she could be lying on the studio floor at this very moment, sobbing her eyes out and screaming your name."

"She's not," I assure her. "She just posted a video two days ago of her and Ollie at Abbey Road."

Roshni *aww*'s, and I don't blame her in the least. Ollie crossing that street was stinking adorable.

"And what about Liam?" she then asks. "Did you tell him about the play?"

At last, my nerves take a back seat as another sensation overrides my system. Strong fondness, lingering longing, and veiled but poignant disappointment.

"He knows I won. He was excited when I told him, but he hasn't asked me about it much of late. I think things between us have officially started to taper off since he extended his time in Paris."

"Well, that's a shame. I miss drooling over that redheaded Chris Evans as I lurk in the background of your FaceTime dates."

"Not everything is meant to last," I tell her. "I just have to remember the good times and accept the fact that I'm now in an established blood feud with that entire family."

"Are we maybe just being defensive because we secretly miss them very much?"

"What's with all the questions?" I whine. "I'm not in my right mind, and you're emotionally waterboarding me in a moment of weakness."

Roshni looks at me with an unaffected stare. "I'm literally asking you very basic, normal human questions."

"While staring directly at me with those beguiling brown eyes and bewitching me into revealing all my secrets."

One-minute warning.

I suck in a breath at the announcement and instantly start shaking. "I'm leaving. I can't do this."

Roshni grabs my hands. "Yes, you can. This is what you were born to do, and no matter what happens or what people think, you deserve to be here. Your art needs to be shared. You've got this. Do you understand me?"

I nod, but it feels like my throat is closing.

"I'm going back to my seat now. I love you, and this is going to be amazing."

"I love you, too. And if at any point you hear the sound of intense dry heaving coming from backstage during the performance, I need you to immediately hunch over and pass it off as your own to the people in the audience to cover my tracks."

"I can do that. Let's not forget, I am an international actress."

"That you are," I agree. "Thank you for coming back here."

"Anytime. Break a leg."

We hug then, tight and quick, before she walks off, and I stay hidden in the wings. I take another breath to center myself, assuring myself that I can do this. I worked so hard, and now it's time to see it through. I close my eyes and remind myself just how far I've come.

This entire year and a half passed in a fast-moving haze, sprinkled with occasional patches of slow-moving sad spells. It was an adjustment. I was so used to being Juliette's assistant—and I don't just mean that as my job, I mean as my actual identity. I wasn't Winnie. I was Juliette's right hand. Her faithful sidekick. A forever aspiring playwright. And I was happy to be those things, but I wasn't challenged. I wasn't pushed. At least, not in the right ways.

Now everything's changed. I'm challenged daily, I'm pushed relentlessly, and I have never been happier. I've learned and developed and grown so much as an artist, and I know that I can handle this.

I open my eyes as the house lights dim, then turn off completely. The stage lights slowly start to rise in intensity, stopping once they're set for the opening scene.

This is it. No turning back. I look across the stage to where the eight principal actors are waiting in the wings. Receiving their cue, they fearlessly step out and get into position. Their breathing is heavy but controlled. They're scared, but they're going anyways. I watch their bravery with a visceral kind of awe and take it into myself before sending it back to them. Because when it comes down to it, that's what theater is all about—drawing bravery from fear and revealing the truth with stirring lies.

The curtains rise, and a tangible hush falls over the room,

so thick and heavy that you can reach out and drag your fingers across it to make a ripple.

It's showtime.

Applause. So much applause. I feel it before I hear it—the vibrations under my feet that crawl up my calves and into my chest from the floorboards. It's like I'm blacking out as the play ends and the curtain closes. Little by little, the sound fills my ears until I'm back in my body and I become overwhelmed by emotion and a life-changing realization—I did it.

I wrote a play and people are clapping and I didn't crumble into a million pieces. I can breathe. I can think. I can relax my entire body for the first time in hours. I smile to myself, delirious and free in my own relief.

The curtain rises again, and the actors run out one by one, each of them getting their moment to find their light. When they've each had their turn, their right arms point to the wing I'm occupying, and I force myself to step out and take a shy bow as I remain to the very far side of the stage. The cast issues one more bow as a group, and the curtain closes for the final time.

The actors hug each other and me, and I thank them relentlessly for their hard work and their unparalleled talent. Half the group is college kids, making up the high-school versions of the characters, and their sheer enthusiasm is contagious. I'm basically levitating from happiness when I eventually head out into the audience.

I meet up with and group-hug my dad and Cassie first, then Roshni and her boyfriend, and end up with my colleagues and group chat friends. A half an hour flies by, and before I know it, it's time to head off to the after-party that we're having at a bar down the street. I tell everyone to go ahead, that I'll be there in a couple of minutes with the cast and that I left my bag backstage.

I've just grabbed it and decide to check my phone when I see two texts from a contact I've barely heard from in over a month. The steady, thunderous pace of my heart skips a beat as I stare down at the phone, pausing before I slowly unlock it to reveal the message.

I knew you could do it. That was absolutely sensational.

Then:

What's proper theater etiquette for requesting an encore? I asked the man sitting next to me, but he only looked at me oddly and said I talked weird.

He knew I could do it. It was sensational. He asked the guy sitting next to him.

Liam is here. Like, here, here. I cautiously step onto the now empty stage, looking out into the audience and feeling my heart drop to my ankles when my eyes lock with his. He's standing there in a side aisle, surrounded by empty seats, and looking at me like it's the first time he's ever seen me after waiting a lifetime.

"Hello," he says. His hair is shorter, and he's grown a light beard. He's wearing jeans and the sweater I sent off to Paris for him this Christmas. His voice echoes in my ears and I feel it in my gut and I'm nervous that I might black out all over again.

"Hey," I answer quietly. I offer nothing else and he seems okay with that, stepping forward towards the stage until he can't go any further. He lifts a leg to climb up, and stumbles slightly as he does. I barely notice. He could have belly flopped up here for all I care. All that matters is that he's now standing less than three feet away from me.

"I may have underestimated the height of the stage," he says, a little out of breath. "And here I was hoping to come off as suave, what with my big surprise entrance and all."

I can't believe this is happening. I can't believe he's here and we're talking and joking in person like it's the most natural thing in the world. I clear my throat and even out my voice. "Well, that'll teach you. I thought everyone knew you always bring a small but trusty trampoline when attending a former flame's opening night."

"I knew I forgot something. Which is odd, because I've done this so many times—attended former flames' opening nights, that is. You'd think I'd have a better grasp on the situation."

"Yeah. No, I couldn't agree more," I tell him. "I'm highly, highly disappointed. Which I'm sure you can tell, since I'm obviously miserable at seeing you again."

He takes in my flushed cheeks and nervous smile, and his ears instantaneously turn bright red. Oh, I've missed those guys. I'm once again tempted to touch them, but I instead wrap my arms around my own stomach.

"When our texts and calls started to slow down over the past few weeks, I assumed that you... I don't know. I don't know what I thought."

"Yes, I'm sorry about that," he says. "I wanted to surprise you, so I thought pulling back a bit might make my showing up tonight seem a little grander, but I see now that I was probably sending you mixed messages. Clearly, I'm the worst."

"Just a bit," I tell him.

"I suppose I also figured a little mystery wouldn't hurt since I didn't exactly play hard to get in London."

"No, you definitely didn't. You were exceptionally easy."

"I thought as much."

We both smile, and a comfortable silence settles between us. "So how have you been?" I ask after a few beats.

"I've been good. Busy with work, if you can believe it. Paris was great, but I'm glad I've finished my commitment. Looking back, I never should have put it off as long as I did."

"And now?" I ask.

"And now I'm here. One of my engineering friends from university lives in the city, and we're going to start up another consulting firm."

"You mean you're staying here?" I sputter out. "In New York? For how long?"

"My work visa just went through, so I can stay for as long as it makes sense." I feel like I've entered another dimension. I'm still wondering how and when we got here when Liam goes on, "Mum had a bit of a fit when I told her, but she's coming around to the idea. She's set up a marathon of apartment tours for me this week with an associate of hers."

"And how is your mom?" I ask, still wildly confused. "Is she doing well?"

"Very good, actually. She's happier than she's ever been."

"That's wonderful."

"It is. It is. Most of it has to do with her and Juliette reconciling. I had no idea how much their falling-out weighed on her, but she's almost like a different person now. Last month she wore jeans."

I take a shocked step back. "Did her personal factory of silkworms suddenly shut down?"

"I don't believe so," he answers with a grin. "She only said she was trying to relax a bit. I think with Juliette around, she's starting to branch out more, which is a nice change. As far as I know, they've been getting together at least once a week."

"That's great," I find myself saying, trying not to acknowl-

edge the swift jolt of jealousy that may or may not be streak-
ing through me. "And is *she* doing well? Juliette? Do you talk
much?"

"We talk fairly regularly, and she's doing great as well.
She's basically creative partners with Eloise now. Did you
hear about that?"

"No, I didn't."

That's not entirely true. In addition to stalking her Instagram, which is essentially an Ollie fan page that's made up of
daily photos and videos of their adventures together, every so
often I also google Juliette to see what comes up. I recently
read an article about a play that she and Ellie have in early
previews, and I felt shamefully jealous then, too. Not due to
her successes or her continued collaborations with Eloise, but
because I wasn't there with them. As much as I'm still mad at
Juliette, as much as I know I should have left her years ago, I
have never stopped missing her.

"Yes," Liam goes on, "everyone's very excited about it.
And Juliette still talks about you, you know. She talks about
you all the time."

I freeze at that, my eyes locking with his—hoping they
don't look recognizably desperate but knowing that they probably do.

"She was so happy when I told her you won the contest
that she more or less knocked me down to get to the computer so she could look up the results herself. I hope you don't
mind that I told her. Maybe I overstepped, but she really was
thrilled."

"I don't mind," I end up telling him, feeling my palms get
sweaty in cautious optimism.

"To be honest, she said that she's kept tabs on you now
and again through some of her theater friends, and she also
mentioned that she started her Instagram page with the sole

purpose of you being able to see Ollie. She didn't come right out and say it, but I think she really just wanted some kind of a connection to you."

My chest constricts. So that explains it. Juliette's sudden Insta-lifestyle that she was always so against. She did it for me. A speck of hope ignites and expands inside me, but I'm quick to keep it in check.

"If that's how she feels, why didn't she reach out to me?"

Liam slides a hand into his pocket. "She said she wanted to make sure that you were ready to talk to her. You know she's not the best with rejection."

"Yes, I'm vaguely aware," I assure him.

"She's also with Paul now. It seems your little matchmaking scheme was a tremendous success."

"Are you serious?" I all but yell. Liam nods, and I shake my head with the biggest smile. "That's incredible."

"It is, in fact. And as it turns out, I think he was a bit of an inspiration to her. She even copied his trademark move."

"How do you mean?" I ask.

Liam then pulls his hand out of his pocket, holding out a napkin that's folded neatly in half. "She wrote this for you," he says.

I stare at it for a couple of seconds until I carefully take it from his fingers. Scared and dying to read it at the same time, I hold my breath as I unfold the napkin completely to see the message that's scrawled delicately across the surface.

You found me mine. I found you yours. I'm so proud of you, Winnie. Now and always.

Tears fill my eyes as I reread the words again and again. I wish Juliette was here. I want so badly to see her face, to talk

to her—not as a boss and employee but as women and equals.
I'm rereading it yet again when Liam speaks.

"What did she say?" he asks.

I force myself to fold the note up and slide it carefully into
my bag. "She says she hates me and that I should bolt away
from you as fast as humanly possible."

Liam looks away with a smile before quickly turning back
to me. "I should have known she'd try to turn you against me
now that she has you back in her clutches."

"And how do you know I'm back in her clutches?"

"Because the way you looked down at that napkin prompted
a whimsical violin melody to be carried in on the breeze."

"That's a spot-on description," I tell him.

"Well, if you're reacting now, I'm very curious to see how
you'll be faring in a few seconds when I tell you my next bit
of news."

"And what news is that?" I ask.

"That Juliette is waiting in the lobby."

For a second, I think I heard him wrong. I mean to ask
him to repeat himself but only manage to watch him as he
reaches into his pocket and pulls out his cell phone. A swipe
and few taps later, he's holding it to his ear as I continue to
stare at him with jumpy eyes.

"It's alright, you can come in now," he says, then puts the
phone away as quickly as it appeared. He's watching me as if
he's trying to gauge whether I'm going to fight or flee, and
I hardly know myself. I'm about to ask him what the hell is
going on when I hear the theater door open and close. My face
whips towards the sound, and there's Juliette. In the flesh. In
New York. In the theater—the two of us once again existing
in the same world after more than a year apart.

I'd like to say that I stand there—that I patiently wait for
her to approach me, but I don't. I keep my eyes trained on

hers as I quickly step forward, then sit, lowering myself off the stage. I walk steadily through the center left aisle. She's been walking this whole time too, and we end up meeting halfway.

Standing across from her, three feet away, I'm at a loss. I don't know what to do or think. Luckily, she's the first one to speak.

"Hi, Winnie," she says.

Her voice is jarring, but I somehow manage to keep mine calm.

"Hi, Juliette."

That's it. Those simple words hang between us for several moments until Juliette speaks again.

"Your play was brilliant. I was mesmerized from start to finish."

I nod almost absently. After dreaming of her approval for so long, I don't quite know what to make of it now that I have it. It feels nice, but not as necessary as I once thought it was. I'm getting what I wished for, only to realize that I never needed it at all. My silence sparks Juliette to go on.

"I should have read it," she says. "I should have read it the first time you asked me. My reasons for avoiding it were so self-serving and stupid, and if I could go back and do it all again, I would in a heartbeat. I should have been the mentor you needed. I held you back when I could have been pushing you forward, and I regret it so much. I need you to know that I regret it."

Tears slip out from under her glasses and down her cheeks, and it's difficult for me to see through my own tears that I refuse to let fall.

"I know that, Juliette. And I believe that you regret it."

She nods her head quickly, wiping her face even though her tears haven't fully stopped. "I hate everything I did to you when we were back in London. I hate that I asked you to go out on those stupid dates, that I asked Phillip to spend time with you, that I told you to stay away from Liam. I was so lonely and so desperate, but neither of those things excuses how I treated you. I took advantage of your loyalty, and I tried to control you for my own personal gain, and when I think of it now, it makes me sick. I just…" Her words trail off, and I can't stop a tear of my own from breaking free.

We both take a few seconds, and when Juliette inhales a big breath to speak, I find myself holding mine.

"I'm so sorry, Winnie. I am so deeply, deeply sorry. You said I was your best friend, and you were mine, too, and not a day has gone by where I don't miss you to a physically painful degree. Whether or not you ever decide to forgive me, I understand, but I want you to know, please know that I love you. You are vibrant and talented and endlessly, endlessly special. And I promise that I will always support you from here on out, whether it be as your friend or just as some maniac lady you used to know. I'll accept either one as long as it's what you want and it makes you happy."

Her words wash over me and through me. An absolute flood after so much drought. I'm terrified but elated. Devastated but hopeful.

"I'm not going to pretend that what happened between us last year was okay," I tell her, "because we both know that it wasn't. I idolized you when I shouldn't have. I cowered when I should have stood up for myself, and you took advantage of that."

She tenses and nods, bracing herself for whatever's about to come next.

"But I'm also not going to pretend that I haven't missed you every single day." Her eyes fly up to mine then, only just brightening with a familiar light. "We both made mistakes, Juliette. I'm not giving myself a free pass either. Our dynamic was deeply flawed, but there was good there, too. And if we can both get back to the parts of our relationship that made us great, then I don't see why our friendship can't get back on track."

Juliette takes a healing breath, sounding like she just broke the surface after being held underwater.

"Can I hug you?" she asks brokenly.

"Since when did you become so sentimental?"

She chuckles and wipes under her eyes once again. "Ollie and the London air have wreaked havoc on my once lifeless heart."

"Sounds like an unbeatable combination if I ever heard one," I tell her. "And that would be a yes for the hug."

We step in at the same time, and I forgot how soothing a post-emotional-breakthrough hug could be. It goes on for several moments until I speak again.

"So, not that I'm not thrilled about your lone appearance, but is Ollie here with you, too?"

Juliette steps back then with a devoted smile on her face. The one that fully demonstrates how Ollie has us all whipped.

"Unfortunately, he's not," she answers. "I took him with me on a flight to Ireland one weekend, and he didn't like it at all. This trip was significantly farther, so I'm letting Isabelle watch him while I'm here. I'm sure she'll have him waiting for me in a custom pantsuit upon my arrival."

I cheese deliriously hard at the thought of it. "He would make any outfit look amazing."

"I'll agree with you on that. Speaking of which, I'm going to head out and give Isabelle a call. I'm only here for four days, so how about we grab lunch the day after tomorrow?"

"I'd like that," I tell her. "We have a lot to talk about."

"Yes, we do," she agrees, looking over my shoulder and noticing Liam as he slowly approaches us. "But right now,

I think there's someone more important that you should be talking to."

I roll my eyes, and she gives my shoulder an obliging pat. "Have a lovely evening, Winnie."

I shake my head and watch as she disappears out the theater door with a wave. I always thought I knew her better than I knew myself, but I see now that I was wrong. I'm very much looking forward to getting to know the person she is now. The person that she should have been all along.

"I wanted to tell you she was here the minute I saw you," Liam says as he moves to stand beside me, "but Juliette made me promise to wait until you and I spoke for a bit. Are you very impressed with my immense willpower?

"Thoroughly impressed," I answer, turning to face him.

"Impressed enough to have dinner with me?"

He looks anxious and unbearably handsome. I wait to reply even though I make my mind up instantly. "I'm impressed enough to let you come with me to the after-party I'm going to."

An uncomfortable wince crosses his face. "Oh, god. The mysterious date to the lady of the hour in a room full of people waiting to talk to her? Do you know how many hellos that's going to be for me?"

"Probably a lot, but I promise to protect you."

"Oh, will you? You're usually the first in line to ramp up my anxiety."

"Well," I say, "maybe I'll take a different approach this time. Plus, how awkward can it be, since my husband is going to be there, too?"

Liam's eyes go cartoonishly wide, and it's my least convincing performance to date when I almost immediately start smiling.

"I honestly hate you," he mutters with a sigh.

I step forward and give him a playful push. "That will be the last time I trick you for the rest of night."

"I think we both know that that's a bold-faced lie."

"Possibly. Does that give you second thoughts about me?"

"Not at all," he answers. "Because in our time apart, I've come to realize that you are more than worth every stomach-turning, sweat-inducing, stress-elevating episode you charm me into. And I wouldn't have it any other way."

I stand there in silence until I speak in a completely awed and steady voice. "That is hands down the most romantic thing anyone has ever said to me."

"I'm glad," Liam says with a grin, reaching his hand out towards me. "So, what do you think? Are you ready to get this show on the road?"

I bite my cheek to contain my blissed-out smile, fully savoring his gloriously cliché question. "Yes," I answer, reaching out to place my hand in his. "I'm absolutely ready."

Epilogue

Five years later

Whenever we arrive at our London apartment, I'm always met with an undeniable sense of elated uncertainty. All of a sudden, a million new possibilities are right at my fingertips, and I'm somehow on vacation, but it's also my daily life. The flat itself is sleek and happy, modern yet charming. It's a comfortable one-bedroom that's a little on the smaller side, but I fell in love with it the moment I saw it. Buying a second home was never a real thought for us when we first got married, but with as much time as we spend here, Liam thought it made sense, and I agreed.

We ended up selling our larger New York apartment in favor of having two smaller homes instead. A two-bedroom we bought in Brooklyn and this one here in Bloomsbury. We come back to London every June, July, and August, and for a couple of weeklong stays throughout the year. Liam works remotely during our trips, and I somehow managed to finagle these unpaid three months off while West Lane hosts a guest artistic director for each summer season. While we're here, I get to focus on my writing, or I collaborate with Juliette and Ellie.

Thinking of Juliette, I reach into my bag to check my phone, finding no new messages as Liam finishes opening the curtains and sprawls out across the couch.

"Are both of them on their way already?" he asks, reaching out for me to join him.

"No idea. I would assume so."

"My money is Mum getting here first this time. I was half expecting her to pop out of the entry closet when we first opened the door."

"There's nothing wrong with a little healthy competition."

"Maybe not, but they could at least give us a couple of hours to get situated."

I squeeze my way onto the couch as well, sitting on the edge beside Liam's shoulder. "Never going to happen. Let the dream go."

"It's gone," he agrees, shifting just enough to wrap an arm around me. "I've learned by now not to swim against the current when it comes to you three."

"Smart man."

I'm about to slide down and nestle further into his side when there's a sudden knock at the door. "Speak of the devils," he says. "Which one do you think it is?"

"We shall find out." I pop up from my sitting position and cross the living room, heading back over to the door and swinging it open. Juliette is standing in the hall with a satisfied smile and with a very excited Ollie.

"I'm here and I have coffee!" she announces, holding up a disposable drink tray with four cups.

I immediately drop to the floor, shower my boy with no less than a trillion kisses, and unclip his leash from his collar so he's free to jump all over me. Once we're both satisfied, I stand back up and look over her offerings with feigned snootiness. "Did you fix my latte the way I like it?"

"Don't get greedy, kid." She gives me a kiss on the cheek and moves towards the semi-open kitchen area, where she places our drinks on the counter. "Morning, Liam."

"Morning, Liam?" he repeats disappointedly, sitting up on the couch as Ollie catapults into his waiting lap. "Oh, how the mighty have fallen. Remember the days when I used to be your favorite?"

Juliette sighs and whips back around to face us. "God, you two are so needy. If you can't tell, I'm extremely exhausted. Carrying those drinks over was no easy feat while walking Ollie and wearing this." She then casually lifts up her left hand and *my* hands immediately fly up to slap over my mouth.

"Stop!" I nearly scream at the top of my lungs. "No! Are you serious?" I'm in the early stages of hyperventilating as I charge across the room.

"I'm very serious," she says as I hysterically grab her hand. "I'm casting off my virgin robes at last."

"This is amazing!" I laugh and yell as I pull her in for a bone-crushing hug. "Wait! We have to FaceTime Roshni! She's going to die when you tell her." I release my hold so Liam can get a congratulatory squeeze in as well. "I can't believe you finally said yes," I gush, elbowing my husband out of the way so I can admire the ring again. "What made you do it?"

Juliette's smile is positively radiant. "Considering he's been asking me for the last three years, I figured it was time to cut him a break. Additionally, I can't stand Isabelle hounding me about it anymore."

"Please, she's going to be on cloud nine planning this wedding."

"Ugh," Juliette grunts, her excitement momentarily lapsing. "I didn't even think of that. Do me a favor and get pregnant to divert her attention."

"Ha," I chuckle, moving to scoop up my latte. "Nice try."

Juliette moans and picks up her tea as Liam and I exchange private smiles. In truth, we have talked about having a baby, but neither of us are convinced it's what we truly want. Maybe being parents will be in the cards for us someday, or maybe not. Either way, it's no one's decision but ours, and as it stands now, we're perfectly happy as a family of two.

"Well," Liam says, crossing the room and scooping up Ollie's leash, "I'll leave you two to gush in private for a bit. I've missed taking this guy on our relaxing strolls, so we'll be back in a few minutes." Ollie is fully up for it and quickly trots over when beckoned.

"Love you!" I call as they head out the door.

"Love you, too," Liam answers. Juliette rolls her eyes, and soon we're both sinking down to sit on the couch.

"You two are adorable," she says. "Tell me, do you wake each other up with butterfly kisses each morning as well?"

"Don't be a hater. It's not becoming of a blushing bride."

Juliette grumbles as she takes a none too happy sip of her tea. "Oh, please. If it were up to me, we'd just go down to the registry office and call it a day."

"And who's saying you can't? If that's what you want, then that's what you should do."

"Well, it may be what I want, but Paul wants to have a small wedding back in Surrey. He moved to London for me, so giving him a nice little wedding seems like a fair exchange in comparison."

"Aw, how sweet," I say goadingly. "And do you wake each other up with butterfly kisses each morning as well?"

That earns me an admiring glare. "Only on birthdays and national holidays."

I lean back into the couch cushions with a chuckle, still amazed by Juliette's news. "Well, look at you," I tell her. "A world-renowned playwright surrounded by her doting family and soon to be married to the love of her life. Some people would say that you have it all."

Juliette scoffs even as she smirks. "Who cares what some people would say? I have everything that matters to *me*. And in the long run, that's what counts."

"I couldn't agree more," I say lifting up my latte. "Here's to you."

"To us," she amends.

I smile at my dearest friend, and she does the same. Life hasn't been perfect or easy for either of us, but we made it through on our own, and now we get to enjoy it together. I'm filled to the brim with contentedness as I lightly tap my cup against hers.

"To us."

Acknowledgments

I can't believe I'm now writing acknowledgments for my second novel, which is out in the world! Becoming an author is 100 percent my dream come true, and it never would have happened without the following people.

My superagent, Kevan Lyon. Thank you so much for taking a chance on me. You don't actually know this, but I've reread your initial query reply email asking me to chat about TBTM a hundred times. And each time I do, it still makes me smile from ear to ear as I shake my head in disbelief that it even happened. Receiving that email from you will forever be one of my happiest memories, and I'm so grateful for everything you've done for me since.

Brittany Lavery, aka the most wonderful editor ever. Thank you for believing in me and my stories. Every step of the publication process has been incredible and that is due so much in part to your guidance, your humor and your kindness. You have absolutely changed my life, and I am endlessly lucky to have you in my corner.

To everyone on the Graydon House Books, Harlequin and HarperCollins teams, thank you for making my journey into publication so entirely dreamy. Your talents and efforts are incomparably amazing, and I'm very thankful for all of you.

Mom, Dad, Bridget and Mary—thank you for always pushing me toward my goals, for celebrating with me and for putting up with me along the way. I love you all so much.

To the people who read drafts of my books upward of five times each and are always there to offer me invaluable feedback and advice—Jen, Mary, Jessica and Aunt Liz, you four are the best!

My grandma, who always believed that our good news would come.

To everyone who encouraged me and had faith that my dreams could become a reality, especially Felice and Paul, thank you so much!

To Roshni, thank for your outstanding insights and for allowing me to sprinkle your real-life wonderfulness throughout this story.

A special thanks to the phenomenally talented actors who helped me understand the glorious ups and downs of theater—Elyse, Joel and Jayme. I'm beyond grateful and inspired by all of you—thank you for giving me a peek into your fascinating world.

And finally, to all the readers out there who gave my books a try. Never in my wildest dreams did I truly think that I would become an author, so to be so embraced and encouraged by so many of you is one of the sweetest gifts my bookstagrammer heart could ever receive. You are all magical and I will forever be thankful.

If you loved *Here for the Drama*, why not try Kate Bromley's laugh-out-loud debut, *Talk Bookish to Me*?

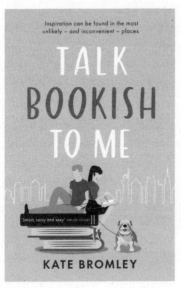

Inspiration can be found in the most unlikely – and inconvenient – places

Kara Sullivan is definitely not using her best friend's wedding to avoid her writing deadline. She's a bestselling romance novelist with seven novels under her belt, so she's a pro. Looming deadlines don't scare her, and neither does writer's block, which she most certainly does not have. She's just eager to support her bestie as she ties the knot. Right? Right.

But then who should show up at the rehearsal dinner but Kara's college ex-boyfriend, Ryan? It's decidedly a meet-NOT-cute.

However, when Kara sits down to write again the next day, her writer's block is suddenly gone. Is Kara's muse . . . Ryan?